Praise for Harper Fox's *Brothers of the Wild North Sea*

"Fox (*Scrap Metal*) sets this gripping, epic tale of love against the backdrop of ancient Britannia. [...] Spirituality and faith are presented thoughtfully in a sensually beautiful recounting of love in a time of austerity and danger."

~ *Publishers Weekly*

"This novel was, simply put, magnificent. It was a well written piece of literature whose characters and story line leapt off the page and thrust its way into your heart and mind leaving behind a lasting memory of a love that is ageless, of a brotherhood that is unbreakable, of a land that is beautiful beyond compare."

~ *Reviews by Jessewave*

"Everything about [the novel] just spoke to me. It is romantic and sweeping and epic, with battles and love stories and even a bit of ancient magic. The story just grabbed hold of me and I was captivated by it."

~ *Joyfully Jay*

"*Brothers of the Wild North Sea* is the latest action-packed adult romance by Harper Fox, who lives in Northumberland and writes gay fiction set in a variety of eras. With this outing she has given us two fiercely determined young men and a love to break the boundaries."

~ *Fresh Fiction*

"...I want to encourage everyone who loves history, pursuit of knowledge, conflicts, brave, righteous men, magic, following your own convictions, and the healing power of love, to invest the time and energy it takes to read this book. Thank you, Harper, for this awesome story."

~ *Rainbow Book Reviews*

Look for these titles by

Harper Fox

Now Available:

Driftwood
The Salisbury Key
Scrap Metal

Brothers of the Wild North Sea

Harper Fox

Samhain Publishing, Ltd.
11821 Mason Montgomery Road, 4B
Cincinnati, OH 45249
www.samhainpublishing.com

Brothers of the Wild North Sea

Print ISBN: 978-1-61921-907-6
Digital ISBN: 978-1-61921-480-4

Editing by Sasha Knight
Cover by Kanaxa

First Samhain Publishing, Ltd. electronic publication: June 2013
First Samhain Publishing, Ltd. print publication: June 2014

Dedication

To Jane, in commemoration of our civil partnership, 3rd September 2012.

Chapter One

Year 687 Christian Era, Britannia, northeast coast

The sea bells were ringing. Caius, walking by the side of a shaggy pony who needed no leading this close to home, listened in wonder. The dunes were scattered with them—fragile purple flower heads the children called hare's bells, dancing in the wind. Twenty summers ago, a child himself, Caius had heard them often. Then time had passed, and like all childhood songs, their music had vanished into the sounds of the world.

He halted the pony on the crest of a dune. From here, the whole coastal plain was laid out before him, a long, wild stretch of salt flats and grassland that paralleled the glimmering sea until both melted into the distance. A vision of heaven, on a spring day like this one. Drawing a deep breath, Caius let himself forget the long winters, when the gale swept down untrammelled from the north, scouring every living thing to tatters in its frozen, sand-filled blast. He did love it here. Unlike his father's stronghold in the hills, his new home stood unsheltered, a collection of low buildings on a small tidal island whose causeway twice a day was sunk beneath the restless sea.

And the tides come highest at the dark and full of the moon, because then both sun and moon line up to pull the water. Caius smiled in pleasure at the memory of his latest heretical lesson in astronomy, taught him in the darkened church with an apple and a candle flame, Abbot Theodosius spinning the round apple Earth by its stalk—*yes, round!*—and Caius and the other monks watching open-mouthed. Cai loved Theo's teachings. There was nowhere else to learn a thing other than farming and warfare in the whole of this bleak northern land, not until you reached the monasteries clustered round the River Tyne fifty miles to the south. Cai couldn't regret the path he'd chosen. The eldest son of a chieftain, he'd walked away from a rich inheritance of land and men. But all old Broccus cared about was feasting, fornication and clobbering the daylights out of the warlords who occupied the hillforts next to his.

Here, the very soil was sacred. Cai was an uncertain convert to the new faith, but he could feel that much, sense the rightness of the ancient name the tidal island bore, a name like the yearning cry of a bird. It rose up in his heart—*Fara Sancta.* The island of the holy tide. Fara.

Movement in the distance caught his eye. The trackway here was lined with odd green mounds. Theo taught that these were the burial places of men and women who'd lived here long before Christians or old Roman warlords had ever been thought of, but sometimes Cai wondered if the local superstitions might be true, tales of fairy creatures you should never name aloud as such, addressing them respectfully as the good folk, the kindly ones. At twilight on the dunes, it was easier to believe in fairy tales than history. And even in the brightness of noon, when a green mound stirred and a shape detached itself from the top, leapt down and began to stump towards him...

"Danan," he called, hoping he'd managed to conceal his nervous twitch. "Why must you lurk there?"

"Where better to waylay a bonny young monk on his way back from trading?"

Cai blinked, not quite trusting his vision, though the air was crystalline. The old woman had an uncanny knack for covering ground. Cai remembered her as ancient when he'd been a baby in the hillfort stronghold, and she hadn't seemed to age since then. Still, she was stooped and fragile, and he couldn't quite see how she'd closed the gap between them so fast.

"But I'm early," he said, watching in amusement while she shamelessly began to open the pony's baskets and leather sacks. "The weaver I was meant to meet at Traprain Law never came. How did you know I'd be here?"

"How do I know that the weather will change? How do I know where to find the snowbound lambs? What's in this satchel here?"

"Don't you know?"

She stopped in her efforts to undo the satchel's thongs. She shot Cai a look of withering scorn and laughter. "You're a devil, Caius, even if you do wear a dress and sing songs to your new god. Is it beads? And gold?"

Cai affected to brush flies from the pony's ears. He was glad of the reminder concerning his cassock, which he'd folded up into a pack in favour of his travelling gear, tough deerskin trousers and a homespun shirt. That was all very well for the road, but now he was within sight of Fara, he'd better soon get changed.

"Perhaps it is," he said mysteriously. Danan had a weakness for finery. She never wore the jewellery she accumulated from traders and goldsmiths, and rumours swirled that she kept them as a hoard for some dragon she'd tamed in the hills. "Perhaps I have old Roman blue glass and nicely wrought gold earrings hung with coral flowers."

"Coral? Or just red enamel?"

Cai smiled. She'd taught him carefully to know the difference. "Coral," he said. "Pink as strawberries."

"And how will you trade those amongst your joyless brethren at Fara?"

"I didn't buy them for the brethren. I bought them to trade with you—depending upon what you've got."

She stamped her foot. "Vows of poverty," she cried, shaking her badger-grey hair into a cloud around her head. "Humility, charity. You're as sharp a dealer as your father, boy, for all your noble ideals. What is it you wish, then? What would you charge a poor old woman for your filthy gold—or tin, I shouldn't wonder, judging by the last sorry bargain you made?"

"The usual. My medical supplies are running low." Cai changed tack and gave her his most charming smile. He'd become Fara's informal doctor in the two years since his conversion. He wasn't quite sure how the role had crept up on him, except that the brethren had lacked a physician, and he'd brought with him a steady hand and a knowledge of herbs gained by tagging Danan around the fields. "Most of all I need the plants and powders only you know how to find and prepare, Lady Danan. The roots that give peace and help for pain."

"Aye, aye. Very well. Turn your back, boy, or see what no monk should."

Cai turned briskly. Danan kept her wares stitched into little pouches secreted inside her voluminous, brightly dyed skirts. Once he hadn't looked away fast enough, and the sticklike limbs in rabbit-skin undergarments had haunted him for days. He cleared his throat. "How is Broccus? Have you seen him lately?"

"Oh, the old fool's well enough. He's got his latest girl with child, if you'll believe it—another little step-sib for you, to add to the clan of them already swarming round his regal mud huts. All right—you may look."

She'd done him proud. Eagerly he eyed the array of vials and pouches she was setting out on the sunny turf. He took the heaviest packs off the weary pony's back and left it to graze, settling beside the old woman on a stone. As always when they met to trade, she handed him the preparations one by one, carefully explaining their use, dosage, effects both good and ill. Extract of willow bark, to cool fevers and inflammation. The powerful juice of foxgloves, an aid to struggling hearts. A dozen harmless tonics, and finally a carefully stoppered bottle in the cloudy, thick glass the art of whose making Cai's people had almost lost along with the occupying Romans, and were only slowly recovering now, for church windows and the most precious of domestic wares. Cai had seen the oily liquid inside the vial before. Essence of poppy, so sweet a remedy for sleeplessness in small amounts. And in large... "Danan, I'm not sure I can buy this from you."

"That depends upon the beauty of my earrings."

"No. I mean I'm not sure that I ought."

"Why not? You've taken it before."

"Yes. I used it up in sleeping draughts and tonics for the nerves. Then when Brother Gregory sickened with the tumour, I wished I'd had more, because..."

"Because you'd have released him?"

"Yes. I was afraid I would. And surely life and death are in God's hands."

"Is that what they teach you? How did Gregory die?"

Screaming and blaspheming, after a life of perfect sanctity. Cai looked away. He hadn't asked to become physician to the Fara brethren, but he took his duties seriously and hated to fail. "I will take the poppy."

"In that case, I will take my jewels."

He unpacked the satchel and watched while Danan transformed from wisdom-filled herbalist to cackling crone. She snatched up the rose-pendant earrings and dangled them from her shrivelled lobes, wrapped the beads around her head in a lopsided crown and danced on the spot, piping out a wordless, tuneless chant. Cai let her get on with it, gathering up his purchases.

He frowned and shook his head. The hare's bells were ringing once more, their silver whisper-music increasing as if in response to the old woman's song. "Lady Danan, can you hear that?"

She didn't interrupt her dance. Her eyes were closed, her expression blissful. "Of course I can." Then she froze. She swung on him. "Can *you*?"

"Yes. I think so. Something."

"Ah, that's not for mortal ears."

Her own looked far from divine in those earrings. Cai grinned. He slung his packs across the pony's back, checking to see the heavy grain bags hadn't rubbed the beast sore. "What is it, then?"

"It means something. Something." She scampered up the side of the green mound closest to the track and stood there swaying, scenting the air. Cai waited. She was prone to sudden bursts of prophecy, mostly too vague to be useful, sometimes clear and starkly accurate. "Ah." She clapped her hands. "Yes. Yes. The *vikingr* are coming."

Cai shivered. He had no idea what they called themselves, the raiders from beyond the northern sea, whose dragon-head boats had haunted the shores of his childhood for as long as he could remember. Cai's people and the brethren used the word picked up from traders to the south, some of whom ventured west to do business with the less ferocious Saxons overseas—*vikingr*, the pirates. The final R was awkward to local tongues and often got dropped. The meaning was forgotten, too, subsumed in the terror the name could evoke. Not just pirates—a race, a force, an implacable visitation from hell. The Vikings... "They always come," he said uneasily. "Not yet, though. It's too soon in the year. The storms are still bad." He took the pony's rein. "Anyway, they always sail past us at Fara. We're too poor to bother with."

"Things have changed. You have something they want. They will come."

Fire, burned-out villages, women stumbling round the charred remains in search of vanished children... Cai shook off the memories. He'd ridden with his father through the coastal settlements on mornings after raids, smelling smoke and blood, Broccus grimly assessing the damage and giving such aid as he could. "Not yet," he repeated flatly. "No."

"Can you hear the music anymore?"

Cai listened. All he could hear was the anxious thud of his own heart and the stir of the wind in the dune grass. "No. Wait, though... Yes."

"That's your own church bell, foolish boy. Seems you'll miss your lunch."

Cai smiled in relief at the rough, ordinary sound. Theo had done his best to introduce Hours, the elegant rhythms of monastic life—matins, lauds, prime and the rest, dividing the day into twelve equal parts—for the spiritual and temporal regulation of his community, but it hadn't worked on Fara. Cai's brethren were subsistence farmers, out in far-flung fields all day, tending such livestock and crops as they owned. Now the bell rang twice a day—once at noon and once at dusk, announcing food was ready for those close enough to come and eat. "That's probably what I was hearing."

Danan looked down at him. Her expression was gentler than usual. There was a trace of pity there, a sorrow whose source Cai couldn't read. "Yes," she said. "Probably that was all."

"I have to go."

"Yes. Be well, Cai. Just...listen for the music of the sea bells when you can. Listen for it."

He shrugged. "I will. Goodbye, Danan."

He was almost at the foot of the dune, the pony trudging patiently at his side, when she called to him again. "Caius."

He turned, shielding his eyes from the sun. She was weirdly outlined by it, her shape seeming to coruscate and shift. She could have been a girl standing there, or a proud young woman. "Caius, your father grieves for you."

"No, he doesn't," Cai shouted back cheerfully. "He threw me out when I converted. Disinherited me too."

"Nonetheless."

"He told me to keep my castrated Christian carcase out of his sight until I'd learned what a real man was. So I shall. You can pass that on to him when you next see him—if he's still grieving, that is."

Cai strode on briskly, the pony breaking into a resentful trot beside him. He always felt better when he'd restated, to himself or anyone else, his reasons for leaving Broccus and the hillfort far behind him. Broc regarded any form of learning as a pitiful waste of time. He lived for hunting, bloodshed and noisy copulation with the endless stream of women he bought from slave dealers or stole along with cattle from his neighbours during raids. Cai had had to get away. And he had to remember the bad things, because the stupid truth was that Cai grieved for his father too.

They were so alike. That was the trouble. Broc could be forgiven for thinking his firstborn son, who resembled him in every detail, would have followed in his rampaging footsteps. Coal-black eyes, hair to match. Strong frames saved from squatness by a length of well-nourished bone carried somehow down the line from Broc's Roman ancestors, soldiers who'd manned Hadrian's great wall in the last days of the empire, married into the people they called *Brittunculi*—dirty little Britons!—and stayed behind when the occupying forces went home. That had been three hundred years ago, but Broc still kept among his prized possessions a Roman army standard, indescribably blackened by time. *Yours,* he'd told Caius again and again. *Yours when you reach manhood and perpetuate my name.*

There was little chance of that at Fara. The perpetuating part, anyway—Cai, at twenty-four summers, had long since attained his majority. Broc had provided him with girls, but Cai hadn't wanted a slave, or worse still some tired, resigned castoff of the old man's. He hadn't really known what he wanted, until...

Swift movement flickered on the white-gold beach that bordered Fara to the north. Cai raised a hand to shield his eyes against the sun. A shiver of pleasure went through him, driving off his shadows. In many ways Broccus needn't have worried—Cai was a very poor Christian still, frequently shipwrecked on the tides of sensual enjoyment that came to sweep his new ascetic principles away. In many ways he was his father's son.

He lifted a hand and waved to the young man running full pelt up the beach, his cassock hitched into both hands, his flag of fair hair flying. "Leof! Leof!"

They met as they always did after Cai's trading trips—arms outstretched, laughter shaking them, knocking the breath from one another on impact. Cai had been gone for three weeks this time, much longer than usual, and their collision was proportionately harder, tumbling them both into the sand. They rolled in the dune grass, little crushed clusters of flowering thyme sending up fragrance around them. "Leof. How are you, you puny Saxon? How is Fara?"

"Oh—the same." Leof beamed up at him. His face was smudged as usual with ink from the scriptorium. "Hengist has discovered a new seaweed we can eat. Brother Gareth has a wart and thinks it's plague. Theo's had me working all hours on his book."

"And is it?"

"What?"

"Plague?"

"Oh, no."

"Thank God for that, then. I don't have to hurry home."

Their mouths met, smile to hungry smile. For Cai there was nothing finer than this—Brother Leof at the end of a journey, a passionate reunion in the dunes. He let the younger man roll on top of him, shuddering with joy at the surrender. Leof was lighter, less huskily built, but it wasn't about strength, and still less force, as he'd have liked to explain to Broc, if it wasn't immediately imperative to thrust all thoughts of his father right out of his mind. "I've missed you."

"I've missed you. Ah, you look fine out of your cassock."

"And so will you, out of yours."

Leof shook with laughter. "Fool. I have to talk to you."

"Talk after this."

"But it's *about* this, Cai."

"Well, then—tell me after, while the subject's still fresh in your mind."

The pony regarded them placidly. Around them, sky and air wove the ancient song of the meeting place of earth and sea—wave-rush on the shore, gulls mewing and sobbing. No more bells, except a last dying peal from Fara.

"You've missed your lunch," Cai whispered, running a hand up beneath Leof's cassock and stroking the skinny belly underneath. "And you're thin. Have you been eating?"

"I forget. I lose myself. It seems of more importance to follow the curve of a letter with my brush than to pursue a clanging, cracked bell to the refectory."

"Very noble-minded. But the curves and the weave and all your wondrous little beasts can't live if their creator isn't fed." Cai moved his hand, and Leof arched his head back, groaning. "At least this part of you is still vigorous."

"For you it is. Oh, Caius—my brother, my brother..."

Caius stripped out of his travelling clothes. The damage to the deerskin leggings wasn't too bad, he noted—just one small damp mark, the rest of his seed spilled blissfully into the turf and the clutch of his own hand, Leof's pouring hotly into his throat, where Cai could still taste it, salty and rich. He shook out his cassock from the pony's pack but didn't immediately put it on. The heavy brown wool was in need of laundering, at his long journey's end, and on spring days like this its weight was unappealing. Still, it was practical, warm in the draughty monastery buildings, and Brother Hengist had perfected a wash that kept most of the lice out. Cai stood naked, idly scratching the pony's ears, enjoying the caress of the warm wind on his skin.

"Cai, please get dressed. No man as beautiful as you should ever be allowed amongst monks."

Caius looked at Leof in surprise. He was sitting curled up on the turf, his skirts firmly tucked around his ankles. He was pale in the sunlight, and Cai put the cassock down again and unpacked the last of his bread and cheese. He had a little wine left too, nice Traprain mead, not as good as the stuff they brewed up themselves at Fara but restorative nonetheless. "Here," he said, dropping down beside Leof and handing him the flagon and a chunk of bread folded up round the cheese. "I am not beautiful. I'm a Roman-Briton mongrel with no grace. Not like..." He pushed Leof's breeze-winnowed hair off his brow. Of all the polyglot men who had gathered at Fara—old-blood villagers like himself, Theo's Greek contingent, the Angles and Danes from the colonies further south—he was the fairest, probably nearest in kin to the strapping great Vikings who tore up the shorelines all summer long. Not that Cai would ever have said so to gentle-spirited Leof, who abhorred their very name. "Not like you, my blue-eyed Saxon. Now eat and drink, and tell me what's bothering you."

Leof wiped his mouth like a child. "I almost don't want to. I feel so ungrateful, when I've been so happy with you."

"You're not leaving, are you?" Cai frowned and cast his mind back over the past few weeks, his own various misdemeanours. Theo was tolerant, but... "Oh. Am *I* leaving?"

"No. Nothing like that. I missed you so much while you were away, but...I thought more too. Prayed more."

"Am I that much of a disturbance?"

"Not you yourself. Your friendship means everything to me. It's just that I can hear the voice of God more clearly when you're not here to make my flesh sing. Caius—*please* put your cassock back on."

Cai got up. What surprised him was that he wasn't more surprised. He unfolded the garment and slipped its familiar weight over his head. In the musky dark of his own scent, a bitter anger touched him. He wasn't quite used to Leof's god even now, and he felt as if he'd lost to a rival. He emerged, tossing back the hood from his head, and saw Leof white and stricken, tears beginning to gleam on his face.

"Oh, Cai. You do still love me, don't you?"

Cai strode over to him. He knelt beside him and hauled him into his arms. "Of course." Yes, he had been waiting for this. Leof becoming his lover at all was an example of something Theo called irony. Leof's gentle teachings about peace, detachment, release from the hungers of the flesh—these had drawn Cai to him in the first place. He kissed the bowed head on his shoulder, remembering his first sight of that flaxen hair across a rowdy marketplace in Alnwick. Cai had bartered with him for Fara mead, and then while the wagons were being packed up towards sundown, had walked with him up onto the hill that overlooked the town.

Cai had had a bad day. He'd gone to seek his father and found him grunting and sweating over a slave girl young enough to be his grandchild. He'd had a bad week, trailing the old goat around the strongholds, joining in brief, bloody skirmishes when Broc took a fancy to a neighbour's cow, plough or daughters. Leof hadn't preached. He'd simply talked about Fara—the wide, quiet spaces, the companionship of like-minded men, the chance to learn. Cai had met him three times after that. On the third occasion he'd decided he wanted to become a monk, and had celebrated by rolling the wide-eyed, willing Leof down into the hay in an abandoned barn. And willing Leof had remained, but Cai knew he had pulled the lad out of his natural ways. "How could I not love you? Please don't weep."

"Don't you mind?"

"Yes." *Just not as much as I'd expected to. You touch my innermost soul, but not like that—even when I'm coming with you, racked by that fierce joy, I still can hear the gulls call, the waves wash on the sand.* "It's your choice, though."

"I want to try to be celibate again. We did take vows of chastity, you know."

"Yes, but that means keeping clear of village maidens, doesn't it?"

Leof chuckled wistfully. "I think it means this too."

"Well, Theo never specified."

"No. He leaves us to choose for ourselves—perhaps too much." He sat up, and Cai offered him a rag from his provisions pack to blow his nose. "Cai—will you try it too? You say you don't hear God when he speaks to you, and maybe that's been my fault, letting us both be distracted by... Oh. Kissing me that way is not a good start, is it?"

Cai sat back, ashamed. He didn't mind Leof's choice, but his own nature was sensual, contrary, his flesh already missing what it knew it could no longer have. "I'm sorry. Come on. We should go, before Theo spots us out here with his spyglass. I didn't tell you—I met Danan on the path not half an hour ago."

"Did you?" Leof put out a hand to be hoisted up, gratitude for the change of subject in his eyes. "What gossip did she have for you?"

"Not much. She did have a prophecy, though. The Vikings are coming, she said."

"The Vikings always come. Not yet, though—it's still much too cold for good raiding."

"That's what I told her." Cai put an arm around Leof's waist. The gesture was only fraternal, and Leof seemed to perceive it that way, relaxing into his embrace and beginning to walk at his side. *Perhaps I'll make a good monk after all. Perhaps I can separate it out—flesh from spirit, and hear the voice of God as you do.* "Oh, that reminds me. I have to listen."

"Wonders will never cease. To what?"

"The music of the bells, Danan said. The sea bells."

The tide was out, the causeway crossing easy. The pony tossed its head in the salty wind that swept across the mudflats and started to pull ahead of Caius on its leading rein. Cai restrained it gently. He didn't want his bottles and supplies to be jostled about, but he shared the little beast's enthusiasm for home. The monastery stood on a vast outcrop of rock—the final flourish, so they said, of a great spine of it that ran right across the country to the west coast, bearing for many of its rippling miles the remains of Emperor Hadrian's great wall. On its northern side, where windswept slopes ran down to the beach, the brethren had terraced the land and persuaded from it—with the aid of many tons of stinking kelp—crops of oats and barley. There was Brother Benedict now, the only one of them strong enough to handle the plough unaided, pacing the length of one terrace behind a patient ox. Beside him walked his inseparable companion Oslaf, chanting Saxon myths and Christian psalms to him to keep him entertained and his furrows running in a straight line. On the rocky landward side where little else grew, Demetrios was collecting scurvy grass and bellowing in Greek at Wilfrid's goats, who also loved the succulent green leaves.

Oslaf spotted Cai and Leof and lifted a hand in greeting. Cai grinned, waving back. Leof was lit up with pleasure too. It was a good place for a homecoming. A hard-worked, hand-to-mouth existence, but a rational one, with time for contemplation and learning. Cai was young enough, sickened enough by his father's bestial ways, to imagine he'd found his path. If he didn't believe as Leof did—if he couldn't yet kneel in Fara's church and truly accept he was bathed in the presence of God—that would come.

A powerful voice boomed out across the salt flats. "Wilfrid!"

Cai was close enough to see the goatherd jump as if slapped. At the top of the narrow trail that led up Fara's western flank, a tall, spare figure had appeared—Abbot Theodosius, never far from the workday crises of his monks. His desk in the scriptorium was placed to give him a view out over the widest possible sweep of the land. "Wilfrid, do you wish a flaking rash to break across your skin?"

"No, my lord abbot."

"Do you wish...? Let me see... Do you wish for loose teeth, a dry mouth, mysterious bruising and seizures?"

"No, my lord abbot."

"Nor do any of us. Keep your goats under control and let Demetrios gather his weeds. Well, Caius, my physician—did I miss anything out?"

Cai brought the pony to a halt. Others of his brethren were running to take charge of the beast, unsaddle him and carry Cai's packages upslope. Theo was bounding down the steps that still divided them.

"Bloodlessness and haemorrhaging in the late stages," Cai called up to him, "but otherwise, well done."

"Ah, you see—I attend, I learn. Still, I'm glad to see you back—Brother Gareth has plague."

"Yes, so I'm told."

"How was your journey? Did you trade off all our wool?"

"Yes, and next year's shearing too, if we'll weave it ourselves for the market."

"Good boy, good boy." Theo leapt the last four steps in one and strode to greet them, hands extended. "Let me bless you. Leof, you too, though I did see you only an hour ago."

Cai hitched up his cassock hem and dropped to his knees on the turf, Leof mirroring his action at his side. Never in his life had Cai knelt to any man, or any god, until he came to Fara. Here, though, in the pure sweet air, the gesture had been stripped of shame for him. He bowed his head and waited for his abbot's benediction.

"Blessed be the travellers who come safely home," Theo pronounced, resting his hands on their skulls.

"Praise be to God," they chorused back. They had all three switched into Church Latin, their only common tongue, Leof and Cai dropping the homely dialect of the northern shores. The transition was a reflex for Cai by now. He'd struggled at first, but a two-year immersion in the language of Bible and churchmen the world over had had its effect, and he'd discovered to his surprise that Broccus had prepared his mind for some of it, with the bawdy old chants handed down to him from his Roman forebears.

The benediction over, Theodosius ruffled their hair, first Cai's dark mop and then Leof's fair one. "I should tonsure you," he said worriedly. "I know I should. You two and all the others."

Cai smiled up at him, pushing to his feet. He'd gathered from his trading trips that certain aspects of monastic life were different here than in other communities. There were no astronomy lessons for the brotherhoods down south—why should there be, when God had fixed the Earth at the centre of creation, leaving nothing new to know?—and Cai had learned to raise his hood when dealing with the monks of Tyne, or risk a storm of disapprobation for his unshorn head.

"I've been thinking about that," he said, setting off with Leof and Theo up the steps. "Don't you think there ought to be some kind of dispensation? For brethren like ourselves, I mean, who tend the fires of faith this far to the north. After all, the bulk of our bodies' heat loss occurs through the top of the skull, I've observed."

"Does it?" Theo glanced over at him, dark eyes gleaming. The scientist in him would defeat the churchman every time, as Cai had also observed. "Have you?"

"I have. When Brother Petros got caught out in the snowdrifts with the sheep, a rabbit skin on the top of his head did him more good than all our clothes and blankets. Even than the fire."

"Is it so? Well, you may have a point. Enough to let me put off the evil day, anyhow—I don't quite understand why our bald pates are pleasing in the sight of God."

"Because, my lord abbot," Leof offered shyly, "he doesn't wish us to be covered up from him."

"Why, Leof, you sound as if he told you so himself. No. It's simply a sign of our renunciation of the world and its vainglory."

"In that case, I should like it to be done." Leof cast a wistful glance at Cai, as if he might like the hair he'd run his fingers through in worldly, vainglorious pleasure to be left well alone. "To me, at any rate."

"Then so it shall be, child—as soon as I get my shears back from Brother Petros. Caius, you've arrived home in good time. Did Leof tell you my first chapter is complete?"

"No, my lord abbot." *We've been a little busy.* Cai pushed the thought away from him. "But that's good news. Did you decide yet on a title?"

"Yes." They had reached a turning in the long stone flight. Theo took up position on a flat rock and spread his arms as if to address the sunny infinity of moorlands and dunes that lay before him. "Poor copy though it is, I shall call it the *Gospel of Science.*"

Leof flinched. Like all the brethren of Fara, he loved and feared Theo in equal measure. He would never contradict him, but Cai had observed how he'd sit in Theo's lectures, head bowed, his hands clasped in his lap, as if silently begging God to overlook the blasphemy one more time. Well—good and conventional churchmen did not get appointed to world's-edge outposts like Fara, and Theo had not been so much sent as banished there. He was a renegade, a once-powerful teacher caught in the rebellious possession of books now deemed heretical by the Roman Church. Stripped of his treasured volumes, his power and authority, he had been shipped off to the far west—where, according to the beliefs of his masters, he might well tumble right off the planet's rim and trouble them no more.

He had noticed Leof's involuntary twitch. Cai tensed. A man of sublime patience, a father to his flock who would help Cai bathe their wounds with his own hands, he could still fly out in rage at wilful ignorance and superstition. "Does my choice trouble you, child?"

"Yes," Leof said bravely. "The gospels are the words of Christ, not...arrows and dots, and long strings of numbers fit to bewilder all God-fearing men."

Theo smiled. "Well, I do hope not *all* of them. Not forever, anyway." He resumed his climb, making room beside him on the path for Leof to walk at his side. Cai, bringing up the rear, looked at them both in affection. "Remember, Leof. All I am doing is trying to recall and write down a fragment of the books that were lost. My gospel—we can call it something else for now—will only ever be a copy, a shadow, of that great wealth. I use mathematics and diagrams because, in their neatness, they can convey what an army of monks writing all day and night could not teach. You, the best and most godly of my brethren, need not be disturbed by it at all."

"Yes, my lord abbot. Thank you."

"And although it would distress me, I will give you dispensation from illuminating my heresies—if you wish."

Leof jerked his head up. Cai could have laughed aloud at his open-mouthed dismay. "Why—no, sir. Please not that."

"Good. Because I value them, your vines and grapes and little dancing stoats."

"Those are foxes, sir."

"Ah. Well, nonetheless. You'll carry on?"

"Of course. I wish I saw what my plants and my beasts have to do with your—your gospel, however."

Theo put an arm around his shoulders. "Science makes an error," he said, the gentle laughter fading from his voice, "in cutting itself off from nature. In thinking of itself as separate. I feel a chill inside my heart when I imagine where such an error might lead. So, my clever painter, though your vines and foxes may not illustrate the turning of the Earth upon its axis, or the distance to the moon, I hope they will remind the men of some future day that foxes, moon and Earth are one, and all the work of one great hand. Yes—I do believe that, for all my blasphemous ways. It's not so hard, as a doctrine—even for the likes of Brother Cai."

Cai, who had been dreaming, surfaced at the sound of his name. "The distance to the moon?" he echoed longingly.

"Indeed. We do it with mathematics, and that triangle whose sides are three, four, five. I'll show you all tonight, after our feast."

"Are we feasting?"

"As far as our duties and our resources allow. A chapter's end deserves a celebration, don't you think? I only wish we had some of old Danan's cure for sore heads in the morning."

"Ah, we do. I ran into her on the trackway coming home. I traded her some jewellery for comfrey, poppy, tonics—everything we need."

"Good boy, good boy."

"Danan told Cai that the Vikings are coming," Leof said suddenly, as if he'd been dreaming too. "It was one of her prophecies."

Theo patted him. "The Vikings always come. We don't need to worry yet, though. It's still too cold and rough for raiding."

"Yes, I know. That's what I told Cai."

Cai left them outside the scriptorium. By then the two were arguing contentedly over the relative virtues of vellum and non-calfskin parchments, and they barely noticed him go.

Shaking his head, Cai made his way straight to the infirmary, to see that his precious supplies were being properly stored away. He glanced in satisfaction round the sunny room, one of the few in the monastery that were glazed, allowing his patients the benefits of warmth and light at once. All but one of the narrow cots were empty, assuring Cai that he was doing his job well. Sitting on the edge of the occupied bunk, he treated Gareth's warts and tried to ease the painful hypochondria that lay behind them with kindly admonitions as to letting the imagination run rife over faith, work and good common sense. Then he discharged him, to his patient's disappointment, and went down to the laundry.

He was sticky and sandy from his interlude with Leof in the dunes. Taking a fresh cassock from Brother Hengist's neatly folded supply, he found himself reluctant to put it on over his dirty skin. He glanced at the angle of the sun and decided he had time to run down to the bathing pools to wash.

He wasn't really qualified to lecture poor Gareth on the perils of imagination. The pools were deserted at this time of day, and the tide had come in far enough to fill their natural granite basins with salty, crystalline blue. Cai swam about among the drifting seaweeds, diving and huffing at the pleasure of the water on his limbs, then scrubbed himself clean as best he could with handfuls of soft sand. By the time he was done, his skin was tingling with wellbeing, and what he'd have liked more than anything else was for Leof to appear, ready to cast off his garments and his new restraint.

Cai drew a shuddery breath. It was all very well to agree on a celibate life not five minutes after satiation. Keeping the resolve would be much harder, he could see. His shaft had risen at the thought of Leof's pale, lithe body in the water with him. Leaning his shoulders on the shell-encrusted rock, he allowed his spine to stretch, his hips to float. His palm ached to explore his aroused flesh, and briefly he reached down, stroking, lifting the warm, compact weight of his balls. An idea flitted through his mind that maybe his own touch didn't count.

He groaned aloud at his own weakness. Of course it did. What chance did he stand of purging his earthly desires, if he couldn't keep his hands off himself? Cursing his father for bequeathing him not only a large, restless cock but a need to use it often and hard, Cai scrambled out of the water. The cracked church bell was ringing again, this time to announce Theo's feast.

Perhaps he'd moved too fast. Perhaps—although he did his best to discourage such beliefs—the fear of the naïve younger monks was true, and undischarged seed *could* rush up into the brain and wreak havoc there. The sunlight around him darkened to black, with fringes and tassels of scarlet. *The Vikings are coming...* He dropped to his hands and knees, lowering his brow onto the stone.

The fit lasted only a few seconds. The sunlight returned. Trembling, he sat up and looked around him at the brilliant day, the rich spring light only now beginning to take on a russet flush in the west. High on the crag above him, Demetrios and Wilfrid were making their way home, to all appearances the best friends in the world, the goats trotting peacefully in front of them. Wilf was even carrying the Greek's basket of leaves. Cai was only hungry, tired from travel. All was well.

Chapter Two

For the brethren of Fara, a feast was a modest affair. Theo, knowing that fields had to be tended and goats fed no matter how many chapters of his book had been finished, allotted his guests one good tankard each of mead and rolled out a small vat of heather ale to be shared around. A sheep had been killed, and Caius finished bottling up his remedy for sore heads, then followed the scent of roasting mutton down to the refectory.

The sight he found there pleased him. He took his place quietly between Brothers Leof and Benedict, and accepted his mead from the abbot's own hand. This was very different from his father's idea of a celebration. By now a drunken, coerced girl would have been dancing on the table. With not enough women to go round between Broc's friends, Cai would have found himself fighting off the sweaty attentions of a warlord before the main course had been served.

Life wasn't perfect here at Fara. Men squabbled, petty grudges were borne. Around him at the long wooden table Cai found every type of human face, from Leof's ethereal beauty to the lumpen grin of poor Brother Eyulf, a halfwit rescued by Theo to work in the kitchens, who closely resembled the turnips of his trade. But they all turned to Theo, as he stood to give them grace, and Cai could see nothing but goodwill, as if by common consent each one of them had left the unworthy parts of himself behind for now, and come with warm fraternal hearts to join the feast.

Theo led the ancient Latin grace with a careful sincerity that made the words new. Then he blessed each one of the thirty men gathered, thanking them briefly for their work—the shepherd and the weaver, the doctor and the cook. He nodded to Brother Michael, who struck up a north-shores ballad on his smallpipes—music during dinner being the rarest of treats—and signaled for the meal to begin.

Caius took an early leave. His long day's walk was catching up with him, and he needed to put distance between himself and Leof, partly for his own sake and partly because Leof, after half a cup of heather ale, was losing his convictions. Cai could see it in the lambent softening of his blue eyes, perceive it in the lingering press of his elbow when he passed the bread. Although on a night like this Cai would gladly have led him out to the moonlit slopes beyond the farmland, he didn't want to be the means of his undoing.

He paused for a moment on his way out of the refectory. A story came into his mind—one of the many Theo had told him, of a sparrow that flew into a king's feasting hall through one window and just as swiftly vanished into darkness on the other side. *Even so, man appears on earth for a little while, but of what went before this life or what follows, we know nothing.*

He shivered. He knew that life was short. That it could be bloody, and grasped in dirty hands until it spilled out its juices and died, he had learned from his father too well. Cai didn't know how he would succeed in his efforts to renounce it, but he could only try, and certainly he could step out of the way of Leof's much more promising struggle. He could see Leof as an abbot himself one day, pure-minded and serene, counselling novice monks of his own. Now he was chattering to Eyulf, who adored him with the mute passion of a hound. Quickly, before Leof could glance up and see him go, Cai slipped away.

The night was calm and still. The shadows in the courtyard were deep, but Cai's feet knew each dip of the well-worn flagstones, and he made his way easily past the well and up the mossy outer stairs that led to the dormitory chambers. He was relieved to have his own cell to lie down in tonight. He'd spent his novitiate year in the communal chamber with only five other brethren, and hadn't exactly been cramped, but tonight he meant to say his prayers as taught and stretch out in solitude, receptive to the voice of God. Cai thought he could give his life away, devote himself body and soul, if he were quite sure he had heard it for himself. *Just once,* he asked silently, letting himself into his cell and pushing the heavy oak door shut behind him.

The dormitory building was perched on the very edge of Fara rock, and Cai's unglazed cell commanded a view out over the moon-silvered bay and far beyond it, right to the glittering horizon. He opened the shutters, leaned his elbows on the sill. *Just once, God*—and the great crescent moon seemed to roll on her back among the clouds and offer herself languorously up to him.

He sighed and turned away. He got undressed quickly, as he'd been taught, paying his nakedness no attention. He lay down flat, placing his hands at his sides. No, wait—he was meant to fold them on his chest, wasn't he? Theo's instructions hadn't been very precise, and Cai had suspected the abbot didn't care much how his novices slept, as long as they did so contentedly and awoke refreshed. Clasped on his breast, Cai's hands were at least out of mischief, and he drew and released a deep, calming breath and closed his eyes.

He just wasn't destined to have this made easy tonight. Even the dried bedstraw herbs in his thin sleeping mat smelled wonderful, heady and sweet. No sooner had he dismissed the scent from his mind when the door of the cell next to his creaked and banged hard against the wall. That meant Benedict, who despite his bulk moved quietly, was drunk. And if he was drunk, caution would be thrown to the winds, his beloved Oslaf clutched tight in his huge farmer's hands and half-carried into his cell.

Cai rolled over. Monks had no pillows, so he pressed his hands to his ears. The cells ought to be soundproof and normally were, their great doors once closed, but Benedict had left his shutters open to the warm spring air, and Oslaf's first laughter-cracked groan carried effortlessly through. Images leapt into Cai's head. It would be so good, to be thumped down onto a bunk tonight and ploughed under by a nice warm weight like Ben's. For the life of him, Cai couldn't see what was wrong with it. Well, Leof had never said that it was wrong—just distracting.

Oh, God. It was very distracting. Oslaf began to moan, quietly but in explicit rhythm. The wooden frame of the bunk cracked off the wall, and there was a short-lived scuffle. Then a cry from Ben made Cai's skin prickle tightly all over in response—the sharp joy of penetration, desire finding target in flesh. Not something he and Leof had ever done. Cai had feared to hurt him, and Leof had shown such confusion when Cai had offered himself in that way…

At least his two neighbours weren't going to torture him for long. The thuds and grunts had accelerated. Then there was a silence that was somehow worse, and a long whooshing groan of utter satisfaction from Ben.

Cai gritted his teeth. He was erect again, much worse than when he'd been down in the pools. Heat like summer lightning flickered all over the surface of his skin. He took hold of the edge of the thin mattress ticking and buried his face in it until the lack of air became more urgent than the ache in his cock. Eventually the miles of road he had covered that day, the hills and tracks and wild moors, came to his rescue, and he fell into a restless, haunted sleep.

He had a strange dream. In it, a wolf came from the sea. Cai, standing on the moonlit beach, felt no fear. He'd met wolves before, during long winter journeys through the forest, and he knew that none would come near Fara at this time of year, and never from the sea. Therefore he must be dreaming. He let himself enjoy the creature's beauty as it bounded from the waves.

It stood still, shook off its fur and became a man. Disbelief held Cai in place. When finally he turned and began to run, it was too late—his feet tangled in seaweed, and the creature caught him easily, knocking him flat. Hot breath brushed his ear. Wolf's teeth sank into his shoulder, but there was no pain. The weight that pinned him was all human. A human arm locked round his chest. A strength like nothing he'd ever felt before restrained him, and he shuddered in terror and pleasure. Rough words resounded in his head, a language he didn't understand, but he knew what he was being told to do and did it, spreading his thighs, lifting his backside to his captor's thrust. He waited to be torn apart.

No pain. A living heat drove up into his core. The creature—the human, the wolf—said his name, and the tenderness of it, the deep vibration, sent a melting rush into Cai's very bones. He pushed up in longing, and there was no pain, only an overwhelming feeling of being owned, claimed, brought home. Thrust after thrust...

He awoke coming. His fists were clenched on the bunk's wooden frame, his body soaked in sweat. Rigid, he rode out his shaft's helpless spending, sweeter and more dreadful than he could bear. It broke him to tears. He lay sobbing, eyes squeezed shut.

He could hear bells. Disconnected thoughts flicked through his head. He would never know the voice of God, not if it depended on chastity. He'd better get the mattress ticking off, rinse it under the pump. Perhaps he should just leave Fara. A wolf from the sea...

A bell, stirring gently on the inshore breeze now tugging at the wooden shutters. Wiping his eyes, Cai struggled out of bed. He went to lean on the windowsill, momentarily dizzy and weak. To climax so hard on his own like that—ah, he was hopeless, the very idea of losing Leof's sweet services enough to drive him wild. From here he could see the church, its reed-thatched roof shining eerily under the moon. The bell in its small, squat tower was ringing passively. An inshore wind—Cai didn't like those, in or out of raiding season. No northern coast dweller did. From instinct and habit, he looked out to sea.

There was a sail on the horizon. A great square sail, pregnant with that breeze. In front of it—impossibly clear to him just for an instant—rode a dragon's head.

They would continue by. They were out of season. Even Theo had agreed on that, the wisest man Cai knew. Fara held nothing for them, not so much as a woman, a jewelled altar cross or a chalice of gold. Cai's heart ached for the villages further north, and for the hundredth time he wished monastic life would stretch to a fast-paced horse such as his father kept. He would fling himself onto it and ride, ride faster than any damn Viking could sail to give warning to...

The clouds shifted. The sea at the foot of the cliffs was suddenly revealed. Cai shrank back from the window, a choked cry dying in his throat. It wasn't the sail on the horizon he needed to fear. It was the great dragon-prowed longship that had come in vulpine silence to the very shores of Fara. She was moored, rocking. Her crew was no longer aboard. That meant they were somewhere between the rocks and the meadows at the edge of the cliff.

And that meant in turn that Cai had a minute. No horse, no real hope—just bare feet and a dead run. He seized his cassock and dived into it, pulling it hard over his head. He wouldn't have spared the instant for that, except that he could fight better dressed than naked, hide up his sleeve any weapon he could find. Harsh laughter burned in his chest—a weapon? He'd be lucky to find a big enough chunk of rock in this sheepfold, this beautiful, soft-bellied refuge for peace-loving men.

A rock would have to do. Cai shot into the passageway and began to pound on Benedict's door. Only a horrified silence answered him, and Cai knew what that meant. Two naked lovers jolting upright in bed, paralysed like fox cubs in a den. "Ben! It's me, Cai. Vikings!"

Another silence, probably of disbelief this time. Cai banged his fists off the woodwork again, and Benedict pulled the door open, his face sleepy and colourless with fright. Behind him, Oslaf was scrambling upright, shielding himself with a discarded cassock. "Vikings? Cai, it's too—"

"I know it's too damned early! Just wake up the others. And send Oslaf to get Theo. Now!"

Cai tore off down the stairs. Moss slithered under his bare soles, but he was faster like this than in his cumbersome sandals. The air hit his lungs, full of nighttime sweetness. Had he really just seen a longship still rocking from the exit of her crew? The dream of the wolf-man had felt more real. Rounding the corner of the main hall, he saw that the refectory was empty, all his brethren gone to their rest.

The church was made of wood frame, wattle and daub. Only the tower at the end was built of stone, to support the bell. Twenty yards of turf divided the church from the hall, a patch of ground Cai flew across without looking back. There was no point. He'd heard the first shouts, and the air he was hauling into his lungs was no longer pure but tainted by acrid smoke. Cai felt a flash of love for the drab little building hunched beneath its thatch, an affection he'd never known on freezing mornings, shivering his way through dawn prayers. He ran through the nave, his shadow leaping round him as the flame from the sanctuary candle danced, grabbed hold of the bell rope and began to pull with all his strength.

The bell rang out into the night. Its voice seemed weak over the roar of Cai's blood in his ears, a whisper when he wanted it to scream. He counted off the tolls. One dozen, two. He wouldn't be allowed much longer. Something thudded onto the roof, like the landing of a heavy bird, the sound followed instantly by several more. The door flew open. Cai tensed to run, but he wasn't worth the confrontation. The soft thumps he'd heard overhead had been firebrands, and the figure in the doorway only paused long enough to toss another inside, this one landing almost at Cai's feet.

The thatch was dry as dust after a rainless spring. The brands on the roof burned straight through. The timber rafters caught alight, one beam crashing down to cut off Cai's route to the door. Dropping the bell rope, Cai leapt out of range of the sparks. The tower had one window, little more than a hole in the wall to let in light. It would have to do. He jumped, grabbing at the sill, got his head and shoulders through and tumbled out onto the turf.

Straight into the path of his first Viking. Cai had a moment to be glad he'd drawn a short one, and startled him by his sudden appearance. He got an impression of animal skins—of a twisted, grinning face beneath a cap-like helmet—hair in a great, thick braid, and then the firelit flash of an axe. He twisted aside, and the blade which would have split his skull in two bounced off the tower wall instead, flying from its owner's grasp.

Cai forgot he was a monk. He grabbed the Viking's plait, whipped him around and smashed his face into the stonework. He didn't stop to look at the result—let the limp body fall and snatched up the axe.

He was his father's son. Broc had been pleased with his prowess. It was part of the old man's rage upon Cai's defection—to lose a warrior child. But Cai hadn't cared about his father's fights, had gone in swinging at his side only from habit and lack of choice. He cared now. He began to run. "Leof! Leof!"

Predictably, Theo and Leof were defending the scriptorium. Cai cannoned into the blazing room, whose parchments and vellums were already burning, the desks knocked to the ground. Leof was grabbing armfuls of books off the shelves, clutching them like children to his chest. A huge shape emerged from the flames, rumbling with laughter, and seized him by the hair. Leof howled but hung on to the books, and Cai solved the problem for him—this one—with a well-aimed slice of the axe, catching the vast raider just at the base of the skull, the gap between his helmet and tough leather jerkin.

"Leof," Cai gasped. "Get out of here, beloved. Just run."

"I can't! I must help Theo!"

"I'll help him. Run!"

Too late. Three more raiders poured into the red-black chaos. Cai didn't take a moment to think—launched himself at them, blood like fire in his veins.

He didn't stand a chance. He hacked and grabbed, gouged and bit like the beast he was beneath his robes, but the flat of a blade slapped his face and he went down. Through a roaring wind he heard Theo, who was yelling back in Latin at grunted demands from the Viking holding him at sword point. Cai didn't understand. His darkening mind tried to grasp at the words, forge from them a chain of sense to pull him back to the surface.

Stop this! Stop it. There's no secret here, no treasure. We have nothing! Stop!

Theo fell silent. Cai struggled over onto his back, and Leof dropped down beside him—limp, discarded, a wheat sheaf tossed on the threshing-room floor. One side of his beautiful face was nothing but blood.

Cai surged to his feet. He locked his arm around the nearest Viking's neck—braced and pulled as Broc had taught him. A terrible, glorious crack of bone rewarded him. His victim fell. Cai whirled to find the next and hit him square on, a roaring, stinking fury in leather and fur. Huge hands clenched on him, a grip beyond evasion. Expecting nothing but a sword through his guts, not caring when it came, Cai fought. The Viking bore him backwards through the flames. For a moment there was a mad beauty to their dance. The burning spaces of the lovely room whirled past Cai's fading vision. He had only ever seen it lit by sunshine, brilliance cloud-muted, coolly reflected from the sea. Rippling patterns of sun on golden sandstone...

The lead was melting in the panes. When Cai and the Viking hit the eastern window, the rough glass cracked. This was Theo's window, from which he'd kept a benign father's watch over his realm. The only large one in the place—it burst outward, hurling Cai into the dark.

There had been nights—just a couple, when joining his father's revelries had been easier than hiding from them—which might explain such an awakening. There was a body under his. It was large and smelly, clad in animal hides. There seemed to be a lot of blood and hair. The halfwit Eyulf was sitting nearby, rocking himself and keening.

The body he was lying on was cold. Cai lurched up. Eyulf gave a squawk and hurled himself into his arms, his cries turning to crowing laughter.

"Eyulf, the kitchens," Cai muttered—all the poor lad understood, and usually enough to send him on his way. But Eyulf clung. Struggling to sit upright, Cai looked around him. He was on the rocks below the scriptorium. Around him, mist and smoke were drifting in pallid dawn light. He couldn't see more than a few yards into the miasma. There were smells in it he recognised and didn't want to, smells that caught in his throat and made him gag with horror. Burned sheepskin—no, burned vellum, subtly different. Behind it, under it and running through it like a shriek was charred flesh. He tried to push Eyulf off him. One of his arms was reluctant to work, though, and every bone in his body hurt.

He'd fallen from the scriptorium window, five men's heights above. Pieces of the thick, cloudy glass were shattered in a wide fan around him. He'd survived because he'd landed on the huge, fur-clad body of his assailant.

Voices echoed in the mist—a rattle of angry Greek, and then a great ploughman's shout. "Demetrios? Demetrios! I can hear Eyulf. This way."

Cai waited. Eyulf had him pinned, and anyway he couldn't

summon up the will to move. If he moved, memory would come. For now he was only a part of the rocks, barely more alive than the crushed flesh and bone that had broken his fall. His lungs filled with pale grey fog. He tried to let it into his mind. He tried not to breathe.

"Caius? Oh, God be praised—Demetrios, Caius is here!"

"He knew it. He said so. Cai, come quickly—he's hanging on for you."

Two shapes coalesced from the mist. One of them prised Eyulf off him and set the poor boy on his feet. The other rolled the dead Viking away far enough for Cai to realise one of his legs had been trapped beneath the corpse. Sensations weren't registering properly with him. As a physician and as Broc's son, he'd observed this happen to men who'd been frightened past their nature's boundaries. For a while they were numb, distant, slow to respond. Cai had considered it a merciful thing, the soul's emergency poultice. He didn't try to fight it in himself.

"Cai! Caius!"

That was Benedict. He was waving a hand in Cai's face. Cai nodded to show that he'd heard. He was very fond of Ben, and even of Demetrios, who had been some kind of prince in the land of Theo's banishment and drove the brethren near demented with his lordly airs. Cai was glad they'd both survived the night. Then a thought pierced to the heart of his detachment, and he sucked in one raw breath. "Benedict! Oslaf?"

"Alive." Ben gripped his hand, and they exchanged a glance. "He's hurt, though. He needs you. We all do."

"Ben, who's holding on for me? Leof?"

Ben closed his eyes. "No. Theodosius. He wants to speak to you."

Cai allowed himself to be hoisted onto his feet. He could walk, he discovered, once blood had been restored to his crushed limb, and he dispensed with Ben's support. He didn't look to left or right, clambering up the steep path. The cries he was hearing from the burning ruins each had their claim on him, but he kept moving, his eyes fixed on the ground.

No one had tried to carry Theo out of the scriptorium. Cai understood why at a glance—the Viking's sword was still buried deep in his chest. The angle was awkward, the haft jammed up against the charred remains of a desk. Brother Wilf the goatherd was kneeling behind him, propping his head and shoulders.

"My friend," Theo said calmly, as soon as he set eyes on Caius.

"Come and kneel by me."

Cai obeyed. He had to—his legs had folded under him. "Let me send to the infirmary. I can get you something for the pain."

"There's no need. This won't take long, and I want to be clear." The abbot's voice was steady, but Cai could hear on every in breath the telltale hiss of a wounded lung. "You mustn't worry, dear Caius...about the book. It's only a copy."

Cai nodded. There were a thousand things he could think of to worry about, and not one of them was a book, not even the precious vellum pages drifting in ashy rags around the room, from which Theo had taught him so much. Had been going to teach him the distance to the moon. "All right." Gingerly he probed the ragged edge of the hole in Theo's cassock, in the pale flesh underneath, but there was no chance. "I won't worry. Don't you worry either."

"You have to find Addy. Addy will give you the treasure—the secret of Fara."

The secret of Fara. In jagged echoes Cai recalled the abbot shouting those words at an enraged Viking face. "Yes, my lord abbot. I will."

"Don't...humour me, you knuckleheaded son of a Roman hill-farmer. Find it. The *vikingr* will raid again and again until you do. Only the treasure can stop them—stop the dark from coming down. Addy has it."

"Who's Addy? Can you tell me?"

"Remember, Cai—the secret isn't in the book. It's in the binding. In the binding."

Theo couldn't speak anymore. A lonely panic seized Cai. How long would this death take? The abbot's lips were moving in silence, bloodstained now, repeating the words that meant nothing to Cai, no matter how hard he tried to focus. *In the binding...*

"Please," Cai whispered. "Rest now, my lord." How long?

A kind of bundle of rags thumped down at his side. Cai jumped, then with a shock recognised Danan. His loneliness eased just a fraction. "What are you doing here? How did you know...?"

"I know what I need to. I have come to help. Why are you letting this good soul die in this way?"

"I can't save him. You can see that."

"Yesterday you bought from me the means to set free what you couldn't mend."

"Yes, but..." Cai shivered. Unorthodox as he was, the abbot of Fara had trusted in a power and mercy outside himself. "Isn't it in God's hands?"

Danan took out of her sleeve a small vial, its contents gleaming softly in the grey light. She uncapped it and took hold of Cai's wrist. She turned his hand palm up and gazed at it intently for a moment. "Yes," she said, gripping it hard. "Yes. In God's hands."

Unsteadily Cai pressed the vial to Theo's lips. The abbot was wheezing now, making faint sounds of incomprehensible pain. The dose ran passively into his throat, but after a moment he swallowed, and his gaze sought Cai's, lucid and full of forgiveness. Barely ten heartbeats later, his anguished breathing ceased.

"Caius?"

Cai looked up. What did Ben want of him now? Danan was gone. He wasn't sure how long he'd been kneeling by the dead man's side. "Yes?" he said hoarsely.

"The others need you."

"The others? What can I do?"

"You're our doctor. Help them."

"I'm not a doctor. I'm a...knuckleheaded son of a hill-farmer." Something about this struck Cai as appallingly funny, and he forced back sobs of laughter. "No one ever trained me. I don't know what to do."

Benedict put down a hand to him. "Well, you're all we've got. I'll help you."

"Ben, you're a ploughman."

"More of a man than you, it seems."

That stung. No one save Broccus had ever accused Cai of any failing there. He got up and almost fell over the blanketed shape on the ground at his feet. "Leof," he said, not as a question.

"Yes. Cai, I am so very—"

"How many are dead?" It came out low and fast, with an odd note of command in it. Ben's response was stranger still—he let go of Cai's hand and stepped back, drawing himself up straight.

"Five of us now. Brother Petros, trying to defend Theo. Andreou, trying to avenge him. Aethelstan, when he tried to stop the *vikingr* from getting to the forge. And..."

"Yes." Cai cut him off with a motion of the hand. Poor Brother Blacksmith, who'd made all the hinges and hasps for the medicine cabinets... He shook himself. "Why weren't there more?"

"I don't understand that myself. They seemed to be hunting something, and when they didn't find it, they left."

"Not without torching us. Is my infirmary still there?"

"Yes. The dormitory wing is down, and the church, but—"

"Get the injured there. Who is worst?"

"Brother Gareth—"

Gareth, with his warts and imaginary plague. "Damn Brother Gareth."

"Gareth has an axe-cut like a slice of pie out of his shoulder, but he says it's a mere scratch and you should tend the others first. Brother John is probably dying. Cedric and Wulfhere too. The rest are walking wounded."

"Very well. Bring them to me in order of need. Get water boiling—lots of it—and send to the village to see what supplies they have there. Did the Vikings raid inland?"

"No." Benedict made a sound in his throat, as if he'd swallowed a *sir.* "The village is safe."

"Good. And what...?" Cai hesitated, but only for a moment. "What have you done with the bodies?"

"The crypt is still standing. We took them there."

"Why not Leof?"

"We were just about to move him when we found out you were alive. We thought you might want to..."

"No. Take him down with the rest, straight away."

"If they come again, they will destroy us."

Cai paused in swabbing down his surgical table. He had changed his awkward cassock hours ago for his travelling clothes, and fastened a homespun apron around his neck and waist. He was up to his rolled-back shirtsleeves in blood. "Perhaps I missed something," he said to Benedict, who was renewing a rope strap at the corner of the table, the one Brother Cedric had torn through in his agony. "I'd have staked my life that we were already destroyed."

"If they come again, they won't leave one stone standing on another in this place. Nor one heart beating in its bone cage."

"That's almost poetic, Brother Ploughman." A trickle of shame made it through Cai's weariness. His friend had been so much more than a farmer on this long, grim afternoon, which was at last melting down into dusk. *Yes—last time the light was angled so, I was a mindless boy with no greater care than my appetite for food and the joys of the flesh. Oh Leof. Leof...* Cedric and John were still alive, thanks to Ben's steady grip on them, the stolid application of brute force while Cai had plied his blade and sheep-gut sutures. "I'm sorry. You've done all you can for now. Go and eat."

"If you will too."

"No. The next few hours will be crucial. I have to watch out for infections, delirium." Was it only yesterday he'd looked around his clean infirmary and congratulated himself on its unoccupied beds? A truly good physician, Danan had told him, would put himself out of a job. As things stood, Cai couldn't envisage ever being able to stem the tide of blood and pain pouring out of his orderly rooms. His patients were quiet now, sleeping or making their silent last dialogues with death, but the walls—and Cai's skull—still resounded with their screams. "I'll be all right. Go on."

The door creaked open. Cai suppressed a raw-nerved jump, but it was only Oslaf, his latest consignment of hot water from the kitchens in a bucket-yoke across his shoulders. He watched while the young man set his burden down, then collected up the soiled rags for the fourteenth or fifteenth time that day. Cai had better things to do, but he couldn't seem to tear his gaze away. He saw that Oslaf made no move without first glancing over at Ben, as if checking that he was still there. And Ben returned each look with an equal warm hunger. Cai was sure they were quite unaware of their exchange. Once Oslaf had finished his tasks, he came to stand in front of Cai. "Is there anything else I can do for you? I'll bring more water once it's boiled."

"No. Wait—ask Wilfrid to come up here, and Demetrios too if he's strong enough. I need them to carry Brother Wulfhere to the crypt."

"Wulfhere?" Oslaf paled. "Oh, Caius. I'm sorry."

"I don't have time to discuss it. We must see to the burials tomorrow. Just go."

Once Oslaf was gone, Benedict turned away and carried on wiping the benches. Cai couldn't seem to move. A bitter black fury was filling him. His hands were trembling, sweat breaking out down his spine. He wanted to take up his cutting knife and drive it into Ben's innocent back. "Why?" he rasped. "Why Leof, not Oslaf?"

Benedict turned to face him. His expression betrayed no anger, but he sat down on the low windowsill as if suddenly worn out. "I grieve for you, Brother."

"Grieve for me? You have no idea. Why is your boy—yours—running around, warm and alive, while Leof, who was worth—?"

"I grieve for you. But mind what you say."

Caius shut up. He pressed his fingers to his lips—to the mouth that had started to spew out such horrors. "Ben," he whispered. "Forgive me!"

Benedict stretched out his hand. Cai stumbled across the room to him and crashed to his knees at his feet. He buried his face in the blood-soaked dark of Ben's apron. "Leof! Leof!"

When he had wept until his lungs were raw and the screams in his head had dulled to exhausted silence, he sat up. Tears were rolling down Ben's face too, tracking clean lines through the dirt. Ben stroked his hair one last time. "Where did they come from, Cai? What did they want?"

"God knows. You're right—the next time will finish us."

"What can we do?"

Cai dragged a hand across his eyes. Already faint moans from the ward were drawing him back to his duty. "I don't know. But when I can be spared from here, I will go and see my father."

Two days later, Cai was on his knees again. In part it was simply exhaustion. Both Fara's ponies had been needed in the fields. He'd made the journey to the hillfort on foot in a bare few hours, and his soles were blistered and sore. In part it was an abandonment of pride. He had made his request, and his father had thumped down in the chair he liked to think of as his throne, burst into laughter and told him to kneel like the Christian he was, if he really desired such a thing.

Cai did desire it. He was no longer sure that he *was* a Christian, and that made submission easier. He lowered his head and awaited Broc's verdict.

He closed his eyes, and that was a mistake. He hadn't slept since the raid, and so hadn't dreamed, but he was beginning to see visions. He was back in the churchyard to the east of the burnt-out church, looking at five shallow graves. Only a thin layer of soil clothed Fara, and although every man who could lift a shovel had taken his turn, the business of digging had been miserable, long drawn out in the rain. Theo at least was at rest in the cool silence of the crypt. The stonemason would mark his tomb. For the others, only a plain wooden cross stood at the head of each pile of earth. Identity was unimportant—each of these men, coming to monastic life, had cast off all selfhood, subsumed who he was in the greater brotherhood of Christ. That was the theory, anyway. It didn't quite work out in life. Wulfhere had sung like an angel. Andreou had been a fat gossip who had loved Theo more than God. Aethelstan's booming laugh had carried out over the noise of his forge, and Petros had made wooden bowls of such exquisite finish that matrons scrapped over them like cats in the village market. And Leof...

In death, the theory worked well. Only Cai and his brethren knew which grave was which, and with them would vanish the knowledge that Leof lay closest to the wall, sheltered by hawthorns, cradled in the sacred ground he had loved.

"Caius!"

Cai jerked his head up. The churchyard dissolved to a firelit hut. All around him, sights and sounds familiar to him from earliest childhood took up their places once again—babies crying, one of Broc's latest wives nursing a newborn at her breast. Shepherds and traders wandered in and out. Broc's great wolfhounds growled at the sheep being driven past the open door. The chieftain's hut was the daily centre of all the hillfort's dealings, and Broc wasn't the man to call a halt to any of that just because his son had turned up, and so half the settlement had seen the proud monk from Fara drop to his knees on command. "Yes, Father?"

"What is there in it for me?"

Cai took him in. *There am I, twenty years into the future,* he thought. Strong as an ox, jet-black hair only now being streaked by a line or two of grey. Indestructible. "I don't understand."

"If I grant these things to you—weapons, horses, men—what will I get in return?"

"You know I have nothing."

"That was by your choice. Before you left me here, you had a kingdom to inherit."

A kingdom? Twelve miserable fields and a hilltop? Just two days before, Cai would have said it. He'd have laughed at the old man's arrogance, certain he had found a better world. He couldn't imagine ever wanting to laugh again, not if he too survived to Broc's late years, his own sturdy frame holding him fast in a life he no longer desired. "Tell me what you want of me. I must have the weapons. I'll do whatever you ask."

"Come back and be my son again."

"You have dozens of sons." Cai glanced around the thriving, bustling roundhouse, from whose every shadow peered a face more or less like his own. "Hundreds by now, probably."

"You were my firstborn."

Cai swallowed hard. What had Danan said—that Broccus grieved for him? He hadn't believed it. All his life he'd been treated like Broc's horse or his dog. A good one, granted—an asset to be shown off on market days and feasts—but nothing more than that. Coldly he said, "May I get up now?"

"You'd never have knelt in the first place if that lunatic Greek hadn't cut the balls off you. Yes, get up. Come and stand before me. You've grown, I think. Started to fill out. It's strange—you still *look* like a man."

Cai submitted to the inspection. He was past being bothered by Broc's words or the spectacle he was providing to the clan. He even stood still when Broc pushed up out of his chair and took his shoulders as if to measure their width.

"How is he, then?" the old man asked idly, tugging at his hair. "Theo, and that little Saxon bedwarmer of yours? Did they get through your raid?"

"No. The lunatic and the bedwarmer are both dead. You were right, Broccus—peace isn't the way. I thought you would help me, but if not... Just let me go."

Caius turned and walked off. He could hear Broc calling after him, but it didn't seem to matter through the ongoing racket in his head. The cries and the shouting had never let up. Sometimes beneath them sea bells whispered, and the bell from the burnt-out church—fallen along with the tower and stolen for melt by the raiders—kept up its dull warning song.

He picked his way around the central fire, around groups of children playing in the dust. When he trod on one, he picked it up out of habit and put it on his hip, jouncing it absently. He'd barely been big enough to walk himself when his first little half-sib had been thrust into his arms, and so it had gone on. He'd lived hip-deep among children all his life. Now he came to think of it, they were the only part of his father's world he'd missed, and he held the small body close, blindly seeking comfort. Probably it was a relative anyway.

The child began to yowl and laugh in pleasure at the ride, and its mother emerged from one of the smaller huts, smiling to see Broc's eldest boy back in camp. "Caius, Caius! Lost your frock?"

Cai handed the infant down to her. "Looks that way, doesn't it? Just for today."

"Ah, won't you stay with us? Don't mind your old fool of a father."

"I don't, Helena. But I have to go."

"You should hear him. Cai this, Cai that, when he's trying to get your brothers to behave. I think he's even proud of you for joining that monastery of yours."

"Yes, he sounded it." Cai looked into her cheerful face, dusted all over with flour. Yes, she'd been one of Broc's women for a while. She hadn't suffered too much, and now she had a home, and this sturdy boy. *Come back and be my son again.* In a way, it would be the easiest thing in the world. If he stayed, no doubt the noises in his head would soon be drowned out by others—the pigs squealing now, for example, as the inept village butcher began his task... Cai's head spun. "I have to go," he repeated, avoiding her kindly outstretched hand. "I don't belong here anymore."

The question remained as to where he *did* belong. Stumbling out of the village, past Broc's ferocious outer defences, the wooden palisade and Roman-style earthworks, Cai tried to think it through. Leof had brought him to Fara. Whenever Cai had doubted what he was doing there, he had turned to Leof and seen, in his friend's devout, loving ways, an ideal pattern for life. And although Cai knew Abbot Theo had never been supposed to tell him that the round apple Earth danced round the sun, his teachings had shown Cai what such a life could be when lit up from within by learning.

Find Addy. Remember, Cai—the secret isn't in the book. It's in the binding.

Cai jolted to a halt on the track. Theo's voice, cutting through his inner racket like a knife, solemn and clear as if the abbot had been standing in the sunshine beside him. Leof and Theo were gone. Cai hadn't been able to save either from a brutal, unchristian death. And his abbot's last command, half-forgotten in the mess inside his skull, meant nothing to him.

He could feel the revolutions of the Earth. He wasn't meant to, he was sure. The vastness of the rock, and the great invisible force that pinned him to it, meant he could spend his days in blissful unawareness of moving at all. Such an illusion was every man's right, Theo had taught. Learning could be taken or rejected. But the choice had to be there. *The treasure. The secret of Fara.*

The sky darkened. The track was empty before and behind him, and he was far enough from the hillfort that no one could see him, but he made his way into the gorse, a painful sickness boiling up in him. He wished the Earth would stop. He wished there wasn't blood beneath his nails, so deeply ingrained that no amount of scrubbing would shift it. He doubled up, his stomach clenching.

He'd forgotten to bring food with him, and Broccus hadn't offered any. Still the efforts to vomit tore through him. He used to suffer from strange, disabling headaches, days when coloured glass had seemed to float in front of his eyes. On those days Leof had sat by his bunk, pressing a cold, damp cloth to his brow. Cai threw up water and stood gasping, wiping away hot tears.

His head had cleared a little. That often happened once the sickness had pitched, Leof cleaning him up and telling him gently how poor an inspiration he was for his profession. Even the bells and the screams inside his head were dying down.

Replaced by rapid hoofbeats. Was that worse? Cai half-fell back out onto the track. A violent four-time percussion... He didn't think he could live with that. With relief he realised the sounds were coming from the hillside above him. One of Broc's wild little warhorses was being driven down over the turf. They'd have made a Roman soldier laugh, Cai suspected, but in their own right they were grand beasts, crossbred down with native ponies through the centuries and still showing some of their imperial blood. An eye for horseflesh was one of the things Cai had been meant to leave behind him in the outer world, but still he watched appreciatively as the horse and cart approached.

No, not a cart. Cai wiped his eyes again, in disbelief this time. Jouncing behind the pony, catching dull flashes of sun on its ancient bronze fittings, was one of Broc's chariots. He had three of them, his legacy from his own father's grandfather. Broc swore they were original and had seen action up near Hadrian's great wall, but Cai reckoned that, like the horse, they were inventive copies. The wheels were broad and tough, better fitted to hillsides than old Roman pavements. Their frames were gaudy with low-relief bronze plates of goddesses walloping nine shades of hell out of a more recent enemy—wide-eyed figures who looked like the very Saxons who had since settled peacefully here, established monasteries and sent their beautiful sons to lighten the lives of men like Cai. "Leof," he whispered, wondering if the name would ever be out of his mind, off his tongue.

Maybe the loss of him had finally unseated Cai's reason. Broc valued these chariots more than his cows and his women put together. They seldom saw the light of day, and were never sent out on errands. Still unsteady, he stepped forwards to meet the driver, a skinny lad struggling for control. "Whoa! Pull her up, pull her up. What's all this?"

"Broccus sent me after you. He says..." The boy hauled back hard on the snorting pony's reins, and Cai took hold of the harness. "He says you're to have the weapons you asked for. He also said..." Frowning, the boy repeated his script. "There's little point, because you and your skirt-wearing friends will probably just chop your feet off, but you're welcome."

Cai looked into the willow containers strapped to the chariot's frame. About twenty broadswords had been roughly packed inside, together with a selection of rusted shields. "He said I was to have all these?"

"Yes. The horse and chariot too. He also said you could have me."

Cai had no doubt in what capacity. "That's nice. How old are you?" The boy looked blank, and he clarified, "How many summers? Since you graced this world with your being?"

"Oh. Fourteen or so, I think."

"Well, go back and have about ten more."

"What? You'll be an old man by then!"

Cai shook his head. He reached up and lifted the boy from his perch. Springing onto the board in his place, he took up the reins. They were soft and worn and came more sweetly to his hands than befitted a humble follower of Christ. He couldn't help but think how much faster he would cover the ground between here and the monastery now. He smelled fresh bread and noticed the satchel of provisions his unpredictable father had also packed in among the swords. Some of his sickness and grief had receded. His imagination pounced forwards to how it would feel to bring a Briton's broadsword slicing down onto a Viking's hairy skull.

"Tell Broccus I'm grateful," he said. "Very." It struck him that Broc had picked out for him a lad with fair hair and eyes as close to blue as the stock of the inland strongholds ever showed. He shivered. "Be sure and tell him I wasn't dissatisfied with you. I can't take anyone back with me, and...I'm done with that kind of thing. That's all."

He shook the reins. The pony danced around, making the harness jingle. Cai had only driven a handful of times, Broc cursing him and bawling out instructions, but he found his balance easily, measuring tension on the reins where they ran through the loops. The boy stepped out of the way, and he drove the chariot sharply forwards, lifting his face to meet the wind.

A mile north of Fara, Oslaf appeared, blue around the lips from desperate running. As soon as Cai saw him, he set the warhorse to a gallop. He'd instructed Benedict as well as he could in the care of the injured men, but knew he shouldn't have left them. Nothing—not even life—had seemed so important as getting to Broc and acquiring the instruments of death. He drove the chariot on to meet Oslaf, reining in hard when he approached the panting monk. "Here," he called, reaching down. "Get in. Tell me as we drive."

"No." Oslaf lurched at the movement of the unfamiliar vehicle, grabbed the rail and hung on. "At least... Slow down. I saw you coming home, and Ben said I should get to you and warn you..."

"Is Cedric worse? John?"

"No. They're healing. Take this side track, Cai. Stay out of sight of Fara for now."

"Why?"

"Follow round so you'll come in at the foot of the cliff. What *is* this devil's contraption?"

"It's my father's, which amounts to the same thing. What's wrong?"

"We have a new abbot."

Cai steadied the pony, who'd enjoyed her wild dash over the

moors and was skittering impatiently in the confines of the lane. He calculated the time it took for a message to reach even the nearest of the brother monasteries. "How? No one can have heard about Theo yet."

"They haven't. This man was dispatched from the south weeks ago to replace him. His name is Aelfric. He's..." Oslaf relinquished his grip to gesture with one hand, clearly lost for words. "Just don't let him see you come in, not with this rig. And..." He glanced incredulously into the baskets. "And an arsenal. Caius..."

"We have to defend ourselves."

"He won't let you. He says the raid was a punishment from God."

Cai almost dropped the reins. "He says *what*?"

"Because we don't obey Rule. Because Theo was wicked and heretical. He wants his body taken out of the crypt and—"

The lane was very narrow. Broc's chariots had been designed for close combat, though, and his horses could turn on a sestertius. The mare swung obediently at Cai's shout and tug on her left rein. The chariot lumbered round, almost tipping Oslaf off the side. "Cai, what are you doing?"

"Going home. The fast way. Where is this idiot from?"

"Canterbury. He has other men with him, senior clerics. Please turn round again. You can't just..."

"Oslaf, be silent. And hang on."

The scene before him was dreamlike. Urging the pony on, Cai struggled to make sense of it. He had been fighting for his grasp on reality all the way down the coastal plain, memories overlaying themselves onto his bleak present moment. He'd driven hard past the place where he'd first seen Leof on his journey home from trading, averted his eyes from the dunes where they'd lain down. Now it was as if time had slipped, doubled back on itself with incomprehensible changes. Men were congregated, motionless but for the wind-driven flap of their robes, in the place where the church had been. Shaken by the speed of his approach, Cai could almost take the vision wholesale, believe in it as he wanted to—the brotherhood nearly back at full complement, close to thirty of them standing in the sun.

But five were strangers. They were gathered around a tall, thin man whose resemblance to Theo vanished after one cruel sting. The remaining Fara brethren were facing them. Through a flash of red fury Cai saw John and Cedric amongst them. Cedric was propped up in Wilfrid's arms, John on his knees, his face grey and drawn.

Cai let the mare pick up speed. She liked open ground, and the church—the remains of it, the undefended space with its tumble of stones and burnt rafters—stood all by itself on the hillside. The monks were beginning to turn in response to the thunder of hooves. Mouths opened, fingers pointed. The thin man pushed back his hood to see, revealing a harsh tonsure and a face like a carrion crow's. Repulsion crawled in Cai's marrow, an antipathy that curdled his blood. Deepest instinct told him that this carrion bird was his enemy, more certainly than the *vikingr* who had plundered and burned with blind malice only. For a moment he wanted to plough straight into the group, smashing himself and the chariot to bits in the process, but he eased the speeding pony's head around, drawing her through an arc to slow her down.

"You," he cried as soon as he was within earshot. "What in God's name are you doing? Why are those men out of bed?"

Benedict detached himself from the group and ran to intercept him. "Caius, wait."

"No! Take the horse. Hold her." Cai leapt down, not caring whether Ben had obeyed his order or not. He vaulted into the church over the tumbledown wall and ran to Brother John. "All right," he said to him, crouching at his side. "Just hold on and..." He broke off, lifting a scarlet hand. "He's bleeding," he yelled, and thrust out his red palm at the newcomers. "Who the devil are you? What have you done?"

The tonsured man stepped forwards. If he was startled by Cai's intervention, his face didn't betray it. In fact he looked coldly amused. "I am Abbot Aelfric of Canterbury, sent to mend the devil's work in this blasphemous pigsty. God and the Vikings have begun my mission for me. Now—before I order you tossed from the cliffs—who are *you*?"

Cai hauled in a breath. Before he could expel it, a shadow fell across him—Ben's huge bulk, interposing itself between him and Aelfric. "My lord abbot," he said, planting a hand on Cai's shoulder and pushing him down. "This is our physician, Brother Caius. Forgive him. The men killed in the raid were his close friends, as—as they were to all of us."

"This wild-eyed savage is a monk? Where is his cassock?"

"He's been travelling. Abbot Theodosius used to permit him to wear—"

"Where is his tonsure?" Aelfric turned back to address the brethren, dismissing Benedict without a glance. "And all of yours? Where are your hours for prayer? Why have I come here to find you doing as you wish, through all the day and the night? You say the Vikings raided here. I say again—God wielded his sword over you, and sent a cleansing fire. In truth..." He paused, eyes shining coldly. "Cast your minds back to that night. In truth, did Vikings come? Or were they demons, cast up from your own blackened consciences to reprove your sins?"

Caius burst into laughter. "You think we *dreamed* this raid?" He stood up, knocking aside Ben's restraining hand. "Wilfrid—press the hem of John's cassock here, as I have been doing. To staunch the hole the dream-demon made in him. Tonsures, Aelfric? Hours for prayer? You try both, in a freezing winter here. You'll want every hair on your shiny pate by the end of it. Ask the newborn lambs in the snow if Brother Shepherd can come home to pray nine times a day."

"Caius!"

"What?" Cai swung round to face Ben. "Why is anyone listening to this man?"

"Because he's our abbot," Ben replied flatly. Cai opened his mouth, but Ben took his shoulders. Low and urgent, too soft for anyone else to hear, he went on, "Besides, what if...? Oh God, what if he's right?"

The sense of nightmare had lifted from Cai for a while, during his wild gallop from Broc's stronghold. Now it came down again, like a killing jar over an insect. Strength ran out of him. If Ben, the strongest and best of his friends here, had fallen under the spell of this lunatic... All the light and warmth in Cai's world lay buried in the shallow mound beneath the hawthorn trees. He had briefly forgotten. "I don't care," he said dully. "I just want John and Cedric out of here. Will you help me or not?"

Ben hesitated. Peripherally Cai saw Aelfric smile, as if winning a finely calculated point. Then Oslaf, who had finished securing horse and chariot to a post, pushed through the crowd towards them. "Benedict," he demanded breathlessly. "What's wrong with you? We must help Cai."

He took Ben's hand. The gesture was potent—much more than

brother to brother. Cai wanted to shield them, but Aelfric had seen it too. His gaze had focussed, knife-blade predatory, upon their joined hands.

Benedict shook himself and seemed to come out of a trance. "Yes. Sorry." He lifted his head. "Forgive me, my lord abbot, but Caius is right."

Aelfric let it go. He did so easily, as if he had found something better to pursue. "Go, then. I have said what I wish to for now. All those who need to, go with your physician. For now."

Cai and Oslaf took charge of Cedric, who had stayed upright somehow, his eyes blank and lost. Benedict picked John up bodily and cradled him. Leading the way out of the church, Cai saw his new abbot's thin lips working, moving as if in prayer. *Abominations,* Cai lip-read, and averted his gaze so as not to know any more. Aelfric was watching Oslaf and Ben like a hawk. *Abominations.* A few of the monks who had suffered no injury during the raid did their best to creep out with the others, but Aelfric's retinue, starved-looking men like himself, moved to block their path.

Aelfric spread his arms. "I will purify this place of all abomination," he declaimed aloud, his voice a crow's caw on the wind. "I will rebuild it in sanctity. You who remain here—never mind your goats and your laundry. Dedicate daylight today to gathering these fallen stones. Your church must be built out of rock, like Peter's of Rome."

Cai stopped dead. Oslaf had started up the stairs to the infirmary with Cedric. He shielded his eyes from the sun. "Don't be a fool, Aelfric," he said. His anger had gone. To himself he sounded reasonable. He had to stop this stranger in such a fundamental mistake. "The Vikings knock down churches wherever they raid. I don't think they care what we worship, or who, but the sight of our churches provokes them. We build in willow and thatch so it won't matter so much—so we can put them back up again."

"Blasphemy!" Aelfric swung a finger at Cai, who thought he would soon become very tired of that gesture. And that word. "Blasphemy, to say the burning of a church matters not! A church built out of faith and sacred stone can never fall. We will build it. You will help us the moment your duties are done."

Cai shrugged and turned away. He didn't know what battle he was facing here, if there was a battle at all. Benedict and all the Fara brethren had been devoted to Theo. A stranger marching into Theo's monastic realm, threatening to desecrate his corpse... Cai would have expected to find Aelfric and his men in a heap at the foot of the cliff, hurled there by Benedict's great hands. How had the crow taken charge? If Cai could bring himself to care, he'd have to find out, discover the nature of his power. And meanwhile... "Oslaf," he called softly, running up the stairs to catch up with him. "I'll take Cedric now. Can you get back down to the chariot—take it down to the stables without our new friend noticing?"

"I'll try."

"Good. And if he stops you—well, for God's sake don't let him see the swords."

To stay out of Aelfric's way was the best. Over the next couple of days, Cai managed this well. John took fever from his enforced attendance in the church, and Cai stayed at his bedside, wrestling away the dark angel more by sheer force than medical skill. Half a dozen times he reached for Danan's poppy vial, but held off, reading the lights in John's eyes as a will to survive and praying he was right. Aelfric didn't intrude into the infirmary, and Cai didn't encounter him again until at last he could leave John for long enough to go in search of food.

His route took him past Theo's office. That was how the brethren had referred to the bare little cell by the scriptorium, though Theo had dispensed most of his administrative wisdom directly, outdoors or looking over his charges' shoulders while they worked. The room had been the storehouse for his curiosities and teaching aids—a row of skulls, some from beasts whose living forms Cai couldn't begin to imagine, some human—and on the shelves below, the array of devices he had used to teach the brethren his wild, anticlerical science. *The* Gospel of Science, Cai thought, Theo's last words resounding in his head again. *Only a copy, dear Caius. Don't worry.*

A dark-robed form was moving round the room. This was such a familiar sight that at first Cai didn't react to it. Tall and thin, bending over the shelves...

Glass shattered on the stone flags. The floor was already glimmering with shards. Theo's bronze spyglass lay in a corner, crushed as if a great foot had landed on it. The device he had called a sextant, the copper arc on its complex wooden frame—the thing he used to tell the distances between the stars—was in pieces against the far wall. While Cai watched in the doorway, Aelfric turned and swept the last shelf clear of its skulls, a single contemptuous gesture.

When he was done, he planted his hands on Theo's desk and glared at Cai as if he had expected to find him there. "You will understand this," he growled. "God made all men—even you, physician—as the sublime peak of his creation. He did not set them adrift on some bare rock to float amongst the stars. He placed them at the centre. The sun...goes round...the Earth."

Cai wanted to weep. He wanted to fall on his knees, scrape up as many pieces of his beloved abbot's precious toys as he could, fold them into his robes and make them whole again. "You're worse than the Vikings," he got out, the words scalding in his throat. "Even they didn't... Even they left these things alone."

"Yes. The demons recognised the devil's instruments."

For once Aelfric was on his own. Every other time when Cai had encountered him, he had been surrounded by his retinue of grim-faced clerics. Cai too was alone. Aelfric was lean, but Cai sensed a strength in him. It would be no cowardice to take him on now—by the rules of Broc's stronghold, not the cloister. Man to man, and the loser to repent the error of his ways as he dropped like a stone from the window.

Caius, don't worry.

This time the voice was almost physical. Cai barely restrained himself from jerking around. He felt as if Theo had laid a warm hand on his shoulder. *Don't worry. Don't let him destroy you or drive you away. Guard my flock.*

Cai decided he was going mad. That was far from unlikely, given his last few days. He had seen better men than himself break down over less. That was fine. If he had to hear voices, Theo's would be the one he chose, unless it had been Leof's. But that sweet soul was resting in a peace beyond Cai's understanding, his voice the sea-wind song among the gorse. Cai went up to the desk. Aelfric tensed for confrontation, but there was no need.

"Have you set a watch?"

"A watch?"

"At night. The raid here came early this year. But now they've come once, they'll do it again. They think we have something they want."

"The demons will not come when men's hearts here are pure. And pure they shall be."

Cai gave it up. He could watch the sea himself. He no longer seemed to need sleep. "By your own wisdom, then. But remember this." He took up the stub of a candle from Theo's desk and put it upright. "Here is the sun. Imagine its light if you can." He placed in front of it the round stone Theo used as a paperweight, and produced from a pocket in his cassock a small pink apple. It was one of Broc's, from the orchard where sweet Roman strains still grew. He set it down in front of the stone, so that all three objects were in a line. "We *are* on the rock, my lord abbot. The apple is the moon. Just now our rock, this stone, sits between the sun and moon, and so the moon is dark. In fourteen days, this apple moon has moved to our rock's other side, and so we see her face in full. So we must be between the sun and the moon—not at the centre of them." Cai paused and drew in a deep breath. "Preach what you will. Darken men's minds if you must—tell them the sun and all creation dances round you. As long as there's a candle, a stone or an apple anywhere in this monastery—I can prove otherwise."

Chapter Three

Cai stood on a fallen lintel stone, his arms folded over his chest. His perch gave him a good vantage point over the ruins where the dormitory chambers had been, and he was watching carefully. One, two, three. Step, parry, thrust. So far he wasn't displeased, except that Brother Wilfrid... "No, no, no." He leapt down and ran across the open, sunlit space. "Wilf, your Viking just ran you straight through the heart. Don't drop your shield."

"Why, you just told me not to raise it, lest he strike me through the balls!"

Cai stepped back, lifting his hands in despair. He let the dozen men gathered around him have their laugh—joined briefly with it himself. In the week since the raid, not much laughter had been heard at Fara. He took up position behind Wilf and covered his shield hand with his own. He nodded to Oslaf, Wilf's fighting partner for this bout. Oslaf came forwards, feinting with his sackcloth-covered sword. "Raise your shield. Now lower. React. You can see what he's going to do from the set of his shoulders." *Especially when he's poking at you like an old woman chasing flies with a broomstick, but that can't be helped.* "Predict him. Better. Good."

Signalling to the others that they should continue the drill, Cai returned to his post. This was his third session, and the best turnout yet. When he'd let it be known two days before that he would be here with Broc's donated arsenal, only Oslaf and four others had appeared, glancing nervously over their shoulders. Cai couldn't blame them for their fears. The ruin was a good place to practise—the one remaining wall shielded their endeavours from the main hall, and rebuilding here was a low priority, the displaced monks sleeping on makeshift cots in a barn, where they rested the more easily for safety in numbers—but Aelfric wouldn't remain deceived for long. A handful of monks missing from their duties during quiet hours was one thing. A dozen, though, almost half the surviving complement...

Cai sensed movement behind him and whipped round. "Benedict," he said in relief, then recalled his friend's behaviour over the past few days and frowned. "Have you come to join us? Or has our lord abbot sent you to smoke us out?"

Benedict looked at the ground. He was very pale. "I should be insulted that you ask. But I understand."

"To join us, then?" Cai jumped down. "Did something change your mind?"

"I am not to touch Oslaf," Ben told him. Cai raised an eyebrow—nobody was touching anybody these days, not now that they all slept like frightened puppies in a barn. "No," Ben said intensely, reading his thought. "Not like that. I am not to lay hand on him even in friendship. Nor am I to speak to him, go near him or have dealings with him at all beyond the absolute necessities of work."

"Dear God. Aelfric told you this?"

"I wasn't accorded that much dignity. It was Laban, his chief aide."

"Will you obey?"

"For Oslaf's sake—yes, I will."

"But...it's brutal. Why?"

"Because if I don't, the punishment will fall on Oslaf, not on me."

Cai shook his head. He could see the crude cleverness of such tactics, but... "Punishment? Look at you, Ben. You could snap Laban over your knee like a twig. Aelfric too, for that matter."

"Yet I can't shelter Oslaf from their condemnation. From being named a pervert, as I have been named. They'll do it before everyone, Laban said. Stand him in front of all his brethren and..." Benedict's voice scraped into silence. Then he looked up, meeting Cai's gaze with hunted desperation. "I can't say any more. What if he's right, Cai? What if we *are* impure in the sight of the Lord? I would send my own soul to hell if I had to, but not his—not Oslaf's."

Shards of broken glass seemed to move in Cai's throat. He stood in miserable silence, trying to work out what had been impure about his love for Leof. "All right," he said eventually. "Do what you think is best. You shouldn't have come here, you know—if Aelfric scares you so."

"Well, he does. But I gave it thought, and the Vikings scare me more." He smiled uncertainly and looked more like his old self. "Will you teach me to fight, Brother?"

Cai smiled too. “Gladly. You present me with a problem, though—we don’t have enough weapons to go round.”

Ben scanned the dormitory ruins. His gaze fell on the pile of half-burned rafters Eyulf had begun chopping up for firewood. “No, but by the grace of God we have plenty of big sticks. Where I come from, those are our weapons. Maybe I have something to teach *you*.”

Cai followed him curiously. For all his size, Ben was such a gentle soul. Cai couldn’t imagine him wielding anything more deadly than a ploughshare. Still, those had been beaten into swords before now. Lifting a long, straight stick from the pile, Ben knocked ash off the end of it and handed it to Cai. “Here. Hold it with your hands apart, like this.”

“Why me?”

“I haven’t been forbidden to look at *you*—not yet, anyway. Or to beat you hollow.”

There was a glimmer of challenge in Ben’s eyes. Deciding he liked that better than the pained anxiety, Cai hefted the stick. It couldn’t be that hard. “Oh, feel free to try.”

Ben grabbed himself a length of wood and grinned at Cai disarmingly. “Well, with a beginner, I’d...”

He moved, and Cai’s legs shot out from under him, swiped from behind by a blow he’d never seen coming. He landed on his backside in the dust. Another clatter of laughter arose from the monks, and he looked around him wryly. Well, he had been drilling them harshly. Maybe the sight of their tormentor knocked on his arse was refreshing to them. “Interesting,” he said, taking Ben’s hand and scrambling up. “Please. Show me.”

“You know, at the very last instant you tripped over your robes. Try tucking them up into your belt—on one side, anyway. You could use the protection on the other. Whichever leg you lead with when you wield a sword.”

Too intrigued to hesitate, Cai hitched up his cassock’s heavy hem and wrapped it once over his belt. Ben did likewise, and Cai nodded at his brethren, some of whom were copying the action. “Yes, you lot. Try it like that. And get on with your drills—no need to watch my humiliation.”

Ben corrected his stance and his grip on the pole. Then the two faced each other, circling warily. Ben came forwards, slowly enough this time for Cai to see his intent, and their sticks locked at right angles with a loud crack. Nodding satisfaction, Ben stepped back and tried for the leg-swipe manoeuvre again. He was taking it easy on purpose, but Cai understood how a twisting dance step would take him out of range—balanced and jumped and got around him in time to try for the drop move himself. Ben sidestepped with unlikely speed, spun round and delivered a thump that shook Cai to the bone through the defending pole.

Fires leapt up in Cai's breast. He hadn't liked fighting for Broc, but those ragged hill-warriors who took him on had soon learned to regret it. He struck back powerfully, knocking a grunt and a startled laugh from his opponent, and they set to in good earnest. Splinters flew from the poles as they clashed. This was a battlefield art, not an elegant one, and after being ditched to the ground twice more, Cai took it to close quarters with a kind of joyous rage. It was good not to think. It was good to struggle hotly with a man of his own strength—stronger, if he let himself admit it. He braced, Ben's corded bare thigh pressing tight against his, then thrust him back, gasping. A heat like arousal flared through him. God, maybe he *was* impure, for such life to be burning in his veins, Leof barely cold in his grave... He tried to retreat, but Ben wasn't having any of that, surging forwards in pursuit.

Oh, it was good. Cai let go and fought for his life. He didn't hear the silence that came down over the ruined hall, didn't notice that the monks had stopped their practice and were standing in a frightened clump. Ben was calling his name, but he didn't want to stop. Why was Ben blocking him, not responding to his moves? One block—another—until on the third Ben's pole snapped under the assault, dropping Cai hard against his chest.

"Caius, please. The abbot!"

Cai froze. Ben's hands were tight on his shoulders, immobilising him. Panting, Cai came back from his fugue far enough to see not just Aelfric but Laban and the three other Canterbury clerics lined up on the far side of the hall.

He pushed out of Ben's arms. He couldn't imagine why he had feared or hated these men for one instant. They were nothing to him—scrawny black-robed skeletons he could knock down with one hand. He strode through the crowd of his brethren, who parted to make way for him, and took a running leap up onto the lintel stone once more. "Good day, my lord abbot," he shouted, cheerfully brandishing the pole. "How may I help you?"

Aelfric stepped forwards. He was pale, and he hadn't managed to compose his face into its crow-like scowl. "What... What is the meaning of this?"

Cai glanced back at the monks. It was well enough for him to take his own monastic life in his hands, wasn't it? But his little army hadn't bargained for this. "It's drill practice," he called out, making sure they heard. "And I am responsible for it. Ben, will you take these men to the armoury and make sure the weapons are all put away? I want to speak to Aelfric."

He waited till the last of the monks had filed out of the hall, their faces averted from Laban's glare. Aelfric didn't even look at them. His gaze was fixed on Cai, as if reassessing him. "Explain yourself."

"I will. I will defend you from the demons—yes, even you—next time they come. Just in case they aren't to be deterred by prayer."

Aelfric seemed to take this in. Cai wondered what had changed inside the narrow, tonsured head—or what had changed in himself, to make those harsh features shadow with uncertainty. "Your faith is imperfect, Caius. Do you not believe these things are in God's hands?"

Cai looked down at his own, clamped tight around the weapon. His faith was in tatters. Was this what old Danan had meant? "Yes, my lord abbot," he said clearly. "I believe that they certainly are."

Cai waited for punishment to fall on him—or, worse, upon one of the brave souls who still joined him each day to learn to fight. Aelfric hadn't forbidden it. He was allowing the rebuilding of the church in timber, wattle and daub, and Theo's bones lay undisturbed beneath it. Still, he spent most of his days in whispered consultation with one or other of his retinue, and Cai had little doubt that whatever balance of power his own efforts had disturbed, soon the scales would swing back with a vengeance.

He wasn't given time to find out. And Aelfric's plans, whatever they had been, died in the bud. On a full-moon night barely two weeks after the abbot's arrival, the raiders came again.

This time they met with a frightened, ferocious resistance. The men sleeping in their makeshift dormitory started awake at the frantic ringing of the bell. Aelfric had allowed a night watch too, and the appropriation of the bell Hengist used in the kitchen to summon Eyulf to scrub turnips.

Cai stood up in the middle of the bunks, gesturing for silence and calm. "We knew this would come," he said softly. "My men, you know what to do. The rest of you—find Aelfric and go with him to the crypt."

Cai had never meant to divide them. He took no joy in military prestige, but he saw the difference in demeanour between those who had become *Cai's men* and those who would go to huddle with Aelfric in the crypt. His father would have enjoyed it—the nervous, proud vigour of the soldiers as they tucked up their cassocks into their belts and headed for the armoury, even the most graceless of them made noble by purpose. Cai followed them out. He found poor Eyulf blubbering in a stack of sheepskins in his favourite storage barn, unearthed him and sent him running with the others for shelter. Then he too armed himself and strode out onto the cliffs.

The longship had ridden in fast on the wind. Hefting his sword, Cai took deep breaths of salt air. By cloudy, scudding moonlight, he saw Benedict at the top of the path, the narrow gully through which the invaders must come. Ben had kept his longstaff in preference to a sword, and was crouched like an avenging troll in readiness, Wilfrid opposite to him. For Ben's sake, Cai had tried to assign Oslaf a safer place away from the front line, but Oslaf, bewildered by Ben's new coldness, had refused to let him far out of his sight, and was stationed on the clifftop. He looked up at Cai's approach. "I can't see them yet, Caius."

"Don't worry. They'll be here."

"Perhaps they sailed by after all."

"No. I saw from the infirmary—the longship is drawn up right under the cliffs. Be at the ready."

Oslaf nodded staunchly, and Cai felt sudden pity for him. "Listen. Aelfric's given Benedict one of his hellfire-and-damnation talks."

"About... About me?"

"That's right. Ben's trying to look after you by backing off, that's all. So be a good lad and play the game. You understand?"

Oslaf looked up at him, anger and relief in his eyes. "Thank you. Oh, I wish Theo was still here."

"So do I, believe me. So do I."

There wasn't time for more. The air beyond the cliff's edge glowed bronze and resounded with shouts. Confused movement filled the gully, and Ben leapt off the rock where he'd been perched, straight into the path of the oncoming raiders.

"No!" Cai yelled. He'd told Ben to wait, wait till he'd picked out the leader and could drop on him from behind, get that stick across his throat. By red Viking torchlight he saw Ben tackle the first huge pirate head-on, as if all he wanted was to kill someone or die trying. Oslaf, instead of holding position to defend the main buildings with Cai, dashed straight into the fray, howling his lover's name like a battle-cry—and Cai, before he could think or reflect, found himself tearing off in Oslaf's wake.

Cai's strategy went to the devil. He should have known. He could wield a sword, more or less, and show others how to do it, but he had no more idea than his father of how to coordinate men. He'd been their doctor, their friend, not their leader. He crashed to a halt face-to-face with a young man whose surpassing beauty was visible even behind the nose guard of his iron helmet. The noble face registered—what—surprise? A strange recognition? Red-bronze hair streamed in the wind. Golden wolf's eyes flickered wide. The moment passed. A lean arm arced up, sword blade flashing, and he and Cai were nothing but beast meeting beast, both rigid with the will to stay alive. The Viking failed to lift his shield. Cai drove forwards into the gap, the burnished flesh for an instant revealed between a leather jerkin and a belt. His sword tip sank deep. He hauled back, ready for his next man—God, another beauty, so like the first they had to be brothers. This time his arm was knocked aside by a vast, roaring mountain of muscle and hide, the leader, who'd emerged from his tussle with Ben in a bloodstained fury.

A pitched fight broke out on the cliffs. Men who'd been ordered to stand guard at the infirmary, storehouses and crypt came racing down, yelling like the blue-painted savages Broc's Roman ancestors had driven from the hills, and joined hand-to-hand in the fray. They were beyond Cai's control, wild with anguished recall of the last raid—of how it had felt to be sheep in the path of these wolves. Most had never lifted a weapon in anger in their lives. They hacked and jabbed indiscriminately, their training thrown to the winds. Cai yelled out orders unheard. The Vikings would slaughter them wholesale, surely. He was too occupied with his own battle to look, to try to save them.

His sword descended through air. Thrown off balance, he staggered. His man—a snarling weasel who'd been doing his best to disembowel him with an axe—was gone. All along the clifftop was unfolding a sight he could never have dreamed of. He sat down hard on the turf, hand going slack round the hilt of his sword. The Vikings were running away.

He leaned back, laughter shaking him. They wouldn't have expected resistance at all, let alone a suicide-dash by madmen. No strategy Cai could have planned for them would have worked so well. He didn't understand the cry going up among the last of the raiders rushing back down the cliff path, but he could guess. *Retreat! Retreat!*

A warm weight hit his shoulder, and he almost turned and ran Brother Oslaf through on raw-nerved reflex. Oslaf skidded to his knees, throwing his arms around Cai. "We did it! They're going!"

"All right. No need to strangle me."

"I killed one myself. I lifted my shield, and I lowered it, and..." Oslaf demonstrated, Cai wriggling out of the way. Then Oslaf's eyes went wide and dark. "I... Oh, God. I slew a man."

Cai took the boy's sword from him. He tucked it back into its sheath. "You helped save your brothers."

Oslaf nodded. But Cai knew for some men that answer could never be enough. It wouldn't have satisfied Leof. Cai dismissed the thought. For himself, he looked at the fallen shapes on the turf with unmixed satisfaction. None of them wore a cassock. Not only had they repelled this raid, but the *vikingr* would think better of it next time. Oslaf would have to work out his own salvation. He was trying now, his gentle face frowning and lost beneath its bloodstains.

Cai put a hand on his shoulder. "You did well."

But Oslaf wasn't listening. A big shape was emerging from the smoke, chilling Cai's marrow until it resolved itself into Benedict's familiar form. Cai hadn't seen him since the beginning of the fight. He hadn't yet had time to fear the worst, but he grinned in relief and waved.

Oslaf's joy burst like a leaping salmon. He shot away from Cai and ran full pelt for Ben, who opened his arms wide to catch him. Cai looked away. So much for playing the game...

And that reminded him. He got to his feet and made his way through the crowd of his laughing, shouting brethren, dodging their embraces and slaps to his back. Once out on the open hillside he began to run. The church was deserted and terribly quiet, though the new construction work was still in place, the door to the crypt intact. Cai raised his hand to knock, then saw candlelight all the way around its edges. That meant the bolts were undone, the wooden bar out of its catch.

He let himself in. Aelfric was kneeling in the candlelight, at the centre of a tight-packed circle of monks. All were on their knees, their faces in their hands. Cai's entrance, the creak of the great door, did not interrupt the low, thrumming chant of Latin prayer, although from the outer periphery—Fara monks, Cai noted angrily, not the Canterbury clerics—a few terrified moans broke loose.

"Aelfric," he demanded, letting his sword drop with a clatter onto the cover of a tomb. "What is happening here?"

Aelfric snapped upright. The brethren jerked their heads up, smiles cracking their pale masks as they saw Cai. Aelfric spread his arms. "*Deo gratias,*" he cried. His hair was standing up like spines around the edge of his tonsure. A light of keen, pure madness filled his eyes. "Praise be to God, we are saved. Did I not say it would be so? Saved, by the power of our prayers."

By the edge of my sword, Cai thought, but didn't say it. There was no point now. Aelfric was lost amidst demons and angels. He turned to the first sane face he saw—Martin, the ancient monk who made up the mead and heather ale. "The Vikings are gone. You can come out now. Why didn't you lock the damn door?"

"He told us not to. He told us to put our faith in God and pray." Martin lowered his voice. "I'd rather have been out splitting Viking skulls with you, Cai. Did you get a lot of them?"

Cai found a smile for the old man's innocent bloodlust. "A nice lot. I'm glad you were here. We can't spare our brewer." He raised his voice. "Come on, all of you. It's safe. And we need help clearing up."

"No!" Aelfric strode through his bewildered flock, knocking the slower ones out of his way. Crazed or not, he looked down through the foot of height he had on Cai with grim power, and he carried his own nimbus of authority with him. "We must all go to our cells and pray in solitude, in thanks for this deliverance."

"Aelfric—they don't *have* cells anymore."

"Then let us go and pray in their ruins."

Cai gave it up. "You must do as you think fit. I have wounded men to tend."

He turned away. A clawlike hand landed hard on his shoulder. Still raw with battle nerves, Cai tore out from under it. "Leave me be, scarecrow."

He hadn't meant to say it. Despite everything, he'd learned—come to believe—that an abbot's place at Fara was sacred. That his person was due all respect. Now Cai had insulted him, in front of the Canterbury crows and his faithful. Worse, if that hand descended again, Cai would lash out. He was trembling still, the scent of blood and Viking torches in his nostrils. Aelfric was silent. With eyes like that he didn't have to speak. Cai read there all his intentions of cold-hearted vengeance.

"Forgive me, my lord abbot," he rasped. "I must go."

Cold-hearted vengeance. Theo had taught that idea as one of his few examples of sin. Men were animals, he had explained—another heresy—and, when injured, turned upon their attackers with words or blows before their better selves could prevent it. That was bad. But to go away and brood upon a crime, and then exact a punishment—no, not even the beasts would stoop to that. Perhaps sometimes the animal *is* the better self, he had mused at the end of his lesson, and walked off abstractedly, leaving the brethren looking at one another in outrage and wonder.

But Caius had taken his point. He'd tried to work on reining in his own quick temper, secure in the knowledge that he'd never be cold, clever or mean enough to have to worry about the greater sin. He'd dared to entertain a little rare pride in his Christian qualities, glad for once that his blood was warm, his reactions quick and instinctive.

He had been wrong. He was as bad as Aelfric. A wolf was howling on the beach, and Cai's blood was ice-cold.

He washed his hands in the bucket for the tenth time, watching red spirals float in the moon-silvered water. He had just dismissed Benedict and Oslaf to their rest. Both were becoming good medics under his instruction, and his patients were at peace. The warrior monks of Fara had sustained a few injuries—some, as Cai had feared, from their own blades—but none would be fatal, and the infirmary had been almost a merry place that night, as they laughed at one another and swapped tales. All were sleeping now, clean and calm and dreaming poppy dreams.

Not a wolf. A man. The cry came again, long and desolate. The Vikings had left behind one of their own.

Cai looked out of the window. He had heard the first cry hours ago. He'd known for all that time that a man was dying on the beach alone. His patients had heard it too, and agreed among themselves, low-voiced and shuddering, that a slow, lonely death was no more than these devil-men deserved. Only Oslaf had looked troubled over the verdict, but Cai had sent him about his errands with a sharp word.

One day, Theo had said, tugging at his hair in frustration, *I will set us all an exercise of treating one another no better than we deserve, and we will see at the end of the day how many of us are left standing.*

But Theo was dead. Leof was dead, killed by a Viking, and with him had been buried the best of Cai's Christian intent. Ben had forgotten all about Aelfric's orders, it seemed, and all night Cai had watched how he and Oslaf worked together, how in every unoccupied moment gaze had found devoted gaze. Cai wondered if they'd found some quiet place in the moonlit ruins to celebrate their impurity, their soul-condemning love.

Leof, killed by a Viking. Cai dried his hands. There on the sand, at the sea's very margin, the wounded man lay. This one was Cai's.

The sand was cool beneath his feet. He could have been alone in the world, one heart beating under the springtime stars. He took time to look at them, as Theo had taught—the little constellation of the lyre, the leaping dolphin and the swan Deneb's great sail, these three in a triangle whose rising promised summer. Mars glowed dully near the horizon, as if pleased with his night's work. Hundreds of millions of others glimmered behind the full moon's cobweb light. *Yes, millions,* Theo quietly reminded him. *More than the grains of sand on this beach, and no matter what you've heard, I don't believe they're holes pricked by the angels in the firmament of night.*

Cai, who had never thought so, but had a hard time believing each star was a sun like the one that lit up his own days, shook his head in wonder. The beach stretched out before him, a long, broad sweep southwards, every grain a tiny star in the silver light. The only flaw in its stillness, its perfect serenity, was the black shape of the man down by the water's edge. He was motionless. His cries had stopped. Cai, who was close enough now to make out his matted hair, drew his sword and began to run.

"No," he whispered, barely audible to himself above the thud of his heart. "Don't die. You're mine."

Red-bronze hair, streaming over a face white as bone in the moonlight. The incoming tide was beginning to lift it, make it drift like seaweed. If Cai left well alone, the waves would do his work for him. But drowning wasn't enough. Drowning wouldn't wipe out the sword stroke that had ripped Leof out of the world. Only another would do that. He skidded to a halt beside the fallen man. He stood still, planted his feet squarely in the sand and raised the sword high in both hands, blade downward. One plunge would do it. One blow.

Cai, stop. You already delivered it.

Cai froze, hands convulsing round the sword. Theo's voice was as real as the wash of the sea, but he couldn't turn to look. The man at his feet was the raider he'd encountered in the gully, the first to engage with him. Torchlight, tawny wolf's eyes. A brief rip and grind of metal through skin, against bone and then out again. On to the next. Cai hadn't thought the blow a fatal one—hadn't thought at all after that. But his blade had put this man here.

Perhaps not. Cai tossed the sword aside, suddenly frantic to know. The fight had been brief but savage—perhaps the raider had sustained some other wound. Crouching beside him, Cai pulled at the thong of his jerkin. Already the salt water had begun to shrink the leather, tightening the garment across the young man's broad chest. Cai pulled out a knife from his belt and quickly cut through the thong. The skin beneath the jerkin was still warm, with the fading heat of an apple brought in from the orchard on a hot day. Smooth as an apple's too, rippling over the framework of muscles and bones underneath—and unmarred, except for the one gaping hole Cai had put there himself.

He sat back on his heels, gasping. He felt sick. When he searched for his cold, vengeful anger, it was out of his reach—not far, but enough, like the sword he'd cast aside. Just beyond his fingertips. He moved to retrieve the weapon, and his medical kit tugged at his shoulders, the strap pulling tight. Cai couldn't remember picking it up when he'd left the infirmary. He must have grabbed it out of habit.

"I've come to kill you, not heal you," he told the pale face hoarsely. "You took my friends, you and your kind. You took Leof." But the beautiful man laid out on the sand had passed far beyond care for such things. He had lost his helmet, the disguising metal stripped from him. His sins, whatever they had been, were smoothing away in the moonlight. The seawater rippled and gathered, and shot out one eclipsing wave to hurry on the dissolution. On an impulse he couldn't understand, Cai lifted the Viking's head clear of the water.

A fist grabbed the front of his cassock. Cai lurched back, and the Viking shoved onto his elbow, soaked hair whipping back off his face. Cai lost balance. He landed hard on his back, the young man seizing the advantage and pouncing up to straddle him. His thighs clamped tight on Cai's hips. The hand Cai had last seen drifting limply in the foam was now clenched tight around a rock. Amber eyes blazed into his, blind with uncomprehending hate.

Cai still had hold of his knife. He was a doctor, and cold vengeance had turned out not to be his gift, but he was his father's son—the dagger's tip was pressed to the Viking's throat. "Go on," he growled. "Brain me with your rock, and I'll slit your gullet with this. Then we'll be quits."

Chapter Four

The wolf's eyes fell shut. A crescent of white glimmered through his salt-rimed lower lashes. The rock splashed harmlessly down into the sand, and the huge, virile tension holding his body taut over Cai's drained away. His arms buckled and he collapsed.

Cai snatched the knife away, just in time to spare his enemy the passive drop onto the blade. He didn't know why—he'd done worse things tonight than cut a man's throat. And this was *his* Viking, the one whose life he'd come down here to take in place of Leof's. He rolled out from under the soaked deadweight, sprang to his feet and stood watching while a wave broke over the young man's face. If he was playing dead again, the game would soon be up. Cai waited. The seventh wave and the ninth one, powerful heralds of the incoming tide, washed right over the raider's body—tumbled him over onto his front. He lay still.

Cai ran to him, seized him by the armpits and dragged him out of the clutch of the tenth wave. This time no hand seized his cassock. That had been a convulsion, Cai thought, a killer's last impulse to kill. Cai could not identify the impulses guiding his own actions now. He hauled his burden up the beach onto dry sand, not caring that the long, well-wrought limbs jolted over rocks. Maybe death by drowning was too good, too easy for this brute. Maybe Cai would find the spark of life in him, fan it up to consciousness and take his cold vengeance after all. There were things in his medical kit, acids, drugs for cleaning dirty wounds, drugs that would burn...

He let the young man's shoulders fall and thudded down beside him in the sand. He wouldn't allow his ragged inhalations to be sobs. He was breathless, that was all. He undid his satchel, reached in and drew out the first vial that came to hand—Danan's poppy, glowing with its own light under the moon. Cai had let a human creature howl in its lonely death throes. He'd done it for hours, closing his ears and his heart.

"I'm sorry," he choked out, not to the Viking but to Theo's ghost and Leof's. He uncapped the bottle, cleared strands of hair and seaweed from the raider's pale mouth and pressed the rim to his lips.

"Gunnar," the young man said, on a note of soft wonder. His eyes opened wide. They were focussed on a distant shore, a homeland far from this bleak coast. "Gunnar," he repeated. Tears filled the amber eyes. He reached out, and Cai flinched away, but this time his scarred, capable hand only stroked the empty air.

Cai poured the liquid down the man's throat. It was a dose for sleep, not death, and he shuddered in bewilderment as he fastened up his satchel and bent down to take hold of the fallen man again. It was a quarter of a mile to the foot of the cliff. If he managed that, there was the path, almost sheer in parts, a tough climb even unburdened. If Aelfric or one of the other Canterbury spooks caught sight of him...

"Caius?"

He jumped and let the Viking drop, nearly hard enough to break his skull on a rock. Staring up into the darkness, he made out a familiar shape, briefly outlined against the sky and then beginning a scramble down the path. Benedict... Cai couldn't have hoped for anyone better, and yet a chill of mistrust went through him. Ben should have been asleep. "What are you doing out here?" he called cautiously. "Where's Oslaf?"

"Praying, as the abbot told him to. It's where you should be too."

"And you. But we don't march to Aelfric's drum yet. Or do we?"

Cai hadn't meant it to sound like a challenge. After Leof, Ben had been his dearest friend at Fara, his advocate in the early days when even Theo's gentle rule had chafed him. But he hated the new coldness in Ben's eyes. He waited warily.

Ben put out one sandalled foot and gave the raider a shove. "Is it dead?"

"Almost. Don't kick him—that's where I hurt him during the fight."

"And you came down to finish him off?"

Cai nodded. That had been his exact intention. He couldn't remember when or how he had lost it. "I can't, though. Help me carry him up."

"Are you off your head?"

"Possibly. I wounded him myself. I can't kill him."

Ben snorted, sounding more like his old self. "You did for three of his friends up there, no bother at all."

"Yes, in the heat of it." Cai glanced back out over the moon-burnished sand. The tide had already covered the place where he had tussled with the Viking. So all earthly struggles would end, Theo had taught—wiped clear, smoothed away by God's hand. "I can't explain it to you. Are you going to help me or not?"

"Where will you put him?"

"To bed, of course. I need to treat him."

"In the infirmary? Where John and the rest of your brothers are still bleeding from *vikingr* swords?"

"I'll put him in the quarantine cell. Look—the moon is setting. Carry him up to the clifftop for me. I won't ask you to have anything else to do with it, except..." Cai paused, wiping salt-stung tears out of his eyes. "Don't tell Aelfric."

"Aelfric is going to notice a six-foot-tall Viking in his monastery. Even in the quarantine cell."

Cai almost laughed. But the Benedict he had once known, that vigorous and hot-tempered ploughman, would have knocked him down for so much as suggesting the betrayal. "I'll deal with Aelfric," he said hoarsely. "Here. You take his shoulders and I'll..."

"No. Leave him to me." Ben pushed Cai out of the way. "You bring your kit and his things. That sword is a good one—the shield too. Is that his helmet down there?"

Cai looked. The incoming tide had washed a gleaming curve of metal up into a niche between the rocks. He went to pick it up. He turned it over in his hands. Yes, he thought it belonged to the Viking. He remembered how the amber eyes had widened and shone out from behind its mask. Would Cai have been able to run the young man through without the disfiguring metal?

It didn't matter. Cai gathered the other weapons and followed Ben up the cliff path, suddenly too exhausted to do more than put one foot in front of the other. Ben had slung the Viking over one shoulder. The matted bronze hair hung down, swinging in time with Ben's movements. The hand that had reached out blindly for a long-gone friend also swung, limp and pale. Cai doubted there was a pulse in its wrist. He wanted to check, but Ben was moving too fast for him. Probably being carried like this would kill the raider off before they got to the top of the cliffs, but Cai could hardly ask Ben to cradle him in his arms.

If he died, he died. The world would be that much simpler for Cai. There would only be a wolf-shaped vacancy, a gap where the sea wind would blow soundlessly through. Cai remembered his dream and caught his breath, stumbling on the track. *The wolf from the sea...*

Yes. The wolf would die. A faint dawn light was filling the infirmary by the time Cai and Ben got there, turning the lantern's flame sallow. Eyes flew wide at their arrival. Bodies stirred beneath blankets, and Brother John, who had never emerged from the twilight world into which a Viking's sword had plunged him, staggered up from his cot, face contorting in bewildered horror.

He tried to block Cai's way. Pushing him gently aside, Cai directed Ben into the little cell off the infirmary. Not many diseases survived long in the salty north-coast gales, but this was where Cai watched over fever cases until he was sure they would turn into nothing worse. He shoved the door shut behind him with his foot. "Set him down there."

Ben dumped his burden without ceremony onto the quarantine bunk. It was a comfortless wooden frame, bare of the mattress and blankets that might harbour sickness. "They won't let you keep him here. Not Aelfric—your own brethren."

"He won't trouble them for long," Cai said grimly. He dropped his kit and the Viking's weapons with a clatter on the floor. He'd seen enough of death by now to recognise its coming—the stillness it set on a brow, the waxen stiffening of lips that looked made to smile and devour and laugh at a world now lost to them. He knelt by the bunk. He pushed his fingertips up under the young man's jaw. The skin was damp, unexpectedly fine-grained and smooth. Beneath it was the faintest pulse, the throb of a tadpole cleaving water. "Not long. Fetch me cloths and some water."

"No."

Benedict had backed away and was leaning by the door. As Cai watched, he crossed himself. "I won't help you treat him, Caius. Not one of his kind."

"They're not bloody demons!"

"They are to me. To all of us here. They surely were demons to Leof. Or do you forget?"

Cai couldn't answer. He waited for Theo's voice in his head, the voice that had bidden him to spare his fallen enemy. But Theo had fallen silent, leaving him only with the vision of Leof's destroyed face. If not a demon, he'd at least brought scarlet-handed murder into his brethren's midst. "I don't forget anything," he said. "Get the others back to bed, and...tell Aelfric if you have to. Go."

He didn't look up as the door thudded closed. He couldn't pull his attention away from the man on the bunk. Was he gone? After taking from his satchel a piece of obsidian glass, Cai held it over the pallid mouth. He couldn't detect a rise and fall in the Viking's chest, and he didn't want to touch him again, to feel beneath his week's growth of soft beard that fine skin. He waited. After long moments, a faint cloud appeared on the glass.

Cai got up. There was a bucket of water in the cell already, and a pile of clean rags. He remembered now putting them in here when he'd been treating the others after the fight. He washed his hands, scrubbing them afterwards with the essence of sage and lavender Danan had taught him would help kill invisible sources of infection before surgery. He had perhaps half an hour before the effects of the poppy wore off. He drew up a stool by the cot. "Stay asleep for your own good, demon. I am going to save you. Or kill you, and I don't care much which."

The sword wound was deep. Dark blood rushed from it when Cai pulled back the Viking's leather jerkin. The bedframe was soaked with it, a black pool spreading on the floor. Another sign of life, Cai noted bitterly, stemming the tide with rags. Pulse after pulse of it, the heart still beating out the dance somewhere within that elegant chest, with its ribs sprung as beautifully as timbers in the keel of a longship.

Stitching wouldn't be possible yet—the edges of the wound were ragged and too far apart. Cai couldn't remember twisting the blade as he'd dragged it back, but perhaps he had. He'd never been confronted with his own battlefield handiwork before. Quickly he soaked the cleanest of his rags in the solution of sage and lavender, wadded them up and began to pack them into the gaping hole. Blood welled up immediately around them. He grabbed a dry cloth and pressed that on top, then another. Both bloomed crimson, like the poppies that opened in one sunny hour around Benedict's barley fields and faded as fast. Cai needed an extra set of hands. For want of them he began to unfasten the rough hemp girdle round his waist, then stopped. The Viking's own belt would do better. Three inches wide and secured on his lean belly by a savage-looking wolf's-head buckle, it would hold the bandages in place, and Cai could tighten it hard enough to hold pressure on the wound.

He undid the belt. The buckle was cleverly forged, the mechanism of it belying the crude silver wolf. Hands slipping on blood, he tried to tug the leather strap free, but it was caught behind the young man's back. Cai reached under him and lifted his hip.

The Viking stirred. It was much too soon for the effects of the poppy to have worn off, but he was built like a young oak tree, his vigour manifesting in every line of his body. Nevertheless he was blind. Cai knew that when the amber eyes opened and searched for a focus, their pupils immense in the lamplight. Quietly, hampered by the rattle in his throat, he asked a question.

Cai almost understood him. The language was like trying to look round a corner in his mind. Theo had taught that the narrow sea between here and the Dane Lands had once been dry, nomad hunters following the herds freely across it, bearing their words and ways with them.

Where am I? Who is here with me?

Cai ignored him. He ripped the sheepskin hook that secured the belt at the back, jerked it up far enough to cover the wound and drew the strap tight through the buckle. The Viking arched and groaned. Blood gleamed on his lips. The words came again, two out of five familiar to Cai's ears. *Who is here with me? Who?*

Cai sat back. He folded his arms and pushed his hands into the sleeves of his cassock. He wanted to stroke the dying man's hair back off his brow. He wanted to lean over him, ease his head up and cushion it on his arm. He clenched his fingers tight round his own wrists to hold himself still—he wanted to kiss this enemy's bloodstained mouth, hold him and bear him gently into death.

Who is with me?

"Gunnar," Cai said softly. He clutched his arms harder, holding himself fiercely still. "I am here with you. Gunnar."

The Viking took a fever from his wounds. Despite Cai's herbs and hand-washing, poisons had entered his blood. By morning, although breath was still rasping in and out of his lungs, his skin was dry and papery, burning beneath Cai's touch. The fire inside released a terrible last strength in him, and he lashed out howling at Cai, knocking a flagon of water from his hands, then lurched upright on the bunk to seize poor Oslaf, the only one of Cai's brethren who had consented to enter the quarantine cell, let alone help.

Cai scrambled up off the floor. He detached the hand that had clenched on Oslaf's robe, narrowly avoiding a blow from the other. The Viking was flailing around for his sword, now safely stowed away in the armoury.

"Stop it," Cai ordered. "Oslaf, fetch me the straps from the surgical tables." He held the young man down by brute force until Oslaf returned, then pinned one wrist long enough to secure it to the frame of the bunk. Oslaf nervously did the same on the other side. The Viking thrashed on the bed, his eyes alight with delirium and hate. He fought his bindings wildly, then suddenly collapsed, expression draining from his sweat-soaked face to leave it serenely beautiful once more. Cai straightened up, breathless. "Best strap his ankles too. I've packed that wound as best I can, but it'll open up if he thrashes round too much."

Oslaf nodded. The raider was still wearing his hide boots and thick deerskin leggings. Cai could have stripped him down while he slept the night before, and for any other sick man he'd have done it—washed him, tended unflinchingly to the inevitable bodily mess of near-death injury. Cai was ashamed of himself for leaving him dressed and filthy, but Benedict's words had twisted together with his own loathing. To save the brute's life was one thing. He couldn't treat him as he had John or Wilfrid, men who had deserved from him a brother's tenderness.

He helped Oslaf tie the straps over the leggings, then glanced up at the younger monk. "Thanks. You should go now, though. Don't make Benedict angry with you."

"It might be too late for that. I know what you told me—that I ought to play the game, but..." Oslaf paled, absently patting the Viking's ankle as if he had been a friend. "I'm not sure it is one anymore. Ben won't let me near him."

"But last night..."

"He pushed me away. Sent me off to pray with the others." Tears suddenly clouded Oslaf's gaze, and he put out a hand to ward off Cai's sympathy. "Do you think he'll live, then? This demon of yours?"

"I don't understand how he's still alive now."

"My grandmother used to say the hair saps strength in fever. She cut mine off when I was ill."

Cai looked at the raider's sweat-darkened mane. "That's nonsense, though, isn't it? A superstition."

"Well, I'm alive. His hair looks the most living thing about him now."

It was true. The tangled curls seemed to have a vigorous existence of their own, glowing rich russet in the delicate early light filling the cell. "All right. It might be worth a try. I'll go and find some shears. Will you stay with him till I get back?"

Cai made his way quickly down to the barn where Brother Petros had kept his shears and shepherd's crooks. He tried not to look about him. The barn was silent now, cobwebs already drifting from its timbers. The Fara flocks were out at emergency pasture under the care of any brother who could be spared to tend them. Aristocratic Petros, so disgusted at first at the task allotted him, had developed a fierce pride in his shepherding skills. His shears were hanging where he'd left them, gleaming and sharp. He'd branched out into barbering too, standing grimly smiling in the courtyard as his brethren had filed up for their monthly haircut. A sense of unreality washed through Cai still when he thought of that night, the first raid, the holes it had torn in the world. He took the shears and hurried back out of the barn.

The infirmary was quiet when he got back. Too quiet—nobody propped on an elbow to gossip with his neighbour in the next bunk, none of the usual demands for his attention. The door to the quarantine cell was shut. Oslaf was in the main ward, eyes downcast, washing bottles with ferocious concentration.

Cai didn't bother to question him. He swept through the ward. Thrusting the door wide, he saw just what he had expected—Abbot Aelfric, crouching over the Viking's bunk, beaklike face avid. Cai drew breath to yell and lost it as a grip closed on him from behind. "Ben," he gasped, trying to twist round. "What is he doing? Let me go."

Benedict shook his head. "Be silent. The abbot must talk to his prisoner."

"His... Ben, for God's sake."

"He isn't harming him. Be still."

Cai twisted like a wildcat, but there was no shifting Benedict's grasp once it had closed. Involuntarily he began to listen to the abbot's voice. It was low, almost tender—a litany of soft-voiced Latin. "What do you want? What do you want, boy?"

He was using the respectful *vultis,* not *vis.* And the Viking was awake again, his eyes wide and lucid. Aelfric's hands were on him. Their movement was caressing. For a moment Cai wondered if he'd been wrong about the carrion bird from the south. Was Aelfric offering help to the injured man—soothing him with that touch?

"*Quid vultis, puer?*"

Cai shook himself. Aelfric had been half out of his wits before the raid, and now—now he was quite insane. He had brought his madness here into Cai's domain, for God alone knew what vile purpose. His grasp on the Viking wasn't kindly. He was putting pressure on his wounds. And the boy was lying silent in his effort not to weep.

Cai had a pair of freshly sharpened shears in his hand. He tossed them aside before he could use them. Fists were better than blades, and an elbow to Benedict's gut best of all. Ben doubled up with a grunt, and Cai sprang forwards, seizing Aelfric by the hood. "Let him be, you savage bloody buzzard. Leave him alone!"

Aelfric snapped upright. He was thin but powerful and his backhanded slap made Cai's nose sting. "How dare you?" he snarled. "Brother Benedict, restrain him. I will have the secret of Fara from this demon if I have to tear it out along with his teeth." He rounded on the Viking again. "What do you want? What are you and your legion of infidels raiding for? *Quid vultis?*"

Not the polite form. The plural. Cai broke into bitter laughter. "You fool, Aelfric. There is no secret. That was poor Theo's dying dream. Who told you about it?"

Benedict hung his head. "I won't have anything more to do with this," he muttered. "Not for either of you. I can't." He turned away. Aelfric shrieked his name, but he ignored it, blundering out through the ward.

The outer door banged shut behind him. Once more Cai hauled Aelfric away from the Viking's bunk. Aelfric struggled, and Cai, sickened, drew back a fist and knocked his abbot down with a punch straight out of Broc's muddy barnyard.

Aelfric sprawled on the flagstones. His mouth opened and closed like that of a fresh-landed cod. Before any sound could come out of it, Cai interrupted, so low and soft that Aelfric blanched still further. "Leave my friends alone, scarecrow. My enemies too, for that matter. If there's any torture to be done around here..." He paused, glancing at the helpless man strapped to the bunk. "I'll do it myself. For a start, I know better than to interrogate a prisoner in a language he doesn't understand. Now get out of my ward."

Aelfric almost choked. "Yours?" He staggered to his feet. "This place—the whole of Fara—is mine now, by God's decree. I can have you banished with a word."

"Say it, then." Cai brushed dust off his cassock. He didn't care anymore about this monster, or the one on the bed. He was tired and lonely, and wanted only to be back in Leof's arms among the sun-warmed grasses of the dunes. "Say your word, and defend Fara yourself next time the raiders come. Otherwise leave me alone."

A silence fell in the little room. Cai didn't look, but he heard the retreating slither of the abbot's robes on the flags. Aelfric didn't slam the outer door as Ben had done. He left it contemptuously wide, as if to let all the winds of heaven come and chill the sick men behind him.

Cai went and closed it. He glanced around the ward to check that no one had taken harm from the draught or needed his immediate help. He waited briefly, meeting each pair of wide eyes in turn, to see if anyone had anything to say for himself on the subject of wolves in the fold. Then he returned to the quarantine cell.

The Viking was sobbing. He would have done anything to prevent it, Cai saw—had already bitten his lip raw. His eyes were tight shut, his face a bone-white mask. His chest jerked in helpless spasms. Tears had carved tracks across his cheekbones, pale in the blood and dirt.

He was trying to curl up around his injury. Quickly Cai unfastened the straps round his left wrist and ankle to allow it. The Viking struggled onto his side. He turned his face to the bare timbers of the bunk, his heavy sheaf of hair falling to shield him. Rough, unstoppable sounds came from beneath it.

Cai's throat ached as if he'd suddenly swallowed scalding water, and he knelt by the bunk. "I'm sorry," he said, his own voice hoarse and strange to him. "I know you don't understand me. I'm sorry. Let me see to your wound."

"I do understand."

Cai jerked back. He sat on his heels, wondering if the clear Latin declaration had come from somewhere else. "What?"

The Viking shoved his hair back with a shaking hand. "I do understand," he repeated, gazing bleakly straight into Cai's face. "I speak Latin. I was taught it by a slave monk in my lord Sigurd's kingdom—the only thing you puny Christians are good for."

Cai swallowed hard. It was as if a wild beast he'd encountered in the forest had suddenly addressed him and opened a discourse. "Why... Why didn't you tell Aelfric?"

"The scarecrow?" The Viking managed a half-choked laugh. "I speak only to men. Because you have aided me, I will speak to you. When I have strength to kill you, I will do that, but until then, listen to my advice, monk—a favour for a favour. Give up the treasure of Fara Sancta. Sigurd and the other Dane Land warlords will keep on raiding till you do."

"There is no treasure. No treasure, no secret. We barely have food to put in our mouths since the last time you savages burned us. Don't you think we'd have surrendered anything we had?"

"Sigurd had to kill many monks before he found one who would teach him. You are strong beneath your skirts, or stubborn anyway. Stubborn and stupid. Be wise, physician. Give it up."

The Viking's eyes flickered shut. Cai reached to ease him over onto his back, but he reanimated. "I am called Fenrir," he rasped, the effort bringing blood to his lips. "Fenrir, after Fenrisulfr, the great wolf of our legends. You must make me well again, monk, and then you have to set me free. I am a prince in my own land—second heir to Lord Sigurd's Torleik realm, and Sigurd and my brothers and my comrades will be back for me. You must let me go."

"Happily. I'd dump you back on the beach in a heartbeat, your majesty."

"A prince in my own..." The Viking writhed, fresh sweat breaking on him. "Oh, gods. Kill me now, monk. I have soiled myself. I am disgraced."

Pity went through Cai like a blade. On its heels came a weird surge of laughter, which he bit back fiercely, bewildered by it. "No, you're not. Your body is tired and weak, that's all. Will you let me clean you up?"

"The work of a menial. A slave."

"Well, you've established that's all we Christians are good for."

"I stink like a pig."

"You certainly do. I've neglected you. I hoped you would just die."

Their eyes met. The faintest glimmer touched the Viking's pain-filled stare. "You're honest, at any rate. What is your name?"

"Caius."

"Caius?" On the raider's lips the word came out like the call of a seabird, and Cai repressed a shiver. "My father's father met a Roman general by that name, a century or so ago. He stuck his head on a spike."

"My ancestors did worse to yours, I'm sure. My father is a chieftain, descended from the Roman army here."

"A chieftain... Then you too are a prince in your own land."

"All five muddy acres of it, yes."

"Very well. I will permit you to tend me."

Cai shook his head. He brought two pails of water over to the bunk and set about his task. The stench in the cell was bad, but Cai had nursed the whole community of Fara through a bout of cholera flux, and not much could turn his stomach now. He only felt sick at having left the Viking—Fenrir, had he called himself?—to lie like this in his dirt. First he cleaned and repacked the sword wound, which was bleeding again after Aelfric's ministrations. Fenrir moaned and passed out during the process, which made the rest easier.

Working as swiftly as he could, Cai stripped him of his boots and deerskin trousers. Underneath them he wore a subligaculum like Cai's own, countering the legend that these *vikingr* pirates had parts so monstrous they had to be strapped up inside a bull's horn. The long strip of linen was stiff with excrement and blood. Cai unwrapped it briskly from round Fenrir's hips, distractedly noting as he pulled away the strip that ran between his legs that the beaten-bronze loin guard stitched into it had protected a splendid, shapely length of cock.

He threw the subligaculum aside for burning, then added to the pile the ruined shirt beneath Fenrir's jerkin. The jerkin itself was good of its kind, well crafted, and would serve again despite the slash through its sheepskin-lined leather. The trousers too. Cai folded these to be cleaned, thinking with a pang of how poor Brother Blacksmith would have exclaimed over the riveted lace-holes and that neat cock-piece.

The Viking was naked, and as finely made as any of his trappings. Just for the length of one indrawn breath, the man in Cai took over from the doctor. Skin a shade between bronze and ivory, marked across the shoulders and chest with coiling blue-black serpents, needle-pricked designs such as Danan's ancestors had used to bear as signs of their warrior caste. A frame of such lean, tensile strength that even half a breath from dying it was beautiful. "Fenrisulfr," Cai said softly, suddenly assailed by memories of a fire-and-shadow dream.

Cai washed him scrupulously, from the crease of his backside to his armpits, and then with a fourth or fifth clean rag took the dust and the traces of tears from his face. He worked quickly, closing the cell's lead-framed window as soon as the air was clear. A fine spring day was rising outside, belying all the torchlit horrors of the night, but still the breeze was fresh, and he shook out two blankets from a wooden chest against the wall.

Fenrir shifted and moaned as the wool settled over his limbs. His fever was mounting again. Cai felt his brow and reluctantly fastened him back to the bed. A wolf in the fold was bad enough, but a delirious one with axe skills didn't bear thinking about. He looked at the curtain of hair streaming down off the end of the bunk. It seemed to be coiling all the more vigorously as its owner lost strength. Well, superstition or not, it was doubtless full of lice, impossible to wash without chilling the Viking to death.

Cai retrieved the shears from the corner where he'd hurled them out of temptation's reach. He sat on the edge of the bed, his thigh pressing gently against Fenrir's ribs. Carefully, untangling each strand as far as he could without tugging, he cut the fox-red mass away.

The mask of a savage archangel emerged. Maybe this creature *was* some kind of royalty in his own world. His brow was broad and capable, his cheekbones sculpted, delicate in their contours as the corners of his mouth. His nose had been broken at some point but not badly reset, its slight irregularity lending a charm to a face that would otherwise have chilled with its aristocratic perfection. Unable to help himself, Cai ran a hand across the shorn hair.

"Gunnar," the Viking whispered, shifting to find the caress.

Cai shivered. This raider—this demon, this archangelic wolf—must have his own Leof, his own beloved bedmate and companion, somewhere in the Dane Lands.

"Gunnar... Bróðir. Bróðir minn."

Bróðir... The word was almost the same in the language Cai had shared with Leof, the familiar rough dialect of the northern coast. Not a bedmate, then—a brother. *Gunnar, my brother.* Once more, unwanted pity assailed Cai. He couldn't understand it. And much less could he comprehend his own brief, blood-hot rush of pleasure and relief.

Chapter Five

The evening light was sweet. Now that June was here, the scurvy grass was in full flower, masses of it carpeting the rocks and turf along the shoreline. Scattered sea thrift broke its fragrant snowdrifts with taller pink blossoms that danced in the wind. The combined scents, blowing in on a warm sunset breeze, washed over Cai where he sat on a bench outside the armoury. Cai set down the axe he had been polishing and leaned back.

He could pretend, here in the last light, that all was well. The armoury was just a barn. Its sandstone blocks had soaked up a day's worth of heat, radiating out now against Cai's spine. The tide was low, the spur of sand that led to the islets exposed. There, beyond the bright green mermaid's-hair kelp and the stones that sometimes yielded tiny, intriguing beads Theo had called sea-lily stems, the first monks of Fara had made their homes. Traces were still to be seen of their cells, not rooms in a dormitory hall but individual huts made out of stone, each one shaped like a beehive. Cai had thought his own life at the monastery tough, after the relative riches of his father's court, but these first comers—holy men from Hibernia and the far west of Scotia—must have existed on little more than seaweed and blind faith.

No, perhaps not blind. There was a peace and sense of purpose on this shore. The Hibernian saints had come here of their own free will, without an abbot or a settled Church to guide them, and here they had lived out their lives, listening to God's word on the wind and the water. A hermit's cave remained there still, marked by a poignant, plain wooden cross. Theo, too lively and sociable a creature to withstand a hermit's life, had spoken with a kind of longing admiration of these men even while he prepared his brethren's next lesson in astronomy or physics.

Music joined the flower scents and skeined itself through them on the breeze. Cai closed his eyes. In this world where all was well, his brothers were singing. The church walls were finished, new timbers arching over the space they enclosed. The work of thatching would take longer, so the voices rose unfettered, a rich chant for vespers. Laban, Aelfric's grim-faced deputy, concealed a pure tenor inside his scrawny chest and an unexpected gift for teaching the ragbag voices of Fara to join in harmoniously with it. The labours of the fields were disrupted, brethren running everywhere in their attempts to keep up with the new routine of Hours, but in spring it could almost be done, and Cai had to admit the music was lovely. Leof would have delighted in it.

He allowed himself to drift, imagining he could pick out Leof's clear note from the mingled voices. He had been up since dawn. The infirmary was clear of all but the most serious cases from the battle a fortnight before, but John required constant attendance, and the Viking, after his wild declarations of princedom and intended murder, had lapsed into a strange, half-waking passivity, watching Cai's movements about the quarantine cell with dull, hooded eyes, accepting from him spoonfuls of broth before turning his head aside. He hadn't spoken again, in Latin or his own language. Cai was beginning to think he'd dreamed their exchange after that night of fever and blood.

He tipped his head back against the stone. As well as doctoring, he'd put in his duty shift as shepherd, helped with the silage crop and carried out his daily drill with the warrior brethren of Fara. At least this last was getting easier. Now that they'd won a fight, his unlikely soldiers trained with confidence as well as hope. They slashed and parried in the ruined hall, and sang like angels for Laban. Wondering at the strangeness of the world, Cai let go, weary nature having her way with him.

He awoke in darkness. No one had come looking for him, but no one would, not now. A figure coalesced out of the gloom—Demetrios, collecting the fresh leaves of the scurvy grass by light of the thin new moon, a trick Danan had taught for capturing their freshness. Cai drew breath to greet him, then changed his mind. Demetrios was pretending with great sincerity not to have seen him. The Greek had been devoted to Theo. So had Benedict and Oslaf. There wasn't a soul within the whole of Fara's bounds who didn't have cause to detest the *vikingr*—and equal reason to mistrust the man who had brought one into their midst, healed him and harboured him there. They took their fighting orders from Cai, did as he bade them on the training ground, and left him afterwards without a word.

Cai didn't blame them. Sometimes he thought back to the night of Theo's feast, the lights and the chatter and the smallpipe music, and a slow ache of loneliness would drag through him. Everything had changed since then. He lived in a world of hard work and readiness to fight, not companionship and learning. Even Aelfric was leaving him alone, just as he'd asked, not harrying him over his haircut or his failure to turn up nine times a day for prayers.

He watched Demetrios fade into the dusk, his basket of herbs balanced on one hip. It was time he went back in too. Oslaf took shifts in the ward, but he wouldn't feed or tend Fenrir. Cai had no idea why he did it himself.

Something clattered in the barn. Cai bolted off the bench and stood rigid, staring into the darkness beyond the open door. He'd thought nothing could scare him after two Viking raids, but like most of his brethren he jumped like a cat at sudden noises. Probably a sword had come down off its makeshift rack. Gathering his robes so he could move in silence, he eased into the barn.

There was just enough light, once his eyes had adjusted. Quickly he worked his way along the racks and shelves, checking that everything was in place. He kept the armoury as orderly as his ward cabinets now, restlessly tidying and cleaning after each drill. He needed to know he could run here and lay hands on any weapon he chose, dole them out in proper order to his fighting men. Nothing was on the floor. Hands outstretched, Cai made a fingertip count of dagger hafts, shields, longstaffs...

And came up one short on the swords. He froze, listening intently. The barn had ventilation windows on its landward side, high up in the wall but large enough to let a man climb through. A tall, determined one, anyway. Blindly Cai counted his broadsword handles again. Broc's were all there, round and crude from the hillfort's smithy. So were the better ones the monks had stripped from the bodies of the Vikings they'd killed. The only one missing had a wolf's-head bronze casting on its hilt.

Cai ran. He didn't try to follow the intruder through the windows. A dash down the overgrown track that edged the barn was quicker, if you didn't mind nettle stings and scratches from the brambles. Lamps were still burning in the refectory. By their golden light, Cai made out a trail of crushed vegetation leading straight up to the main hall's southern door.

The refectory was echoingly empty. No—there was Eyulf, sieving flour for the morning's bread, his face as usual covered with white dust.

"Eyulf," Cai called softly. "Have you seen...?" He remembered who he was talking to and shook his head. "Never mind. Just go to the dormitory barn and make sure the door is barred after you."

He was turning away when Eyulf banged on the table with his spoon. He got up from the bench, stood on his tiptoes to make himself taller, drew down his brows in a terrible scowl and took a couple of prowling steps forwards. Then he pointed to the stairs.

At any other time, Cai would have laughed. "Thank you. Leave your bread for now, all right? I'll find him."

He should have rung the warning bell. He could have had a dozen fighting men at his side in a minute, helping him track down the rogue. Instead he padded softly down the torchlit corridor that led to Aelfric's office and the rooms where the Canterbury men had established their base. No chance of those high dignitaries bunking down with the brethren in the barn. Maybe this was the night they would learn to regret their splendid isolation. Maybe they had already learned. Aelfric allowed only one torch to burn in each corridor, and only until the lights had exhausted themselves and burned out. It was a good economy. Cressets and lamp oil were lasting much longer at Fara these days, and darkness shut down all reading and study at sunset, as Aelfric's God intended.

Cai slipped past Theo's study, where lights used to blaze in improvident splendour halfway through the night. He rounded the corner into the narrow passageway beyond. Empty, and the doors to the clerics' cells intact, as far as he could see...

Firelit shadows patched themselves into the shape of a man. The Viking, naked but for a blanket he'd hitched round his waist like a kilt, was leaning in a corner, his back pressed to the wall. His sword was clutched in both hands. His face was gaunt with pain, and Cai could count the hollows between each rib. "Fenrir!"

The Viking's head jerked up. He swung to face Cai, raising the sword in a movement of practised, murderous beauty. "This isn't your business, physician," he hissed. "Go back to your ward."

Cai strode to meet him, disregarding the blade. The Viking was about to drop it anyway. He was ready to fall. "You shouldn't be out of your bed. What in God's name are you doing here?"

"I have come to slay the scarecrow. My honour demands it. So should yours, but you are soft and puny. I shall do it for us both."

Cai grabbed him. He took the sword from his hands before it could clatter onto the flags and wake the whole corridor, got a steadying grip round his waist. "I'll show you how soft and puny I am in a minute, you stupid bastard. Nobody's going to do any slaying here tonight. Come with me."

"No. My flesh remembers his torment. I shall murder him, and then the one who held you back from aiding me. Then the one who walks past my bed without seeing when I thirst or hunger. Then the ones who do not meet your eyes when you speak to them, or turn away from you discourteously, or..."

"We can't murder men for bad manners. As for Aelfric, I'd like to kill him too, but the others..." Cai pulled Fenrir's arm around his shoulders. "The others are afraid of you." He tucked the deadly wolf's-head blade into the girdle of his cassock. "I can't think why. Now come with me."

"No. If you won't let me slaughter these fools, turn me loose. I will go back to the beach, fend for myself until my brother comes back for me."

"Gunnar?"

Fenrir twitched. He emitted a faint growl, twisted out of Cai's grasp and slammed him against the wall, just below the guttering torch. "You will not say that name!"

Cai couldn't say anything at all with a sinewy arm pressed to his throat. He couldn't breathe, either. The Viking stared hard into his face. Freeing himself would have been easy—a knee to the groin or a jab to the healing wound—but he couldn't bring himself to move. He wasn't afraid. The press of a living body against his was a terrible comfort, even like this. A hot pressure like tears built up behind his eyes, and he ran his hand down Fenrir's arm.

The vulpine features altered. It wasn't exactly a softening—more the relaxation of a snarling hound bewildered by a caress. "You will not say the name," he repeated, and sank to his knees at Cai's feet.

"Oh, God." Cai crouched beside him. The makeshift kilt was soaked with blood. "You've torn out your sutures. Come with me. Hold on to me. Come on."

The journey back across the courtyard and up to the ward was painful. Oslaf met them in the doorway, his eyes wide. "Caius, forgive me. I only just noticed he was gone."

Cai hefted his burden over the threshold and back into the

quarantine cell. Fenrir was stumbling, barely conscious. "That's because you didn't look. Is his bunk mat clean? Fetch a fresh one before I lay him down." Oslaf ran to obey, and together they eased the Viking flat. Cai began to examine his wound. "I understand your hate. I won't force you to help with him, but if you can't, you have to tell me, so he's not left on his own."

"Where did you find him? Why... Why are you wearing his sword?"

Cai had forgotten that. He undid the awkward weight from his girdle. "I need fresh sutures. Quick, before he comes round properly. He was outside our new abbot's rooms."

"With his sword? Cai, don't you see? He's going to murder us all in our beds."

Cai couldn't argue. "Well, just now he'd have a hard time getting back out of his own. I don't care what you think, Oslaf—as long as he's in here, he must be treated like anyone else."

"Why?"

Cai frowned. It wasn't like Oslaf to argue or question him, not like that. Maybe Benedict's new chill was rubbing off. "Because I'm a doctor. Because—"

"No. Why bring him in the first place? Everyone loves you here. And they know it's you they have to thank that we lived through the last raid. But they can't forgive this."

Threading a strand of sheep gut through a fine bone needle, Cai bent over his task. "I'm not looking for forgiveness," he muttered. "Sage oil, please. Rags. As for my reasons..." *I wounded him myself. He was alone. Theo spoke inside my head and told me to.* None of these would do. *Because he was beautiful, my wolf from the sea, and I couldn't bear him to die.* Cai bit his lip. "I don't know. I don't know."

He plunged the needle into the pale skin. Fenrir jerked on the bed. Oslaf was ready to hold him down, but this time instead of lashing out, the Viking only clutched the edges of the bunk.

"Sorry," Cai told him, pulling the new suture tight. "I didn't want to sedate you again. But I can, if you can't bear this."

Fenrir gave a low rumble of laughter, such a contrast to his pain-racked face that Cai and Oslaf both jumped. "I've felt your blade, monk. Your little prick...doesn't bother me at all."

Cai worked on. With an effort he kept his face straight. "Ah," he said, when he thought his voice would be steady. "Viking humour. I've heard of this."

"We do not call ourselves Vikings. We bear the names of our ancestral clans—Hallgrimr, Vigdis, Torleik. Nor do we raid in horned helmets, as your foolish Saxon bards would have it. The horns are for rituals only, the worship of Thor. Can you imagine—in a packed longship, or close-quarters battle..."

He couldn't go on, and Cai finished stitching as deftly as he could. He pressed a wad of soothing willow extract onto the wound. "Yes. I suppose you'd have someone's eye out."

Fenrir smiled. It was the first time Cai had seen him do so naturally, without his lupine snarl. He turned away quickly, astounded at the charm of it—ashamed of his response. He shook out a fresh bandage and began to bind the wound up.

Oslaf was staring too. "He *does* speak like us."

"Yes. I told you. His Latin is better than mine."

"I thought him merely a beast."

"Well, he isn't." Cai dared a glance into the gleaming agate eyes. "He's a man, and a bloody dangerous one. So. Can you keep a watch on him while I'm not here, and treat him like a man as well as guard him?"

"Yes. Ask him to pardon my neglect of him—and my help in keeping him prisoner."

You could ask him yourself. But Cai knew he was placing a huge burden on Oslaf as it was. He gestured to the younger monk that he could go, and returned his attention to his patient.

He worked on for a while in silence. As well as his pulled stitches, the Viking was covered with other cuts and grazes, trivial in a healthy man but each a possible gateway for infection after long illness. He cleaned the injuries methodically, making quite sure not to linger or let a swab become a caress. "Why am I not allowed to call your brother by his name? Am I considered too lowly?"

Fenrir focussed on him with an effort. He'd exhausted himself with his abortive hunt and was on the edge of sleep. "No. Well—yes, you are. But that isn't the reason."

"What, then?"

"My brother is the heir to Sigurd's Torleik clan. Our lands are wider and richer by far than all Sigurd's rival tribes put together. I wish my lord Sigurd health and long life, but when he dies, my brother will be powerful beyond imagination."

Cai shrugged. "I'm pleased for him. Even a king has a name, though, and any peasant may use it."

"You don't understand. Gunnar is more than..." Fenrir's brow furrowed as he searched for the word, or perhaps steeled himself to use it. "He is mine—*bróðir minn.* He is coming back for me. Until he does, his name belongs on my tongue only. How did you find it out?"

"You called it when you had a fever. And you still do, in your dreams."

For the second time that night, Fenrir's mask softened. Then he flushed in what could have been shame or anger, and he turned awkwardly away onto his side—not before Cai had seen the glitter of tears. "I forbid you to listen, then."

"I'll try."

"And while we are discussing names—do me a kindness and stop trying to call me *Fenrir.* You cannot pronounce it, and the sound you make pains me."

"What shall I call you, then?"

"Fen will do."

"Very well. And since you sound like a sheep giving birth when you say mine, you'd better call me Cai."

In the morning Fen was better. Cai, who had fallen asleep on a spare cot in the ward, awoke to the commanding ring of his voice. "You! Physician Cai's dogsbody, Odleaf or whatever you are called—fetch him to me instantly. What has he done with my hair?"

Cai swung his legs off the bed. There were days at Fara when things were more difficult than others, and this one was off to a rare start. He took a moment to splash his face with water, then strode to Oslaf's rescue. Fen was bolt upright on his bunk, his eyes bright with imperious life. Cai pushed the door closed behind him. "Keep your voice down. What the devil is wrong with you now?"

"My hair. Where is it? Where did you put my sword, and where is my fine helmet with the chased-silver cheek guards?"

"Your sword is locked up out of your reach. Your helmet..." Cai hesitated. He'd thought about using it, giving it to one of his warrior monks, but somehow the thing had repelled him. Behind its cruel mask, even a friend's face would become a stranger's. He'd locked it up inside a chest in the armoury. "Your helmet was lost. And as for your hair, I gave it to the tanner to stuff saddlebags." That wasn't true, but the look on Fen's face was worth the price of the lie. "Don't worry, it'll grow back. You can look like a great louse-ridden thug again soon enough."

Fen's brows shot up to the place where his fringe had once been. "You're a fine one to talk about lice. I've heard about you dirty Christians, mortifying your flesh beneath your robes until it rots—using your vows of poverty to excuse yourselves for sleeping in flea-ridden filth."

"There, Oslaf. Aren't you glad he's started talking? Go and get your breakfast." Cai advanced on his patient. "And you—keep a civil tongue in your head when you're talking to the men who help you here. There's precious few willing to do it. Have you passed water this morning? Was there blood in it?"

"You have no right to ask me such questions. You must show respect for me. You must—"

"A simple yes or no will do."

Again, that unlikely blush. Cai couldn't tell if it was rage or mortification, and wished he didn't find so fascinating the movement of blood beneath the pale skin.

"Yes, then. And no."

"Well, that's good. You can get up. I'm about to teach you a few things about dirty Christians." He hoisted Fen off the bunk by his armpits and deposited him on a bench. "This mattress—which I'm about to change for you yet again—is filled with the dried flowers of a plant called bedstraw, a natural repellent to fleas and other vermin. If it smells sweet, that's because of the *Tanacetum vulgare*—tansy—that drives away ticks. We also use it to flavour our bread. As for mortifications of the flesh..." He threw a blanket at Fen and shook out the new mattress. "I can't answer for the abbot and his clerics. But the man who used to rule us here—Abbot Theodosius—forbade us all such things. He said..." Cai paused, waiting till his voice would be steady again. He was remembering Theo catching Wilfrid by the arm one day, asking him why he was limping, and with gentle firmness making him hitch his cassock up to show the circlet of bramble thorns round his thigh. "He said it was monstrous to misuse the bodies God gave us. Like breaking a beautiful gift. Now, do you think you could walk with me down to the courtyard?"

"Walk with you? I could sling you over my shoulder and carry you there," Fen returned, but with less of his customary snarl. He was watching Cai oddly, as if reassessing him. "Why should I, though?"

"I haven't finished teaching you. Come on."

"In my blanket?"

"No. In one of these." Cai took a fresh cassock out of the linen chest. He waited for the outcry, but perhaps he'd shocked his patient speechless. Making the most of it, he shook the garment out. "As you say, it has a skirt. It's also warm, comfortable and practical. Put it on."

"Where... Where are my other clothes?"

"Incinerated, mostly. We salvaged what we could, but you're not walking round this monastery dressed like a pirate."

To his surprise, Fen took the garment from him. He stood up, letting his blanket drop. He showed no sign of consciousness at his nakedness, and Cai studiously failed to notice it either, waiting while Fen pulled the cassock over his head.

"With what shall I gird up my loins?"

He made a fine figure in the long brown robes. They had belonged to Brother Petros, who'd been about the same height. With his shorn head and his direct gaze, he was pleasing to Cai somehow in the way of an oak sapling—young enough to bend, set to last a hundred years. "You'll gird them as you usually do. The linens are in that box. But don't bother now—I'm taking you for a bath."

Fen refused assistance down the stairs with a haughty gesture that made Cai want to slap him. In the fresh air of the courtyard, though, he swayed and grabbed at the low stone wall that surrounded the well.

"Sit down," Cai ordered him, looking out across the fields. The little packhorse he used on his travels and the monastery's only other pony were both hard at work in the hay pasture. "Wait. Sit there, and..." He tugged up Fen's hood to conceal his bright hair. "Just for a moment, try not to be conspicuous."

Broc's chariot horse was feeding her head off in the paddock to the south. She had proven useless between the shafts of cart or plough, rearing and kicking in a fit of royal rage to match Fen's own. Cai had expected from day to day that Aelfric would order her slaughtered and salted away for winter meat, but there she was, looking glossy and bored in the sun. She came when Cai whistled, as if he might at last have something interesting for her to do, and bumped her chestnut muzzle hard against his chest. As far as Cai knew, she'd never been tried as a saddle horse—not that Fara, or indeed Broc's stronghold, ran to saddles. He clambered the drystone wall and took her by the halter.

The Viking sat up straight at the scrape of hooves in the courtyard. He pushed his hood back, his face becoming keen and intent. "Roman," he declared, as Cai led the mare up to him. "Yes. Roman, with two hundred years of your Briton puddle-jumpers mixed in, and..." He pushed upright, pain and weakness forgotten. "And a strain of the Barb. You won't know what that is, monk. You think the world ends at the Oceanus Britannicus."

"I do know. My abbot Theo told us of places far beyond that—Barbary, Arabia, where men called Berbers live in silken tents and ride about the desert on beasts that can gallop as easily on sand as soil. What does a *vikingr* pirate know of horseflesh, though?"

"It's true that we are masters of the sea." Fen ran a thoughtful hand down the mare's flank. "And the ponies we use for raids are scrappy beasts, not like this. They take us to the battle, then we fight on foot, our stupendous skills in warfare bearing all before us. This explains what I saw in your weapons barn. I thought it a fever dream."

"The chariot?"

"Yes. What does a Christian monk know of those?"

"I told you—my father is no Christian. He's a Roman warlord, or he likes to think he is, and he gave me this beast and the chariot to help me defend Fara against monsters like you." Cai paused, distracted. The morning breeze was full of the scent of kelp and thyme, too pleasant in his lungs to fuel hostility. "You really think she has the Berber strain?"

"Mm. Look at her high forequarters, her crouped rump." He leaned stiffly, patting her fetlocks, and Cai crouched beside him to take a closer look. For a moment monk and Viking dropped away and they were simply men, heads together over an intriguing piece of horseflesh. "Her hooves are rounder than the Roman breeds. What's her name?"

"I don't know. I don't think she has one."

"You should always name things—beasts, ships, swords. It brings down the spirit upon them. Speaking of which—where is my wolf's-head blade?"

"Safely locked up." Cai took a step back, renewing the distance between them. This man was his enemy. He had forgotten. "Out of bounds to you. Listen—while you're healing, I can treat you like any other sick man. But once you're well, you'll be a prisoner here. You'd better behave like one, or..." Cai fell silent. He had to have imagined the flicker of hurt in those dark eyes. "Here. I'll give you a leg-up."

"I can manage for myself." Fen grasped the horse's mane just in front of her withers. He braced to spring up. Then his knuckles whitened, and he let go a gasp that would have been a scream from a lesser man. He rested his brow on the mare's flank. Cai reached for him, but he flinched away and scrambled, grey-faced, to stand on the low wall that bounded the well. "I can do it from here, if you will hold her."

Cai held the mare's halter while she danced and sidled. She wasn't used to a weight on her back, but Fen sat quietly, and after a moment she settled, head high, exhaling in wide-nostrilled snorts.

Cai led her out of the courtyard. Once out on the wide sweep of turf, the salt wind warmly buffeting his face, he was ashamed. "All right," he said, not glancing to see how his magnificent prisoner looked on horseback. "What is its name, then? Your wolf's-head sword?"

"*Blóðkraftr dauði.* The mighty blade of blood and death."

Cai shook his head. "It would be."

"And I shall call this horse *Eldra*—the fire."

There was no one else at the bathing pools when Eldra had picked her way down the cliff path and onto the rocks. Cai was relieved. He knew that every kindness shown to Fen was an insult to the memory of his slain brethren, and more so to the living ones who had to witness it. He looped the horse's leading rein round an outcrop of rock in the shade, then turned to Fen, who had remained silent for the last part of the journey. "I know you wouldn't let me help you up there. But I think you'll have to let me help you down."

Fen regarded him blankly. "Yes. To my undying mortification."

"For God's sake. All right. Swing your leg over her forequarters, not her rump. It'll pull your stitches less that way."

"It is an unmanly way to dismount."

"So is landing on your face in the kelp. Come on."

Cai held his arms up for him. Reluctantly Fen consented to be aided down, slithering into Cai's embrace, where he stood for a moment, trembling. "Enough. I can stand now. Let me go."

"Is *every* little thing a matter of life-and-death Viking honour for you?"

"Of course."

Cai led him down to the pools. The tide was rising, as it had been on the day when he'd come here alone, yearning for the earthly pleasures Leof had just renounced. The water in the rocky basin was bright with the same green-blue reflection of sky. But Cai's world had ended since then, burned to the ground and grown back again in a shape he still could barely comprehend. Who had that boy been, stretched out in the pool with nothing more on his mind than the hungry tension in his loins? All such needs had fled from him. In the few short hours of sleep he got, his cock remained quiescent, and the idea of his own touch scarcely occurred.

Ironic that he'd achieved his monastic ideal in such a way. Leof would have said it didn't count, if he was no longer tempted, but that was one of the many nuances of Christian thinking Cai had never understood. Achieving the result was surely good enough. "Take off your robe and get into the water."

"Into the..."

"Yes. Come on. It's not too cold on a day like today."

The look Fen gave him could have been bottled and used as a wound-cleansing liniment. "My whole body? Into that?"

"Yes. We dirty Christians do this once a week, whether we need it or not. Theo insisted on it. Come on—the salt water will help heal you."

Fen put out a defensive hand when Cai reached to help him lift the cassock over his head, so Cai stepped back and let him get on with it. He kept his attention on the rocks, the rainbow gleam of sea urchins and cockleshells through the sunlit water. He'd seen a hundred naked men before, and once they passed into his hands as patients their bodies lost all significance to him but the parts of them that needed healing. Fen's splendid shadow was only an image, a thing to admire from his new, cold distance.

He took the cassock wordlessly, choosing not to complain that Fen had thrust it at him with a princely disregard. Not this time, anyway. "All right. Get in slowly. If you stay off the kelp, you won't slip."

"You too."

"What?"

"You too. Prove to me that this insane immersion is truly your practice, and not just your effort to freeze me to death, or drown me."

"Oh, for God's..." Cai began to strip off his own robe. He didn't want to get into the water. He didn't want to be reminded of his last visit here, the warmth inside his marrow, the pleasant exhaustion that came after loving. Now that he'd gone to the trouble of getting Fen down here, he didn't really care what happened to either of them. If this was the quickest way of dealing with him, so be it. He splashed into the water, slithering himself on the seaweed, righted himself and reached up his hands. "Here. Get in."

Fen picked his way down the rock. For a big man, he moved with a cautious grace that made Cai want to laugh despite the chilly numbness in his breast, and he clutched Cai's wrists like a scared child. "Gods, monk!" he rasped when he was knee-deep. "No wonder you can keep your vows. Who would care for the pleasures of frig after this?"

"That's not exactly how it works. Anyway, how can a rock pool be so cold to you after you've crossed the North Sea on a raid?"

"We cross the sea in boats, in case you didn't notice. How is it that your bollocks haven't crawled up into your belly forever?"

Cai, not quite hip-deep in the water, struggled not to follow Fen's gaze. "Well, if yours do," he said, pulling him down to stand beside him, "it's surely the least you deserve." He waited till Fen was off balance, then put a hand between his shoulders and shoved him into the pool.

He listened with interest. Some of the language he was hearing was similar to Broc's, when a horse or a dog had annoyed him beyond endurance. Fen struggled in the water, submersing completely, then flipping back out like one of the silver-skinned porpoises Cai saw from time to time on fishing trips out beyond the islands. He shouldn't have been out of his depth, and even if he was...

The fear that this great seafaring pirate couldn't swim seized Cai like a cold hand. He plunged in after him, stilling his frantic movements with an arm around his chest. "Easy. Don't thrash about so. What's wrong with you?"

"Nothing." Fen fought for a few seconds more, then lost a sobbing, coughing breath, the back of his skull resting on Cai's shoulder. "I am cold. I hurt where you stabbed me. And I don't..."

"Yes?" Cai was interested in this string of nothings. "What else?"

"I don't understand why my brother hasn't come back to slit all your throats in the night and rescue me."

It was on Cai's lips to tell him that one Viking raider was as treacherous as the next—to ask him what he had expected. The ragged wound with its crude stitches gaped a dreadful blue-black beneath the water. *Where you stabbed me...* Fen had never said as much before, as if he hadn't taken the injury personally, accepting it as one of the chances of war. "What happened that night? Why did they leave you behind?"

"They did not. They would not."

"And yet here you are."

"Through no fault of Gunnar's. Or Sigurd's, for that matter. They must have thought I was dead."

"I've heard legends that your kind leave no one behind. Not even a corpse."

Fen dispensed with his grasp. After an ungainly movement or two, he seemed to find his rhythm. Of course he could swim. He struck out across the pool, putting as much distance as he could between himself and Cai. On the far side, he tried to haul out, finely corded muscles straining in his back. Then his strength failed him. He slid halfway back into the water, clutching at the rocks. "You will get me out of here, monk."

"In a minute." Cai swam over to him. Before Fen could object, he turned him, seizing his narrow hips and settling him so that he was sitting on a ledge, in the place where the jade-blue water was most strongly warmed by the sun. Cai scooped up a handful of sand and rubbed it over Fen's thigh, or tried to—he dodged a cuff aimed at his head and retreated. "Do it yourself, then."

"What is it for?"

"It cleanses you. Scrapes all the scabs and the lice off you." Treading water, Cai watched him. He needed some attention himself. He hadn't cared, over the last couple of weeks, whether he was dirty or clean, and Aelfric certainly hadn't taken any trouble over the matter. He rubbed sand onto his own limbs, and Fen did the same, hands moving uncertainly over his powerful shoulders. When he tried to reach down, though, pain shadowed his face.

"I cannot."

"Let me. You must know by now I'm not going to hurt you."

"No. But you shame me—every day, with your touch and your interference about my person, and your questions about my water and my bowels."

"I'm a physician. There's no shame in that."

"A Dane warrior should need no physic. A Dane warrior should need no..."

Cai let him run on. His voice was somehow consonant with the wind and the splash of the water, and if it helped him to complain and lay down his warrior's laws while he submitted to having his legs rubbed with sand, so be it. Cai allowed his mind to drift. These beautiful limbs were longer than Leof's, carved with a strength Leof's quiet life had never demanded of him. Badly scarred from what looked like untreated axe wounds. The big, tense muscle that ran up the back of the thigh made Cai's ache in sympathy—and something darker, a vibration of longing. But all that had died in him, hadn't it? Cai was glad that Leof had been his last, that he'd bear onwards into his life with him memories of such purity.

"Who is Theo?"

Cai looked up. Fen was regarding him, his gaze like sea-light through honey. Salt had caught his lashes together, and his shorn hair had grown out enough to spike as the sun dried his crown.

"You wouldn't be interested."

"Theo who makes you bathe. Theo who thinks man's flesh is a beautiful gift from God."

Surprised that he'd remembered, Cai shrugged. "He used to be our abbot here. Before Aelfric."

"Aelfric the scarecrow?"

Cai almost smiled. "I didn't think you were listening then. Yes, Aelfric the scarecrow."

"I shouldn't think you ever called your abbot Theo names."

"No. He was a good man. He taught us about the movements of the stars, and how to treat one another well. I loved him." Suddenly Cai recalled who he was talking to, and he finished the rubdown ungently, making Fen wince. "Much good it did me. Your lot killed him in the raid before the one that bestowed your gracious presence on me."

"He's dead?"

"Yes. He died defending our library and scriptorium. He was armed with a book. You can get out of the water now."

Fen couldn't. Cai watched him struggle for long enough to satisfy the new surge of pain and hatred in his heart, then went to give him a hand. He thrust Fen's discarded cassock at him, and bent to pick up his own.

"Is that why you took up the sword, warrior priest?"

Cai couldn't read Fen's stare. It was comprehensive—taking him in from the top of his head to the soles of his bare feet, paying thorough attention to those places where he was much less priest than warrior. His shoulders, the musculature of his arms, as if any moment he might be recruited for some lightning raid up the coast...

"That's right," he said coldly. "The only throats that will get slit around here will be Viking ones. Fara is defended. Tell that to your brother, if he ever comes looking for trouble here again."

Chapter Six

Dark of the moon, a month after the second raid. The church was completed, and Cai knelt on its stone-flagged floor between Benedict and Brother Martin. This was midnight office, the most ungodly, to Cai's mind, of all the new canonical hours. He'd stopped objecting to them. He could see how they might work and be beautiful, in a monastery with plentiful resources and time on its hands—a kind of circle-dance of prayer so that no hour would pass without praise of God's name.

Matins, prime, terce, sext, none, vespers, compline, midnight office. The names had their own music. They blended with Laban's plainsong chant and the flickering torchlight. No one needed Cai's attention in the infirmary, and no less than three men had been set to watch the coast for raiders. Freed for once from anxiety, Cai felt the tug of sleep. Subtly he eased his hood forwards. Beside him, Martin emitted the tiniest snore. Theo had used to provide a chair for him during mass, but the old man had learned the art of sleeping on his knees whilst maintaining an attitude of perfect devotion.

On Cai's other side, Benedict knelt with spine erect, tension radiating off him. These days he spent more time with the Canterbury clerics than amongst his brethren. Aelfric spoke to him often, too quietly for anyone else to hear, and Ben would listen, head bowed. Oslaf kept bewildered distance from him, lost weight and grew pale. Cai opened his eyes again. He'd never be free from worry, would he—not at Fara, not now.

The chanting stopped. That was the signal for the monks to rise and return to their bunks until matins three hours later, the real start of the monastic day. Cai put a hand to Martin's elbow to wake him and help him up, but Aelfric stepped forwards from the shadows. "No," he commanded, his voice more like a crow's caw than ever. "Remain on your knees."

Cai bit back a groan. Three hours was little enough time to prepare for a day of farming, weaving, rebuilding and all the other duties that fell upon the brethren now, with their reduced numbers, and no Theo to point each man to his right task and ease the labour. Normally even Aelfric released them without a further sermon.

"Remain on your knees. It is thus you must hear God's word on the ultimate fate of your souls. Your former abbot, thinking to spare you, never taught you the one truth that could bring you to salvation. He knew his own heresy, and so he kept silent on the truth of hellfire. He knows it well enough now."

Cai tried to lurch to his feet. Ben gripped his arm, and he subsided. Why should he care? Theo was safe, far beyond the reach of the carrion crow. The more Cai objected, the more of Aelfric's grim attention he drew to himself, and he wished only to slip unnoticed through his shadowed days. Those were the terms of his uneasy truce with the abbot—silence and cooperation, in return for Aelfric's blind eye to his various privileges. He was still allowed to train his men to fight—to keep a warhorse and chariot, and a wounded Viking raider in a quarantine cell. He lowered his head.

"Each one of you here will have undergone pain. Perhaps you have broken a bone, or had a colic fever in your guts, or burned yourselves with hot fat from the kitchen fires. Is it not so?"

Martin suddenly stirred. "Aye, aye. But we have our Caius to mend all of that for us."

A ripple of laughter went through the congregated monks. "Hush, Martin," Cai whispered, giving the old man's hand an affectionate squeeze. "Just listen. We'll be out the sooner."

"The brother is old, and therefore we forgive him, although I see no need for a band of holy men to keep a brewery, and it is my intent to shut it down. Imagine the worst moment of your pain. Bring it back to mind and feel it now. What made you endure it?"

Silence fell in the church. Most of Aelfric's questions during sermons were rhetorical, but he seemed to want an answer to this one. An owl hooted off among the ruins, and the torches rustled. Cai couldn't think of a thing to say.

"Because it passes, my lord abbot."

Oslaf had pushed back his hood. His pain-filled gaze was fixed not on Aelfric but on Benedict. "We endure because it passes. And..." He paused, focussing for an instant on Cai, a faint smile flickering. "And, in truth, we do have Caius."

"I forbid further mention of Caius." Aelfric took another step towards the congregation. The torchlight cast his shadow up across the ceiling until he was tall and thin as a storm-blasted ash, and his outstretched fingers sprouted long, clasping claws. "We endure because it passes. Yes. But I am here to tell you this—in hell, there is no such mercy as the earthly passage of time. You are pinned like an insect upon the most terrible moment of your agony, and...it will last forever."

A sound like a low-moaning wind filled the church. The light of the torches remained steady, though. After a moment Cai identified the source of the keening. Laban and the other clerics had drawn close, heads together, faces invisible beneath their hoods.

"Forever," Aelfric repeated, and their voices rose.

Cai went cold with disgust. Surely men who had been taught by Theo to think for themselves could never fall prey to such theatrics. He began to get up. He would take his brethren with him out of here and into the clean night. Vikings and darkness were less to be feared than these lies.

But Ben was moaning too. His sound was deep and real, full of grief-stricken terror. Cai took hold of his wrist beneath the sleeve of his cassock. "Come with me," he whispered. "It's all right."

"No! I can't move. Don't leave me."

Cai knelt still. Aelfric's shadow-arms extended, up and across the raftered ceiling, enclosing the whole congregation. "Brother Benedict knows," he intoned. "He knows the sins that plunge the soul into hellfire. Worst among them all is impure love. What is impure love, Brother Benedict?"

"All love of the flesh is impure," Ben gasped out. This was a lesson he'd clearly learned well. Rocking, clutching Cai's hand, he began to recite. "All fleshly love is lust, a perversion of God's love. Our bodies are sacred to Christ. To lie with a woman condemns our soul. To lie with one another as with women impales us like insects in the hellfire. Forever. Forever."

Cai had had enough. He tore his hand out of Benedict's and stood up, ready to take on Aelfric barehanded if he had to. Anything to stop this.

But Aelfric was already on the move. His face was calm and satisfied, as if he'd achieved his goal. The clerics had stopped keening and formed up into a protective phalanx around him. Together, like a river of black pitch through the very firelit hell Aelfric had created with his words, they swept out of the church.

Benedict sprang up to follow. Cai tried to stop him, and Oslaf, pale as death, made a helpless grab for his sleeve, but Ben left at a run, clumsy, a broken-down piece of machinery shambling in his master's wake.

The rest of the brethren gathered together like frightened sheep. They too began to move, Oslaf in their midst. They bumped against Cai, who was rooted where he stood, jostling him blindly. Only Oslaf seemed to see him. They exchanged one glance, and then Oslaf too was gone, melting with the others into the night. A gust of wind rushed through the open door, extinguishing the last torch, and Cai was alone in the dark.

No. Not quite alone. At his feet, Brother Martin gave a twitch and woke himself with one mighty snore. He looked up peaceably at Cai. "Ah. I was sleeping. Is it over, then?"

Cai picked him up carefully, waiting till his legs were steady under him before letting him go. He brushed the dust and cobwebs off his robes. "Yes. Yes, it's over."

"You're in a bad fettle this morning, monk."

Cai looked up from the cabinet of herbs and potions he was rearranging. He had plenty of everything, having seen Danan the week before, but he felt a restless need to rattle bottles and slam doors. Just now there was little else for him to do. He had arrived in Fen's cell that morning to find his patient on his feet, voluntarily washing his face and limbs with a cloth and a bucket of water. He had already fastened a clean linen strip round his loins. He had stayed still when bidden for Cai to check his wound, and dressed himself without complaint in a fresh cassock.

He was healing well. Cai, squinting fiercely into a bottle of willow salve, tried to forget the sight of him in morning light, splashing water into his face, the droplets in a rainbow aura round his head. How he had looked as he had straightened to greet him, something like a smile touching his elegant face. He could stand up properly now, not leaning to favour his side. For once Cai's ward was empty, and he hadn't objected when Fen had followed him out of the cell, seated himself on one of the bunks and watched him begin his routine.

"What is it? Has the scarecrow been after you to shave your head again?"

"No."

"Good. Because..."

Cai tried to analyse the silence behind him. It was warm, he decided. Warm and getting tighter... Before he could turn, Fen's hand was on his shoulder. Cai would have to remember how quietly he could move. The hand passed briefly, gently, through his hair.

"Because that would be a shame."

Cai almost dropped the jar of valerian root powder he'd uncorked. "Careful! Do you know how long this stuff takes to grind?"

"It stinks of mouse." Fen had calmly retreated to the window ledge, as if his caressing touch had never happened. "What does it do?"

"It soothes troubled spirits and promotes the health generally, as its name suggests."

Fen gave this a moment's thought. "*Valetudo*," he said. "Yes, I see. You look as if you could use a dose of it yourself. What's happened to trouble your spirits, then?"

"Apart from you?" Cai firmly corked the jar and set it back in the cabinet. He'd barely slept in the few hours between midnight office and matins. He'd come as a novice to Fara with every intent to become a good Christian. Much of the doctrine—subjugation of earthly desire—had been strange to him, but between Leof and Theo he had learned to see the beauty of it too. Aelfric's version was completely alien to him. With his lover and his teacher gone, why should he stay, to see his friends tortured by threats of eternal damnation? "Nothing. I'm busy, that's all, and I can't concentrate with you asking me all these questions."

"You're thinking of leaving."

Cai repressed a twitch. How had Fen plucked that newborn thought from his head? "I'm thinking of remedies for constipation. You'll see why, after a few more servings of Brother Hengist's egg bread."

"That stuff would bung up a bull. Maybe you *should* leave. I don't see what a decent soldier's doing amidst all these eunuchs anyway. But I for one am glad you were here on the night I arrived. Now—do you think you could take me for my daily walk?"

Closing up the cabinet, Cai turned away. He didn't dare meet Fen's eyes. There was a painful prickling behind his own. He was lost, if he let words of kindness from this enemy—however rough and fleeting—touch the loneliness gaping under his ribs. One of the blankets on the cots was rumpled. Cai snatched it off, shook it out hard and threw it back into place. "Go and put on your sandals, then."

Cai had negotiated with Aelfric that the Viking prisoner should have an hour of exercise each day. He would get better sooner that way, Cai had argued, and then Cai would no longer have the flimsy excuse of protecting him as his patient. After that, Aelfric could do what he wished with him. Cai had enjoyed the furrow that had crossed the abbot's brow at the thought of dealing with a six-foot Viking restored to full health. All the Canterbury clerics combined would be like gnats on the hide of a warhorse. Cai had to escort Fenrir personally during these outings, and any trouble that came from them would be visited—as usual—not on Cai himself, but on one of his friends.

Aelfric had wrapped chains around Cai. They were thin and meagre as the abbot himself, but he had chosen them well. They could tighten like wire, and none of Cai's strength could avail him. Remembering poor Benedict moaning in the firelit dark, Cai realised that Aelfric knew how to choose the right chains for each man. Yes, it was time for Cai to go. Not back to his father's stronghold but somewhere free. He'd take his chances among the robber bands who roamed the sunlit uplands of Cheviot and Traprain Law if he had to, shake off the shame and dust of this place forever.

"Cai. I need you to slow down."

Cai had set off blindly across the courtyard and continued from habit along the track that led to the clifftop. Fine rain and sea fret were blowing into his eyes. Normally Fen walked beside him on these trips, his air one of resigned, almost exaggerated obedience—Cai's prisoner, even if he could have picked his captor up and slung him off the cliff with barely an effort. Now he was lagging behind, one hand pressed to his side.

"What's the matter?"

"You're meant to be guarding me. I can't keep up with you."

"Oh. Sorry." Cai slowed up and waited until Fen had limped to his side. Fen's breath was rasping in his throat, his lips tinged with blue. Cai hadn't intended to offer his arm, but the gesture came naturally, and Fen took it easily, as if their bodies had been made to fit together like this. They stood in the rain, both surprised by their sudden proximity. “Are you all right?”

“Yes. I thought that perhaps the next stage of my healing was...a route march.”

“No. You should still take things slowly. Lean on me.”

They set off again down the track. The north coast was wearing her wild summer face this morning, sealskin greys fighting it out with green and startling violet among the breeze-whipped waves. The wind was fierce but not cold. The sea met the sky with such purity here, and for all its austerity, its vivid scents and colours had pierced Cai’s heart from his first hour within Fara’s walls. He couldn’t imagine life anywhere else.

“If such a man as your scarecrow had been set in charge of the clan of Torleik,” Fen said, his voice still ragged, “we would have taken him and pulled his lungs out through his back. It is called the blood eagle.”

Cai frowned in disgust. “I’ve heard of it. Charming practice though it is, it’s not my solution to Aelfric.”

“Why not? Because of your faith? Your Christian convictions?”

“More than that. My convictions as a man.” Even as he spoke, Cai wondered if he was telling the truth. If he had Leof’s murderer in front of him, the heat of battle upon him and an axe in his hand...

“It wasn’t the Torleik who came here. That night—when your abbot was killed, and your boy—it wasn’t my men. A different tribe.”

Once more it was as if Fen had pulled a thought from Cai’s skull. This time Cai felt it as a violation, and he dropped Fen’s arm, striding on ahead. “Who told you about my...about Leof?”

“Your brethren are gossips. I hear many things in my cell. Many reasons why you’d just as soon poison as heal me. But it wasn’t the Torleik.”

“What difference do you think that makes to me? Would your lot have treated them any better—Leof and Theo?”

“No. Perhaps not. I only wish you to know, because...”

Whatever Fen’s reasons, they were lost in a rumble of hooves. Reflexively Cai drew Fen to the side of the track, out of the path of the monastery’s single overworked plough ox trotting determinedly towards them with her broken harness trailing in her wake. Normally the most stolid of creatures, she was moving like a compact landslide, the earth vibrating under her feet. Behind her ran Benedict, his face distraught.

"Catch her," he yelled, as soon as he saw Cai. "Something scared her. She bolted." Benedict stumbled and fell, then dragged himself upright and staggered on. "I couldn't stop her. I can't do anything. I am useless—a sinner—a worm."

Cai caught Benedict, and Fen caught the ox. He seized the beast's trailing harness as she passed, and without seeming effort pulled her head round, forcing her to a snorting halt with her great-horned head leaning into his chest. Cai dropped to his knees with Benedict. "Ben! For God's sake, what's the matter?"

"I am nothing. All the works of my hands fail me. Aelfric said it would be so."

"What has he told you?"

"Enough. Enough. A life of sin here, and an eternity in the fire."

He was shuddering, sobs racking his big frame. Cai rocked him, clasped him roughly. "You know better than that. How often have you helped me in the infirmary? You've seen what happens when men die. All pain of that kind—burning, hurting—it stops when the body does. None of it could possibly follow the soul."

"But what if it can, Cai? What if it's true? In that case I've not just damned myself to eternal torment...I've damned Oslaf too!"

"I swear, I *will* make a Viking eagle out of that scrawny..." Cai fell silent, fire rising up in his throat. He looked over Benedict's shoulder to Fen, who was now watching from a few feet away, the ox standing tamely at his side. What could he say to wipe off Aelfric's dirt from his poor friend's soul? He wasn't Theo, with philosophical arguments at his fingertips for any occasion.

But Theo had never turned to philosophy when faced with unhappy men, had he? He had listened, then asked questions. Simple ones that brought forth equally simple, powerful answers. "Don't you believe in a merciful God?"

"What? Yes, but..."

"An infinite God, infinitely merciful. Come on, Ben. It's one of the dearest beliefs we hold, the first things they taught us."

Ben caught his breath. "I...I remember."

"Then how can that same God do as Aelfric teaches? How?"

Benedict didn't reply. But his rigidity eased, and after a moment he laid his brow to Cai's shoulder. Fresh sobs shook him, but they sounded easier now, less fraught, as if a dry riverbed inside him had suddenly flooded after rain.

Fen gathered up the ox's reins. His expression was unfathomable. "I will leave you," he said softly. "I will mend this beast's harness and hitch her to the plough."

Cai glanced up at him. "Can you do that?"

"I can. Princes are farmers in my land too, just as they are in yours."

Caius left Ben with the plough. The ox had been harnessed to it and tethered, the rein repaired and one wayward ploughshare knocked back into place, but the field was empty. Distractedly bidding Ben to mind his work and not think, Cai scanned the landscape. Fen was nowhere to be seen. Cai set off at a run.

On instinct he headed for the armoury. Fen's sword, *Head-cleaving Bloodsucker* or whatever vile thing he'd named it, was still safe in its rack, and that was something, but...

But Eldra and the chariot were gone, and that was something else entirely.

Cai bolted out of the barn's shadows. He was breathless from his dash down the hill, and now his heart was trying to punch through his ribs with fear. Had he managed to unleash upon his brethren and the coastal villages a Viking raider with a chariot and warhorse at his command? And worse than the fear of that, sliding around in Cai's guts like a hungry snake—betrayal, tiny and cold. What had he expected? The softening in amber eyes, the brief touch to his hair—what had Cai taken from that, to make him think Fen would do anything other than rob him and run at his first chance?

Hoofbeats again. Cai whipped round, expecting to be mown down, not by an ox this time but by his own father's horse. There in the pasture that edged the sea, sudden sunlight flashing off her trappings, Eldra was circling. She had been expertly hitched to the chariot, and Fen was standing casually on the footboard, guiding her round in a wide arc. He saw Cai, transferred the reins to one hand and raised the other in greeting. "Come along, physician. I've just been warming her up for you."

Cai stumbled across the grass. He was dreaming, surely. Fen trotted Eldra over to meet him and drew her to a halt at his side. "Come on. Jump up."

"No. God almighty, Fen—you jump down. Quick, before somebody sees us."

"Who? The scarecrow?"

"Anyone, you idiot. I'll be killed for letting you do this." Cai made to grab Eldra's bridle, but Fen edged her deftly out of his reach. "Besides, I have duties. The infirmary, and..." He paused, listening, as a bell began to clang. The tower was still in ruins, but Eyulf had learned how to climb to the top of it and ring his refectory bell to summon the brethren to prayer. "It's time for terce."

"Oh, more God-bothering... Do you think he likes being woken up nine times a day by your importunities? If they're all in church, no one will see us go."

"Go where? I can't just leave. I can't—"

Fen held out his hand. It was wide and capable, and Cai knew the heat that coursed beneath its pale skin. "Oh, I've no doubt that you're needed here, even if you've started to doubt it yourself. But you have to get away for now. Look at you—hollows under your eyes, half the life drained out of you. A gallop on the sands will set you right. And unlike you, I really know how to drive this thing."

Cai let Fen take his hand. He used it for balance only, not wanting to pull at his patient's healing wound, and he leapt up onto the board. He took his position at the rail next to Fen. "This is madness. I'll be defrocked."

"Defrocked..." Fen grinned and gave the reins a shake so that Eldra trotted forwards out of the paddock. "That would be a sight to see. Is that what happens when you disgrace yourself beyond forgiveness?"

"Among other things. Fen, you'd really better stop."

"Once we've had a run. Did you manage to console him—your friend with the ox?"

"Not much."

"What ailed him? Why does he think himself a worm and a sinner?"

Cai adjusted his grip on the rail. Fen had the chariot going at a steady pace, as if they had all the time in the world, covering the turf between the outer walls and the long stretch of beach to the north. If this was madness, Cai couldn't deny that it was sweet to him—the sense of movement, the rush of the salt wind. Of leaving everything behind. “Aelfric preached us a sermon last night. About hellfire.”

“Hellfire? Ah, not that again!”

Cai broke into laughter. He couldn’t help himself—the fresh air, and Eldra’s lively shift from a trot to a canter, shook his spirit loose. “What? Last night was the first I ever heard of it. How does an infidel Viking raider know?”

“That slave monk of Sigurd’s. The one who taught me Latin… He used to rant about the eternal torments of hell that awaited us infidels.”

“Well, I’m sure you gave him good reason.”

“We thought at first he meant our goddess Hel, or the Hel river to the underworld. When we understood him at last, we laughed at him. As if any god—or even your Christian devil—would spend all eternity spiking mere humans with forks, or burning them on fires.”

“I suppose the arrangements for *your* damned souls are far better.”

“Oh, we have our Underworld. It is called Helheim—the house of Goddess Hel, and so you Christians haven’t even come up with an original name for the place. I am not sure that we have damned souls, though. Only those unfortunate enough not to die a hero’s death in battle.” Fen snapped Eldra’s reins, and she picked up speed, neatly rounding an outcrop of rocks. “The rest of us gallop straight across Bifrost, the rainbow bridge into Valhalla. So no fears of the afterlife trouble *our* hearts, monk.”

“I should’ve let you talk to Ben. I brought him little enough comfort.”

“Ah, half of it depends upon the man. You heard the same sermon, and you are not on your knees weeping over your sins. Are you?”

No. Cai was bolt upright, his spine straight. He could see for miles, and he felt fine. “Maybe I ought to be.”

“Nonsense. Die on the battlefield—you seem fond enough of fighting—and you too might fly to Valhalla. I’m sure Thor will overlook the skirt.”

Cai didn’t point out that two sets of skirts would have to be overlooked at present. Fen was beaming, thoroughly pleased with his joke and his spiritual prospects. Cai let him get on with it. Somebody around here should be happy. And Cai could see the virtues of the warrior's way. It didn't have to be the same as Broc's, low and dirty, though Broc had shown him enough of it to give him the skills. Speaking of which... "Who says I can't drive this thing?"

"I didn't. I just said I would do it better."

"And what makes you think so?"

"I have to do it better than a monk. You're free to prove me wrong."

Fen offered him the reins with exaggerated courtesy. Cai stepped into the place he'd conceded. The leather was warm and smooth where Fen had held it, Eldra's mouth a willing, vigorous tug on the bit. Instinctively Cai adjusted his grip so he wouldn't restrict her. He leaned forwards over the rim. "Go on, girl," he called, paying her out a little more rein. "Go on!"

Fen had left him with the easy part. The rocks and the turf were behind them, the beach ahead. The tide was out, the sand hard-packed and firm. Eldra stretched her pace out to a battlefield gallop and took off.

It was a beautiful run. Eldra, sturdy and tireless, flew across the strand. Cai straightened her out along the water's edge, so that her hooves sent up explosions of spray. The chariot wheel hit a stone, jouncing the carriage, and Fen yelled with laughter and slung an arm around Cai's waist, steadying himself, securing them both.

He didn't take the arm away when they were running smooth again. Cai didn't question the continued embrace. It felt right, to be pelting through the hoofbeat thunder with a brother warrior's hold on him. Doubts and tormented thoughts dropped away from him. He drew deep breaths of the rich air. Spray and sand stung his face, and he drove Eldra on, faster and faster. He was pinned from the waist down between the chariot's rail and Fen's warm, whipcord frame. The rhythmic jolting made his flesh begin to ache, a yearning like music, like the relief of tears. He was still alive, wasn't he? No matter how hard he'd wished himself buried under the hawthorns at Leof's side, here he was. Energy surged in him.

"Still think you can do better, then?"

"I don't want to try. I'll just watch you."

Cai sent Eldra flying out along the strand. Here, if he'd wished, he could have galloped for hours—the sea margin ran flat and golden-white all the way to Berewic in the north, a great, long, welcoming smile of a place, now at this pitch of late spring nothing but wide, empty beauty, singing to him from the sky. He wasn't sure what impulse made him turn the horse's head a little inland, so that her hooves struck softer sand, the drag on the wheels slowing the chariot up. The dunes were tall here. Their crescents echoed the crescent of the great bay, music in shapes and forms. When Eldra tore along their edges, following their curve, she and Cai and Fen were part of the music too. This conviction seeped into Cai's blood, and he eased back on the reins to listen. Oh, it was like the sea bells, only deeper, overwhelming...

"Had enough, monk?"

No. Cai was quite sure that he hadn't had enough—not of anything. He was young. He'd barely had a chance to set his lips to life's cup, and he was hungry and thirsty in a hundred ways at once. Ignoring Fen's laughter and tightening grip round his waist, he drew Eldra to a trot, and then a sweaty, snorting standstill. He hitched the reins to the rail. You never left your horse loose, no matter what tides were rising inside you. Beyond that, Cai's thought systems failed him. His mind was a dazzled blank when he turned, eyes closed, mouth opening like a rose, into Fen's arms.

Fen grunted, as if despite everything, this had surprised him. It was only for a heartbeat. He seized Cai hard. He closed his hand on Cai's throat and jaw, tight enough to send a splash of fear into Cai's arousal, and stilled him with a grip to the back of his skull. Their mouths met in hot, salt-rimed impact. Cai groaned, pushing back at him, shoving off the chariot rail to meet him. He wanted to kill him, devour him, pounce with him into the sand, wolf to wolf. Violent images flashed through his mind, cravings and needs he'd never come close to feeling when he'd gone and lain down in the dunes with...

With Leof. Oh, God. Cai tore back, so hard that Fen's restraining grip on him almost cracked his ribs. "Stop. Let me go."

"What? You're stiff as a spear."

"I know. But I can't—"

Fen released him. Cai was briefly relieved—disappointed—but only long enough for Fen to leap down off the board and hold up one imperious hand to him. "You can. Come here, monk. Do as you're bidden."

Cai sprang down. "Do as you're *bidden*?" he echoed incredulously. He knocked aside Fen's grasp and seized the front of the raider's cassock. "Who the devil do you think you are?"

"A prince of the Torleik Danes," Fen informed him. "I honour you with my touch." Cai tried to punch him to show how honoured he felt, but Fen didn't blink, catching his fist in midair. "I am not like some of my kind, who rape the Saxon peasants in their huts. I will lie only with my equal."

"Whether he likes it or not?"

"A prince in his own land, and..." For the first time Fen's voice faltered. "And a fine man who has healed me. Besides, he *will* like it."

Cai crashed down with him into the sand of the dunes. Only one sea-grass ridge shielded them, but no one came out here. They were alone in the sight of God, a god Cai knew from the marrow of his bones did not send men to hell for love. Had he dragged Fen the last few yards off the beach, or had he succumbed to the Viking's grip? He couldn't remember, and it didn't matter now. Fen rolled on top of him, and that was a first—that full weight, a man of his own size and strength pinning him down. He moaned in fear and pleasure, turning his face to find the rough kiss he'd broken off before.

Fen met him hungrily, tongue thrusting deep. "Caius!"

Not like a sheep giving birth now. Now the sound of his full name made Cai's shaft lift still harder, as if summoned by royal command. "Say it again," he growled, biting at the side of Fen's neck.

"Caius. Caius. You fine man... Lie on your belly for me."

"Oh, God. No."

"Are you afraid? Did Leof never fuck you?"

Leof. Cai froze, clutching at Fen's shoulders. That ancient word *fuck*, the same in both their languages, rang in his ears. They weren't far from the place where Cai had last loved him. Just over the dunes from here, the boy's fine hair fanning out on the turf as he lay down in surrender. "You know how you won't let me say your brother's name?"

"What of it?"

"Don't say his."

"Why not?" Fen tugged at the girdle of Cai's cassock, then gave up on that and ran a hand under its hem, his palm warm as life on Cai's chilly thigh. "I can do anything for you he did. More."

"I don't doubt it. He was gentle. There was no fucking."

"Pitiful. Wasn't he able?"

"Shut up." Cai pushed Fen off him. "He was... You've no idea what he was." And the thing Cai couldn't forgive was not Fen's ignorance but his own forgetting. "He's only been dead for six weeks. And your lot killed him."

"I told you, not the Torleik."

"I don't care! You're all the bloody same to me!" Cai scrambled upright. When Fen reached to grab him, he slapped him aside, the blow connecting this time, a sharp crack. "I loved him. And now you've turned me into a beast like yourself."

Fen stared at him. Cai struggled to read the changing lights in his eyes. Fires of lust were blazing there—a heat to match his own—but what was the darkness behind? He couldn't have caused this creature serious pain. Not that kind—not a raw hurt of rejection.

"I loved him," he repeated. "I shouldn't have come here. Take... Take my horse. Take the damn chariot if you want. You're not my prisoner anymore."

Fen stood up. He had consented to being shaved once a week along with the Fara monks, and the mark of Cai's blow stood out clearly on his white skin, a crimson handprint. Cai forced himself not to step back in fear of him. Whatever barbaric world had spawned him, he was the prince of it—a real one, unlike Cai, with his few muddy acres and his brawling sot of a father.

He looked down on Cai from a pitch of enraged royalty. "Your horse? You think I'd consent to take that mongrel nag—or your father's hay cart?"

"All right. To hell with you. Don't."

"Do you imagine I offer myself—my flesh, my manhood—without meaning? For a brainless fuck on the sand?"

Cai swallowed hard. "How do I know what you do? You're my enemy. I should never have forgotten it."

"I would have made your blood sing."

Cai turned away blindly. He grabbed the chariot's rail and hauled himself aboard. He was shaking in every limb, barely able to untangle Eldra's harness. She didn't respond to his shout, as if holding opinions of her own about his decision to leave, and for the first time he struck her—the lightest sting to the rump with the loop of the reins, but enough to make her start forwards, dancing in outrage. "Go on," he called again, voice breaking like a boy's. "Get on with you. Go!"

Fara was in sight before Eldra slackened her pace. The stark outlines of the monastery—more than half in ruins now—broke Cai from a trance.

He hadn't meant to come so far. For the last couple of miles, rage dying out of him, he'd known what he was doing and let the horse thunder on anyway, hiding his thoughts in the beat of her hooves. But he'd abandoned a wounded man. Friend, enemy, lover—it didn't really matter. He was a doctor, and Fen had been under his care.

He turned Eldra and drove her back the way she'd come, cold fear tightening his throat. If Fen had gone into the dunes, Cai's chances of tracking him in the soft, windblown sand were slim. There would only be a gap in the world, as Leof and Theo were now empty spaces to him. Cai didn't feel as if he could bear another hole. He was a cobweb already. The next gale would blow him away. As he approached the place where he and Fen had parted, he gripped the reins hard, legs weakening. He didn't know how it had happened, but if Fen was gone, Cai had lost far more than a patient or a prisoner. The beach was empty. He felt sick.

He could hear something. He pulled Eldra to a halt and dismounted, this time forgetting to tie up her reins. It was a kind of chanting, not melodious like Laban's plainsong but broken and rough. The sea fret was thickening now, riding the incoming tide. Spectral figures danced in it, and Cai shielded his eyes against the glare from the cloud-wrapped sun. Far out in the water, just before the place where the beach shelved down to unknown depths, a solitary human figure was standing. He was breast-deep, his hands raised and pressed to the back of his head in an attitude of prayer—or desperation, Cai realised, beginning to run. The dark shape at the water's edge was a discarded cassock. Barely breaking pace, Cai hitched up and tore off his own. The heavy wool would drag him under instantly once it got soaked through.

He ran until the resistance of the sea against his thighs became too strong, then arced forwards into a dive. Waves slapped him hard in the face, and his lungs and gut clenched at the chill, the implacable north-shores bite that never eased, even in the heart of summer. Brine flooded his sinuses, and he coughed and forced a rhythm on himself, four powerful strokes, then a breath. Four and a breath, looking for his target each time he surfaced. Expecting each time for Fen to be gone.

When he was close enough, he stopped and trod water. Fen must be on a spar of sand—Cai was out of his depth here, the riptide current tugging at him. He made one last effort against it. "Fen! Fenrir!"

Fen didn't move. Cai could distinguish individual words now. Words for gods, and darkness, and revenge. He covered the last space between them and seized Fen's shoulder, anchoring himself as best he could on the sand underfoot. "What are you doing?"

Fen's hair was slicked down, his eyes wide and vacant. It took him a moment to focus, and when he did, an expression of mild surprise crossed his features, as if he'd encountered Cai unexpectedly in a corridor of Fara. "I am placing a curse upon my comrades. They should have returned for me by now."

"All right." A swell of the tide tore at them, and Cai fought to hold him still. "But can't you do it from the beach?"

"No. The sea must bear my vengeance away to those who deserve it. To Sigurd, to the Torleik warriors who swore their loyalty to me. To... To Gunnar."

"Don't. You love your brother."

"You may say his name now. He is nothing to me."

"You don't mean that." Fen was warm beneath Cai's hands, his skin burning under the water's chill. "You're feverish again. Come ashore with me."

"I haven't finished cursing."

"Well, you can do the rest some other time." Cai took his shoulders and turned him around. "Come on."

Cai got him back to shore with a mix of persuasion and brute force. He was shaking with exhaustion by the time he pushed him up the final rise of the beach. Eldra was waiting patiently where he had left her. He paused for long enough to dry Fen down a bit with one cassock and bundle him into the other, then quickly got dressed himself. He climbed onto the chariot's board and hoisted Fen up after him. There was barely room for a man to sit, but Fen didn't fight when Cai eased him down so he was huddled at his feet.

"You've undone all my good work," Cai told him, pulling the hood up over Fen's head.

"I don't care." Fen blocked Cai's next move, thrusting his hand away. "Don't touch me."

"Very well." Cai shook Eldra's reins. She set off at a smooth-running canter, as if aware of her precarious load. Cai guided her onto the firm strip of sand between the high-tide seaweed mark and the incoming waves. Soon this flat strand would be under the water, but perhaps he would have time to get Fen home. He didn't really care about anything else. He didn't want to think any further than the next few yards of sand ahead of him, any deeper than the warmth of Fen's shoulder pressed against his thigh. Cai had found him. He wasn't drowned or lost. He was here, awkward and fever-racked, simmering with almost-palpable rage. For the first time in a month, Cai was happy.

"I retract my curse on Gunnar."

"That's good. I don't know much about cursing, but Danan says they can come back and strike you."

"Danan?"

"A friend of mine. You'll meet her."

"Ah. A girl."

Cai bit back a smile. There, on the crest of the furthest dune he could see, a female figure was standing, long grey hair blowing in the wind. Had she been there all along, watching over the beach and everything that had played out there today, or had Cai's naming just conjured her up? "No. Very much not a girl."

"I understand now. About Gunnar."

Cai didn't prompt him. He let Eldra run on in silence, and the next time he looked Danan was gone.

"I have been here long enough to know...you have no treasure in Fara, secret or otherwise."

"I did try to tell you. My abbot Theo thought there was something too. Believe me, I'd have handed over anything we had to stop the raids."

"So Sigurd will have taken the Torleik men to raid elsewhere in search of it. But my brother would have come back anyway. You understand nothing about him. No puny Christian could. He had a warrior's heart. He could lift a sword as soon as he could walk. He never ceased in slaying and striking from that moment on."

He sounds lovely. Cai kept that thought to himself. Fen was shivering now, a tense vibration where he was pressed against Cai.

"So he would have come for me. There is no doubt. I am still here, trapped among you paltry excuses for men, and therefore... Therefore Gunnar is dead."

Cai took the reins in one hand. Blindly he put the other one down, seeking Fen's head. It was lowered, pressed to his knees. This time Fen didn't push him away.

"Listen," Cai said. "I can't be your lover. But I won't be your captor, either." He ran a rough caress over the bowed skull in its hood. "Once you're well, I'll help you leave here. You're not my prisoner anymore. I'll help set you free."

Chapter Seven

Step, parry, thrust. One, two, three. Cai glanced over the top of his shield at Brother Gareth, broke the rhythm of the drill and drove a slicing stroke downwards. Gareth didn't so much as blink. He spun and knocked Cai's blade aside.

"Good," Cai gasped, gripped his sword hilt fast and carried on.

That was the trouble. They *were* good now, his little band of warriors. Cai had taught them everything he knew, and he couldn't take them further. Cai's fighting skills were those of a quarrelsome hillfort chieftain. They had served well enough in the last raid, but what about the next? One, two, three... It was hard, even with surprise attacks like the one he'd just launched on Gareth and one-on-one test fights that came perilously close to the real thing, to sustain his men's concentration. Benedict no longer joined them. No sign of Oslaf this morning either. Would they lose momentum, one by one, fall under Aelfric's influence and wait for God to save them?

Gareth, grinning, his hypochondria long since blown away in the pleasures of action, jumped to one side, broke drill and made a sly jab at Cai's ribs.

"Good!" Cai said again, only just evading him. "Insolent, but...very good."

"No. No, no, no."

Cai jerked round, signalling Gareth to stop. From the shadows by the wall, a lean shape was emerging, one hand impatiently extended. The rest of the monks stopped their drill and turned to watch.

For the last few days, Fenrir had accompanied Cai to the training ground. He'd asked to do so politely enough, and Cai had been content to let him. Fen had been very different since their return from the sea. His belief in imminent rescue had been destroyed. He hadn't spoken to Cai again about Sigurd or Gunnar—had barely spoken at all—but his silences had been thoughtful, and instead of holding himself proudly back from the daily life of the brethren, he had started to appear amongst them, in the kitchen garden and at the refectory table. He had gone out once with Benedict and the plough. A few of the men recoiled from him, but those who knew and trusted Cai took their cue from him, and carried on about their tasks while their Viking enemy—now clad in a cassock, hard to distinguish from one of their own number unless you looked into the amber-fire eyes—began unprompted to work at their side.

In the ruins where Cai trained his warriors, he'd remained on the sidelines. Cai wasn't sure why he'd wanted to come, but it meant at least that he was within sight and out of trouble. And although for the last week he'd barely opened his mouth, and not once laid hand on him, still his presence was pleasing to Cai—a warmth like the glow in the air after sunset, the promise of morning to come. Now he was striding towards the gathered men, his passivity thrown aside.

"No," he repeated, taking Cai's sword from him. "You hold it badly. I've been watching you—trying to work out why. Now I see."

Cai folded his arms. He was peripherally aware of murmurs from the group behind him. A Viking in the vegetable patch was one thing. Here in their midst with a sword in his hand, he was a bad memory, a vision from nights of smoke, blood and fire. "Well?" Cai challenged, making sure he kept himself between Fen and the others. "Are you going to tell me?"

"Since it irks me beyond endurance to watch you, yes. Come here."

He stood behind Cai. It was the best position for correcting grip, and Cai braced himself not to notice the heat at his spine. He remembered a sea-fret breeze, and a promise—*I would have made your blood sing...*

"You think of it as a weapon. An object."

"Yes. What else?"

"It is not," Fen said. "Put your hand on mine." Cai obeyed, and instantly Fen lunged forwards, making the monks scatter. "There. Did I move, or the sword?"

"I don't know. Both of you."

"Exactly. Both, and each as alive as the other. The blade is a part of you." Fen thrust again, bearing Cai forwards with him. This time the action felt natural and easy, the leap of energy palpable between man and sword, and no, Cai couldn't tell which was which.

"I'm not sure..." he gasped, "...I want my brethren thinking of their weapons as part of themselves. We're men of God."

Fen handed the sword back to him but didn't step away. "When the *vikingr* next come, do you think they will care? Go easy on you because you are poor men of God, fighting against your will? Don't hold it as if you wanted to cast it away. Take the hilt in your palm as if it were part of the bone running down from your elbow."

"Like that?"

"Yes. It hurts me a bit less to see you, anyway. Show your men."

He turned and made his way back to his seat among the ruins. He was favouring his side again, and his final demonstration thrust had made him go pale. Resisting the urge to run after him, Cai faced the brethren, who were gathering round, interested to see what a Viking had had to teach on the subject of dealing with Vikings.

"Well," he said reluctantly. "He's right, isn't he? We have to go into battle as warriors, not monks, no matter how we would wish to live the rest of our lives. Watch me. Take the hilt in your palm like so—as if it were a part of you, an extension of your bone..."

"And where will you be? When the *vikingr* next come?"

They were descending the slope from the training ground. Cai had a patient waiting for him in the infirmary, Fen a stint with Benedict behind the plough. There was no reason for them to be lingering here, taking the walk slowly, shoulder occasionally brushing shoulder in companionable bumps. The morning sun was pleasant, though, belying grey clouds gathering out at sea.

"I will be long gone by then. As soon as I can walk more than a few fields' length."

"You can almost manage that now. And I've told you, you can take Eldra, if you're so anxious to be gone. A chariot horse is no use for close fighting, not on this type of ground."

"Very well, I will. If you're so anxious to be rid of me."

They stopped and looked at one another. Cai tried to interpret the glimmer in Fen's eyes. Was that suppressed laughter? "No. I mean, I know you can't stay here. But..."

"Caius! Brother Caius!"

Cai turned in time to see Oslaf taking the steps from the main building at a run. Oslaf's skirts were flying, his face a colourless blank.

“Oslaf? What’s wrong?”

“Ben. Was he with you for drill practice?”

“No. He doesn’t come anymore.” Cai steadied Oslaf as the young man halted in front of him. “Why? Can’t you find him?”

“He should be out in the fields, but the ox is still in her stable. I haven’t seen him this morning at all.”

“All right.” As soon as the words were out, Cai knew that it wasn’t. The ground seemed to shift beneath his feet, a shadow to pass over the sun still struggling against the coppery eastern clouds. “We’ll help you look. You run up to the infirmary, check that he’s not there. Fen, will you go and look in the barns?”

Cai set off downslope again. Oslaf disappeared across the courtyard. Barely five seconds later, Fen emerged from a gap between outbuildings and fell back into step at Cai’s side. “You don’t think Benedict’s in the infirmary.”

“No.”

“Or in the barns either.”

“No.”

“Where, then?”

Cai couldn’t tell him. His mouth and throat were numb, as if he’d been swimming in icy water. He could only keep walking. In the bright sweep of open ground below, the newly rebuilt church shone innocently under its thatch. A sanctuary, a place of rest and prayer. Or so it had been, until Aelfric had opened up beneath it the burning pit. He broke into a run.

He was blinded from the sunlight, and his vision flashed red and green as he stared around him in the shadows. The church was cool and silent, the lull in the canonical tide between terce and sext.

It was also empty. His eyes cleared enough for him to be certain of that much. The doors banged behind him, admitting a wash of clean air and Fen, gasping for breath, one hand pressed to his side.

“I couldn’t keep up with you.”

“Sorry.” Cai too was breathless, now he had time to think about it. He leaned his hands on his knees, dizzy with relief. “I thought… I don’t know what I thought. But he isn’t here.”

Fen came to stand beside him. Through the thump and rush of his own pulse, Cai became aware of his stillness—his absolute, focussed rigidity. The tension of a wolf scenting blood…

"Cai. He is."

The doors thudded open again, and this time stayed wide, each of them caught and submissively held by one of the Canterbury clerics. In the middle stood Aelfric, cutting out a thin, mean shape from the brilliance behind him. Aelfric too scanned the church. "Brother Benedict is missing," he said harshly. "I will not have such abandonment of discipline. Where is he?" His attention fastened on Cai and Fen like a grappling hook, and he gestured to Laban to take hold of Fen, who for once offered no resistance, falling back against the wall. "You, physician—I've turned a blind eye to your harbouring of this monster. His brute strength has its uses. But don't you dare bring it in here, with its heathen corruption. This is holy ground."

Cai began to chuckle. He couldn't help it. He was still elated, and Aelfric was so vile, so rich a contradiction of everything Cai had been taught about his new faith. "Aren't we *supposed* to bring them in here if we can? The corrupt heathens, so we can convert them and..."

He faded out. Aelfric wasn't listening. Wasn't looking at him either. His gaze was suddenly fixed where Fen's had been. Where a faint, slight movement was now catching at Cai too, forcing him to look up—up and up into the shadows of the roof space.

A human shape was hanging from the rafters. Cai took this much in, and then the sight and all it stood for seemed to rush to the far distance. He whipped round, looking for a human face. Not Aelfric, not Laban. They wouldn't do. The third of the clerics, a Roman called Marcus, had sometimes seemed less sombre than the rest. Cai seized his shoulders. "Keep Oslaf out of here."

"Which... Which one is Oslaf?"

There are so few of us, and you are our masters. How can you not know our names? Cai shook him. "Benedict's friend. The young one. God, ask anyone—just keep him away!"

Marcus stumbled out. Now that Cai had done that one vital thing, the distance closed, sweeping his next duty in on him. With it came hope, stabbing and hot. Hangings didn't always work. Knots slipped, men were incompetent. Drops were too short to crush the trachea and break the neck. For as long as Cai had known him, Ben had never been the most deft or thoughtful of men. He was a ploughman. A staunch-hearted warrior when forced, and by nature a lover. All the actions of his hands had tended to life, not death. "I have to get him down!"

Ben had used the pulpit, the makeshift stairs and platform where Theo had nine times out of ten laid aside his sermon, folded his arms and addressed them agreeably, man to fellow men. He'd kicked it aside with great force. Cai dragged it upright from the place where it had fallen and pushed it back into place. He clambered up its steps, sick fear slowing him, filling his limbs with lead. The pulpit wasn't tall. Nor was Cai, especially—not by contrast with Ben, who'd been able to stand here, string himself up, and...

"I can't reach him." He tried anyway, leaning far out over the pulpit's edge, grabbing a handful of Ben's cassock and pulling him into his arms. He could only stretch as far as Ben's hips. He took hold, desperately trying to lift him, to relieve the pressure on his neck. "I can't reach him. I can't get him down."

"Caius. I can."

Cai looked down. The church was filling now, men arriving, drawn by the chaos, taking a few steps and falling still. Aelfric remained rooted where he was. White faces stared, thank God none of them Oslaf's. At the foot of the pulpit, Fenrir stood waiting. He had recovered from his fright. He was solid and strong, and he sought Cai's gaze warmly. "Let me. I can bring him down."

Cai couldn't let go. He stood aside to make room when Fen climbed up to join him, but he kept his hold on Ben, lifting, lifting. Only when Fen produced a bronze-handled knife from somewhere within his robes and reached up did he relinquish some of his burden, easing it into Fen's free arm. Fen cut the rope with one savage gesture, and together they caught the body as it fell. Fen eased the bulk of it over his shoulder. "I've got him. Go down now."

Cai stumbled ahead of him down the pulpit steps. Together they laid Benedict out on the flagstones. Cai dropped to his knees, vaguely aware that Marcus was holding back the crowd. Now he could see Ben's face. In that moment he understood that his friend had got it right after all—that he'd tied his final knot, and made his last leap, with perfect efficiency.

Still he tried. He listened at his chest, silent as an empty barrel. He felt for the pulse at his throat and his wrist. Theo had taught him a heretical manner of calling back souls whom God had decreed drowned by breathing with his own lungs into their mouths, and he did that for a while, until the deadly cold of Benedict's mouth under his, the unnatural movement of his head when he let go of it, finally bore it in that he would be recalling the spirit into a body so destroyed that revival would be cruel, an obscenity.

He sat up. Full sunlight was blazing into the church now. The day would be hot. "Fen," he said, his voice echoing hollowly in his ears. "Help me carry him down into the crypt. I have to..."

There was no one there. No—the church was thronged now, but the one face Cai needed was missing.

"Not in the crypt," Aelfric was croaking at him. "Not a suicide. Not in holy ground."

Cai thrust him aside, his scrawny body as insubstantial as his words. Maybe Fen, having seen the worst that could happen on this holy ground, had taken advantage of the chaos and run. Cai didn't blame him. It was time for him to do the same.

He pushed blindly out into the light. He didn't blame Fen, but he wanted him, and he loathed him in that moment for creating the bitter desolation in his heart, a hunger he'd never have known if they had never met. He set off uphill at a dead run. He kept going until he reached the outhouses, until his hands were tearing at the well-known latch of the small barn where he kept his supplies for journeys, his packs and his secular clothes. He tore off his cassock and tossed it as hard as he could into one corner, sending up a cloud of spiders and dust. Beneath its heavy wool he was sweating coldly, stinking of shock and misery. He'd walk into the first water he came to, and he didn't much care if he came out. Perhaps he could use his last breath on a few of Fen's curses, and trust in the sea to bear them home.

There on the shelf were his shirt and deerskin leggings. He pulled them on with shaking hands. The shirt fastened with a fine leather strip across the chest. He had to lace it through fabric loops on each side, a task that proved impossible when he tried. Swearing, he tore the lace out altogether and threw it onto the ground. He'd do without. He'd do without the pack, for that matter—it wasn't as if he'd be stopping off at the kitchens for supplies, or buying things from the settlements, or ever coming home. He was done here.

Someone was blocking the door. Not a scarecrow shape this time—a graceful one, tall and straight. He had picked up Cai's lace from the ground and was holding it, a delicate thing in his big hands. "You are leaving?"

Cai didn't answer. He kicked off his sandals, replaced them with the boots he kept in a wooden chest, safely out of reach of mice. Now he was ready. "Get out of my way." Fen didn't move, and Cai marched up to stand in front of him, not meeting his eyes. "I thought you were gone."

"No. I saw Oslaf heading for the church. Brother Wilfrid had just told him. He...required restraint."

Cai swallowed hard. "What did you do to him?"

"I restrained him. I took him up to the infirmary. I gave him the poppy, the drug that brings sleep."

"Oh, God."

"A little."

"How did you know...?"

"I took note when you gave it to me. He's asleep. I left Wilfrid to watch over him. Now, do you want help with the body of your friend?"

"No!" It came out as a shout, scaring the doves in the rafters. "Aelfric won't let him lie in holy ground."

"Why in Thor's name not?"

"He took his own life. Another new rule, I suppose. I didn't know. No one ever... No one ever did that here before." His voice shook. "There was never any need."

Fen didn't touch him. He bowed his head a little, so his brow was almost brushing Cai's, and in a concentrated silence broken only by the wing beats and the music of the doves, he passed the leather lace through the first loop of Cai's shirt. Then the next, and the next, until he drew the strands together in a knot. He repeated, his voice rough and low, insistent—"So. You are leaving?"

In a bunk in the infirmary, Oslaf lay waiting to wake up into hell, a world of unimaginable pain. Wilfrid, whose sympathies and skills were those of a goatherd, sat helpless by his side. In the church, the ruined shell of a fine man lay, defenceless to the black-robed buzzards who believed him too corrupt to lie in his own monastery's soil. None of this had anything to do with Cai anymore. This place was Aelfric's now—it belonged to the crows. And yet... "No," he snarled, stepping back out of range of Fen's warmth. "I just have to get off this damned holy ground for a while." He shoved his hands into his pockets and thought for a few moments, frowning at the hard-packed earth. Water. He wanted water, to be clean again, or at least away from the mud. "I'm going fishing."

"Fishing?"

"Yes. I go out sometimes and fish. Food, you know? Meat that hasn't been strung up in a cellar for three months. Let me past."

"There's going to be a storm, Cai."

"Nonsense. The sky is clear. Do I have to knock you down, or...?"

"No." Fen stepped aside.

A few yards down the track that led to the boathouses, the weather-beaten sheds where the monks kept their fishing creels and lobster nets, Cai turned. Fen was watching him intently, beautiful in the sunlight. Cai would have given anything to run back into his arms. "Do something for me, will you?"

"If I can."

"Oslaf has family. He comes from farming stock up near Berewic. Find one of the lads who runs errands between here and the village, and give him a message. Tell them to come for him. Tell them to come now."

At last he was alone. Nothing and no one could touch him out here. Cai let the oars rest in their rowels, muscle spasms chasing one another down his back, arms throbbing. The monastery had one small sailboat, but Cai had taken his usual coracle. It was little more than cattle hides stretched over a wooden frame. One man could handle it, though, and he hadn't wanted the intricacies of sail. Just to run the craft down the causeway with a tremendous scrape and rattle, leap into her at the last second, and row and row. He lowered his head. Sweat trickled down between his shoulder blades.

The sunlit waters held him. He felt their movement under the keel, one tiny part of an unimaginable whole of movement, a rocking and surge that could bear him—if he had strength and fair weather—right to the frigid wastes of the north, or south to the Mid-Earth Sea, where Theo had told him, eyes distant with longing, that dolphins leapt and the sun shone all year round. Far to the east was Fen's home, the land of the Danes. Perhaps he ought to head there, surprise the *vikingr* by going to them. They couldn't be worse, them and their dark gods, than the nightmare unfolding itself at Fara in the name of Christ.

No. He wanted to stay here and feel that mighty rocking, greater than any man or god. He also wanted to stop crying, because that was what he had been doing since he cast off, raw sobs racking him. His chest was sore. Strength was leaching out of him. With an effort, he caught his breath. Nothing in his heart or mind would accept that Ben was dead.

"Ben," he called out, as if his friend's spirit might still be nearby and could come back to set things right, wipe out the atrocity. "Benedict!"

Only the wind answered him. He curled up, laced his fingers round the back of his head and closed his eyes.

A thud on the prow of the boat brought him round. He didn't know how long he'd been sitting there. He was sleepy, and a kind of numb peace had come over him. He didn't think it was the holy serenity Leof had said was the goal of their religious lives, but he would take it. It would do. Leof, Benedict, Theo. Gone. A bird was sitting on the prow. It was one of the fat little creatures that haunted the group of rocky islets two miles or so out from Fara. Their beaks were striped in vivid rainbow colours, their movements comical. The puffin watched him curiously, shifting its weight from one outrageous bright pink foot to the other. Then it took off, short wings beating frantically, towards the nearest island.

The seals were hauling out there too. It wasn't basking time. Cai knew the rhythms for this far better than he knew his canonical hours, the tidal intervals when the rocks below Fara would almost disappear beneath the furry, mottled bodies. As he watched, a small flotilla of beautiful black-and-white ducks bobbed past the coracle's prow, calm on the surface but heading purposefully inland.

Get out of the water. Cai received the message loud and clear from these three harbingers, and he set it aside in his mind. The day was still lovely, if he didn't look behind him to the place where surly clouds had been gathering since dawn. The ducks became a glimmering patch in the distance. Eider, they were called, their feathers highly coveted stuffing for pillows. Addy ducks, the locals sometimes called them.

You have to find Addy. Addy will give you the treasure—the secret of Fara.

Cai sat still. Theo had been silent in his head for a long time now, as if leaving him to deal with his own problems. In a way that had been good, because his voice—so close, so vivid—had made Cai fear for his sanity, but he had also missed him. This was just a memory, though, an echo. He reached for it, and like a dream it dissolved from under his grasp, leaving him desolate.

He had come out here to fish. That was what he'd told Fen, and he would do it. He got up stiffly and shook out the net from its heap on the deck. He was a good fisherman, adept at spreading his nets against the current of the sea. *Get out of the water,* the creatures of the islands said. Well, he would when he was done. And if in the meantime the tempest chose to break on him, he would take that as God's word. The Viking had sparked something in him he had thought was dead, some instinctive yearning to friendship and life, but he was tired now, and Fen was far away. Yes. He was done with the fight.

The sun turned copper green and vanished. Out of the darkness came a voice—one note, low and huge, filling the horizon. Cai's fishing boat sat still in the midst of it on water turned suddenly, deadly calm, and he listened. This was the voice of the wind, not upon him yet but racing blackly towards him over the waves.

A visceral terror awoke in him, nothing to do with his life on the shore but a blood-simple message from his bones, lungs and heart that they did not want to be out here, exposed like a cork, with that demon gale bearing down on them. That they, no matter how tired Cai's spirit was, did not want to cease. He grabbed the oars. He didn't stand a cat's chance in hell now, but he began to row.

The storm broke like the end of the world. The voice became a shriek, and the millpond water boiled. Just for a moment Cai had the advantage of it all—the wind was howling landward, pushing him. Then the first wave heaped itself out of the mouth of the demon.

It smashed over the coracle. Cai ducked and clung to the little craft's hull while its force thundered down on him and spent itself. For seconds the whole boat was under water, then she somehow righted and heaved back to surface. Scrabbling for purchase on her soaked deck, Cai managed to look up.

Straight into the demon's maw. A wave the size of Fara's church was rearing over him. Half-blinded with salt, Cai stared at it. He had time to hear its snarl, its hungry, sucking roar as it gathered up, tugging the coracle into its undertow. Cai waited. He would meet his end as Theo and Leof had met theirs—upright, unafraid. He wouldn't look away.

Chapter Eight

He was swimming. It might have been for minutes or for years. His sense of time had gone down with the coracle, shattered to shards.

No. Not even swimming, not anymore. His arms were numb. He was clutching a spar from the wreckage. Each wave drove him under for longer, left him less time to suck lungfuls of air in between. He was starting to like the submersions. It was quiet down there, out of the shriek of the wind, the brutal chaos above. Down there was a memory, one that branched off from reality and blossomed on its own. Down there he hit the sands again with Fen, and this time no guilt about Leof rose to stop him, because Leof knew all, understood all, forgave all, and was no more likely to condemn him than the sun or the marram grasses waving over his head. Down there Fen's arms closed round him, and even better than the sweet rush of hunger and release was the reality of that body on his, as if all his life his flesh had yearned for this brother, this counterpart, a missing piece of himself at last returned to him.

The memory-dream was waiting. The spar became an obstacle to it, a grudging barrier, and he started to push it away.

A wall sliced down into the water barely a foot from his skull. By lightning flash and tarnished light, Cai saw it—a timber wall, curved and glistening. A voice close to his ear said, "No, you don't," and a hand locked into the back of his shirt.

A huge strength hauled him upwards. No more tender than the waves had been, it dragged him over the top of the wall, bruising his ribs and hips. A boat, Cai realised, when he was more in than out of it, and the strength let him go, dumping him onto its deck. He landed facedown and lay still.

A boot promptly shoved at him. "Physician!"

He kept his eyes shut. He was done for, his lungs flooded. The deck beneath him heaved, and he rolled with it, nothing more than flotsam on the tide.

"You! Caius! Dead or alive?"

He got his head up, coughing and choking, and shoved onto his arms. "Dead."

"Get your arse up off that deck and help me anyway."

The next flash revealed a Viking in the prow. He was soaked and resplendent, his jerkin and leggings clinging to him, cassock discarded God knew where. With one hand he was clutching the mast of Fara's only sailboat. He was holding the other out to Cai. "Come on! Help me raise sail."

"Sail..." Cai grabbed him and hauled himself up. "You can't. Not in this."

"How do you think I got out here?"

That smile could dazzle the lightning. His fingers were locked round Cai's arm, a hold that would never grow tired. "You came after me."

"What?"

Cai repeated it, yelling through the spray. "You came after me. In a storm."

"Call this a storm? Torleik babies sail their coracles through worse than this." Again, that flash of a grin. "Having said that, grab the rope. We might get the chance at one run."

"To shore?"

"No. We'll never make it. That island, the long, low one to the east."

Cai shielded his eyes to look. Another wave tipped the boat through the height of its mast, but Fen rode out the lurching movement easily, holding Cai fast. By harsh copper light he made out the shape on the horizon. "Not there. That's East Fara. There's no safe anchorage—just rocks."

"Maybe not for fisherman monks." Fen tossed him the rope that would haul up the boat's ragged sail. "I am a Viking. And we have no choice."

He was right. Cai backed off with the rope. The boat's next lurch knocked his feet out from under him, and the sail unfurled as he slithered aft, instantly snapping belly-tight with air. Fen ran back to join him, and together they wrenched the canvas round far enough to reap the gale without capsizing, to find and ride the angle of the wind. The boat jerked forwards twice, like Eldra impatient of her harness, then shot through a gap in the waves.

Fen roared with laughter. Cai joined in. Fear fell away from him, dirty old clothes he had no use for anymore. Fen had come out for him, out through the storm, and the upshot of it all—life or death, the future Cai had spent all his life grabbing after, striving to control—didn't matter. He was here in Fen's moment, tearing through the lightning, and all would be well.

All would be well. Belief sprang up in him. It was nothing like the faith he had been taught. Wild and hot, it had as much to do with the sea as his salvation from it. Depended on nothing—held no God outside himself accountable. He didn't have to reach for it at all. It was simply here, like the seals and the birds and the storm. Like Fen. It burned and hurt, then leapt up high like fire and made him laugh still louder, hauling on the rope, his hands working so close to Fen's that when the flicker of sheet lightning came, he couldn't tell which pair was his own.

It sustained him even when the boat's keel struck off the rocks that guarded East Fara. A stretch of beach he hadn't known was there gleamed briefly beyond them, and he joined frantically with Fen's efforts to guide them there, to fly them to it while the wind ripped the sail from the mast and the boat heeled over. All would be well... The words were ringing in his head when the boat ran aground, smashing to a halt, pitching him over her prow into the dark.

"Caius. Cai!"

Hands were shaking his shoulders. He was propped against a rock. Every bone in his body felt bruised, and it was easier to stay under. To sleep. One of the hands—and he knew them, was beginning to know their touch better than his own—delivered a smart slap to the side of his face. Fen. Cai surfaced, gasping, ready to hit him back.

He was waist-deep in water. Fen must have dragged him this far ashore, far enough out of the roaring surf to set him down. The black rocks rose all round him like a jagged, burned-out forest. Waves were crashing to oblivion on their spines, rushing between them. A huge foam-topped crest heaved up out of the dark as he watched, the tempest hungry for their lives even now. Fen hadn't seen it. He was leaning over Cai, holding him out of the water. Cai didn't bother to try and warn him. He got his feet beneath him—surged up, grabbed Fen and shoved him ahead of him up the beach.

Neither had much running left in him. Up ahead was a crescent of rocks whose outer edge was turned to the storm-driven tide. A wave broke over it just as Cai and Fen fell into its sheltering curve, but it would do. The wind howled a little less fiercely there. The sea still stretched out its paws, but couldn't drag them back. Sand was piled up here, strange rippled structures marked with kelp and a million fractured shells.

Cai pulled Fen out of the storm. They dropped to their knees, huddling against the rock. This time when Fen's mouth sought his, he turned to him with a cry of joy and relief. Fen had been right—his blood was singing already, so loud the angels must hear. His skull banged off stone, and he reached up through exploding stars to grab anything he could of the Viking's hot muscle and bone. Fen resisted him, tearing back to arm's length, far enough to see him. "Caius."

"My wolf from the sea."

"Yes."

"You came for me."

"Well, none of your other lily-arsed brethren would do it. They saw you, and they ran around like headless chickens, but..."

"They're not sailors. They're not..." *Not you,* Cai wanted to finish, but his throat had seized up.

"Not pirates. Not *vikingr.*"

Cai nodded. Like their shelter, it would have to do. Another wave broke, spray arcing high, landing with a seething crackle all around. Fen's mouth was salty with it when it next landed on Cai's, and he moved like the thunder, bearing Cai down onto the sand. But Cai was full of newborn faith and certainty. He rolled on top, pinning him, and Fen looked up and whispered, "*There* you are," as if in recognition. As if at the end of a long, lonely wait.

Cai shuddered. He straddled Fen's thighs and ran a hand down over his stomach, over the hard plane that rippled and arched to find his touch. Fen was erect beneath the leather thong of his leggings. He moaned when Cai freed him, sea-chilled fingers clumsy on the lace. His cock lifted stiff and full into Cai's grasp, a vision seared into Cai's brain by the lightning. In the green-flashing darkness that followed, Cai plunged down on him, shifting to allow him access in return. He buried his face on the side of Fen's neck. That great, strong hand was on him now, between their bodies, undoing him.

There—flesh to flesh, Fen letting go only long enough to grab him by the backside, hauling him into place. Bucking up as if he meant to dislodge him, at the same time holding him tight enough to keep him there forever. Gasping, Cai thrust back, for the first time in his life with all his strength. Leof would have broken beneath him. Fen only shouted in pleasure and rose up to meet him again. After one more kiss and shove of his tongue beneath Fen's ear, Cai sat up to get his back into the rhythm, laying hold of both of them. He fastened a fierce grasp on Fen's shoulders. The heated length trapped against his belly hardened still further, summoning his own to one last delicious stretch, a storm to match the tempest around him gathering in his spine.

"Fen!" he yelled, and in the next lightning flash saw him, face wild with consummation, all the amber in his vulpine stare turned silver. Climax started, a surge too huge to sustain, and Cai let go, surrendering to the inner leap.

Fen curled up from beneath him and seized him tight into his arms. They thudded down together onto the sand, wrestling in feral joy. The wind shrieked unheard. High above them in the tormented night, the moon sailed clear out of the clouds.

Pater Noster, qui es in caelis…

Cai twitched and stirred. His face was buried deep in Fen's shirt, and if that was Abbot Aelfric, they were both in trouble now.

Sanctificetur nomen tuum!

Aelfric didn't belt out his Our Fathers like that, as if the words were rocks he could throw to ward off the devil. The distant voice faded, and Cai decided he'd been dreaming. He pressed tighter to Fen's side, moaning softly when the arms around him locked him more firmly into place. The storm was over. The tide had gone. The sand was softer than his bunk at Fara, Fen's hold on him warmer than sunlight, and he could fall back into sleep.

Something tugged at his sleeve. Still not looking, he jerked his arm away. The scrabbling touch came again, this time at his belt. Trying to pull it free. Well, Fen was welcome, if he wanted to start over. It had been years since Cai had awoken with another body next to his. Hundreds of mornings trying to quell his waking erection in the name of God. Burrowing against him, Cai shivered at the powerful lift of his own flesh. The tugging came again—insistent, more like a bird plucking at him than Fen's frank grab—and he cracked one eye open to look.

A monster was standing over him. He sat bolt upright, tearing out of Fen's embrace, scattering sand. The monster jerked back. It put its head on one side. It wasn't afraid—just startled by Cai's sudden movement. It considered for a moment, then opened its toothless mouth wide and emitted a weird cry. Four others exactly like it emerged from the pale dawn light.

Cai's erection died. He snatched for the fisherman's knife at his belt. Behind him Fen was waking up, scrambling onto his knees. "Cai, what the hell—"

"Fara devils! I've heard of them. They eat shipwrecked sailors."

"Devils? They look human to me. Almost."

There were eight of them now. Yes, almost human. All of them skeletally thin, dressed in a few rags of sealskin. Horribly alike in the twist of their wasted features, their narrow, hairless skulls. Two of them had harelips, stumps of rotting teeth showing in the gap.

Instinctively Cai got to his feet and pressed his back to Fen's, and felt him doing likewise, getting ready for defence. "I can take three of them. You?"

A contemptuous snort. "These bags of bones? I'll take what's left and come back for *your* three."

"Wonderful. What are you going to do about the dozen more that just climbed up over those rocks?"

"*Pater Noster, qui es in caelis!*"

The devils nearest to Cai started and cringed at the voice. It was much closer now. Cai's vision was still blurred with sleep and salt, and he dragged his sleeve over his eyes. An old man had appeared at the crest of the nearest dune. He could have been brother to Danan. His wild white hair flew with the same vigour, and he came leaping down the sandy slope with much of that lady's unlikely speed. His hands were raised over his head. In one of them he clasped a staff like a shepherd's, and he gesticulated with it powerfully, gestures of banishment that came in time with his shouted prayers.

"*Sanctificetur nomen tuum! Adveniat regnum tuum! Fiat voluntas tua...*"

Now he was on the flat, his ragged brown robes flying to expose skinny ankles. The devils began to fall back from around Cai and Fen, whimpering sounds emerging from their twisted mouths. "*Sicut in caelo et in terra!*"

On earth as it is in heaven. Too much for the devils of Fara, who turned in one ungainly movement and began to run, hopping and stumbling in their haste. The old man galloped after them a little way down the beach, then came to a gasping halt, arms still upraised. He dropped out of Latin and continued, sadly, as if to himself, "Give them this day their daily bread. Just not the flesh of these sailors."

His arms fell. He turned, leaning on his staff. "Are you all right? Did they hurt you?"

Cai glanced at Fen, who was staring at the old man in disbelief. Perhaps they both were dreaming. Benedict had died, and perhaps Cai had gone down with the coracle. This was a strange afterworld, with snaggle-toothed cannibal denizens and fleshly joys beyond imagination in the sea foam, but he would take it over Aelfric's hellfire.

"No," he called, steadying himself against Fen. "What are they? Why are they afraid of you?"

"They don't seem to like the sound of Latin prayer. I use it to chase them off." He shrugged despondently. "I might as well give the poor devils a blessing while I'm at it."

"They *are* devils, then?"

The old man stumped towards them up the beach. "Not in the sense you mean. They're as human as you are—the first people of these islands. Heaven knows how they came to be cut off here, but they only breed among themselves, and it damages them."

"Would they have eaten us?"

Another shrug. "They eat what they can. Speaking of which, you boys will want your breakfast. I wondered why he dropped me such a big one this morning. God provides."

Cai shook his head. "I don't understand."

"The eagle. Such a big fish," the old man told him easily, as if he ought to have known. "He brings me one each day, clutched in his great claws. This morning, a salmon the size of a young seal! Well, sailors have grand appetites. And being washed ashore is hungry work. Come along."

The old man set off at a brisk pace. After an exchanged look, Cai and Fen followed him.

"Do you think he knows Latin for more than his prayers?" Fen asked quietly, dropping into stride at Cai's side. "I understand a bit of your uncouth north-shores tongue, but clearly not enough. I thought he said an eagle dropped a fish for him."

"He did." Cai jogged ahead and caught the old man up. "Sir, we're grateful for the rescue. My friend isn't from here. Do you speak Latin, so that he can understand?"

"Of course. *Ita vero.*" He switched without effort, the neat Roman syllables falling more naturally from his mouth than they ever would from Cai's. "But I'm surprised that sailors do."

"We're not sailors. We're..." Cai looked back over his shoulder, daring Fen to argue. "We're monks. From Fara monastery. We were out fishing, and we got caught in the storm."

"From Fara?" The old man's gaunt face lit up. "Fortunate boys! You study under Theo, then—Theodosius of Epiros, a most learned man."

"Yes. He told us about Epiros." Cai's throat ached and closed. If this was the afterworld, Aelfric had been right in part, then—pain *could* chase and follow men there. The cry of the seagulls became desperate shouts from the scriptorium, and Leof whispered to him from out of the surf. "But...Theo is dead, sir."

The old man stopped short in his tracks. Cai would have stumbled, but Fen was close behind him, catching him by the armpit. Cai turned to him. Only yesterday, he thought he would have to face such things—his grief, and the pain of others—alone. Always alone. *No,* Fen's burnished gaze told him silently. *Not now.* His grip on Cai turned to a hold, and together they watched the old man, who was now stalking unhappily back and forth along a few feet of sand.

"My friend. Ah, poor Theo, my dear friend. I met him on my way back from Rome, when my elders in Hibernia sent me to study there. What was it? The cholera? He never did like this climate. He missed his dolphins and the warm sea. Was it flux? A pneumonia? Or..." He turned himself around, bare feet carving out an agitated circle in the sand. "Wait. Ah, that's what the damned old woman wasn't telling me. There was a Viking raid, she said, then she shut herself up, like the old clam she is. Was that how Theo died?"

Cai couldn't keep up. His head was spinning, with exhaustion and hunger and the energies he'd spilled out with Fen during the night. "Which old woman?"

"Who? Oh. Danan, she's calling herself this time. The herbalist, though some would say witch. A gossip, but not enough of one. Starts a story but then doesn't tell you it all, curse her bones."

"Danan comes out here?" Cai had never seen her anywhere near a boat. "How?"

"Only the ancient creature herself knows that. Tunnels, she says, though I've never found any. Probably she flies. Ah, poor Theodosius! So much learning, to be wasted and spilled out by a..."

He fell silent. The following quiet was terrible, even filled with wave-wash and the breeze. The old man stopped his pacing and drove his staff into the sand. Then he folded his hands into the sleeves of his robes. He stepped up and halted in front of Fen. "Not a sailor," he murmured. "No, and no monk either." He was as tall as Fen and could look him straight in the face. Fen remained still beneath his inspection, even when the old man reached to push back his fringe. "Square brow. Straight nose, high cheekbones. Red hair, but not like the western Keltoi. Red like the fox, and like blood." He shuddered and retracted his hand. "*Vikingr.*"

"*Ita vero,*" Fen growled in return. Cai heard the danger in it and got ready to restrain him, but there was no need. The old man stepped back, lowering his head. His face was deeply marked with the lines of an old, hard-learned lesson in forbearance.

"I have been discourteous," he said. "Whatever your origins, the wind and the waves have brought you here, and you're my guest. Do you have a name?"

"Fenrir. This is Cai—Caius."

"Ah. Caius, a fine old Roman name." The old man turned his attention to Cai. "And this one *is* a monk, though unshorn and out of his cassock—a man of God, no matter how he feels right now. I am Aedar. Yet for many years now, the villagers along these shores have called me Addy. I've come to prefer it."

"Addy..." Cai ran a hand into his unshorn hair. Another wash of vertigo went through him. "*You're* Addy? My God... Theo talked to me about you just before he died. He said..."

The old man's brow furrowed, waiting for him to go on. But the sea and the gulls, the cries from the burning scriptorium, grew too loud for Cai to think past them, and he sat down hard on the sand.

"Caius?" Addy's hand closed on his shoulder. He glanced in appeal at Fen. "What's wrong with him?"

"I don't know, do I? He's the doctor, not me."

"Is he sick?"

"No. He loved this Theodosius, though, just as much as you do. And yesterday another friend of his died."

"A monk of Fara?"

"Yes, by his own hand. They have another abbot there now—a damned scarecrow called Aelfric. I'm not of your faith, and they don't let me into the church, but I've been watching. He's a brute. Cai's been trying to stop him."

"This Aelfric—did the churchmen of Canterbury send him?"

"Aye, that was the place."

Addy sighed deeply. "So it begins. And I am little better, with my questions and my selfish grief, when this boy is half-drowned and wholly starved. You too."

"Such things don't bother me, old man."

"Hm. Tough pirate. Immune to the pangs of love too, I hope."

"What?"

"Never mind. Just help him up and bring him with you."

Cai tried to say he didn't need the help. But he was so tired he could barely see, and when Fen bent down for him, he reached up gratefully, skin heating with memories of that strength closing round him in passion. "I won't let love give you any pain," he said indistinctly, as Fen hoisted him to his feet. "I won't let anything hurt you."

"Quiet. You're half-asleep. Let's just go with this old lunatic and eat his fish, if he hasn't dreamed it."

The fish was real, and one of the biggest Cai had ever seen. They ate it solemnly by Addy's fireside. For a long time silence held sway, made peaceful by the whisper of the flames in their stone pit and the sense of a vast golden day beginning all around. The dawn mists had cleared. The sea was returning pink lights to the roseate sky, as if neither had ever roared and convulsed and tried to consume them whole.

Addy's cave lay in the shelter of a dune. No more than a deep hollow in a rocky outcrop, its sole comfort was the well-made fire pit outside it. Cai couldn't see how the old man lived. Addy, a big chunk of salmon gleaming in his hand, returned his gaze tranquilly. If he noticed that his guests sat shoulder to shoulder while they ate, he didn't remark on it. He passed them a flagon of cold heather ale, and when they were done, produced a bowl of fresh water and a piece of homespun linen so they could wash. "How is it with you now?"

Cai nodded, wiping fish grease off his fingers. "Better. Thank you." He gave Fen a violent nudge, and the Viking stopped appreciatively tugging bits out from between the salmon's bones long enough to grunt an acknowledgement too. "But how can you afford to share your food with strangers? And how do you come by the ale?"

"I have plenty." Addy spread out his robes and settled himself more comfortably by the fire. "As for the ale, that old woman I told you about brings it to me on her devilish visits. Mead from Fara too, in which I can still taste the good work of Brother Martin, though he must be very old now. Is it so?"

"Yes. Martin's still brewing, though Aelfric wants to shut him down."

"The Fara mead?" Addy chuckled. "He'll have an uprising on his hands. Tell me more about him—this new abbot of yours. What does he profess?"

Cai hardly knew how to begin. Fen was warm and solid at his side, though, and not so occupied with his fish that he couldn't spare Cai a gentle shove. "That we're all sinners, I suppose."

"And didn't Theo teach you the same thing?"

"Yes. Yes, if we did something wrong to one another. But with Aelfric, everything's wrong. Everything that comes from our bodies, that is. If we want it with our flesh, it's sending us to hell."

"He teaches you the doctrine of hellfire?"

Cai hadn't realised Aelfric's grim vision was a doctrine. Belatedly he noticed that Addy's robes were a cassock like his own, patched and worn almost beyond recognition. "I've heard of you," he said wonderingly. "When I was growing up. A crazy old hermit, a holy man who lived on the islands alone. How long have you been out here?"

"Long enough to gain a reputation, it seems." Addy poked the fire and gave Cai a wry look from under his wiry brows. "I was a missionary, a priest in far west Hibernia. For a while I was at Fara. Then I found that I could hear the voice of God much better in the silences out here, and I stayed. The years have flown past me—how many, I couldn't say. Certainly more than your lifetime." He sighed. "And the truth is that my chosen seclusion has now become necessity to me. They want to make me bishop, you see."

Cai, who had just been about to apologise for calling him crazy, caught Fen's sidelong look. "Bishop?" he echoed. "Who does?"

"The high men of the church. I prefer my solitude, though, so I am in hiding from them. The beasts of the islands take care of me. As I've told you, the eagles bring me fish to eat, and the seals come also, to receive my benediction and sing me their songs."

Once more Cai nudged Fen, in warning this time. However insane this old man might be, he had rescued them, shared with them his fireside and his food. "Wouldn't it be better," he said cautiously, "to come back and live on the mainland? To have shelter and companionship?"

"In my lunatic dotage, you mean?" The old man grinned lucidly, making Cai blush. "Possibly. But the church I knew has altered so much in her ways." He paused and frowned, as if this was a puzzle he'd tried to work out for himself many times before. "Not that they're all bad ways. The word of God must reach the whole world, and you can't do that with a handful of crazed Hibernian saints and visionaries, can you? So the church—the Roman church, in her wish to reform our wild island ways—is sending out men like your Aelfric. And since the voice of the wind and the sea won't make men behave themselves, they bring with them doctrines like Aelfric's, to hasten them into the fold."

"Like sheep," Fen said suddenly. "To frighten them into belief—whether the creed be good or bad."

"I've lived in this creed all my life. I have to believe it good. But yes—like sheep, Fenrir the wolf."

They stared at one another—the holy hermit and the Viking, each on his own side of a divide whose ancient depth Cai could sense almost as a physical thing. Into the crackling silence, he said, "Fen doesn't see men as sheep. Nor do I, and...nor did Theo. He tried to teach us to think for ourselves."

"He was a good man. A Gnostic, if you understand what that is."

"Yes, thanks to him. One who finds God for himself through learning and prayer, not following in blind obedience."

Addy's eyes gleamed in what might have been approval. "As good a definition as any. Now, Caius—the monk who sits at the side of a Viking wolf, and understands gnosis, and has no truck with sheep or bad shepherds—what do you want to ask me? What did Theo say to you before he died?"

Cai drew up his knees. Theo's last behest had been such a weight on him, and yet now that the time had come, he was reluctant to speak. His abbot had been living proof to him that a man could combine deep religious convictions with sanity. Cai was quite certain that Fara held no treasures, and it hurt him to think that Theo had believed otherwise—that such a chimera had been his last thought. "He said there was some kind of treasure at Fara. A secret. The *vikingr* believed in it too—it's what they were raiding for that night."

"That was all?"

"No." Once more Cai hesitated. He hadn't told even Fen this much. "He said this treasure would stop the raids, and I don't think he meant the *vikingr* would just go away when they got it. I think he meant it had some sort of power. And—he was delirious by this time, dying—he said that the treasure lies not in the book but in the binding."

He waited. His heart was thumping. He didn't want to look at Fen, because something in his words had made a difference—Fen was listening intently, all the weight of his attention suddenly brought to bear. The old man too had leaned forwards, about to speak.

Then he looked both of them over. His examination was compassionate, but unhurried and stripped of all sentiment. He released a long sigh. "I am sorry," he said. "My poor Theo. He was a rational man. But he loved his books above all else, and I fear his last thoughts became tangled up in them. Were they all lost?"

"Yes. But he wasn't worried about that—at least, not about the one he was writing. He said that was only a copy."

"Theo's book? What was it?"

"He called it the *Gospel of Science.*"

Addy almost laughed. He caught the reaction, pushed it firmly down. Cai saw himself and Fen through the old man's eyes—a dishevelled, faithless monk in fisherman's clothes, and a barely tamed Viking raider whose face had lit up at the idea of treasure. "A little blasphemous of him," Addy said, settling back. "Very typical, though. I wish he'd had time to complete it. And I wish I could tell you his message means something to me, but I know of no treasure. No secret. Young men, I must think about this, and pray, and I must do so in solitude. You lost your boat last night?"

"Yes. She was smashed to pieces."

"How you escaped the same fate is a mystery greater than Theo's.

God cares for children and fools."

"It was not God." Fen clambered onto his feet, hoisting Cai easily up with him. Cai remembered how he'd blanched with pain on the training ground just the morning before, and wondered if the shipwreck had been good for him. "It was me. I am an excellent sailor."

Once more the old man fought laughter. "Well, whichever of you takes credit," he said solemnly, "I'm glad of the result. Companionship is rare for me, and I will gladly shelter you here for the night. But go away now. There is a stone hut down by the shore with the remains of some boats in it, perhaps belonging to the devils when they were still human enough to know how to sail. You may be able to patch one together for yourselves." He nodded, gazing into the ashes of the driftwood fire, where spectral blue-green lights were shimmering against the morning sun. "Yes. Yes, go away now."

Fen leaned over the hull of an upturned boat. He braced, muscles cording up and down his bare arm, and tore a length of planking away. He examined it critically. "Rotten at both ends, but sound enough in the middle."

Cai put out a hand. Fen tossed it to him, and he fitted it into a gap in the ancient fishing boat they were repairing. He hammered it into place with a rock, crushing the rotten ends tight into the good wood. That would form a kind of seal, and the clay pit a little way up the shore would provide caulking for the rest. He sat up. "That's the last of the holes. The big ones, anyway—for the rest we can just bail. It's not a long trip, if we catch an incoming tide."

"All right. Let's haul her out and have a look."

Cai got out of the hull where he'd been working. He picked up the prow, and Fen went to grab the battered stern. They dragged her out of the crude drystone boathouse that had stopped her from eroding to splinters and dust over the years. She was heavy, but Fen didn't flinch, and he set her down on the runway outside with a dazzling grin. "She looks good."

"Better than she has any right to." Cai eased down his end, grateful that none of his repairs had snapped out of place. "Speaking of which..."

"Yes. I am better too. Your stitches came out somewhere last night, and beneath them I am healed. Maybe you were right, physician, about the benefits of salt water, or...of something."

Cai had begun to wonder if *something* had been consigned to the seabed along with their boat. They had come down here in silence and worked quietly, only exchanging the words they needed for their task. Maybe a *vikingr* pirate could grasp at a brother-in-arms in a moment of danger, rekindle the fires of life with him, but afterwards... "I should come and have a look. May I?"

"You never asked my leave before."

"My patients have to do as I say. If you're well again, I don't wield the same authority."

Fen examined him from the far side of the boat. The morning was brilliant now, a brisk wind dancing in the light. There wasn't much chance of concealment, for damaged vessels or for men. It didn't seem likely to Cai that Fen had shared his doubts, but there was a trace of uncertainty on his brow, in the corners of his mouth. He took a couple of steps back and sat on the remains of the hut's seaward wall. "Yes, then. You may look."

Cai knelt in front of him. It felt natural, and it was the best place from which to undo his leather jerkin and the top strand of his leggings. Lifting both garments far enough aside, he saw that the wound had closed, its edges ragged but clean. New flesh, pink and healthy, had formed inside. "It'll scar," he said roughly. "I'm sorry."

"For what? Thor counts our scars in our favour when we die."

"No. That I did it to you."

"We were in battle. And we were nothing to one another then."

Cai looked up. It had been on his lips—*what are we to one another now?* But he didn't need to ask. Answers to questions he hadn't even known were forming inside him were there in Fen's eyes. Fen put a hand on top of his, pressing it to the warm skin inside his jerkin, laying it over the wound. He leaned down, and Cai stretched yearningly up. They kissed with brief ferocity, then Cai sat back on his heels. He tugged the front of the leggings open with his free hand. He'd noticed in some lightning-flash instant the night before that Fen had dispensed with the subligaculum cloth, just as he'd left his own behind him with his cassock on the storeroom floor. Easier to get to... He gasped and swallowed hard as Fen's shaft rose, then without hesitation—the moment before memories of Leof, of doing this for him, could rush in—he dived down.

Fen grabbed the hair at his nape. Pulling away, not claiming him.

Cai sat up. "What's the matter?"

"This..."

"What about it?"

"Among the Torleik, it's...something a lesser man does for a greater."

Cai stared at him. In Leof's case, that had probably been true. No, certainly true—as time went on, Cai understood more and more what strength had lain in that gentleness. What strength such gentleness took, to survive unsoured in a rough world. "Do you think," he growled, "a lesser man is about to do it to you now?"

Again, that silent answer. Cai would never have believed that face could soften in surrender. The clasp at his nape became a caress. "No. Please."

He was big, and Cai took him carefully. The small noises he made sent red pulses of arousal into Cai's groin, but he kept his hands off himself, stroking and grasping Fen's thighs until he'd accommodated what he could of the long shaft. Fen kept very still, electrical as pent-up lightning under Cai's touch. What was it costing him not to grab, paralyse, thrust? The great hands released him and fastened convulsively on the stonework, a clutch that would have cracked Cai's skull. And now he did move—small shifts of his hips, the movements of Cai's peaceful ocean yesterday before the storm, infinite power stored up and waiting. He braced his feet on the sandy floor and let go one desperate moan.

The sound of it washed all of Cai's caution away. He closed his mouth hard around Fen's straining cock and let him slide deep into his throat. He couldn't breathe, but that mattered less than getting him inside, sucking him, making those half-anguished cries rip from him. Tears burned him blind. He hung on, twisting his fists into the deerskin, the swollen shaft-head ramming further and further into him—unbearable, perfect.

Fen went rigid, muscles of his thighs locking tight. The pressure in Cai's throat became a rush, a melting heat, and he swallowed and swallowed to keep from drowning. Red haze threatened him, but he hung on still, pushing through it, wanting every wild pulse of Fen's coming, meeting every one of them halfway.

Fen caught him. He dropped to his knees with him onto the sand. Cai leaned against him, brow pressed to his shoulder, coughing and snatching great lungfuls of the sun-bright air. Fen was shuddering, his own breath ragged. He felt at Cai's groin. "You're still hard."

"Yes. I was..." Cai waited till the words would come out whole. "I was...occupied."

"Aye, almost suffocating yourself on me. Gods! I thought you would eat me alive."

"Maybe next time."

"Or I will eat you."

Cai raised his head and looked into the eyes of the wolf. A deep, delicious fear unfolded itself, stretching his erection harder. "Will you?"

"Maybe I will start right now. You smell good enough. Lie down."

"Here? It's damp."

"You did it in the sea last night."

Cai grinned and subsided onto the stones. The moment's resistance had been feigned—he'd have lain down in fire if Fen had asked. He spread his thighs, moaning, while Fen unfastened him and leaned in close.

The hot mouth engulfed him—paradise, with a sharp scrape of teeth. He grabbed Fen's shoulders. "Careful, you savage."

Fen sat up briefly, his face avid, a wicked smile curling one corner of that handsome, dangerous mouth. "Forgive me. I've never..."

"Never been the *lesser man* before?"

"If you must put it so, yes."

"Well, take some instruction. Run your tongue up me first. Open a bit wider and... Oh, God," Cai breathed. Fen had obeyed him on the instant, putting the lesson into practice. "Let your lips cover your teeth. Yes."

Yes. Cai fell back, raising his arms over his head in surrender, hiding his face in the crook of one elbow. He forgot Leof and Ben, and Theo, and the secrets and treasures of Fara. He forgot about death, in the rising flood of red-hot life Fen was calling up from his bones. He angled his hips, and Fen seized his backside, lifting him to be devoured. His vision blurred, and the flood rose high, and just for a while he forgot.

It took all afternoon to caulk the boat. The walk to the clay pit was a rough one, and the business of scraping damp clay into a makeshift pail arduous, straining backs and shoulders. Cai and Fen spoke very little, and looked at one another less. The work needed doing. Back at the boathouse, they took up position on either side of the repaired vessel's hull and began the laborious task of spreading the clay. Cai's hand brushed Fen's, and the spark leapt, the flash of a flint striking stone above dry kindling. Their hands clasped tight.

"No," Cai whispered, still not daring to look. "Not unless you want to spend the rest of your life on this island."

"You're right. The clay will take some time to dry."

"The rest of the day at least. So..."

"So?"

"So you have to let me go."

They went back to work, and this time didn't pause until every crack and hole in the woodwork was packed tight. Then Cai straightened up, rubbing a handful of dry sand between his palms to clean them. The sun had passed zenith and was blazing over the monastery to the southwest. Only a narrow stretch of sea divided Addy's retreat from the mainland, but in this light the Fara buildings, all the pain and joy that had reverberated within their walls, were nothing but a handful of glitter. Even the great rock on which they stood could have been cut from papyrus in this light. *If you want to spend the rest of your life on this island...* That was old Addy's desire. Cai too could see the charm.

Fen came to stand beside him, and the charm became clearer still. "We have hours of daylight yet."

"Yes. The boat should dry."

"Our work is done, then. I don't imagine your crazed hermit will want to be disturbed in his prayers, so..."

"I'm not sure he's all that crazed. So?"

"So...we have time. Sunlight. Sand dunes and soft beds of thyme. I would do with you..." He faded out, voice roughening, a little rasp that raised the hairs all up and down Cai's spine. "What you could not do with Leof."

He'd used the word *fuck* without hesitation before. What had changed? *Everything,* the wind-voice breathed in Cai's ear. *Everything has changed.* "What—with an old man running around, and bands of inbred cannibals prowling?"

"We will find a place. I will keep watch."

"Even while you're..." Cai shook his head. He couldn't say it either. He wondered if Aelfric had ever experienced desires of the flesh so intense that they passed into the spirit, and then beyond words. "Even while you're doing that?"

"Yes. And so will you. You were a warrior before you became a monk, and long before you lay down with me. That's what you'll be when everything else is gone."

Cai frowned. It was a solid Viking compliment, but he wasn't sure he liked it. "That doesn't enthrall me."

"What else would you have?"

"Your idea of a beautiful death might be a battlefield one. For myself, I'll take a long life and a warm bed at the end of it."

"Would you? When you left Fara yesterday, I didn't think you wanted to last until sunset."

"Well, I almost got my wish." Fen passed an arm round his waist, and he shivered in surprise and then returned the gesture. "But everything's changed. Come on."

"Where are we going?"

"The dunes. The soft beds of thyme."

Fen was right—they both were inveterate warriors. Cai caught himself assessing their chosen dune for defensibility even before they'd reached it, and he knew he'd have done so without the Viking's suggestion. High, isolated a little way from the rest. Good lines of sight all around, and plenty of crisp marram grass to give away intruders.

Tucked away behind its crest, a perfect crescent of white sand. Cai stepped carefully around its edges. Its surface was unmarred, shining like the inside of an oyster shell in the sun. He didn't want to disturb it till they both did. Then they would rip it to hell. He didn't know how it would be, but he knew there'd be a fight, a combat he longed for and hungered to lose. "Fen..."

Fen was immobile on the ridge of the dune. His back was turned, his attention fixed on the mainland. Afraid their peace was already about to be shattered, Cai scrambled up to join him. "What is it?"

"I have understood something."

He was quivering finely, like an arrow drawn against a string. Cai wouldn't have known it, but the tense vibration transferred itself when he laid a hand to his arm. "What? Is something wrong?"

"This island—they call it Fara, yes?"

"Yes. Well—all this scatter of islands are called the Faras, but this is the largest, so yes."

"Fara, the island. And the place where the monastery stands..."

"Fara too, but not an island. Peninsula, not *insula*." The words felt more than usually awkward in Cai's mouth. He didn't want to be up here talking Latin to this man. He was sure that, a little time more in each other's company, they would smooth out the differences in their north-lands tongues and be able to speak as their natures intended. "What about it?"

"The Fara treasure. Our legends say it lies on the island of Fara. *Insula*, not peninsula."

Cai chuckled. It wasn't funny, but he could see a bitter irony. "Great. So you lot have been knocking seven bells out of my poor monastery for nothing? Didn't you know the difference?"

"It looks like an island from the sea."

"Well, next time you see them you can tell them to leave off, can't you? They can come and raid..." Cai fell briefly silent, his mouth drying. "Oh, for God's sake, Fen. You can't think there's anything *here*."

Fen took hold of his sleeve. He pulled him down into the bright crescent, rucking up its surface. "Sit," he said, a trace of command in his voice Cai was more than half-inclined to argue. "There are things I haven't told you about the Fara treasure—just as you didn't see fit to tell me all the things you said about it to the old man."

"That wasn't on purpose. There hasn't been time, and—"

"And you hardly knew me. Very well. The same constraints have been on me, but now you have to listen. I need your help."

Cai couldn't understand the change in him. He'd perked up at Addy's fireside, but this was different—a feverish distress beneath his eagerness. "You'll have it, if it doesn't mean outright murder," he said, trying to smile, immediately regretting his choice of words. What did he expect of the wolf? "Tell me now."

"According to a prophet of my people, the Dane Land tribes once held a treasure, an amulet of infinite power. It could even bind our gods. And many years ago, one of the followers of Christ stole this amulet and buried it on a holy island off the east coast of Britannia."

"But there are dozens of those. Why are *we* feeling the business end of Thor's hammer?"

"Our prophet had a new revelation over the winter this year. He named Fara. You do not understand about this treasure, Cai, and nor did your abbot. No man not born a Dane could ever understand. In our enemy's hands, it has the power to bind our warriors' might. To suck the wind from our sails, cause our swords to snap and our proud manhood to wither."

Cai looked innocently out to sea. He still had hopes of this refuge amongst the dunes. He said, thoughtfully, "God forbid."

Briefly he thought it had worked. The fever-lights in Fen's eyes warmed to gold. He was laughing softly when he took Cai into his arms, and his kiss was so thorough and carnal, the push of his tongue so deep, that everything else faded away. Then he pulled back. He kept a warm grip round Cai's shoulders, but he was pale in the tapestried patterns of the marram-grass shadow, his profile set and fierce. "Well, it hasn't happened yet. But my people—the Torleik men, Sigurd and Gunnar and all my clan—believe in it. That's why the monastery raids have been so unrelenting. But this is the island of Fara, right here." He got up, letting Cai go. He took up position on the dune's western ridge, the light wiping out his details from behind, leaving only a black silhouette, the ageless shape of a warrior. "I will find the amulet. Then Sigurd and Gunnar will come to me, and they will find it in *my* hands. And the world will change."

"I thought... I thought you'd decided your brother was dead."

"What if he is not?" Fen didn't move. He might have been cast in bronze there and left as a warning, a memory of fear. "What if he lives, and...he ditched me here, like a dog or a broken shield? Like a thing?"

"He wouldn't have." Cai sprang up. The faceless statue spoke like a man, a living soul stricken to the core by something far worse than Cai's sword. Cai climbed up to join him, took his hand—more like a child than a lover this time, folding his fingers tight into his own. "He loved you. You told me so yourself."

"He loved power."

"Fen, come on. Never mind ancient treasures and fantasies. Lay me down here and show me what I've been missing."

Fen tore his fingers free. He gave Cai one look—half-anguished, half-amused, as if Cai had come up with the one proposal that might have slowed him down, diverted him from his purpose. Then he turned away. He set off down the slope of the dune, his long stride devouring the ground. The lowering sun struck blood-scarlet lights from his hair.

"Help me," he yelled back to Cai, not glancing round. "I'll lay you down later, and you'll never forget it. But for now—we're going to find this damn treasure!"

Cai couldn't sleep. He was dirty and bruised, and darkness had fallen too suddenly for him to go and bathe in the sea as he'd wanted to do. Addy, sharing with them a fireside supper of scurvy grass and salmon, had warned them against venturing too far from the cave in the night. The devils were restless then and prone to hunt, their weakened eyes more effective in torchlight than under the sun. The old man had seemed different when Fen and Cai had returned. His air of distracted hospitality had vanished, and he had eaten in silence, watching them gravely from his own side of the fire.

The cave was barely wide enough to accommodate the three of them, and Fen had offered to take a watch, although Addy had assured him that wasn't necessary. He was crouched outside in the cloudy moonlight now, his tense, powerful shape just visible. Cai was relieved not to be forced into close quarters with him. He felt as if some kind of padding had been stripped off his nerves, leaving them naked and vibrating to Fen's slightest touch. In the boathouse that morning it had been wildly pleasant, and now...

Now he was afraid. He'd gone with Fen, and he'd done his honest best to help him find the secret of Fara. All afternoon and into dusk they had quartered the bare little island. He had turned over rocks, followed streambeds to their source. He had met Fen coming up to meet him a dozen times, his face a baulked blank, frustration coming off him in waves. A dozen times he'd told him to give it up, and a dozen times been ignored.

To say that he wasn't the man Cai knew would be absurd. What did Cai know of him? Shifting uncomfortably on the cave's rocky floor—how luxuriant even his own thin mattress at Fara, by contrast—Cai remembered a beautiful hound his father had traded for and brought into the hillfort camp. The seller had been evasive about the beast's ancestry, although her upswept yellow eyes ought to have given her away. She'd been good for a while, herding Broc's cattle and sleeping at the foot of his bed, and then one full-moon night she had plucked up a baby by its nappy rags and trotted away with it into the unknown. *A wolf in the fold,* Broc had fulminated for weeks afterwards, damning the trader to a hundred gory deaths, never seeming to realise that he'd opened the gates to the sheep-fold himself and let the creature in.

Cai dropped into exhausted sleep at last, and dreamed restlessly of a man with golden eyes who followed him into the dunes, brought him down with one breathtaking pounce and began to tear him apart. The dismemberment was painless, the rip of sharp incisors a shuddering delight, and when he protested—painlessly bleeding, dying—the wolf looked up at him and said, *But you let me in, you fine man. You lay down with me. You let me in.*

He woke up, throat convulsing in a choked-off howl. The cave was full of cobweb light, delicate as pearls. Every detail of the scene before him was perfect, so lucid he would take it with him to his grave. Addy was lying flat out on his back. His mouth was open, his long, thin frame nothing but a loose collection of bones beneath his cassock. And, rising up from a crouch of dreadful, virile beauty beside him—Fen, a fisherman's knife clutched savagely tight in his fist. Before Cai could move or make a sound, he was gone, silent and swift, dissolving into the sea mist that had come in with the tide.

Chapter Nine

Cai knelt by the old man on the cave floor. He couldn't breathe, not even to let go of the horrified sob wedged tight in his chest. He didn't know where to touch him. His throat looked intact, but there were a dozen places in his cassock's folds where the wound might be concealed. *You're a doctor,* he told himself fiercely, but it was no good. All hope was gone, all life long fled from a face like that—ravaged and hollow, grey as the dawn.

The sob tore free. Addy snorted himself awake at the sound, opened his eyes and stared up at him. A beatific smile spread across his face, as if he had expected this morning all his life, anticipated everything and awoken full of joy to find it fulfilled. "There's a good boy," he said, lifting a bony hand and patting Cai's face. "There, you see? Don't worry."

Cai leapt to his feet. He cracked his head off the cavern's roof, but the pain was meaningless. The thing that got released in men's bodies in extremity, the heat in the blood that made them fight or run away like deer—he could feel it, raging through every vein. His heart would rip out through his ribs if he didn't move. He gave Addy one last look and half-fell out of the cave.

The beach was empty, swathed in mist. No Fara devils seemed to be around, but God help them if he found any now. One line of footprints faded off into the distance. The blood-heat in him pitched, and he took off, heedless of the stones on his bare feet.

Fen had got far enough to let Cai run off some of his terror-born rage, but he was still throbbing all over in the grip of it when the lean figure emerged from the mist. Fen was motionless, his head down. He didn't flinch or glance up when Cai tore across the last stretch of beach between them.

The knife was still in his hand. Cai knocked it free, and it sailed end over end to bury its blade in the sand. He crashed to a breathless halt beside Fen. "What were you going to do with that?" he yelled. When Fen didn't stir, he grabbed him by the jerkin. "What were you going to do?"

Fen animated. He shoved Cai's hand away, and Cai got ready for a fight. Instead Fen fell back a few paces. His eyes were wide, a lostness draining their amber fires to grey. "This... This is all your fault."

Cai swallowed hard. The mist was catching in his lungs. "*Mine?*"

"Yes. You, with your blasted Christian ways—your doctoring, and your healing, and your damned compassion. With your body that makes me feel as if my own doesn't belong to me anymore, and yours does, so that I feel your pain more than my own..." Fen paused for breath. "So that I feel another man's pain before I inflict it! Damn you—I cannot even raise a knife to a useless old man!"

"Am I meant to be *sorry* for that? Fen—you murderous bastard..." Desperately Cai choked back the laughter that was trying to rattle out of him at Fen's discomfiture, his baffled rage at not being able to commit cold-blooded murder. "Why the hell would you have wanted to?"

"Can't you see? That old lunatic knows about the treasure. He's hiding it somewhere on this island, and the only place we haven't looked is inside that cave, the place where he sleeps. He's defending something there."

"Don't be so stupid. There's nothing in there but damp."

"At the back, in the shadows where we couldn't see. And you heard what he said about tunnels. Don't look at me like that, monk—I wasn't going to torture him for what he knows. Just kill him and get him out of the way."

"Oh, is that all? Why didn't you say?" Horror and laughter were winding themselves around in Cai like drunken serpents. What was he doing, out here on a barren island with this creature? Why did he want to take him in his arms? "My God. He's just a poor old man."

"I know that. Look, you've gained your point. I haven't harmed him, have I? I...I couldn't."

He sounded so mournful. Cai reached out to him. "Come here." Fen obeyed as far as coming to stand in front of him, but wouldn't take his outstretched hand. "He isn't hiding anything. Listen—our boat might be ready. I think the sooner we leave here, the better."

"Why? In case your castrating bloody influence wears off?"

"You were going to murder our host. It might make things awkward over breakfast."

Fen smiled—an involuntary flicker, quickly erased. "He was sleeping like a dog. He didn't know."

"I think he did, Fen."

"All right. If you want to walk away from so much power, we'll go."

"Not yet. First we go back and see that he's all right. Thank him."

At last Fen took his hand. He did it reluctantly, but their palms met with a sensual warmth, and after a moment he gripped tight. "Very well, Saint Caius of Nowhere."

Addy was pacing back and forth along the high-tide line, the hem of his cassock snagging on dried seaweed. He was anxiously watching the sky. He didn't appear to notice his guests' approach until Cai called out to him, and then spared them only a distracted glance. "He is late. He is late, and you two must be hungry."

"Who is late, sir?"

"The eagle."

Cai shot Fen a warning look. "I see," he said cautiously, getting into the old man's path and stopping him gently, afraid his restless movements would wear him out. "You know, if you wished, Fen and I could patch together a fishing net and..."

"Ah, no. No. If you provide for me, how will I know the love of God in the beat of the eagle's wings?" Cai couldn't answer that. After a moment Addy returned his attentions to earth and gave him a wide smile. "But I would have liked to have given you your breakfasts. Perhaps you had better pursue your own ways now. You mustn't starve here."

"We can catch this next tide, if our boat holds up. Are you sure you won't come with us?"

"No, no. These fools who wish to place me on the bishop's throne would find me too easily on the mainland. You won't tell them I'm here, will you? If anyone asks, you will say you met a mad old hermit, and Addy is a legend."

Cai shrugged. "I promise." It seemed true enough to him now. Perhaps some shipwrecked monk had become marooned, assumed the name and grown old here in his delusions of power. "Well, if you change your mind or you're ever ill, light a signal fire on your western beach. We'll see it from Fara." Once more he looked around the featureless strip of dunes, where not so much as a rabbit or a goat cropped the turf. "I still don't see how you live."

"I told you. God provides."

Even if He's a little late this morning. Cai had been turning away. Then something in the old man's voice made him pause. There was such certainty in it, the deep note of conviction that had drawn Cai to him the day before.

"Caius, listen. I have said that your new abbot Aelfric is a poor example of the coming faith. Whatever *you* profess—even if it's no more than belief in yourself as a man—you must be a good example. Do you understand?"

"No," Cai said honestly, spreading his hands. "Even if I did...I don't know how."

"We can't lead men to purer lives unless our own are pure." His benign gaze encompassed Fen, and he smiled. "I don't mean the flesh. For myself, I believe the flesh must have its way, governed by love and by will. But I am a heretic. By the example of your own life, I mean. Cai, you grieve over Theo, and I thought I did too—but there is really very little need."

"Why?" Cai could hardly get the question out past the pain in his throat. He didn't think he'd ever grieved for him more poignantly than now, when for all his words the old man's eyes were bright with tears for him too.

"You'll see. You'll see. Now, catch your tide. Unless..." He suddenly focussed on Fen, his smile broadening. "Unless, son, you would like to go and take a look around inside my cave. It's daylight now, and your search will be easier. Caius and I will wait."

Fen's lips parted. Then he stared at the ground, his brow knitting ferociously. "I don't wish it. No."

Cai had seen him flush before, in rage and arousal, and sometimes mortification at the forced intimacies of medical care. But this was pure shame. Cai hadn't thought him capable. Shame at his aborted deed, or only at being found out in it? Addy didn't seem to care. He was chuckling now, rocking himself back and forth in amusement. "Poor wolf, poor wolf. I would have made a sorry meal for you. Tell me, Fenrisulfr—there being no secret of Fara, what would you have by way of treasure? Can it be attained in this life? I'd grant you it myself if I could."

Fen looked up. "Vengeance," he said suddenly, as if Addy had fished the word out of him on a hook. "My kinsmen who abandoned me here among Christians and lunatics—I would have revenge."

"Ah." Addy sobered. He folded his hands into his sleeves. "That, I can't grant. But you will have it one day. Yes—knee-deep in water and blood."

"Fen, come on." Cai took hold of him, a firm grip on his rigid arm. "Sir, we should go now."

"Yes," Addy said absently, distances opening up in his eyes. "Go in God, blessed be Her name."

"And you." Cai hesitated, wondering if he'd misheard. "*Her* name?"

"Ah. Yes. I forget sometimes—forgive me. But that reminds me. That old woman Danan—you said you know her."

"Yes. I'm a kind of physician at Fara. Not much of one, but..."

"She has told me you are very good. A healer by spirit as well as by skill."

"Really?" For a moment Cai was distracted. She'd called him a hit-and-miss quack last time they'd talked about his medical skills. "Yes, I know her. She trades me the herbs I need for my work."

"Take care of her. It matters little really—she'd be back with the corn in spring—but I wouldn't wish her to die that way." Addy shivered. "How strange, that the word of God should be put into practice so! No, not that way. Keep watch, Cai. Look out for her."

The incoming tide ran strongly, but it was still a long haul from the island of Fara to shore. The sun had driven off the ghostly fret and was making the sea dance in sapphire and green before Fen called a halt. They had passed a halfway point. Cai, glad enough to take his cue from so superior an oarsman, stopped rowing and rested his oar. Fen had pulled rhythmically all the way out, patterns of purposeful muscle rising to meet each stroke. He hadn't so much as broken a sweat, and now he was looking at Cai as if in surprise that he was tired.

"I'm not," Cai said defensively, trying to hide the tremor in his arms. "Who the hell could keep up with a Viking, though?"

They were side by side on the boat's wooden bench. "Only another Viking," Fen admitted easily. "Maybe it's best you don't try. I can take her from here."

"What? No. I just need a rest."

"At risk of wounding you, I may be better on my own. A second oar who isn't quite as..."

Cai broke into reluctant laughter. "Oh, God. Don't start worrying about my feelings now."

"Very well. A weak second oar can unbalance a strong one, make his job harder. Just go and sit in the prow."

Cai got up, still smiling. "Are you saying I've been holding you back? Let me see your wound before you take over this longship. You can... You can just lift up your jerkin for me this time."

Their eyes met in burning recognition of what Cai's routine check had unleashed yesterday. Fen did as he was told, and Cai crouched in front of him long enough to ascertain that the vigorous rowing hadn't done any damage. No—the muscle was repairing itself, smoothing out. "You're fine," he said, glad his recent exertions allowed him to sound breathless. "You can cover up. We'd better not rock the boat."

He went to sit. Fen watched him closely. "I was afraid," he said, "that you wouldn't wish it. To lie with me anymore, I mean—knowing what I am."

Cai glanced up in surprise. "I *don't* know what you are. I only know what you did. Theo used to say that was what mattered—what we did, not what we'd thought about doing."

"That's good. Because if we are judged on our wicked thoughts, I am headed fast for Aelfric's hell."

"With me right behind you." *And yes, I would lie with you there, though you were the devil himself.* Cai couldn't say it, but he held Fen's gaze until he was sure the message had got through.

"I feel as if I know your Theo. Through you, and everything you've said about him. Maybe that's what the old man meant when he told you there was no need to grieve."

Cai shifted in the prow. He dipped his fingers into the water, thoughtfully fretting its surface. It was lovely here. Fen picked up the oars, and Cai almost put out a hand to stop him. What was it all about—this effort to get back to a shore, a home, where he had lost all sense of belonging? What awaited him at Fara? "I'm beginning to think," he said slowly, "that my poor abbot—though I loved him, Fen, and I always will—might not have been sane when he died."

"Well—for what it's worth, I too am losing certainties. I believed in the legend of the amulet, the treasure. But perhaps it was only an excuse for rapine. Our prophet did come up with Fara this year. The year before, he was just as convinced it was White Bay."

A helpless chuckle shook Cai. "Really? He said a different place..."

"Every year. Yes."

Their laughter rang out across the water, scaring up a piebald cloud of Addy ducks. "Oh, God," Cai managed at length, wiping his eyes. "Have we both been such fools? And as for that old lunatic in his cave, with his seals and his eagle..."

"Cai. Hush."

Cai frowned, leaning forwards. He could hear something. Was it the echoes of their own voices off the distant rocks? No—more musical than that, familiar to Cai and yet strangely altered. He shaded his eyes against the sun.

The seals were hauling out onto the rocks. They had come in their droves, the light striking off their sleek fur. Instead of tussling for the sunniest places on the rocks, flopping and jousting with one another on the way, they seemed to be moving as one.

Their focus was the old man standing on the rocks at the top of the beach. He was only a skeletal outline at this distance, but Cai could make out that his hands were extended, as if in benediction. "He said... He said the seals came to sing to him."

"Which would be madness, except..."

Except that they were singing. It was a music Cai couldn't have imagined in this world. Their eerie barking stretched out and clashed in wild harmonics, as if the great North Sea itself had found a voice. Cai got up, making the boat lurch wildly beneath him. He pointed, unable to get a word out, and Fen stood beside him, grabbing his arm. They were just in time to see a vast sea-eagle sail out of the dawn, golden talons wrapped around a fish.

The monastery was silent, its tumbledown buildings held in quiet sunlight. It was like a future vision of itself—moss beginning to take hold among the ruins, the pride of human life that had built her long vanished, sleeping beneath the hawthorn graves. Cai and Fen dragged the boat ashore, then climbed the steep path up the cliff face without meeting another soul. At the top they came to a halt, looking around them. Cai hadn't expected to be missed, for anyone to be watching or waiting on their return, but this was a better opportunity than he'd anticipated. He turned to Fen.

"This could be a good moment, you know. For you to go, if you wish."

"I…I could still have your horse?"

"Yes. I told you. If you wanted."

"And what if I didn't want?"

"The horse, or…?"

"To go." Fen evaded Cai's look. He was surveying the barns, the fields and the infirmary building that had been his prison for so long. He still slept in the quarantine cell, Aelfric having forbidden him to join the others in the dormitory barn. He was still locked away from compline to matins, though Cai knew he could make short work of the window and the ivy beneath it if he wished.

"You're strong now. I can't believe you'd want to stay."

"Would you come with me?"

What a wild, strange thought. It sent a shiver down Cai's spine and he briefly closed his eyes to savour it. He'd been on the verge of departure when Benedict had come to cling to him, renewing for a time his sense of a place here, an obligation. But whatever Ben had needed, whatever guiding light or rock, Cai hadn't been able to provide. No—he hadn't been expecting a lookout, much less a welcome party for his return. For the place to be this quiet, all his brethren must have gone about their usual daily tasks. "The waters close over our heads, don't they?"

"Not over yours. Not if I can help it."

Blindly Cai put out a hand. Fen took it immediately this time. "No. You didn't let me drown, did you? I like to lie with you. I think you're a dangerous, bloodthirsty nutcase, but…I see in colour again when I'm with you."

"So?"

"So… Yes. I will go."

He didn't have a thing to pack. All he had to do was walk with Fen down to the armoury, collect a few weapons—Broc's sword, Fen's ancestral head-splitter—and help him pull the chariot out into the yard. He could see Eldra from here. The only living creature to remark their arrival, she at least seemed pleased to see them, trotting the length of her paddock with her head held high. Cai had no right to either of Fara's ponies, but Eldra was his, and between the shafts of the chariot she would take them anywhere. South, perhaps. There were cities down there, places where if Leof's gentle god was long dead, Aelfric's monstrous one was not yet in the ascendant—Roman towns, where for every Christian you met you would find five who still bowed to the ancient shrines of Jupiter and Mars. Zoroastrian cults too, followers of the soldier's god Mithras, Broc's particular favourite. The world was large.

Yes, large. But all the voices of this little one were rising from the timber church. Cai drew Fen to a halt as it came into view. They stood together, wordlessly listening. The church doors were wide open. Only this way could the building accommodate the full complement of monks. It seldom was required to, even when Aelfric made Eyulf ring the bell and stood eagle-eyed with his great black staff, counting his flock through the doors. There were always tasks to be done that Aelfric still recognised as essential, or at any rate didn't dare yet deny. But everyone was there today, the stragglers crowding on the steps outside.

Fen was still holding Cai's hand. "What's going on?" he asked softly. "Is it a holy day? Some saint's miserable, pointless bloody death to be celebrated?"

"I don't think so." Cai found he was grinning. He didn't see things quite the way Fen did—not yet, anyway—but he'd come to appreciate the external point of view. Men like Aelfric could hammer down a black iron bowl across the whole world, and so far God hadn't seen fit to help those trapped underneath. Poor Ben... "I don't know. It's not even a prayer hour."

"Well, it's good timing for us, whatever the fools are about."

Cai hesitated. If Aelfric had herded his brethren together for another dose of hellfire, didn't Cai, their physician, owe them whatever antidote he could give? Then again, he'd learned to his cost that he could only doctor their bodies, not their souls, and sporadically at that. Whatever Danan had said to Addy about his skills, he really was only the hit-and-miss quack she had called him to his face. He rubbed his thumb gently over the top of Fen's hand. "You're right. Come on."

Eyulf was perched on the tower, the dinner bell laid neatly in his lap so he wouldn't forget it or what it was for. As soon as Cai noticed him, he sprang to his feet, sending the bell flying, dislodging stones in a terrifying scatter. He let go one yell of mixed joy and fear, slithered to his backside and began to fall.

Cai ran. Fen was on his heels, and Cai had a moment to reflect on the strangeness of that—as far as the poor Viking was concerned, this flight was in the wrong direction. But there he was, a shadow, then a force that took substance and shot right past him, far faster than Cai could hope to run, and so it was that Eyulf tumbled down into the most unlikely salvation of all—the arms of a Viking, who went down quite gracefully beneath his weight and rolled them both out of danger, shielding the howling lad's body with his own from the last few plummeting rocks.

Coming to a halt, Cai let the laughter building in him surface. The danger was over, and Eyulf clearly didn't appreciate his rescuer—had recoiled from him as soon as Fen had let him go, and now they were both on their feet, was circling him, face contracted in the hideous scowl that meant *Viking*. Cai went and stopped the boy, brushing dust out of his robes. Eyulf stood on tiptoe in his agitation, attempting to reproduce Fen's height and prowling walk, pointing frantically at him over Cai's shoulder, as if Cai hadn't noticed he was there.

"I know," Cai said. "It seems odd to me too. But he's..." He paused, long enough to meet Fen's eyes. "A good Viking. Sometimes."

"It was instinct," Fen growled. "Next time I will let him fall. Cai, you idiot—we've missed our chance."

Cai whipped round. All his surviving brethren were standing in the sunlight, staring at him as if he and not Eyulf had just dropped down from the sky. Wilf the goatherd was in the front line. A handful of others were still emerging from the church, among them Oslaf, pale as death, supported between Gareth and Demetrios.

Cai spread his hands. "What's wrong?" Still Wilfrid just gawped. "Where is Aelfric? Has he got you all here to listen to more of his ranting? Gareth—that boy should be in bed. Who made you bring him down here?"

"He wanted to come," Wilf answered at last. "No one made us. The storm, Cai—we thought it had taken you. And Fenrir went after you—the only one who dared. We thought you were both lost to us. We came here to pray for your souls."

Cai pushed his fringe back. He couldn't take this in. Not so many faces breaking into astonished grins, not for such a reason. "And... And Aelfric allowed you?"

"No. But he couldn't stop us. He can't, can he...?" Wilf paused, as if realising this for the first time. "Not if it's all of us." He stepped forwards and suddenly enveloped Cai in a painful embrace, redolent of the barnyard and warm goat. "You came home."

The brethren crowded round him. Cai resisted for a moment, trying to step back, but then he saw that the circle of chattering, smiling men had absorbed Fen into its boundary too. Fen was wide-eyed, attempting to look haughty. Cai doubted he had ever been clapped on the back by a man half his size, or told—as old Martin was telling him, beaming at him toothlessly all the while—that he wasn't so bad after all, for a murdering infidel pig. Brother Cedric, who had lain so deadly ill in the infirmary after the first raid, came jostling up to grab Cai in his arms, and the small, unruly sea began to bear him and Fen off.

Cai extricated himself far enough to get to Oslaf. Gareth stepped aside for him, allowing him to give the stumbling boy his arm. "Oslaf. Forgive me for leaving you. Benedict—"

"Don't, Cai. I can't hear his name."

"I should have stayed and looked after you."

Oslaf shook his head. His face was calm, but Cai had seen that deadly serenity before, in men tried beyond their strength, their passions poured out into a well that knew no filling. "He loved you," Oslaf said. "I do too, and I prayed so hard for you to be safe. Nobody can look after me now, though. Do you understand?"

Cai understood with painful clarity. To deny the boy's despair would have been a further outrage, and he didn't argue—just put an arm around his waist and led him on gently. "All right. Where is he?"

"Aelfric wants him buried on the north side of the church. He hasn't done it yet—Gareth and Wilf and Hengist have been watching over him."

"In the crypt?"

"Yes. But I don't know how long they can keep watching. They're afraid."

Cai had heard of north-side burials. The need to place the dead in earliest morning sunlight to the east was older by far than Church doctrine, and doctrine rode easily on those beliefs to assign the north to winter, darkness, a fit place for suicides and lost souls. Theo had done his best to blow away the cobwebs of such superstition, but they clung, always the stronger in dark times. "The north side is sacred too.

All earth is holy."

"But how will he know where to rise on the last day? And...he'll be all alone."

"Oh, Oslaf." Cai tightened his grip. "I don't believe that's how it works. We'll have him buried with his brothers, though—I swear it. Where is Aelfric?"

"I don't know. He came down to the church—he didn't want us all together like this, praying for you. But Wilf said we had to, and then one of his own men—Laban—came and joined us."

"Did he?" Glancing back, Cai saw a black-robed figure being borne along with the rest, looking mortally embarrassed but not displeased with himself. "We're making strange friends, aren't we?"

"You made the strangest of all. And yet your Viking shamed us with his courage, and when he didn't return, we grieved for him too. Look, Aelfric is there, down by the..." Oslaf stopped dead. He would have fallen without Cai's embrace. His eyes opened wide. "Oh, God. No."

An odd group had gathered by the monastery gate. On one side of the drystone wall—nominal barrier between the sacred and profane worlds, easily scaled by the smallest errand boys but in general respected—Aelfric was standing, flanked by his clerics. They looked like four burned larch trees, black and bare of ornament, stiffly upright. On the gate's far side, gaudy and chaotic by contrast, a stout old woman had planted herself, fists bunched tight on her hips. She was dressed in bright north-village weaves, holding a donkey on a long, frayed rein. At her shoulder, a young man in shepherd's breeches and waistcoat was casting a shadow to match his formidable height. She was red in the face, expostulating loudly with Aelfric. As Cai watched, she unclenched one strong hand and poked a finger at his chest to emphasise her words.

"Oslaf, what is it? Do you know them?"

"Yes, but it must be a dream. My grandmother, Hilde. My brother Bertwald. What are they doing here? Oh, no. He'll hurt them. He'll—"

Cai cut him off. "I know what they're doing here. They made good time. And nobody else is going to get hurt." He transferred Oslaf's weight—not much, just grief-stripped bones and a cassock—to Fen, who was at his shoulder, waiting. Cai didn't have to look. He knew the Viking would be there, would make the catch and follow him. Striding ahead of the group, he made his way across the tussocky ground. He felt as if native Saxon sunlight were springing back at him from the buttercups, dazzling flakes of release and relief in the yarrow. Aelfric had put out the lights in Oslaf's life, and now his family had come, nature reasserting herself, rushing to fill the gap. "Aelfric!"

The abbot turned. He caught his heel on the hem of his robe and almost fell over, arms flailing to save himself. Something had changed, shifted—not one of the obsequious Canterbury clerics put out a hand. "You," he snarled, when he'd regained his balance. "I might have known. Not even the ocean could swallow your disobedience and pride."

"That's right," Cai called cheerfully into the breeze. "She spat me out, and here I am. Welcome, *hlæfdige*. You must have travelled all night."

The old lady stopped in her diatribe at hearing a word of respect in her own language. Aelfric looked from her to Cai. "You know this woman?"

"No, but I invited her here. She's come to take Oslaf home."

"So she says. I tell her—and you listen too, you serpent, striking at the faith that has fed you and sheltered you here—no man leaves. *Tu es sacerdos—*"

"*Sacerdos in aeternum!*" the old woman snapped, to Cai's surprise. She didn't look as if her grasp of Latin was broad, but Cai guessed she might have heard the phrase a few times since beginning her confrontation with Aelfric. "A priest forever!"

"Yes. The truth of it penetrates even to these vulgar ears. Those vows once taken, no man's soul escapes the service of God. No matter where his body lies—and I forbid any member of this community to take one step beyond its boundaries—his spirit belongs to the priesthood." He threw out one hand in a gesture of banishment. "Be off. The boy belongs to me."

"*Sacerdos in aeternum...*" Now that Hilde had a good hold on the words, she rolled them round with a kind of disgusted relish in her mouth. "He wasn't anybody's *sacerdos* when his mother squeezed him out of her belly and into my hands, wet and red and raw." Aelfric blanched, but she ploughed on. "And in my hands he'd have stayed, if the wench hadn't kittened off three more and died and left them to starve. I sent him here to get learning and his dinners. Why does a child bring me a message to fetch him home, if I care for his life? Where is my boy?"

Bertwald the shepherd suddenly came to life. He seized Hilde's shoulder. "Grandmother. Oslaf is there!"

Shielding her eyes, Hilde searched the group of men on the hillside. She emitted a shriek. "That skeleton? No!" She tried to seize the gate out of Aelfric's hand, and when that failed, dodged aside and started scrambling over the wall. Bertwald gave her an assisting shove from behind, and Cai, seeing that nothing would prevent her from barrelling down the other side, darted to catch her. Bertwald followed her, and the two ran off upslope.

Cai was left standing with Aelfric. Alone? No, not quite, although the abbot seemed suddenly deserted, the clerics fading off into the background. Fen had left the others. He had taken up position a few yards away and was watching Cai unfathomably. Cai remembered the sea, and the broad, windswept moors, and Eldra waiting in her paddock. He thought about freedom. Looking at Aelfric, but speaking more to Fen, he said, "I think the men here will obey me. They know me, and they know I mean them good. I think they will do as I say."

Aelfric gaped. "What do you mean, you heretic?"

"You can frighten them into submission for a while. I don't doubt that. And I have no desire for leadership. You will remain abbot, with all due deference paid you."

"You... Are you daring to *offer* me this? My own God-given place?"

"Yes," Cai said frankly. He didn't want to. He wanted to run to Fen where he was waiting—yes, waiting for whatever the outcome of this would be, his own freedom granted and untaken. "It's not much of a place, Aelfric. A handful of monks on the edge of the world. But you've failed with them, haven't you? Not even your own men have the heart to help you now."

"Be silent, you cur."

"In a moment. You can leave if you wish, take back the news of your failure to your masters and leave us in peace. I don't think you will, though. These men need a leader. I can do it kindly, and you'll have a community here, under your authority in name if not in fact. I won't humiliate you."

"You won't *what*?" Aelfric began a low cackle. It was a terrible sound, hysteria and madness seething an inch from the surface. "Kneel to me, brute! Abase yourself!"

Cai shivered. The breeze was warm, and Aelfric was making this so hard, holding open a door onto the whole wide world. Cai's resolution wavered, his newborn ideas of his duty too fragile to bind him down. Fen was waiting. He began to walk away.

"Caius!"

Thin fingers closed on his sleeve. He shook his arm free, but came to a halt, watching the sun burnish Fen's hair to copper and fire.

"Brother Caius. If you do this...what is it that you want?"

I just want Fen. Cai almost said it, the wave of need so intense he wondered that it didn't knock Aelfric down. Aelfric had run after him. Cai doubted he had ever run a step after any man in his life. His eyes were murderously bright at having been forced to it now.

"I want," Cai began, choosing his words carefully, "for my abbot Theo's body to be left in peace in the crypt. I want my brother Benedict given his funeral rites and sanctified burial in our graveyard here." He waited, but Aelfric just stared. "And I want you to step aside and let that woman take her grandson home, with no more threats or fulminations from you to darken his mind."

A keening wail from up the slope made him turn. Oslaf had fallen. The old woman, her face a mask of grief, was hauling him up across her lap, so pale that Cai wondered if grief and shock had snapped the fragile cords of life in him. The other monks were clustered round, not touching or helping—bewildered at having a woman in their midst, even one like this, as plain and good as the bread they all had been brought up on. Even Theo had taught that a monk should stay clear of them. For the first time, a flame of impatient questioning sprang up in Cai's heart. What kind of faith made strangers, enemies, of half the world?

He was about to run to Oslaf's aid when Bertwald stepped forwards. He leaned down over his fallen brother, raised him tenderly off Hilde's lap. He lifted him effortlessly, and Oslaf gave a short, lost cry and hid his face against his shoulder. Without a word, Bertwald set off, cradling his burden, Hilde scrambling to follow.

Cai stopped her as she passed. "You must be weary." He glanced at Aelfric, who had stepped aside as bidden and was waiting with his hands locked white-knuckle tight by the gate. "The abbot will give you shelter for the night."

"Shelter?" She peered at him from reddened eyes. "You're a good boy. You sent that message, didn't you? But there's no shelter to be had here, not for our kind."

"All right. In that case...the abbot will send someone after you with food and drink." He waited. After giving him a look that should have shrivelled him to dust on the ground, Aelfric turned and stalked off in the direction of the kitchens.

Cai sank down on the turf bank that curved round inside the monastery wall. The bank was ancient, the wall by comparison new, the invention of yesterday. Untold generations of men and women had found this place desirable, worthy of defence, had built their banks and grown their crops and lived and died, long before the creed of Christ had been thought of. Cai put his face into his hands. What had happened to them—all those people? He envied them their peace, their very absence. They were nothing but the traces they'd left in the sunny earth. "What have I done?"

A warmth settled by him. "You've taken this place for your own." A low, rumbling laugh. "And no blood spilled. My people have no word for such a victory."

"Victory..." Cai clutched at his skull. Soon he would start laughing too, and that was no good—it would undo him, and then he would weep. After Bertwald, good brother shepherd, had loaded Oslaf up onto the donkey and led him away, Hilde bringing up a dignified rear, Cai had found the whole remaining congregation of Fara looking at him, awaiting their orders. He'd given them—quietly, hands spread in surrender—*What are you waiting for? The beasts in the fields are hungry. Bread needs to be made, mead brewed for the market. Go to your work.* "I don't want such a victory. What are you still doing here?"

The warmth became a pressure. Fen's arm closed around his shoulders, so deep a pleasure that Cai swore he wouldn't look, not until he had to. He would have this moment, and not see the farewell in Fen's eyes.

"Caius."

"What?"

"You're staying, aren't you? Since you just made yourself the abbot of this place."

"No! I did not. All I did was help them."

"You took them into your hands." Fen tightened his embrace. "You're not a man to let go of them, not after that. You're going to stay."

Cai lifted his head. The tears had come anyway, shaming him. He knocked them away. "Well?" he asked roughly. "What of it?"

"Aelfric has taken your terms. He had to. But he isn't sane, and you have made him hate you. Such natures breed poison, and can poison men's minds even in their own madness."

Cai looked at him in disbelief. "Thanks," he said faintly, the marrow of his bones trying to melt in the heat of the amber gaze fastened on him. "You think I don't know all that? Why are you telling me?"

"Because you'll need help."

"I don't doubt it."

"And if you need mine, I will stay."

Chapter Ten

Full moon, midsummer—the Feast of St. John, and a sweet, sultry darkness had come down at last. The sea stirred restively, little white horses whispering to painless destruction on the warm sands. Bronze wands of hypericum nodded in shifts of night air too lazy to be called a breeze, the tiny glands in their leaves glistening with oil. Great trumpets of bindweed gaped their silent music, and silvery seedpods of honesty, their skins already shrivelled after a fortnight of heat, gave the moon back her light. In the spectral, shifting radiance, the so-called abbot of Fara crouched by a stream, washing streaks of afterbirth from his hands.

A lantern appeared briefly in a gap between the dunes. Brother Hengist's broad face shone beneath it, grinning. On his hip he bore the grain sack for the night's baking, ten good loaves that would rise in the dark hours and be thrust, as if into the fires of dawn, into the monastery oven at first light. "Is all well, Abbot Cai?"

Cai plucked a water-lily root from the streambed and lobbed it at him accurately, muddy end first. "Yes, all's well. Once there was one ox and now there are three."

"Nature is bountiful. Good night, Abbot Cai."

Another lily root, this time bouncing harmlessly off the baker's broad rump. Alone, Cai finished washing his hands, then splashed water into his face for good measure. "Abbot?" he said to the moon, who seemed to be expecting conversation, her weary face attentive. "I'm not sure an abbot has to doctor beasts as well as men. Or spend his day up to the hips in mud before that, helping dig ditches and drains."

"But you looked so fetching while you were about it."

Cai jumped. He tried to smooth the reflex away but knew he failed. He didn't look up—plunged his hands into the stream again and watched smilingly as the water wove patterns through his fingers. "How would you know? You were off with Wilfrid."

"The view is good from those hills. A handsome soldier with his cassock hitched up and a spade in his hand… A much finer sight than the goats."

"I should hope so. But I notice they fascinate you, whenever there's work involving mud, blood or innards to be done."

"Abbot Cai, you're a false-tongued excuse for a Christian."

A shadow fell over the water. Still Cai didn't look. It had become a complex pleasure to deny himself the sight of his lover until the last instant. He didn't want to see too soon. He didn't want Fen to know the changes seeing wrought in him each time—the heat, the helpless flush. And Fen was right—he was a liar. There wasn't a single task the Viking had evaded since their return from the sea. He had built walls, helped unblock the channels that ran from the latrine, turned his hand to the dozens of jobs where his strength and persistence had been needed.

Fara was coming to life again. All the daily work that had fallen into abeyance after the raids, set aside through grief or lack of manpower… It wasn't so hard, Cai had discovered, to see where men should go and send them there. With Fen at his side, he had even been able to do it, overcoming the shame of giving orders to his friends. He had told Aelfric—dispassionately, standing in the abbot's study while the old man looked at him like a snake—that the monks of Fara would come to prayer when they could. That prayer in a field or a ditch was as good as—better than, maybe—prayer in a church, under God's clear skies.

Aelfric had conceded. The brethren had gone willingly to their work, their new leader amongst them, as embroiled as they were in the labour and mud. Cai didn't know how Fen's presence had made these things possible, but he felt the Viking's power like his own, like sunlight. They had seldom worked together over the last two weeks. Fen could administrate a task as well as carry it out, and had gone without Cai's request to the field where the new dormitory hall was rising, or tumbled drystone walls being repaired. To Cai, their separation had been essential, and Fen hadn't questioned it. They were leading by example, and Cai knew—as Leof had known, as even broadminded Theo had taught—that to live as a monk in this church of Christ, a man ought to be chaste.

They had barely touched one another. Had spent their days apart, their nights in the communal hall. But Fen was here now. "Yes," Cai said softly, looking at him at last. "I am a very poor Christian indeed."

"How did your mother ox fare?"

"Very messily. The twin was a surprise. Would you like to see them?"

They made their way quietly back down the track to the barn, pushing aside the long stalks of hypericum as they passed. St. John's wort, Danan called the plant, the power of the ancient sun god disguised behind the name. As if the thought had summoned her, there she was—far off on the seaward slope, moving like a ghost through the moonlight. This was a fine night for gathering herbs, she had taught—full moon, and the midsummer tides of the earth at their height. The oil from the hypericum leaves made a tonic that eased men's griefs, caused the sun to shine within them and disperse their sadness. She had a basket on her arm. The moon lit up her cloud of white hair like a halo. Cai wondered how Addy was, and if the old woman had lately brought him mead, threading the legendary tunnels beneath the sea or sailing the night air on her broom. Then Fen's shoulder brushed his, and all thoughts beyond the moment deserted him.

He'd left a lantern burning in the barn, hung safely from a rafter while he worked. The ox dam had taken hours about her labour, finally depositing one slithery bundle into the straw, the second one coming so fast after it had almost dropped into Cai's hands. Now the pair were on their feet, their eyes wide in the lamplight, their matching expressions of astonishment so absolute that Cai began to laugh. "There they are. One of each. The bull looks a bit like Eyulf."

"Don't wish that on him." Smiling, Fen went to look them over. Neither they nor their mother flinched at his approach. His touch was careful, almost tender, as he felt the little limbs, brushed drying afterbirth out of the silky coats. Cai was surprised. Fen had liked Eldra, but she was a war machine. His pleasure in these domestic young was unforeseeable, so far a cry from the man who had wanted to slay Addy that Cai struggled to fit the two images together in his mind. *You don't know him,* his fading sense of self-preservation warned him. *Knowing should come before love.*

But it was too late for that now.

Fen looked up. "Are you all right?"

"Yes. Tired, maybe."

"They're fine little beasts. Shouldn't she be up and feeding them?"

"Aye, that she should, the lazy old girl." Cai slapped the ox dam's rump. She turned her placid head in his direction but lay still, chomping serenely. "She thinks she's earned a rest. Come on, your ladyship. Hup!"

Fen took hold of one great curving horn. "You heard him, Dagsauga. On your feet." Immediately the beast gave a snort, spread her hooves on the packed-earth floor and lurched upright. Her calves needed no second invitation, wobbling over on uncertain legs, bumping bony brows against her udder.

"All right. What magic word was that?"

"Just her name. All female oxen are called Dagsauga in my country, or Smjőrbolli." He paused as if struggling for the Latin words, then said in Cai's own language, "Daisy. Buttercup."

Cai gave a snort of laughter. "Viking raiders call their oxen Buttercup?"

"No. Viking farmers. We only raid in season, and then we tend our homes and crops, just as you do. So that takes care of the little heifer. What are you naming the bull?"

"I hadn't thought about it. He's just a farm beast—he'll go to market when he's weaned."

"Still, you should name him. It—"

"Yes, I know. It brings down the spirit on him. Well, we'll call him Yarrow, then, if that isn't too ordinary."

"No. Very suitable." Fen gave Dagsauga an encouraging pat. Then he rested his hands on his hips and looked around him into the barn's golden shadows. "It's late. Will you be missed in church? Or the dormitory hall?"

Why are you asking? The words burned on Cai's tongue. He had kept his distance. Yes, he and Fen had been busy, but there had been times, solitudes. Fen had made no move. It was one thing, Cai supposed, to seize a man after a storm, or on a wild island with no one to care for but the gulls. "No. I told Aelfric I'd be out here all night, making sure the calves are safe. And you?"

"I told him I was going out to hunt."

Cai swallowed. They both still deferred to Aelfric, paid lip service to his authority, and so kept within the terms of their uneasy truce. He wasn't here now, and the night—for both of them—was secured. "Hadn't you better get on with it, then?"

Fen raised one finely marked brow. "With what?"

"With your hunt. While the moon is still high."

"Caius..."

It was low and soft, a plea not to be teased further. Cai surrendered, letting go a breath. "Sorry. I thought maybe we had to be shipwrecked first."

"Everything's changed here. You've been busy. I didn't wish to...disturb your balance."

"My balance?" Cai chuckled. "What happened to the man who knocked me onto my arse in the dunes?"

"Still here."

"And offered to do to me things I was stupid enough to refuse?"

"Still offering."

The barn was large, extending off behind Dagsauga's stall into deep, fragrant spaces. The year's first cut of hay was loosely piled and drying all around, muffling footsteps to silence. Cai unhooked the lantern from the overhead beam. He held it ahead of him and concentrated on that, on following his own light. Lupine shadows leapt and crouched all round him—some his own, others cast by the man moving noiselessly behind him, and soon Cai couldn't tell which was which, and fear clashed with the arousal mounting inside him. Why was he afraid? He could handle himself—handle Fen if he had to. He'd done it before. Their very first meeting had been a fight, and Cai had won.

He would lose against the man restored to health. The conviction of that made every tiny hair on his shoulders and spine rise, as if Fen were already touching him, brushing his palms down his naked back.

In the barn's furthest reach, he eased the lantern into a niche in the stonework. Then he turned. Fen was standing a few feet away from him, waiting. A cassock was as impractical for hunting as for delivering cattle, but for Aelfric's sake he and Cai had conscientiously worn them, traveller's and raider's clothing folded away out of sight, since their return. Either Fen was getting used to his or had found one that fitted him better. He wore it with an insouciance that was anything but holy. He was beautiful.

Cai cleared his throat, which seemed suddenly full of golden motes of dust from the hay. He said, dryly, "What are you waiting for?"

"Did it ever occur to you, Abbot Cai—these things I could do to you, these things you want and fear so much...?"

No use in denial. "What about them?"

"They are things that you could do to me."

Cai's lips parted. He felt all expression drain from his face, and suspected that he looked about as bright as Yarrow, and twice as astonished. Fen was holding out a hand to him. Cai ignored it. He closed his eyes—strode blind and bruising-hard into his arms.

The freedom offered was all Cai had needed. Spectral thoughts about greater or lesser men, comparative physical strength, evaporated in Fen's heat as they landed in the hay. Cai wasn't sure who had knocked who onto his arse this time, and it didn't matter—he clutched Fen's shoulders, rolled luxuriantly with him, letting the pent-up wildness surge and surge. Fen gave it back to him, thrusting to meet each wave. The heavy cassock fabric caught and restrained them, but even the friction of that was good, a sweet torture Fen brought to an end by hauling up Cai's hem and crushing their bodies together, flesh to engorged flesh. Too hot a day for the linen-strip undergarment—Cai's shaft plunged straight between Fen's thighs, the place where lean muscle would grind hard enough to bring him over in a second.

"No!" Cai gasped. "Not like that. Do them to me—the things you said."

Fen went still. Their struggle had left Cai on top, and Fen gazed at him, hands securely spread and holding his backside. The flickering lamplight met the amber fires in Fen's eyes. "Your choice."

"Yes." Cai didn't know how this creature had come to be waiting beneath him—this barely tamed man, not a bit of his wildness abated, letting him decide. It felt like embracing a storm. "This time, you show me. Fuck me."

Fen's pupils widened. He took Cai in for a long moment more, as if assessing him—for strength, intention, what his flesh, bone and muscle would withstand. Then he pushed up, rolling him powerfully down onto his back. "I want you stripped," he growled. "I want to see every inch of you. Now."

Now the cassock fabric was unbearable, a hot, tight skin. Cai sat up far enough for Fen to start ripping it off him, and they fought over girdle, sleeves, the tussle of getting the thing off over his head. Immediately Cai seized Fen's robe to return the favour, but Fen stopped him, hand locking hard round his wrist. "In a second. Gods, Caius—let me look at you."

Cai propped himself on his arms. He bore the inspection as best he could, although blood seemed to rise and burn beneath his skin wherever Fen's gaze focussed. He wished he could see himself through those firelight eyes, see whatever it was that was making sweat sheen on Fen's brow, in the hollow of his throat. All he knew of himself was that he was ordinary—hair rumpled, bits of hay caught in it, his body just the stocky, tough framework that had carried him about his business for so long in a difficult world. He was scarred. The hair that marked his chest and a midline down his stomach was black and wiry, an inheritance from Broc. But Fen was running his fingers over the old injuries, that dark line. His face was rapt.

Cai shivered. "You've seen it before, you know."

"Yes. Down at the rock pools, when you decided to wash me. But I was sick then. I couldn't appreciate it all."

"It's not so much. Just a hill farmer."

"You have no idea."

Cai released a groan. He tipped back his head and shut his eyes. Fen continued a fingertip caress down across Cai's navel. He bypassed Cai's shaft with a brush of his knuckles. Cai gasped in frustration, but Fen reached deeper, closing a short-lived grasp on his balls, then pushing up between his buttocks, one finger finding target.

"God!" Cai managed, with an emphasis that startled them both. "Yes. There."

"Very tight. Not your first, am I?"

"No, but it's been a long time." He writhed, trying to find the beautiful touch again. "I know it'll hurt," he added stoically, to prove that he wasn't afraid. "I won't mind it. Go on."

"I won't hurt you."

"How can you not? It's not like with a woman. And Benedict's cell was next to mine. Oslaf sometimes sounded as if he was dying."

Fen quirked a smile. He leaned forwards and kissed Cai's throat, then the sides of his neck, all the while rubbing at the entrance to his body, until Cai thought his heart would tear out through his ribs. "You don't think Benedict and Oslaf found ways to ease such...dreadful suffering?"

"I don't know. I never thought about it. I..."

"Be quiet. Here, my unimaginative doctor. Look."

Fen let go of him long enough to reach into his cassock's side pouch. He withdrew a glimmering bottle Cai instantly recognised. "That's the wheat oil and rosehip I get Hengist to make up for me for winter, to cure coughs and chest ailments. It lubricates... Oh."

Fen made a valiant effort not to laugh at him. His hair had grown back, long enough for a bright bronze curtain to shield his face as he turned aside, uncapping the bottle. "I took the liberty of stopping by your supply cabinets on my way out here. And I made no assumptions, before you get your back up, you stiff-necked Celt. But the moon was full—the night so warm—and I knew you were out here alone."

He was pouring the oil into one palm. Cai's protest about the raid on his supplies died unspoken. The next time the touch came at his body's entrance, it was warm and slick and he had no resistance to it, the tight ring of muscle convulsing but not rejecting the inward slide. The first pang of broaching over, the push was delicious, as if Fen were reaching for some stray fragment of heaven—the golden fruit that had suddenly grown deep in Cai's guts, perhaps, pulsating just in front of Fen's reaching fingers. "There. Ah, there!"

"Yes. I know about *there*."

Cai gave a sobbing chuckle. "Not *your* first, either, then."

"No. Many fine brother warriors. None of them anything like you."

"And your people don't mind it?"

"No. Not any more than yours do, outside of mad enclaves like this. It's expected, among men who travel without women, although..." He leaned forwards and kissed Cai, lingeringly, tongue shoving deep in time with his fingers. "Although Sigurd was fretting that I'd never get him heirs."

It was the first time he had said his lord's name without bitterness, and Cai, although he could barely speak, tried to attend him. "Your brother, though—"

"Ah, yes. Gunnar has done it for both of us, time and time over, the women willing or not. But men fall fast among the Torleik, and Sigurd likes a brood growing up around him, of good blood and ready to replace us. Now—before you die of this, my beautiful monk—kneel for me. Up on your hands and knees. Now."

Cai couldn't have done it except at those soft-voiced commands. His limbs had turned to water, desire washing strength out of him. He grunted in protest as Fen withdrew his fingers. The emptiness inside was unbearable, his cock so stiff against his belly that one touch would have finished him. Fen was sitting back, stripping off his cassock, and Cai closed his eyes to that in case it had the same effect. Awkwardly he scrambled onto his knees. He *would* die if Fen kept him waiting, die of shame at being so ready, laid so open.

"Fen," he rasped, a dream coming back to him—the dream of the wolf from the sea. "Fen, for God's sake, fuck me now."

The wolf had turned into a man. This man, whose advent had been written into Cai's dreams, his very blood, before he'd ever seen him. Crying out, Cai lowered his brow to his wrists, his hands clenching and unclenching in the hay. The wait ended instantly. Fen's thighs pressed to his. The oil's warm musk filled his nostrils, and he knew without looking that Fen was rubbing his shaft with it. Fen's hands closed on his hips, holding him still.

The push of that great cock inside him burned the touch of Fen's fingers to an ashen memory. The mounting pressure would destroy him. He felt with anguished detail the gape of his arsehole to accommodate the head, and he stifled a yell as his muscles clamped down afterwards, a reflex of shutdown and repulsion. "No! Stop. I can't."

Fen went still. He released Cai's hips and put his arms around his waist, the hold at once so powerful and so tender that tears blurred Cai's vision. He kissed a hot track between Cai's shoulder blades, up the back of his neck. "Pain?"

"No. Just...too much. Too much inside me."

"I will stop. If you are sure."

"No, I'm bloody not." It came out on a sob. The only thing worse than this overwhelming pressure would be the loss of it, the emptiness of that. Fen had sounded breathless, his voice ragged. "Am I hurting *you?*"

"The muscles inside you are strong. And you're fighting me."

"I'm not. I want you. I..."

Fen took hold of his cock. His grip was hard. Shocks of pleasure went through Cai, undoing the iron lock of his arse around the penetration. More oil came, Fen releasing his embrace long enough to pour it over his shaft where it was holding Cai open. His fingers pushed gently against the ring of strained flesh, rubbing the oil in. Fen said something in his own language, deep and rough, and once more Cai almost understood it, the words following Fen's touch, the fullness inside which suddenly was not unbearable but essential, perfect, the one thing that Cai had to have.

"Fuck me," he commanded again, this time knowing exactly what he was demanding. "Yes. God, all the way, Fen. Now!"

Fen moved, a deep thrust that drove the heat into Cai's core. Cai gave a cry of astonished relief. He stopped crushing the hay in his hands and flattened them to the barn floor, taking his weight on his palms, lifting his hips to meet Fen's next great push, up and in, then drawing slowly back so that the strange golden fruit swelled up again beneath the friction, throbbed and threatened to burst. He moaned and shook his head, the pleasure harder to endure than the pain had been.

Fen began a rhythmic movement. He kept his grip on Cai's shaft, wrapped the other arm tight round his waist and secured him. His breath came and went against Cai's ear—shuddering breath and more words in that wild tongue that sounded like the sea, and then a low growl of oncoming release.

Cai couldn't tell him to wait or to let go. He wanted both—to make the pounding fuck go on forever, and to have Fen explode into his body now. Then all choice and words dissolved as a climax like nothing he had ever felt before began to claw its way up out of his bones. It seemed to come from every inch of him—his marrow, his lungs, the place where his backside was locked and convulsing round Fen's shaft—tearing him up by the roots, ripping raw shouts from him as bolt after thunderbolt of ecstasy hit. His cock spent into Fen's hand, into the grip that never faltered even when Fen choked out his name, broke rhythm and rammed to completion.

They hit the barn floor hard enough to skin Cai's belly. Fen landed on top of him, knocking the air from his lungs, and redeemed the pain of withdrawal with an impassioned clasp of his shoulders, tenderly brushing back the hair from his face with his free hand. "Caius!"

Cai grunted. His face was buried in the crook of Fen's arm, and he never wanted to see daylight again. Fen's skin was as fine as a butterfly's wing beneath his lips. Life streamed in the pulsating vein. The salt of his sweat lay on Cai's tongue like a benediction. "Yes," he managed, raising his head a reluctant fraction. "Here. Alive."

Fen's laughter held a note of relief, as if he might have been in doubt. Gasping for breath, he rolled onto his back, pulling Cai with him to lie in his arms. "You bloody beautiful thing."

Chuckling, Cai wrapped an arm across Fen's broad chest. Unlike Cai's it was hairless, ivory smooth except where the nipples rose, brown as hazelnuts, contracting even now when Cai's fingers brushed them. "You're not so hideous yourself."

"Better than your first?"

"My first was..." Cai had to stop for a moment. His lungs were still labouring, his throat sore. "One of Broc's lecherous old cronies, up against a wall when I was barely fifteen. So you didn't have much competition there."

"Oh." Fen's embrace tightened. He pulled a face and gave Cai a look of wry, grim sympathy. "Sorry."

"There were others after him. Better. Nobody who..." He pushed up onto one elbow, picked a hayseed out of Fen's hair with unsteady fingers. "Nobody who reached in and almost ripped the soul from me. Nobody who nearly stopped my heart."

Fen took Cai's face between his hands. Fen's mouth was red, deliciously swollen with excitement, nothing of the wolf left in those depthless eyes but a trace of glowing amber. He drew Cai down. Their mouths met—carefully at first, almost with delicacy. Then Cai pressed passionately down. Words like flickering lamplight went through his mind. He wanted to say them and was glad his tongue was paralysed, pushing against Fen's in a silent battle that ended only when scarlet splashed across his vision and he had to break away to breathe.

Not words he could say to a Viking, not now. Maybe not ever. He mouthed them for his own satisfaction, invisibly against Fen's shoulder. Sleep was washing over him, and Fen had made them comfortable in their hollow, pulling the nearest discarded cassock over both of them to keep them warm. The words made a shape against Fen's skin—a shape in Cai's own language, not chilly Latin, which Fen might have read and understood. Not *te amo, te amo, te amo...*

Fen groaned deeply, a sound of exhaustion, relief, some indefinable yearning thing that made Cai's sinuses prickle with tears. He buried his face in Cai's hair.

The lantern had almost burned out. In its very last light, blue summer dawn shining through a gap in the barn roof, Fen stirred and sat up. He ran his hands and then his mouth over Cai's chest, and then when Cai was hoarsely protesting that he couldn't—not again, not so soon—lithely straddled his lap.

"You can."

No point in further argument, not when Cai's cock was rigid and straining to lift against Fen's thigh. "What do you do to me?"

"Very little. You woke up with this one."

Cai laughed painfully. He didn't doubt it. A besetting problem for him, that, sending him scrambling down to the rock pools to plunge his errant flesh neck-deep in their chill. He'd even told Theo about it—not in so many words, stumbling, awkward—and the abbot had listened kindly, prescribed him meditations and prayers to redirect his dreams. They'd helped a little for a while.

But he was strongly made and full of life, and it was so damn good to ride with his body's energies instead of quelling them. To have a destination, an immediate use, for this big morning erection... Fen shifted, releasing him. His shaft sprang up, probing into the crack of Fen's arse, seeking a target Fen was already offering, his powerful crouch angled just right to receive him. Cai grabbed for the oil, and their hands met clumsily over the task of spreading it. The bottle had gone over during their exertions last night, and there wasn't much left.

"Is it enough?" Cai rasped, sitting up, easing Fen's buttocks gently apart and drawing him down. "Can you...?"

"Yes. I've dealt with worse with none at all." He groaned, Cai's tip pushing into him. "Nothing bigger, though. Gods, I take back...everything I said about...castrated monks."

To be conjoined with him like this—slowly, lit by common day—was more shattering to Cai than their wild encounter in the lantern's flame. Fen sank down on him until Cai was buried in him to the root. For a long time both sat still, the only sound their ragged breathing, Fen plying unsteady fingers through Cai's hair. Then he began to rock himself. The movements were tiny, but Cai felt each one as a sweet, wrenching grind, crushing his cock in its tight engagement. He wrapped his arms round Fen's waist. A ray of dusty sunlight found its way through the window to the east, setting the pale skin alight with unearthly radiance.

Cai kissed his collarbones, sucked briefly at the hollow of his throat. "You look like the god of dawn."

"That's a goddess. Ēostre. And...not very Christian of you."

"I don't care. Come for me. Come."

Fen rose up, arching his spine. He put his head back and let go in a silence more intense than any scream. His cock jetted hard, whiplashing Cai's stomach and chest with his seed. When he was done, the last spasm finished, his flesh hot and tight all up and down the length of his impalement, he took hold of Cai's shoulders. "Lie down with me," he whispered, his voice in rags. "Lie down, like we said."

"But you're finished. I..."

"Just come here." He fell back, lithe and irresistible, part of the force that drew all things down into the earth. Cai went with him, shuddering, still buried deep. Fen opened his thighs, wrapped his legs round Cai's hips. "That's it. God, yes—put your weight on me. Fuck me till I can't see or think anymore. Do it, Cai, beloved—do it now."

The dew was still heavy on the grass when they left the barn. Cai looked at the glistening strands of marram in disbelief—that a world could be transformed before the day had properly begun. *Cai, beloved*—he had taken the words, folded them carefully and placed them in the back of his mind. Endearments blurted out in passion's extremity were too sweet, too fleeting to set store by. And yet still the world was transformed. He yawned, stretching, and Fen came and caught him from behind, nuzzling the side of his neck.

"Stop it," he said half-heartedly, watching a spider swing one silver thread from fern to flowering bramble. "We have to be monks again. Our day's labours start now."

"We just mucked out a cowshed. What more do you want?"

Cai grinned. It hadn't been the most poetic termination to such a night, but he'd felt guilty about the beasts he'd supposedly been out here to tend. The calves were none the worse for the strange noises that had issued from the back of their barn all night. Dagsauga, however, had bestowed upon them sly, placid looks from under her lashes, making Cai laugh as he and Fen shook out the straw and filled the manger. "Well, I'm certain it will go downhill from here."

"Until tonight, perhaps. Can you find more pregnant oxen to look after? Kindly remember—I never *was* a monk."

"*Fen.* Let go of me. Maybe we have time to go and wash in the rock pools."

"Mmm. I like the sound of that much more now than when you first suggested it."

"Bloody insatiable," Cai said wonderingly, aware his struggle to be away was unconvincing, his disapproval undermined by the new rush of blood to his groin. "Wait till I get you in that water. The sun hasn't touched it yet. The last thing on your mind will be—"

"Caius! Cai!"

They sprang apart at the voice, just in time to see Brother Gareth come pelting through the gorse bushes, his cassock hitched inelegantly up above his knees. "Oh! Cai, there you are. Thank God. Brother Hengist's gone and chopped off his finger with a butcher's knife. And, Fenrir, begging your pardon, but Wilfrid says, if you're back from your hunt, please to help him fetch back the goats, which ate their way out of their pen last night."

Cai exchanged a look of weary amusement with Fen. He set off down the track, the Viking falling into place at his side as if he'd walked there all his life, Gareth jogging impatiently ahead. "Hengist has actually cut his finger *off*, Gareth?"

"Well—maybe not all the way *off*. But there is an awful lot of blood, and he's fainted, and Eyulf is screaming. And Wilf doesn't know how the goats chewed a hole through a new willow fence. But the moon was full last night—everything was strange. Brother Demetrios swears he heard wolves howling."

Chapter Eleven

Another full moon, this time golden as the barley Danan said would ripen in the husk by such light. Cai wasn't so sure of that. All his life he had worked alongside the farmers at the hillfort to get the crop in at harvest moon, but only because mornings could dawn grey and stormy at this time of year, the summer beginning to wane. Tonight Cai would roll up his sleeves and join his brethren in the one field well enough favoured by the sun and good soil for the barley to grow. He stood in the window of the scriptorium, the empty arch that had once glimmered with sea-green glass, and he watched the gilded orb rise from the sea.

He was tired, but he didn't mind. Since the moon's last waning he had worked wherever he was needed. He could see traces of Theo's monastery rising up around him, and there was no amount of time and energy he would begrudge to restore that. Aelfric kept mostly to his study, a brooding adder. Fen had warned that there was venom in him yet, but Cai thought the man's will had crumbled along with his little empire, built on the sands of fear. He and the Canterbury clerics—including Laban, whose rebellion had been short-lived—observed the canonical hours and did not complain when the church was not full, although Cai had observed that a surprising number of his brethren did go out of their way to meet the new rule. Cai did it himself when he could. There was a great beauty to it, a kind of stately dance, and there were no more teachings of hellfire.

Freed of Aelfric's interference, Cai had given his orders with more conviction. Now if he hesitated, one or the other of his brothers would come and demand to be told what to do. So it was that he had begun the restoration of the scriptorium. He had wondered at his own temerity—their bread and butter didn't depend on it, or even their education, since they had no books to put in it. Still, it brought him a keen joy to see the burnt-out chamber swept clean, the tumbled masonry being mortared back into place. And perhaps the books would come.

Over winter, when there was less to be done in the fields, he might journey down to the Tyne monasteries, examine the libraries there, renew Fara's supply of inks and vellum. Brother Wulfhere, their carpenter, had died in the first raid, but his apprentice was at work on a new writing desk in his spare time. There was a man at Traprain Law who knew the art of glass. Cai allowed his attention to drift, picturing the room in all its glory, men working peacefully over their script and illuminations, the light of knowledge kindling here again.

There was a bloodstain where Theo had fallen. Cai blinked, coming back to himself. None of them had tried to scrub away the mark. If Cai breathed deeply, he would catch the lingering stench of smoke and charred flesh—real, or just a memory embedded in his senses, he couldn't tell. He turned back to the window. The clean sea air could continue to sweep through the chamber for now. He leaned on the sill, let the salty evening breeze cool his brow.

He wasn't the only soul here with solemn thoughts tonight. On the rocks below, the shadows had gathered into the shape of a man—Fenrir, emerging from nothing and almost disappearing into it again, halting at the very edge of the cliff. There he sat and drew his knees up to his chest. Cai could scarcely make him out from here. Conspicuous by day, with his height and his bright hair, at dusk he became part of his surroundings, as if...

As if the night could swallow him. He was looking out across the sea. Even in the melting, merging light, Cai read lonely yearning in the set of his shoulders. Oh, they had had a month of it, he and his Viking. Cai didn't think there was one concealed refuge in the monastery grounds, one secluded hollow of the dunes, where they hadn't found each other—stripped and sucked and fought their way into each other's flesh. Cai was still bruised from their last encounter. He had inflicted marks of his own, and discovered that he too could make a man's blood sing.

He still didn't fool himself that he could fill up the empty spaces in Fen's soul. Fen no longer spoke about his brother or the Torleik tribe. His talk with Cai had ranged broadly, and Cai had found himself expressing ideas and thoughts no other companion had inspired in him, but Gunnar and Sigurd had been consigned to silence. Cai hadn't tried to rescue them. They were the unknown forces still acting on Fen's soul, and how could Cai compete? All the life Fen had experienced before his abandonment here, that whole world of seafaring, conquest, brotherhood... No, much easier to let it fade.

As if poor Fen could forget. Suddenly ashamed of himself, Cai turned away from the window. The steps from the scriptorium were still ruinous, half the stairwell burned away, and he made his way cautiously down them, slipping out through cobwebby shadows into the night.

Fen didn't stir at his approach. Cai had made enough noise not to startle him. He crouched on the rocks behind him—hesitated for a moment, then put his arms around him. "Fen."

He made a deep sound of welcome, turning far enough to rub his face against Cai's. "Is it time for us to go and start the harvest?"

"Not yet. I know you grieve for your comrades and your family. Forgive me if I haven't spoken of them."

"My comrades..." Fen's smile brushed Cai's cheek in the dark. "In fact I was thinking about you."

Something shifted in Cai's chest, a relief and pleasure so pure that it hurt. "Were you?"

"Yes. The moon casting her track across the sea like this... It seemed so strange to me that the waters divided us for so long, I had to come and look at them. Maybe there is an earthly bridge as well as the rainbow one into Valhalla. Maybe the moon creates it, and allows men's souls to know one another before they meet in the flesh. Even... Even if they never do."

Cai remembered the dream of the wolf, and he nodded. "Maybe," he said hoarsely. "I rejoice that *we* did."

"As do I. Even if I was trying to kill you at the time."

You're killing me now. Cai kept that thought to himself, his throat aching and burning. "I've been in the scriptorium. I want to rebuild it, but Theo died in there. Leof too. And I felt such sorrow for them, but then I saw you out here, and..." He shut up. What had he been about to say? His tongue kept bringing him to this brink, as dangerous as the cliff edge where they now sat. He rested his brow on Fen's shoulder, closing his eyes.

Fen laced his fingers through Cai's. "I too am struggling to understand. I am a warrior. And, yes—I have lost my comrades. I ought to be dead—from shame, if nothing else."

"There was no shame in it. Not for you."

"I will never make you understand our laws of battle. Sigurd would say the weakness was in me, to permit them to leave me behind.

Hush, Cai—I *know* what you think of that. It's not what concerns me. Despite all these things, I am happy here. I wouldn't leave if I could. I...I wouldn't leave *you*."

Cai didn't move, not even to open his eyes. If he stayed quite still here, the world might never move on. He might remain in this moment, hearing the song of his own blood, or perhaps of Addy's seals far off over the glittering sea. He didn't want, didn't need, didn't think he could bear anything more. But Fen tightened his grip, binding them together, making Cai see in the dark behind his eyes the intricate knotwork Leof had used to paint down the margins of Theo's book.

"I am trying to understand," Fen said, "just as you are. So much grief, and such a waste of water that divided us! And yet I have come to love you. And you, my fine man, whispering in the dark, as if I couldn't read your words on my skin, even in your own language... How have we come to this?"

"I don't know," Cai whispered. "Is it...bad? Do you regret it?"

"I regret the years without you. I used to see the other young men bind themselves to one companion, whether in lust or friendship, and I tried to believe I wasn't made like that. It was my last thought on the beach that night, while I lay dying in the waves—that if I'd had such a companion, he wouldn't have allowed me to be left behind."

"I never will."

"And you—I will fight for you until we are stricken down together and our spilled blood mingles in the sand."

"That's a lovely thought."

Fen caught the tremor of laughter in Cai's voice. "It is not given to me to express my feelings more gently. Will you accept this?"

"Absolutely."

They knelt for a long time in silence, only the rush and in-breath of the moon-swollen tide to accompany their thoughts. Then Cai smiled, recalled to the moment by the demands of his importunate flesh. "This is all very noble and pleasant, isn't it?"

"Yes, I suppose so. What about it?"

"It makes me want to fuck your noble Viking bones right through the nearest rock."

Fen gave a bark of laughter. "That would seal our bargain very well. Do we have time?"

"No. I can see the men coming down for the harvest. Addy said we have to lead by example."

"To be accurate, I believe he said *you* had to. But come along. The rock will still be here when we are done."

Their path took them down through the churchyard. Out of habit, Cai paused by Leof's grave. The small mound was greening over now, merging back into the moorland. All summer wildflowers had blossomed around it, a handful of campions or sea pinks to gather, and now the hawthorns were starring the night sky above the wall with moonlit fruit. Cai broke off a stem and laid it at the foot of the plain wooden cross. When he looked round, Fen was brushing fallen leaves and clumps of moss off the grave. The last time Cai had gone through this ritual in his presence, Fen had stood aloof, as if bewildered by tenderness shown to the dead.

Cai was about to thank him. Then he stopped, his attention caught. Between Leof's grave and Benedict's—still raw, painful to see—a scatter of withered herbs lay on the turf. Cai crouched to look at them. "These look like Danan's."

Fen came to stand by him. "How can you tell?"

"They're medicinal plants. This is valerian, and this lady's mantle. She likes to get them at full moon and from a graveyard if she can. They're at their most powerful then, and... Well. They're well-nourished."

"She must have dropped them."

Cai chuckled. "You haven't met her. She never lets go of anything. I'll send to the village tomorrow and see that she's all right."

"Addy said something to you about her, didn't he?"

"Yes. To take care of her, and about a bad death." Down in the barley field, the villagers were streaming to join the monks in their labour. A song much older than any of Fara's hymns was rising up in the warm air. *We have sworn a solemn oath, our lady Gráinne must die...* Scythes were gleaming in the moonlight. Cai shook his head. "He also said she'd rise up with the next harvest, and that won't happen unless we get this one in. Come on."

On the third morning after the harvest, the milk from the villagers' dairy herd refused to come to butter. Cai frowned down at the small, panting boy who'd been sent to inform him of this, as if it was anything to do with him. Still, on previous occasions Theo had been known to go and say some words of benediction over the churns. The brethren were dependent on the villagers' few cows for their butter and cheese, and so Cai went down, blushing with embarrassment, and did his best, the entire population turning out to watch in critical expectation.

He was no Theo, that was certain. He should have sent Aelfric, whose face alone would have curdled the milk. He said his Our Father, hands outstretched over the churns, and added for good measure a bawdy chant Broc sang to get the bull to go to work in the springtime, translated into Latin to render it holy, but the paddles continued to splash in the churns and still no butter came.

Reduced to practicalities, Cai advised them to empty out the buckets, churns and troughs, clean them all and try again. He was lifting the first churn to give them a hand when Brother Hengist slipped into the dairy barn, moving as discreetly as such a big man could, and took up position on the other side of the barrel. "Caius! There's ergot in the grain."

It was meant to be a whisper, but Hengist was used to bellowing out to monks three fields away that their dinners were ready, and the villagers tending to the cows around the barn looked up.

"Hush," Cai admonished him. "What, in the crop we brought in the other night? There can't be. We'd have seen it."

"I know. But look!"

He pulled from his sleeve an ear of golden barley. Cai set down his barrel and took it from him, his heart sinking in dismay. The purple-black fungus pods scattered in among the healthy grains were impossible to deny. Cai had seen them before, and their effects on the men and beasts who consumed them. Danan had taught him to make that his first diagnostic check, in cases of hallucination and sudden madness. He crumbled the dark pod between his fingers. *Danan...* Where was she? The messengers Cai had sent to Traprain and the hillforts hadn't returned, but that could simply mean the old woman was out on one of her long peregrinations among the hills, or drinking mead with Addy in his cave. "Find Fenrir. He will help you start bringing the crop back out of the barn."

"It was Brother Fen who spotted it. He's already put some of us to work. He says we'll have to go through it ear by ear."

Brother Fen... Cai almost smiled in spite of his anxiety. Had any of them dared call him that to his face? "Well, he's right. We have to save what we can, but it mustn't get into our bread or our grain stores."

"Is it really so bad? My mother ate it once, and she dreamed she was flying."

"One kind can do that. But it gives you seizures too, and the other sort brings on fiery pain in the limbs and makes your toes drop off. So let's not chance it."

"No," Hengist agreed, wide-eyed.

"Go back and help them. I'll be right behind you, after I've—"

"Ergot?"

Cai and Hengist turned at the shrill cry. Godric, the village's informal leader, had scrambled onto an upturned bucket. He was a fat, mean-eyed little man whose authority was largely self-assumed, and the people normally paid him no attention. They were turning to him now, though, the fearful word echoing among them. "Ergot—the punishment of holy fire!"

Cai released a breath of irritation. He wiped his hands on a cloth and stepped into the middle of the barn. "There's nothing holy about it. And it's a fungus, not a punishment."

"Holy fire!" Godric shouted again, making Cai wonder if he'd been at the infected grain already. "And milk that will not churn. And Friswide's hens have stopped laying, and last night my hearth burned with a cold green flame. Perhaps there is a witch!"

Cai had never heard the word spat out in such a way. *Weika,* the Saxon villagers said, and with reverence—men or women who could take and turn the forces of nature in their hands. Cai took a good look around the circle of faces in the dairy barn. Fears and doubts were dawning there, a darkening of innocent eyes. "A witch?" he queried grimly. "I think perhaps we are lacking one. And—tell me, *Hlæford* Godric—has anyone from the monastery been down to preach to you here?"

Godric had plainly been told to keep his mouth shut. He did so now, smugly, enjoying a secret. His wife, less subtle, and indebted to Cai and Danan for the safe delivery of her three children, gave him a shove, which knocked him straight down off his bucket. "Aye, Brother! That new one that looks like a crow. He has been here—not preaching, but telling us strange tales."

Yes. Once more Cai felt a bitter twist of admiration for the real abbot of Fara. Whether some among these villagers were nominally Christian or not, they were all of them too hard-nosed and busy to make time for a sermon. Offer them a story, though, and there they would be, gathering round the fire, their Saxon blood hungry for narrative. Not one of them could read or write, but their recall of a song or a story-telling poem was instant, perfect and largely uncritical. You had to be careful what you told them—unless it suited you not to be.

There would always be somebody to listen, if you chose the right sort of tale. And there would always be somebody like Godric to let you in. "All right," Cai said. "Do you remember Abbot Theo?"

Godric's wife beamed. "Of course. A good man. *He* could always make the butter come, no offence to you, Brother Cai."

"None taken. Do you remember some of the things he said—about thinking for yourselves? Deciding for yourselves what's right, no matter what others may say?"

"Oh, yes," Godric grunted. "A good man, but a fool. He even used to tell us we should disagree with *him,* if we wished. Aelfric says we should obey."

"And is that better?"

"I don't know, but it makes more sense. How are we to know what to do otherwise?"

Cai resisted the urge to run his hands into his hair. He had only just been beginning to work out his own notions of right and wrong when he had lost his teacher. He didn't mind acting abbot when it came to work schedules, but he wasn't in any way ready for preaching or the cure of men's souls. "I've told you. Just try to think for yourselves. Just..." The barn faded out from around him. He was back on an island beach, locked in conflict with a Viking who had just decided not to kill. Fen was wild-eyed, glaring at him. *You, with your blasted Christian ways, your damned compassion! I feel your pain more than my own. I feel another man's pain before I inflict it!* "Just try to imagine whatever you're about to do to someone else is happening to you. If you don't bloody like it, then stop."

He paused for breath. Nobody seemed impressed. Perhaps he should have said it in Latin. Only half-convinced himself, he gave it up in favour of practicalities. "Friswide, your hens need more oyster shell in their feed, I should think. And—no offence to *you,* Barda—your fire could use a good clean. Sea coal does burn green, and gives precious little heat on a blocked hearth." He turned on Godric. "And you—if an order's what you want, I'll give you one. Finish your work here, then bring anyone who can be spared up to the barns and help us save our crop."

Cai pulled Fen into his arms. He tightened his embrace, and Fen let go a shuddering moan and subsided against his chest. His hair was damp with sweat—Cai ran his fingers through it, marvelling at the virile strength of every strand. He was letting it grow, avoiding Brother Cedric with his shears. Soon it would be a Viking mane again. "Are you all right?"

"Gods, yes." Fen coughed and caught his breath, which was coming as fast as Cai's. He stroked Cai's belly, caressing the dark fleece at the base of his cock. "I must send you away more often."

Cai chuckled. He'd had a lonely week of it, out among the hills. And for all the gnawing fear in his mind, all the way down from the top of Dragon's Tail Ridge to the lights of Fara, to the very door of his weary pony's stable, one need had been consuming him. And there, desire made flesh, a wish granted, had been Fen, leaning in the doorway, pale skin glowing in the lantern's flame. They had waited until the pony was rubbed down and fed, but no longer than that. Cai frowned, suddenly doubtful. "Did I hurt you?"

"A little. But we can manage on passion and spit, and I sucked you magnificently before you began, did I not?" Fen gave the curling black hair a tug when Cai groaned. "What—do I offend you, mealy-mouthed monk?"

Smiling, Cai ignored the jibe. He had learned to express himself plainly enough to satisfy any Viking. "No. You make me want to go again."

"Mm. So I see. Is there something in the water, on top of those lonely hills?"

"There's precious little of anything up there." Cai took hold of the exploring hand trying to assist his newborn erection. Reluctantly he drew it away, lifted it and kissed its palm. "And there's no Danan. I followed all her usual trails, all the places she showed me where the best herbs grow. No sign of her in the villages either, not for weeks. Did you fare any better here?"

"No. I did as you asked and made my way into all the cellars and hidden chambers of this place."

"Did you do as I asked and do it discreetly?"

Fen stretched luxuriantly, settling himself in Cai's arms. He had come in a stormy rush, pressed tight to the stable wall. His belly was still damp and glimmering with seed. "I didn't have to. Nobody challenged me."

Cai surveyed the beautiful frame of him, strength manifest in every limb, even freshly drained and sleepy as he was. "No. I'm sure they didn't. You were meant to be subtle about it though, Fen."

"Subtle wouldn't have got me into the Canterbury crow's chambers."

"Oh, God. What *did*?"

"A fat bribe of your poppy draft to Laban. He's got a taste for it, you know."

"Is that who's been siphoning it off?"

Fen nodded, the silky shift of his hair over Cai's chest distracting. "He's a troubled soul."

"What did you tell him?"

"Just that I'd keep his secret, if he kept mine. And that I was looking for something, which is perfectly true. I checked the studies, the storage rooms, everywhere. Even beneath Abbot Aelfric's sacred bunk."

Cai snorted with laughter. "What did you find there?"

"A few miserable spiders, discussing how best to spin their way out of hellfire. I don't think your old lady's in this place, beloved. I've looked everywhere."

Beloved. Cai closed his eyes. Fen's easy, sincere delivery of the word sent it straight into his heart. Since that harvest-moon night, they'd kept silent on the nature of their bond, but there was that word, that name Fen pronounced so freely. Cai kissed his brow. "All right. She may have taken a longer journey, though I never knew her to travel far from here before. How was Aelfric while I was away?"

"Quiet. Up here, anyway." Fen eased away far enough to look at him. "He concerns me, though. He's been down to the village every day."

"What—preaching to them?"

"No. Doing as you said Godric's wife told you—sitting amongst them and telling them stories. I followed him down once, sat in the shadows and listened. He told about a woman who was faithless to her husband, and her thigh and her belly swelled up and rotted." Fen gave a twitch of displeasure. “Where does he get such a tale?”

“From the Bible, unfortunately. Though you’d have to dig deep to find such a foul one. Ugh—why doesn’t he tell them about loaves and fishes, or making the blind man see?”

“I don’t suppose those ones are frightening enough. They all looked whey-faced by the end of it, especially the women.”

“Curse him. Why is he doing this? Are they taking him seriously?”

“I think if the crop hadn’t failed, they wouldn’t be. And other things happened while you were gone. The children have come out in an itching rash, and one of Barda’s goats has died.”

“For God’s sake. Those goats were ancient. I’ll take a lotion of zinc down for the children tomorrow—it’s probably fleas.” He sat up, Fen shifting with a grunt of protest to accommodate him. “Damn it, though—we could ill afford to lose that grain. The farmers at Traprain can sell us a little, but we’ll be badly off over the winter. Anything else?”

“Well, I wanted you to sleep before I told you this, but we’ll be worse off still if the apples don’t ripen. Hengist says they should be turning sweet by now, but they’re still green and sour.”

For the first time, Cai ran out of reasonable arguments. A primal fear touched him—of a long, dark winter with no grain or fruit. And, this winter, twenty-nine hungry men looking at him to ask him why. “Fen,” he whispered uneasily, the warmth of their joining draining away from him. “What’s going on around here?”

“I don’t know. But it was different, wasn’t it—before the men from Canterbury came?”

Before the raids, too. Cai didn’t say it. His lover was here, shoulder pressed to his shoulder, never less of a Viking pirate than now, with lambent eyes fixed on him in concern. But Cai often thought as Fen had done beneath that golden moon—*how have we come to this?* “Yes,” he said. “I’ve tried to make it as it was, restore it a little. But...”

“But Aelfric and the crows infest it and undo all your good work.”

“Not quite so bad as—”

“I tell you what we should do. No—what I should do, since you’re a monk. One night I should drug their ale with something from your cabinets. And then, while they’re asleep, I should take my sword *Blóðkraftr dauði* and—”

“Fen!” Cai couldn’t repress a spasm of horrified laughter. “Stop it.”

"What? I have said I will drug them, haven't I? They won't be in any pain. And then you could be abbot here in truth, which is what your brethren and these villagers need."

"Hush, will you?" Pushing up onto his knees, Cai put his arms around him. Cai never had come quite to terms with Viking humour and couldn't tell now if he was serious. He held him, trying to enclose within the circle of his embrace all that was noble in him, the dawning compassion that had made him spare the life of old Addy, everything that made him a man Cai should love. He pressed his lips to the graceful arch of his collarbone, looked into the darkness beyond his shoulder. "We can't do such things."

"Why not? Your world is so hampered. These men are parasites, poisoning the minds of your friends. With a few swings of my blade..."

Cai pressed a silencing hand to his mouth. Fen chuckled and pushed his tongue against his palm, sending bolts of arousal down his spine. "Demon," Cai whispered. "Be still. There's somebody coming—one of the parasites, I think."

The track below the stables was dark, hard to negotiate on a cloudy night. Nevertheless, a black-robed figure was tearing along it as fast as he could go. Drawing Fen out of the stable doorway where the lantern made such glories of his skin and hair, Cai listened, his hand still pressed tight despite the patterns Fen was now tracing on it with his tongue tip. "It sounds like Laban. What's he doing out here at this time of night?"

"What do you care?"

The question was only a muffled vibration, but Cai knew all his sounds by now. "Less and less by the second. But he may be ill." Cai recalled the last man he'd found sobbing and distraught on a pathway at Fara. "I'd better go and see."

"Please yourself, physician."

"I won't be long. Will you wait here?"

"Mm." Fen settled himself on the straw. He stretched out one arm along the top of a bale and drew up his knee, the better to display his hips and thighs, somehow more powerful to Cai in their lassitude than when they had been taut and convulsing in the throes of their fuck.

"Don't," Cai rasped, struggling into his cassock. In reply, Fen only grinned and ran a hand down his own body, then took hold of his rising cock in a grip Cai knew from vast experience felt bloody wonderful. "Please."

"Well, hurry. Yes, I'll wait here. But I can't promise you that I won't start by myself."

Cai ran out into the night. At that moment he hated not only Laban and the Canterbury clerics but every duty, every obligation, every man, woman and child who might get between him and the magnificent creature he'd left behind him. He hated the stony path for stretching out beneath his feet—the very air, for being closer to Fen than he was, for wrapping itself in summer-breeze embrace around him. Visions of rebellion danced through his head. He would take Fen and leave this place. Perhaps Broccus wasn't so wrong about the mindless life of the senses—perhaps Cai too would become a hillfort chieftain, fight all day and roll Fen around in his barbaric wolf-skin bed all night. Where was the world where they could leave Viking and monk far behind them and live freely as men—where even Cai's own questions and doubts would be silenced in his heart? He thrust away the vision of Broc's beautiful yellow-eyed hound. His very guts burned with the need to run back to the stable, fling himself into Fen's arms, impale himself on that waiting shaft. *We can manage on passion and spit...*

Shuddering, he took up position on a twist in the track. Laban, if it was him, would have to come through here. Cai didn't feel like offering comfort, no matter what the problem. Perhaps for once his duty to his fellow man could be discharged simply and fast. "Laban," he called, stepping forwards as the dark figure rounded the corner. "It's me—Brother Caius. What's wrong?"

Laban almost knocked him down. His head was lowered, the hood of his cassock raised and flapping into his face. Cai seized his arm to steady them both, and Laban came to a choking, sobbing halt. "Leave me be!"

"Are you ill?"

"No. You don't have to tend me. Just let me go."

"Where? The last man I let go strung himself up in the church."

"Oh, if I could be so brave as that... No, Caius." Laban doubled up, coughing. "I'm not going to hell with Benedict."

"You don't believe Ben's in hell. When Aelfric wanted him buried away from his brethren—you helped stop that, didn't you?"

"Aye, and brought down Aelfric's curse on myself."

"I'm sorry."

"I thought I could be part of your world, your life here. I wanted your brethren to be my friends, far more than I wanted the Canterbury men to be." He stopped fighting Cai's grip and looked at him properly. "I grew up in a village like the one down the track. My church was a church like yours. Then I was sent to Rome, and..."

"Forget Rome. It'll take Rome a long time to catch up with us here."

"Less time than you think. The missionaries are coming, telling even the priests of Iona that their ways have been wrong. And they're not cruel madmen like Aelfric. I've met them. They're good. Oh, so good, so holy. But they don't believe that common men should read, or think, or learn anything outside the Holy Bible..."

"Or the parts of it they're taught, because they'll never be able to read it for themselves."

"Yes. And they'll win, these sacred demons. They'll put out all the lights."

Cai took his shoulders. He'd never even spoken to Laban, beyond the day's civilities. And yet here he was—intelligent, full of solemn anxiety, the same hopes and fears as Cai's own. "Stay with me, then," he said. "Help me fight them."

"They can't be fought. You'll learn." He detached Cai's hold on him, gently, as if he'd much rather have remained. "I don't belong in your world, and I can't be part of *his*. Not now."

"Aelfric's? Why not now?"

"Not now he's doing this. You don't understand, Caius. There's only one way from now on. And everyone who doesn't follow it will burn."

The breeze shifted. It brought on its wings a scent familiar to Cai as his own flesh—wood smoke, resiny and pleasant, the promise of a warm hearth, a good meal. But all the fires of Fara were shut down for the night and would stay that way until Hengist set his baker's ovens roaring at first light of dawn. He turned. Far off in the darkness, a red glow was kindling. It wasn't on the monastery lands, or in any of the scatter of villages that could be seen from here. Cai checked his inner calendar, the ancient wheel of ritual that had shaped his year until he'd learned a new one from this new, strange church. Too late for Lugnasadh, too soon for Samhain...

"What is Aelfric doing?" he demanded. "What is that fire?"

But Laban was gone, the track as dark and empty as if he had never been there.

Chapter Twelve

Cai ran. He knew he wouldn't be fast enough—not to close the distance between himself and that fire and stop whatever hellish thing was in the offing there—but his heart was easy. Fen would aid him. Fen would find a way. His strength met Cai's own like the confluence of two rivers. Fen had saved him twice now—pulled him up, body and soul, from the sea of his grief for Leof, and the swamps and quicksand that men like Aelfric created, reminding him lustily every day that his flesh was not a punishable burden but a joy. There wouldn't be time to harness up the chariot, but Fen would help him catch Eldra, and together they'd fly across the spaces of the night—she would bear both of them, they'd discovered, provided Fen took the reins, an arrangement Cai had argued then acceded to, laughing and chagrined. They would get there.

The stable was empty. The lamp still glowed on the hollow in the straw where Fen had made himself comfortable and promised to wait—patiently, if not chastely. His cassock was gone, and there was no other sign of his existence.

Which meant nothing. Fen could have got cold, or gone to humour Aelfric by locking himself up in the quarantine cell where he was still supposed to spend his nights. Perhaps he too had seen the fire and gone to investigate, in which case Cai would encounter him somewhere on the track leading out across the salt flats. The light was brighter now, golden flashes dancing in the ruby glow. A massive bonfire, a waste of wood and resources where there was no need for it, out of season and fierce...

"Fen," he called, fear trying to close his throat, but there was no reply.

Eldra wouldn't come to him. He thought he could hear her, but the waning moon was cloudy, the field a patchwork of shadows. After leaning over the fence, whistling and jingling her harness for as long as he dared, he gave up and tore back to the stable. The pony would have to do, weary though the poor beast was after their journey home. She eyed him in disbelief as he unhooked her bridle again, but once he was settled on her broad back, she caught his sense of urgency and clattered out into the yard.

No sign of Fen on the slope down to the tidal flats. Still Cai disregarded the chill in his throat. He couldn't have the Viking at his side all the time. Best if he remembered that now. His soul, his very thoughts, had begun to shape themselves to meet a shadow *other*, something outside himself, and what would he be if it was gone? A shadow too. Whatever was left after the subtraction of Fenrir.

He slapped the pony on the rump, and she surged to a choppy gallop. He focussed on the difficulty of staying aboard her, bareback, his cassock slipping underneath him. The tide was low, drawn out as far as it would go by the weak quarter moon, but the sand it exposed could turn to treacherous mud, requiring him to ride carefully from one pale stretch to the next. Whoever had built that fire must have come this way too. He was beginning to make out hoofprints and footprints in the drier places. Who would brave the flats on such a night, and what fire needed to be kindled so far from Fara and the villages?

The nebulous shape of the flames resolved itself. On a broad sweep of turf at the foot of the dunes, driftwood had been piled high, and into the centre of it someone had driven a single tall post. At the foot of the post—God, and they could have made it shorter for so pitiful a captive—a shape barely recognisable as human was huddled, bound round the waist with crude fisherman's rope. Its feet were invisible, hidden by flames. A cloud of white hair, drifting in the updrafts, haloed its bowed head. *Danan.*

Cai began to shout. He was still too far off for the men and women gathered round the pyre to hear him, but one yell tore from him and then another, raw sounds he had thought only Fen could rip from him. His lungs convulsed. He was trying to hurl his voice ahead of him, make it do what his hands could not. He leaned close over the pony's neck. Her mane whipped into his face, stinging him, and he clasped her flanks with his knees and drove her on at a speed neither of them had known she had in her. She was snorting and flecked with sweat by the time she had carried him within earshot of the crowd. Cai kept on yelling, an incoherent roar that had *no* at its roots but made no more sense than that.

It didn't have to. It only had to make them see him. If they saw him, they would stop. Cai was in no doubt of this—the people in the firelit circle were villagers, the ordinary souls he met and dealt with every week. They knew him. More crucially, he knew *them*, and not a single one among them would have done this. They were kind, flawed, human. If they saw him, they would break whatever trance was holding them. They would cut the ropes and let Danan go.

Not one of them turned. The thunderous splash of the pony's hooves must be reaching them by now. Desperately, in flashes between the blinding whisk of the pony's mane, he tried to make out what was fixing their attention. Not the helpless little figure in the fire, as if she were somehow unimportant... Cai caught his breath on a sob. Had they already killed her? Tied up her body to burn, for God knew what hideous purpose? They weren't even watching her. They were watching a dark shape perched halfway up the side of a dune.

Aelfric was preaching. Cai had never seen him in full flight before. He'd never had the right congregation—only a bunch of half-heathen monks, their minds corrupted to rebellion by Theo's rule. No, he needed men and women like the ones before him now. Theo had never tried to teach the villagers. Cared for them, answered their questions, but even in his enlightenment believed that some men were born to be priests, and others to tend cows, and best if each remained in his station. And so the villagers of Fara were here, their eyes and minds—and, Cai could see quite clearly now, most of their mouths—wide open.

Preaching or not, the abbot was ready for Cai. He didn't glance at him or break off his monologue until the pony was within twenty yards of the group. Then he ceased to stab the air with his claw, and pointed it straight at Cai. "Stop him!" he screamed, his voice a thin blade that sliced the night. "Stop the profane consort of the witch!" The finger swung to Friswide. "You, woman—take your children and stand in his path. He won't run them down."

She actually did it. She had one dirty infant by the hand, two others, half-asleep, hanging on tight to her skirts. Without a flicker of change in her vacant expression, she swung around to plant the whole fragile group of them directly in the pony's way.

Cai hauled back on the reins. The pony chucked her head up and bunched her hindquarters. They were too close—Cai's momentum bore him on and he pitched over her shoulder, narrowly missing one child while the pony veered off to the other side. He broke his fall with his hands, ducked his head and crashed onto the turf at Friswide's feet.

She bent with genuine concern to help him up. "Brother Caius!

What are you doing here?"

"Me?" Cai coughed and spat out bits of grass. "What are *you* doing? Godric—Barda—all of you, come here. Help me untie Danan and put out that fire." He tried to run and found his path blocked by Godric, fat and serenely smiling. "Out of my way, man. Are you responsible for this?"

"No, Caius. Abbot Aelfric summoned us here. He has captured the witch."

Cai grabbed him. He bodily set him aside, but somehow the move put him into the arms of the next smiling, muscular farmer. "Aelfric!" he yelled past them. "Tell them to let her go." He struggled against a surrounding wall of flesh. "In God's name..."

"It's in God's name that I act, blasphemer." Aelfric leaned forwards in his sandy pulpit and transfixed Cai with a blank, triumphant gaze. "I caught her digging up dirt from holy men's graves by light of a full moon."

"She was gathering herbs, you idiot. Let her go before she burns. *Danan!*"

"There is no help for her. She will burn, and her curse will be lifted from these people. The grain will be cleansed. The apples will ripen on the bough. The children—"

"Stop!" Frantic, Cai cut across him. No grains or apples here, but he grabbed the nearest of Friswide's infants and held it high, quickly glancing at the rash on its cheek. He'd been wrong about the fleas. "These children have scurvy. They need to eat green plants, that's all. It isn't a curse or a..." The child gave a wriggle of discomfort, and he took it into his arms, unable to handle it roughly even while visions of taking it hostage flashed through his head, of threatening to chuck it onto the fire with Danan. "Danan is a healer. She'd never... Wait. When did you take her, Aelfric? Last full moon?"

"Aye, and kept her where neither you nor your savage could find her."

Cai dumped the child into Friswide's hands. If mad, empty preaching was all that worked here now, perhaps he had some of his own. He was being hemmed in by the villagers—not angrily, but absolutely—and he struggled to get enough distance from all of them to see into their faces. "Last full moon," he repeated. "Think, all of you, for God's sake. When did we find the ergot in the corn? When did your children fall sick and Barda's goat die?"

"Why, it was after full moon," Barda said. She was the only one amongst them who had looked troubled at the prospect of burning a human being alive, who seemed to be unswayed by Aelfric's power. She reached out and gave Godric a slap, which almost knocked him down. "It was after full moon, husband!"

He turned and hit her back. It wasn't a slap but a punch to the face, and Cai saw he had wanted to do it for years. She was twice his size, formidable. He would never have dared touch her outside of Aelfric's charmed circle. "Hold your lip, wench," he hissed at her. "The abbot has told us. She worked her evil spells from her captivity, to make us set her free."

Cai grabbed Godric by the scruff and hauled him back. "Right," he shouted. "This woman—Danan, who pounds up rosehips to cure your children's colds, and has never harmed a hair on anyone's head all her life, has suddenly taken to cursing and..." He gave Godric a shake. "And what? Evil spells? God help us. Did you ever think your trees might have blossomed and your children thrived *because* of her? And—and when this monster stole her and hid her away in some hole beneath the ground, the very earth began to die?"

It wasn't working. The trouble was that Cai didn't believe his own words—not as Aelfric believed in his. It would take a madman to hold such convictions, on either side. A creature who could blight the land or nurture it according to her will... No. He twisted around to look at the pyre. Danan hadn't moved. Perhaps the smoke had killed her, or rendered her insensible—he prayed so. She was just an old woman. Cai ran out of words and reasons. He dropped Godric like a dead rat and threw himself at the crowd.

He could hear thunder. At first he thought it was only the pounding of blood in his ears, and redoubled his efforts to tear through the thicket of bodies, the hands that were holding him back. No one was hurting him. The women were even patting at him soothingly, as if he'd been a distraught child. They were just *there*, solid and stupid and immovable as cattle. "Damn you all! Let me go!"

"Blóð ok sorg!"

Cai jerked his head up. No Saxon throat could produce such a sound. The thunder grew louder. The barricade slackened around him, hands falling away, mouths opening. Astonishment and fear—at last, the placid, dreadful smiles disappearing, like cobwebs in the blast of a good north wind.

Godric waved a plump paw back in the direction of Fara. He gaped like a fish, and after a couple of efforts got one word out. "*Vikingr!*"

"*Blóð ok sorg!*" The battle cry rang out again. A thrill of terror shot down Cai's spine, stiffening the hairs on his nape. He knew the words. They were very like his people's own, and he'd been taught many blood-hot Viking ones now, shuddering with passion in sand dunes, stables, barns. *Blood and woe*—yes, pure oncoming hell, bearing down out of the night. *Blóð ok sorg*, the long, lonely syllables drawing out, like...

Oh, God, like the cry of a wolf. For a flashing instant even Cai was fooled, the villagers' terror transmitting itself in a wave of primal body scents. They were scattering around him. He was free now to move, to run to Danan and try to set her free from the pyre.

There was no need. The *vikingr* raider swept down. In his leather jerkin, his bare arms taut with muscle, he was every shore dweller's nightmare. Eldra was surging beneath him, her movements so blended with his that they seemed like one creature. His wolf's-head sword was buckled at his side, and in one hand he swung an axe. "*Blóð ok sorg!*" he yelled one last time, blazing past Cai at a gallop, sparing a second to flash him a lunatic grin. Then he drove Eldra straight at the fire.

He was as likely to decapitate Danan as save her. The blade of the axe flashed once as it fell, and a hollow thunk of metal on wood made Cai wince. He cried out in fear as Danan's lifeless form drooped forwards, but Fen hauled down hard on Eldra's rein, sweeping her round in a tight circle in time to grab the old woman before she collapsed. He shouted again—formlessly this time, a roar of victory and laughter—and hoisted her up like a bundle of rags beneath his arm.

The fire leapt skyward, as if in rage at the loss of its prey, blinding Cai to everything beyond it. Fen was gone, the only trace of him a dying percussion of hooves. He turned. The villagers were all staring in the same direction, the terror in their faces dissolving to confusion—and, at last, a different kind of fear, as if awaking from a dream. They began to look like themselves again.

"It was Fenrir," Cai choked out, only then fully realising it himself. "Fen took her. He saved her."

Aelfric let loose a shriek. There was something deathly in the sound—a kind of despair, as if some fibre within him had reached a breaking point and snapped. "Thou shalt not suffer a witch to live!

Thou shalt not—"

The tuft of marram grass on which he'd been perched tore out of the sand and gave way. For one eerie moment he remained suspended, that clawed finger swinging to find its next target, feet poised over nothing. Then he dropped like a bundle of sticks in a sack and rolled to the foot of the dune, limbs flailing.

The villagers watched in horror. Then—easily roused, easily swayed—they began to laugh. Cai pushed through them. This time they let him, and he shouldered his way to where Aelfric lay, twitching and panting.

"No," Cai said, desperately stifling laughter of his own. "Don't you see, he's not well in his head? Don't follow his orders, but...don't laugh. You, Godric—Blacksmith Wynn—take hold of him. Help him back to the monastery and call his brethren to take care of him."

"No!" Aelfric lunged into a sitting position. He was like one of the fearsome creations of the Jews, the mindless, unstoppable golems who would carry out their makers' vengeance to the ends of the earth. "The Bible commands! Thou shalt not suffer a witch to live!"

Cai could snap too. His doctorly compassion dried. He took the abbot by his scrawny throat and shoved him back down onto the sand. "You think you know the Bible?" he snarled. "No man alive today knows the Bible. That's what Theo taught us. A book written in Aramaic—translated through Hebrew and Greek into Latin... All it can be is God's guide to us, not his sacred bloody word-for-word commands. Things get lost. Words change. And Theo taught us those ones straight away, to show us an example. The word is *poisoner* in Hebrew. Thou shalt not suffer a poisoner to live."

"Is it so, Brother Caius?"

Cai glanced up. Barda was listening, hands on her hips, her expression thoughtful. She was nursing a split lip, which Godric would have cause to regret later on. "Yes. It's so."

"It's very strange."

"Not as strange as what you people tried to do out here tonight." He let Aelfric go and got up, trying to wipe the memory of his bony gullet off his hand. "I'm asking you, as your friend...don't follow Aelfric. Don't follow *me*. Just for God's sake try to think for yourselves. Now, I have to find Fen and see if you've managed to kill that old woman between you."

Eldra's hoofprints lay crisp on the damp sand. A direction would be easy, though the great, bounding distance between each set of prints told Cai he might have a long walk. And where would Fen have taken her? Back to the monastery and the infirmary there, if he had any sense. But the deep-gouged marks were headed south, so unless he'd doubled back among the dunes...

The four-time drum began again. It was so faint that Cai briefly wondered if Eldra's prints had somehow retained their sound and were echoing it back to him. The uncertain moonlight was illuminating a thin stretch of the strand, the place where the incoming tide was sweeping up the beach. The percussion gained a dimension—a wild splashing, flying hooves cleaving water—and out of this premonitory sound-ghost came a shape, a moonlit vision of a man on horseback. Fen was coming back.

He was riding unburdened. Cai began to run towards him. It was too soon for him to start demanding where he'd put poor Danan, if she was dead or alive, but he raised a hand and hailed him. Alive or dead, Fen had tried to save her. Had come tearing to the rescue when Cai had given up on him, had been stupid enough for one instant to think himself abandoned. His heart leapt. "Fenrir! Fen!"

Fen didn't slow. He and Eldra swept past him, Cai getting one more glimpse of that mad, beautiful smile. Then Fen bore back on the reins, his obedient warhorse once more responding, beginning the battlefield manoeuvre she'd learned with Broc's chariot behind her and had used tonight to let her master get behind Danan, scoop her up and go. It was a trick to rescue comrades cut off by a skirmish. Broc also used it to round people up.

The horse was rushing down on him. Cai stepped back, already knowing it useless, trying to get out of her track. Fen was leaning forwards past her shoulder, one arm stretched out. "Blood and sorrow, monk," he cried, his rich voice cracking with laughter. "Your turn now!"

"Don't you bloody dare." Cai backed up further, hands raised defensively. Once more Eldra passed him, but slowing now, turning neatly to cut off his retreat. "Fen—I am serious. You are not carting me off like a damn bag of flour... Fen! Do *not*!"

"Save your dignity, then. Jump."

There was one moment when Cai could do it. The villagers were roaring with laughter. If he glanced at them, took the time to tell them to shut up and be about their business, he would miss this ride. And he didn't want to. Even less than being borne off from the scene like a struggling sheep by this insane Viking did he want to be left behind, alone on the sand. He seized Fen's arm. Fen hoisted him and he leapt. He landed with a ball-jarring thud across Eldra's rump and almost slid off over her tail. He seized Fen's belt and hung on.

Fen took off with him into the night. Cai wrapped his arms round his waist. He had no idea of where they were heading but he didn't care—closed his eyes and pressed his brow to Fen's shoulder to increase the feel of the unknown. Let Eldra bear them off into the void. Theo had said the earth was round, but that was hard to believe on a north-lands beach, where the moonlit horizon stretched out forever on a pure, empty plane. Let Fen drive Eldra on and on, and perhaps they would hurtle off this world's edge. Leave behind the place where it was possible for good human creatures to set an old woman to burn, where knives of guilt pierced Cai for not having somehow taught them better, as if not only Fara's monks but her villagers too were burdens on his soul... "No!"

Fen spared a hand from the reins. He rubbed his fingers over Cai's tight-clenched knuckles. "No what?"

"Don't stop. Take us away."

"Too late, beloved. We're already here."

To come from a gallop to a dead stop was also a battle manoeuvre, and Eldra was good at it. She propped her forelegs and commenced a graceful skid, and for the second time that night Cai was hurled down from horseback and into the dark. This time he landed in soft sand. He scrambled to his feet in time to see Fen make an elegant warrior's dismount and pat Eldra's neck as if she'd done him proud. He was smiling broadly—beginning to shake with laughter.

"Fen, you...you *arse*!" That was no good. Cai's own voice quivered. He tried to find the fury that should have been burning him up. "You arrogant Viking savage! How dare you sweep in and grab a..." He floundered for words, then took inspiration from his damp, sand-covered cassock. "A man of God, as if he'd been nothing but—"

"A shrieking virgin nun? That's what you think of us, isn't it?"

"Oh—and that's wrong? A slander upon your good name?"

"Not at all. But not me. Not the Torleik. We only take such plunder as will be useful to us, and I chose to take a fine man."

Cai stared at him. He hadn't heard *Torleik* in some time now. He'd been starting to think those ghosts were laid for Fen, exorcised by newer, brighter experience. He hadn't heard that proud, easy *we* that told him where his Viking's blood loyalties still lay. His own blood chilled. But Fen gave him no more time to think about it. Chuckling, he advanced across the sandy crater in the dunes. "Look at you, my man of God—all on fire with outrage, your hair in spikes. You have seaweed in it." He reached out as if to pick some out, then gave Cai the lightest shove, just enough to tumble him backwards. Cai took the opportunity and seized Fen's jerkin as he fell, dragging him down on top. They crashed together into the sand, laughing and scuffling.

"Puppies!"

The voice stopped Cai between one playful punch to Fen's ribs and the next. He flipped over, dumping Fen off him. Extricating himself, he pushed up onto his knees. "Danan?"

"Puppies," she repeated sadly. "Supposedly men, and yet—puppies in a basket. It isn't enough, you know, Caius of Fara."

She was perched comfortably atop the dune. Her hands were folded in her lap, as if she'd come here and settled down to watch a show. Cai undid the grip Fen was trying to fasten on his girdle. "Let me go, you fool. Danan—are you all right?"

"She's fine," Fen answered for her, giving up and helping him to his feet. "I don't know how. But there's not a mark on her. She's a salamander, or a witch indeed."

"That can't be." Cai ran up the dune and knelt beside her. "Danan, my lady. You might think you aren't hurt, but you've been breathing smoke. And—you're burned, or scorched at the least. You must be."

She sighed. Without warning she hitched up her skirts and stuck out her bony legs. "See for yourself, physician. If it will make you feel better. Your tame raider swept me off in time."

"Impossible." Cai inspected the gnarled toes with their goat's-hoof nails, the ancient, calloused feet. He shot a glance at Fen. "And believe me, I wish the bastard was tame. I don't understand this. Your lungs should be burned. You were lifeless on that pyre when I got there."

"It seems not."

"I called to you. Why didn't you show me you were alive?"

"Perhaps I was not."

He sat up. She seemed to read his bewilderment and have pity on it, or on something about him—reached forwards and brushed one hand across his hair. "Don't let it tax your brains, boy. Perhaps I was feigning. Your villagers were strange tonight—perhaps it seemed best to me not to provoke them."

"*Strange...*" Cai shook his head. "I never saw them like that. How could it happen?"

"Because they have no leader."

"Nonsense. People shouldn't need a leader to be good. Decent, at least." Cai resumed his examination of the thin but healthy limbs, the flesh that should have reeked of smoke and charring but didn't. The old woman's skirts smelled a little of fresh comfrey leaves and bedstraws, and that was all. He knew what was coming next and didn't want to hear.

"In a perfect world—that of Theodosius—that is true. He was perfect in his way. You are grossly imperfect..." She waited till his eyes met hers in sarcastic acknowledgement. "And better suited to your times."

"Why does it have to be me?"

She shrugged. "Why should it be anyone? You are right. People shouldn't need a leader. But where there are men who would lead them astray, they do. Addy hoped..."

"You do know him, then? When did you last see him? What did he hope?"

"So many questions. You exhaust me."

"I'm sorry. But—"

"I must go. I have herbs to gather. I was interrupted, if you recall."

"Where was Aelfric keeping you, Danan?"

"Somewhere dark and silent. Don't scowl, boy—I found it restful." She shook off Cai's restraining hand and stood up. "Ah, wait. In return for this rescue, I will give you something—you and that redheaded beast. Come here, both of you."

Fen left off checking Eldra's limbs and came to kneel at Cai's side. His expression was mild, as if he'd never rode up and down a beach roaring and swinging an axe. "I don't understand how it is, old salamander," he said, "but I am glad you're unharmed."

"Unharmed?" She gave him a cuff to the face. Cai flinched—anyone else would have drawn back a stump—but Fen only beamed. "I shall bear the mark of your knee in my arse to the grave."

"There was no time to stop and help you to a more maidenly

posture."

She broke into wheezing, rasping chuckles. "Maidenly! Well, I'll forgive it in the circumstances. Now, where is the damn thing...?" She dug like a weasel into a pocket of her skirts, threw out a half-eaten apple and a barley ear, then extracted a long red ribbon. "There. Do you know what this is?"

Cai did, but was too taken aback to say so. Fen, less inhibited, took the worn length of silk between his fingers. "Yes. Our custom is the same. This is for handfastings." Silent laughter shook him. "I'm honoured, lady, but perhaps I'm too old for you. And my preference lies elsewhere."

"Yes. Even my Caius here had a few girls before he was certain, but you...you knew."

That silenced both of them. Fen lowered his gaze, and Cai took his hand. He'd grown used to having secrets pulled raw out of his head, but the process was new to Fen. Cai wanted to tell Danan to leave him be. There was something painful in the thought of Fen, young and far away from him, yearning from the first awakening of his flesh for other men.

He held tighter, and Danan nodded approval. "Aye, that will do."

"What will? Danan, what are you up to?"

"It will help you. You must lead, and you will be the better for a good man at your side."

Light dawned on Cai. His mouth dropped open. "Oh, God. Danan, no. Look, he *is* at my side. He doesn't want—"

"Who says I don't want?"

Cai started. Fen was still holding the ribbon. He looked at Cai with fire and cloud-swept moonlight lighting up the amber of his eyes. "Who says I don't?" he repeated, turning his hand in Cai's grasp so that their fingers meshed. "What better? It will bind us closer than brothers."

The secret of the book is in the binding. Cai stared at the ribbon drifting in the offshore wind, coiling as if with a life of its own. It felt like an answer, or part of one, but it faded as he tried to follow it. Why did it leave him so chilled?

"A battlefield marriage, Fen?" he said faintly, rubbing the strong fingers between his own.

"Many such have been made. And, if it fails to suit, it's only for..."

"Only a year and a day. I know." *But it will suit. That's what makes me afraid. I will be here on my knees, asking for its renewal, every year and a day for the rest of my bloody life.* "Aren't we already closer than brothers?"

It wasn't the right question. The moon-clouds won out over the fire. A sorrow whose depths Cai now knew he had barely comprehended darkened Fen's gaze. "Please. Let her make us so."

Cai raised their joined hands. He hoped there was nothing for him to say as part of the rite. His throat was closed, an aching pressure of tears building up behind his eyes. And Danan, after examining both of them with a solemn anxiety Cai had never before seen her display, bound the ribbon once around Fen's wrist.

"Solstice to solstice, hand to hand, from blood-mother earth to the heart of man..."

Cai closed his eyes. He tried to let his doubts go, to lay them on the warm night wind that was stirring his hair, pushing the wool of his cassock against him in all the places where he longed to be touched. If Fen wanted this, then what *could* be better? The ritual words, older by far than monastery stones or even the hillfort's walls, rolled out around him. *Bud into bloom, bloom to decay, round the great track for a year and a day...* Danan's voice altered, losing its rasp of age and smoke. It gave Cai a vision of oak saplings springing up, each on its own side of a stream. Winter passed, suns and moons, and in the heat of summer each tree leaned across the stream and enmeshed its young foliage with the crown of its brother. More summers, more winters, more suns and moons, and the two had grown together, their great trunks fused, the stream parting now to flow round them. *Hand to hand and pledge to pledge, from home and hearth to the bright world's edge...*

Danan stopped. When Cai opened his eyes, he half-expected to find a priestess of the Druids before him. They had not all been slaughtered or driven back to their mountains by the Romans, and she had sounded so young. But there was only an old woman, looking scorched now after all. She sat down suddenly on the sand. "No."

She hadn't completed the loop of the ribbon around Cai's wrist. She let it go, and it drifted from Fen's like a trace of blood in the water. Fen picked it up and offered it to her. "Go on, old woman."

"No."

"No what? Go on. It isn't finished."

"It can't be. The time isn't right."

Fen chuckled. He made as if to fasten the ribbon himself. "Time? I may be a faithless *vikingr* pirate, but even I can promise a year and a day."

"No, Fenrisulfr. You can't. Not even that."

Shuddering, Cai unfastened the silk binding. He took it from Fen's wrist too, fingers clumsy on the intricate weave Danan had made. "Leave it," he whispered.

"No! I want us to be more than brothers."

"We are."

"And how does she know my full name?"

"She knows Addy. Just leave it. Come on."

"How did Addy know it?" Fen turned to face him, eyes wide, suddenly full of angry fear. "Why did he say I would get my wish of vengeance, knee-deep in water and blood? I don't wish that anymore. I want to stay with you."

Danan staggered to her feet. Her movement released a tang of singed fabric onto the air. "I must go," she rasped, and broke into a fit of coughing.

"Stay. Finish the rite."

"Fen, let her be." Cai held out the handfasting ribbon to her, and she took it, pushing it frantically into her clothes. Cai would have helped her, but she whipped away from him into the shadows, too swift for him to follow. He took a few steps in the strange tracks she had left. There on the sand were her apple and her ear of barley corn. He picked them up. The apple was hard and green, the corn riddled with dark pods of fungus. "Danan!" he called, hardly expecting to be heard. "Is it true? Does the land die without you?"

A weird rush of laughter rippled back to him. "Of course not, stupid boy."

Cai bowed his head. There went another miracle.

"But check your orchards and your barns. You'll find the wind has changed."

It did, in a buffet of air so strong it almost knocked Cai down. He stumbled, and Fen caught him hard from behind. There was a wash of freshly broken comfrey stalks, and then of ozone, and then the breeze was blowing sweetly from the sea once more.

"What was that?"

Cai turned in his arms. Fen was shivering, staring into the

darkness Danan had left behind her. “Nothing,” Cai told him fervently. “Nothing. Everything’s all right.”

“It isn’t. Why wouldn’t she bind us? Why did she say—?”

“Hush.” Cai stroked his hair, then hauled him into a ferocious embrace. “Didn’t we agree she was crazy—her and Addy too? Forget them.”

They were folding down together in the shelter of the nearest dune when the hare dashed by them. It was a big one. It scudded past their hiding place, close enough to kick sand into their eyes. For a moment it sat poised at the dune crest, gilded eyes glowing.

Fen sat up, unhitching the knife from his belt. “That’s a beauty. Shall I get it for us?”

Cai had seen him fell a smaller beast from twice the distance. He grabbed his arm and bore it down. “No. No, love—not this one.”

Chapter Thirteen

"Caius! Brother Caius!"

Fen yawned and sat up. Quickly Cai put a hand on the top of his head and pushed him down again. He didn't want that fox-bright hair appearing among the ripening ears of wheat, giving their game away.

"It's Hengist. He might want something."

"He always wants something. And if I leave him alone for long enough, he finds it all by himself." Cai picked out the ripest apple from the four they'd brought out for their midday meal. It was hard to choose. The orchard had given with such abundance that they'd had stock to sell, after drying all they needed for their own winter needs. The apples weren't big, but they had blushed a sunrise pink no one at Fara had ever seen before, and they tasted of summer distilled. Cai offered the best of them to Fen, who snarled playfully and snatched an enormous bite. He held it between his teeth, eyes shining an invitation. Cai chuckled and groaned—after a moment gave in and tried to seize the morsel back. Their mouths met. Juice ran sweetly down Cai's throat. Brother Hengist's running footsteps faded off into the distance.

They didn't have much time. The villagers' wheat lands too had ripened with such unexpected vigour that the Fara brethren had broken off their own labours to come and help fetch it in. Today was the equinox, daylight and darkness in balance, the time for second harvest, and after this only the third one, the Samhain-tide slaughter of beasts. Then Cai's world—monastery, village, the handful of men and women who gave it its pulse and its life—would crouch down for winter, provided for, safe. Fen and Cai had been working in the fields below the village since dawn. Soon they would have to get up, join the others, form up into the scything line and cut their refuge down with their own hands.

"Caius! Brother Cai!"

God, Hengist was coming back. That was too bad. Cai had lost the fight over the apple and was flat on his back. Fen was pinning him down, growling softly, sharp incisors skimming his jugular. Every brush, every barely restrained bite, was jolting Cai closer to the brink. He couldn't speak. If he opened his mouth, he would give them away with a howl. He buried his face in Fen's cassock, clutched at his backside, at the taut surging muscle thrusting down on him again and again. The homespun fabric was in the way. If they came like this, they would leave marks. And Cai wanted to feel him—needed, had to have, that long, hot shaft pounding up against his, even if Hengist had found them and was standing looking on. He tore the cloth out of the way. Fen, unleashed, gave a cry and an unrestrained shove, driving against him with all his strength. Cai arched his back, ecstasy squeezing his eyes shut. He convulsed. Behind his eyelids the sun turned crimson.

Brother Hengist's footsteps faded again. Cai could hardly distinguish them from the slowing thump of Fen's heart. His head was on Fen's shoulder. Fen was running unsteady fingers through Cai's hair, the bites transformed to kisses to his brow and lips, just as devastating. More—the wolf became gentle, all wildness spent.

"Stop," Cai whispered. "Stop. We have to go back to work."

"Did I hear Hengist again?"

"Yes. He's gone."

"Was it just the rushing in my ears, or...did he sound a little desperate?"

Cai had thought so too. But his own blood had been rushing, and he hadn't cared. He didn't care now. He pushed up onto one elbow, suddenly resentful. "What of it? Why is it my problem? Why do they always come calling for me?"

Fen smiled. It was a particularly beautiful, lazy smile, and it left Cai in no doubt of his thoughts. He snapped off the head of one scarlet poppy and tucked it behind Cai's ear, so that neither of them could take him seriously. "Is it because they love you and trust you? Poor lamb."

"Well—isn't it enough that I doctor them, work for them all day long? Do I have to...?" There it was again, that word Addy and Danan had spoken, the word he heard echoing round his own head all day long and on Theo's lips in his dreams. "Why should I lead them too? All right, men need leaders when there's someone around who wants to lead them straight to hell, but Aelfric's locked up. He can't do anyone any more harm."

"Locked up?" Fen's derisive snort sent a quiver through Cai, a glitter of unlikely new arousal. "Oh, yes. Because you're such a hard-arse, aren't you—holding him captive in his own rooms, with meals brought to him daily, and his clerics for company any time he wants them."

"What would you do with him?"

"He's a serpent. I would crush him underfoot, then chuck him off the cliff." Fen ruffled Cai's hair, knocking the poppy aside. "It would cost us less too."

"Oh, I don't begrudge his keep. He's out of the way. I should be too."

"What do you mean?"

"It's the equinox. Everything is in balance—summer with winter, night with day. I think men find their balance too, if they're not being dragged off to one side or the other. I give it all up." Cai bestowed one last, lingering kiss on the corner of Fen's mouth, then helped him up. "Come on, before we get scythed." Together they made their way out of the waist-high forest of gold and onto the track. "I'm not going to lead. There's no point to it, and leading means I have to pick a—"

"Caius! Brother Cai!"

Fen broke into laughter. Cai groaned and raised a hand in surrender to poor Hengist as he trotted once more across the wheatfield. "Third time lucky, Brother. Here I am."

"Oh, Caius." The late-autumn heat had been almost too much for the bulky cook. "I'm glad I found you. I didn't want to frighten any of the others, and yet..." He looked shyly at Fen. "May I speak to you alone?"

Cai was surprised. The brethren of Fara treated their raider as one of their own now, their fears of him forgotten. "There's nothing you can say to me that Fen can't hear, surely, unless..." Cai paused. Hengist suffered badly from piles and was mortified by them. "Unless it's a medical matter. Do you need some more celandine oil?"

"No. Er, no, but thank you. It's Eyulf."

"Is he sick?"

"No." Hengist shuffled his feet. "Two or three times today he's come to me, though. He's been standing on his toes and making faces, doing his sign for..." Contracting his brows, Hengist managed a pale imitation. "His sign for Vikings. Your pardon, Brother Fenrir. And he keeps pointing out to sea."

Cai went cold. He tucked his hands into the sleeves of his cassock and took a few steps down the track. From here, Fara's great flank blocked the seaward view. He wanted to tell Hengist not to fear—that Fara had been stripped of all of its few assets in the raid that had brought Fenrir to their shores, that there was nothing left to take, not even the memory of a legend. But the truth was that this season often brought down a last flurry of raids before winter weather set in, and the monastery's grain stores were full.

"All right," he said at last. "Thank you. I should think Eyulf's been having his nightmares again, but we'll post extra lookouts tonight."

He watched Hengist jog away back to the crowd of villagers and monks gathering in the field for their afternoon's labours. When Fen came and put his arms around him fiercely from behind, he didn't look at him.

"I am not going to lead," he said grimly, "because leading means you have to pick a side." Bitterness rose up in him, sharp as bile. The balance of the equinox was fleeting, wasn't it? And after it came the long nights. "Where will you be, Fen? If the raiders come—which side?"

Fen's grip tightened. "I will be at yours."

Feint, parry, thrust. Cai had let the battle drills slip over the past weeks, in the flurry of the harvests, but Eyulf had given him a healthy reminder. The poor lad was perched on top of a crumbled wall now, scowling and twitching and glaring out to sea. Cai hadn't been able to get anything more from him, and three days had passed since the harvest. He might have seen a *vikingr* sail on the horizon, or only a passing merchant ship. Or maybe some memory ghost had risen up in his addled brain to scare him, but Cai wasn't taking the chance.

Feint, parry... He was partnering Marcus, another of Aelfric's cleric's. Laban hadn't been seen since the night of the pyre, despite the best search Cai could spare for him, and the rest of the Canterbury men had come to a clear decision over which side their bread was buttered on. They visited their captive master when he asked but kept their distance—wore brown robes and took up quiet roles in monastery life. Marcus was good with a sword. Roman blood in him to match his own, Cai thought, clapping him on the shoulder and pointing out to him the man he should take on next.

That left him face-to-face with Fen. They didn't fight in the drill yard, unless it was to demonstrate something, both of them usually kept too busy instructing the others. But they both had done the rounds of every other man this afternoon. They squared off against each other mockingly. Fen was wielding his wolf's-head sword, Cai his favourite from the hillfort forge. No one trained with his blade sheathed in sackcloth these days. That time had gone.

Fen leapt, and Cai took the force of his blow down at the root of his sword, jarringly, sparks flying. Muscles wrenched in his back with the effort of defence. Bright anger splashed through him. He knew what Fen was doing—their encounters, demonstration fights, had become too ceremonious. They were too well matched. They would end up in a dance out here, each aware of what the other would do next, their shared glances sending signals of brotherhood, not challenge. Now Fen had hurt him—deliberately called up the fire from his blood. "Very well," he growled. "Guard yourself, Viking."

Fen took his first sword cut on the rim of his shield. He made it look easy, though Cai could tell from the force of his recovery that the strike had told. He pounced back at Cai with battlefield violence. Their weapons clashed again. An equal strength, Cai would have sworn, and yet in the moment when his own would have run out, there it was—the simultaneous melting of Fen's.

"Don't you hold back on me!" Cai ordered, slipping out from under the lock.

"Do you think I would dishonour myself?"

Cai grunted under the impact of a new attack. "You might try not to dishonour *me*. Fight me! I have to know."

"What? You've already faced me in battle."

And run you through. Cai missed his next thrust entirely and almost fell. "Not a fair fight. An ambush in the dark."

"The best way to deal with my kind, I promise you."

"Don't..." Whipping round, Cai blocked three rapid feints. He did it well, but the fourth brought *Blóðkraftr*'s tip to his throat, and he froze, gasping.

"Don't what, monk?"

"Call yourself that. *My kind.*"

"Don't tell me with one breath to be what I am, and with the next forbid it."

Up on the wall, Eyulf uttered a long, dismal groan. Instantly Fen put up his sword. Cai swallowed. A delicate stinging told him the blade had just broken his skin. Marcus had leapt up onto the remains of a parapet and was gazing off to the horizon, shielding his eyes against the sun.

"Marcus," Cai called, not taking his gaze off Fen's. "What can you see?"

"I'm not certain. There's a fret, and... Wait. I see sails."

"What shape are they? How many?"

"Square. Five. No, seven. No—oh, *Domine adiuva me...*"

"Marcus?"

"Yes?"

"If you see more than seven, kindly keep it to yourself."

Marcus remained silent. Cai straightened up. He sheathed his sword and turned to the white-faced men dropping their drill postures and looking out to sea. "Brethren of Fara!" One by one they fixed their attention upon him. He felt it like separate weights, barbs sinking into his flesh. "How many times have we seen Viking fleets on their way to the fishing grounds north of here? And even if it isn't so—even if they're bound for shore—it's broad daylight, and they're a long way out. When have we ever had this much warning? Every man here knows his task." No one stirred a muscle. Eyes fixed unblinkingly on him, as if he on his own could make the nightmare disperse. "What's wrong with you? Come on!"

Fen touched his shoulder. The caress was hidden, warm, the press of a palm to his spine. "Fear wipes men's minds," he said softly. "Fear can drag them to hell even faster than Aelfric would want."

Cai took one long breath. "Wilfrid," he began, if not with kindness, then calmly at least. "Don't be afraid. You know the men appointed to you. Take them now, and herd the goats and the sheep into the caves at the foot of the cliffs. Gareth, you and Cedric tell the villagers to do the same, then help them pack what they can carry and send them on their way inland. They should head towards Traprain Law—my father might take them in, if worst comes to worst. Hengist, have your men carry all our grain, our fruit and salted meat into the cellars. And you, Marcus, stop gawping and do as you've rehearsed—gather all our weapons at the armoury and see they're clean and ready. Well, what are you waiting for? Go!"

They turned and filed out. Even Eyulf knew his place in this emergency and ran off after Hengist to help carry the grain. Cai looked after them. There was order and purpose in their departure. He didn't fool himself that it weighed in the balance against seven or more Viking sails—the fret had closed in now, sealing him off from the truth—but he'd done what he could. In the silence of the drill yard, the sea wind moaned. "I'll go and fetch Dagsauga and the ox calves. If I set off with them now, I might get them to safe pasture by dusk. Do you think Eldra will be of any use to us?"

"In a foot battle? No. I could do some damage, but they'd cut her out from under me."

Oh, you assume you'd be riding? But there was no point in challenging Fen's arrogance there, not having been on the receiving end of those battlefield horsemanship skills. "I don't want to use her like that."

"Neither do I."

"Then can you take her out to the fields beyond the Coldstream ford—you know, the place where we..."

"Er, yes."

"And take the farm ponies on leading reins. The further we spread our assets around..."

"Yes. And yes, I will come back."

Cai flinched. "I never asked that."

Fen stepped up close to him. He brushed one fingertip across the tiny cut on Cai's throat, then passionately took his face between his hands. "Your eyes ask it. Your bloody beautiful mouth asks, in all the words you don't say, every time you look at me. Caius—you and your brethren took me in. You saved my life. You could have tied me up in a wickerwork boat and shoved me out to sea, but you didn't. You gave me food, clothing, work to do. My own kind abandoned me. Who am I going to fight for, if these sails don't pass by?"

Cai unfastened his sword belt. He couldn't bear the dragging weight of it round his hips. He struggled out of it and dropped it on the turf. He'd have torn a strip off another man for treating his weapon so, but he was blind with tears. He had cut Fen too—a thin red line across his cheek only now starting to bleed. He leaned his brow against Fen's, and Fen took hold of the hair at his nape and held him strongly. The wind spiralled up from the cliffs—a raider's wind, inshore, rich with scents of autumn. It vortexed around them where they stood motionless, a season's first leaf-fall blowing in its wings.

Chapter Fourteen

One man too many. It was better than one too few, but Cai couldn't work it out. The night had come down black and hard, and in his urgent tracks from lookout posts to armoury to storerooms, he didn't have time to worry too much about the unknown figure. It was quick and thin, familiar somehow in the glimpses he had of it. Only when Cai rounded the stairwell of a firelit corridor and crashed right into the fragile shape did he realise. He snatched back the cassock hood before the stranger could try to dodge past him. "Oslaf!"

"Yes. Forgive me, Cai."

Forgive him? Cai could have kissed him. He still looked frail, but a few weeks of his grandmother's care had taken the death-shadows from his eyes. "What in God's name are you doing here? Why have you been hiding from me?"

"My brother came back from shepherding with tales of a fleet on the horizon. I had to come. I was afraid you'd pack me off home."

"No, not this time. We need every man we can get. Are you strong enough to lift a sword?"

"I think so."

"Go and find Fen and make sure. He's down at the armoury. He'll put you through some drills."

"They are certainly coming, then?"

"We still don't know. At nightfall they were still a long way out, but..."

"Caius?" That was Gareth. He was such a changed man from the night of the first raid, when an axe through the shoulder had driven out all trivial fears of the flesh from him. He was pale now, but Cai noted with gratitude his soldierly bearing. He came up close before he spoke, kept his voice low. "Cai, Brother Fen says we should make ready. The tide has turned. The Vikings are making for land."

Cai had to conduct himself at least as well. He braced against the painful leap of his heart. "Understood. Go at once and give the signal."

He turned to the boy. "Oslaf, I'm sorry. We don't have time to make a warrior of you just now—will you go and help Hengist guard our stores?"

"Whatever you command. But I wish I could have fought with you."

"I know. And you will again one day. But you're too dear to me, for Benedict's sake and your own."

Cai watched him dart off. From the newly built bell tower, a low, insistent tolling began. The bell was new too, or newly purchased—a tradeoff from the smith at Berewic for part of their rich apple crop and some mead. Cai had watched his brothers proudly lift it into place only the week before. Had these things been done just in time for hell and death to rise up out of the waters and knock them back down? At least the upper level of the church had been built in willow and daub, not stone. That would save them some trouble next time.

He caught that grim thought on the hoof. Fen had been right about fear and its power to distort the mind, and Cai wasn't immune. Cedric was waiting in a doorway, watching him for his cue. Curtly Cai gestured him to be about his business, and strode off to find his own.

The bell rang softly, its tongue muffled up in a sack. The strangled note of it lent a dreadful tension to the night, pulsing out across Fara's dark, huddled buildings. Only a few lanterns shone from windows on the landward side, casting a fitful light on Cai's path as he made his way to the cliffs, one man then the next running out at the signal to join him.

The sea bells... How Cai had made them ring that first night, screaming out the monastery's whereabouts to any ship not yet come in to land! And even the second time, how they had left all their lights burning, a gesture of defiance before they had joined the attack... Not this time. Not this time. More men poured in from their posts around the buildings, and Cai fell back, making room so they could run with him in the shadows. Only the monks of Fara would hear this bell, would see these lights. From the seaward side, Fara would be only a cluster of ruins, the burnt-out husks from the last raid. There was just an outside chance that the blanket of night would shield them, and the fleet pass by.

Fen stepped out to meet them in the place where the track turned to a narrow defile at the top of the cliffs. His hair had grown long enough to drift in the night wind. Cai had faced him half a year ago in this very place—had for one instant met those eyes, which took fire into themselves when there was none, and kindled fires in Cai that would burn him to ash before they died. He took up a stance of soldierly respect in front of Cai—a deputy to his commander—and one look at him told Cai the truth. "They are coming."

"Yes. Only two ships, thank the gods, but putting in hard and straight for us."

Cai drew a breath. He looked at Fen, one eyebrow on the rise. They shared the silent thought. Only two? That was the difference between an immediate wipeout and a decent fight. Two might almost be enjoyable.

He saw the same idea flashing round the brethren waiting behind Fen, drawn up in orderly fashion, their skirts hitched into their girdles, weapons ready. "Gentlemen of God," Cai called to them. "Each *vikingr* ship bears about twenty men, and none of them are passengers. We are thirty. We can do it, but not a man here is to relax. I want stealth, brutality and a most unchristian attitude from all of you. Is that understood?"

It wasn't the time for a battle cheer. Cai saw it coming and hushed it, grinning. "Later. When we're bearing down on them like skirt-wearing demons from Abbot Aelfric's hell. Now get into your places, and wait for Fen's signal and mine."

The raiders would make landfall in the bay below the cliffs. Cai knew that from bitter experience. It was the natural place, the beach sloping smoothly there, offering easy anchorage, a fast run in to shore. On a dark night like this, only the thinnest waning moon to light their way, the broad white sands would gleam temptingly, and there beyond them Fara's great rock—a desirable stronghold, inhabited or not.

Cai signalled his division of the men off to the left. Fen was crouched at the top of a whinstone outcrop. He had already directed the brethren under his command to their hiding places among the dunes to the right. The bay might be wide and hard to control, but it could be used as a trap, with men positioned correctly in places leading up to the defile. Timing would be crucial. Fen knew more about that than Cai did—he and Cai had agreed, just the night before in a brief interval of their loving, that he would give the sign.

Cai clambered up the rock and knelt beside him, taking care not to break the skyline. "Do you see them?"

"Yes." Fen gave him an odd, amused sidelong glance. "How do you not?"

Cai looked again, this time following the set of Fen's shoulders and head. A cold thrill seized him, a mix of nausea and excitement. It was like learning to see the passage of a serpent through water, a creature he'd been taught was only mythical. And, as Fen said, now he'd got the trick of it, how could he not? Two great vessels, their lines like water, like billowing sails. They forged a path along the troughs of the waves, the diagonal drift of the tide. Their uplifted prows bore bestial heads—one a square-mouthed dragon, gaping, crudely hewn, the next a spiral of surpassing beauty with a swan's head at its centre. Their timbers fanned out from these delicate points to broad, sturdy hulls. Cai had never seen his enemy, not until he was face-to-face, breath to breath, locked in bloody combat. He had never really seen the ships. "They're beautiful."

But Fen had turned away. He had slumped down against the rock. His fist was clenched tight around the hilt of his *Blóðkraftr* sword, his knuckles white and stark.

"What is it?" Cai whispered, ducking down beside him. "Is your belt loose?"

"No. The first boat—does it have a wolf's-head prow?"

"No. A dragon, I thought." Cai risked another glance. "I don't know, though. A godless heathen beast of some kind—I can't tell."

"It's a wolf. The sail bears the signs of the Torleik."

"Is it...? Do you think they've come for you at last? To rescue you?"

Fen shook his head. "Not in that kind of battle array. And the second boat, the beaked dragon..."

"I thought that one was a swan."

Fen chuckled painfully. "That one belongs to the Volsung. Vicious bastards who pirate with us in the summer, then steal our damn cattle all winter. This is a raid, not a rescue."

"Fen—what are you going to do?"

Their gazes locked. "I never thought I'd see that sail again."

Cai put a hand on his shoulder. "*Fen.*"

He struggled out from under Cai's grasp and crouched a few yards away, hunched up, hair concealing his face. And in that moment Cai's world, from church to dunes, from turf to cloud-shadowed sky, fractured and began to crack apart. He had asked. He hadn't understood how a loyal Viking, with ideas of brotherhood higher and nobler than any Cai had attained about God, could change sides to fight alongside a foreign monk. Even if they were lovers—even if they had lain in the fragrant barn last night and sworn to one another blood faith till they died, even if Fen had done that while he was coaxing one last come from Cai's exhausted flesh, and Cai had given it back to him in the teeth of ecstasy. *Yes, yes, yes.* Still Cai had asked him. *Where will you be? Which side?* And Fen had answered, and Cai had believed.

But Fen couldn't fight the Torleik. Of course he bloody couldn't. Cai lurched to his feet and almost fell at the rip of sick vertigo through him. Fen's back was still turned, his head down. He looked scarcely human—an outcrop of the dunes or the rock. Cai would remember him that way. He wouldn't think of him anymore as a living creature, the wolf from the sea who had become his companion, so dear to him he would wake with the bastard's name on his lips, fall asleep saying it instead of his prayers. Cai would never think of him again at all.

He had a war to win. All round the bay, like fox cubs in holes, his men were waiting. They were men he'd trained and put there himself, and just now they were waiting for a signal that was never going to come, not from the lump of dune sand or stone wrapped up in its cassock and rocking, the only living thing about it its bright hair. Cai turned his back. He wanted to spit out the terrible snake-venom taste from his mouth, but he was afraid to find out that he could never rid himself of it. He controlled his breathing, the heave in his lungs that wanted to burst into sobs or retching.

He mustn't break the skyline. He had rehearsed all this—his own track down from the defile to the place where he would be able to see Fen, ready and waiting in his appointed foxhole. Only the smallest change was needed. He made one last check of his sword belt with cold, steady hands. Then he ran silently down the track. Instead of turning right he ducked into the dune grass at his left, found Fen's empty place and slipped into it. He was the son of Broccus, the scion of a race that had been dealing with barbarian invaders for seven hundred years. Goths, Vandals, Huns—fireside tales around the hillfort's hearth, of noble Roman emperors beating back the alien hordes. Even as a child, Cai had believed maybe one word in ten. Maybe one in a hundred now. But one in a hundred was better than nothing, now that he was left with nothing, and he could assess the moment to strike as well as any other man. He had to believe that.

Here came the boats. He leaned forwards, crouched in readiness.

God, they were beautiful—fine beyond the craftsmanship of any western shore dweller, Saxon or Roman. The plain, strapping ugliness of the men who poured out of them was almost a relief. They were huge for the most part, jerking Cai back into his flesh in visceral fear of them. There were a handful like Fen, lean and graceful as they saw to their anchorage and leapt over the prow, but for the most part they were the men of their legend, hairy great axe-swingers, thick manes drawn into plaits or horses' tails, bulky shoulders straining leather jerkins.

Not afraid, and not in any hurry. They grinned as they waded in from the boats, took a moment to splash one another and bark cheerful insults back and forth. Darkening the monastery, muffling the bell, had been good strategy. These men thought they were coming to claim an empty rock. "Geiri, you son of a goat. If I'd had to share that oar bench with your great farting arse for one more league..."

Cai shook his head, as if he could rattle the understanding out of his ears. Fen had taught him too much. He didn't want to know about these brutes, their discomforts or their humanity. "I could drink a river. I'm sick of the taste of my piss."

"Hogni started drinking his before we ran out of water!"

A roar of laughter. Cai squeezed his eyes shut. He fought the urge to ball up. He'd only met his Vikings in combat until now. It was easy to hate with a bellowing axe-man roaring down on you. How Fen had hated every living Christian at Fara, until one of them had cared for him! The laughter rolling up at Cai was rich and familiar. It could have been Fen's.

When Cai looked again, the world was in darkness. Briefly he wondered if he'd wished himself blind as well as deaf, and had his prayer granted. The moon was gone, a great black cloud whose advance Cai hadn't seen devouring her whole from the west. Down on the beach, the raiders were cursing, blaming one another for failing to notice the weather. One of them was calling for a light.

"Bring the torches from the ships."

Cai clutched hard at the roots of the seagrass. This changed everything. Many torches, casting flaring firelight up the flanks of the dunes, would expose the monks in their hiding places as the dull moonlight could not. Fen's stratagem of waiting, the moment he and Cai had worked out so painstakingly when enough of the Vikings would be clustered together in the defile—all that would fall apart. One torch, though... Cai knew how one torch in blackness could blind you before it began to help you out, how it cast everything beyond its own nimbus into a void.

He took Fen's plans and snapped them, crumbled them to dust, mentally brushed his palms together and cast off their ashes into the wind. Cai would give the signal on his own judgement now. The lighting of the first torch would save them. There was no moon now—in the dunes nearby he could hear someone panting in panic at the lack of it, and sent out a silent plea to him to wait, have faith, to believe—but the raiders' first torch would show them to one another, light up their target before they themselves could be seen. In its way it was perfect. Better than any tactic of Fen's. Cai could be better without him. He could survive.

He was sobbing when the torch flared up, but so deep down inside himself that it didn't matter. So dryly that it didn't blind him, and the leap of battle fever in his blood came at the moment when his heart would have shattered. He felt nothing.

His men were waiting, terrified in darkness. Fen wasn't in his appointed place and neither were the damn Vikings. Cai had to make his move, and now. To make it strong and good. He sprang upright. He flung a hand into the air and loosed a cry his father would have been proud of, a bestial howl that brought the monks leaping out of their holes as if stabbed. For a second it could all have gone to hell. They staggered on the dune slopes, discomposed, black rabbits as likely to run for cover as to fight. But Cai yelled again, this time pointing to the clustering men on the beach. They were shielding their eyes, blinking—too dazzled to see what creature was shrieking in the night above their heads. Cai seized his moment, and the warrior monks of Fara attacked.

They blazed in on their wave of surprise, and it took them further than Cai could have dreamed. What warriors he had trained! Wilf took the first kill, goatherd turned berserker, lashing about him with his broadsword as if born to the trade. Feint, parry, thrust—he dropped his target with the gawp of astonishment still on his handsome Viking face. Gareth rushed in after him.

Demetrios the Greek, leaping about like a deranged mechanical scarecrow, forgetting every damn thing Cai had taught him but somehow making progress anyway, staying out of reach of returning strikes. Yes, they were fine. Cai, wading in, had an instant to love and admire them. The torch was out, knocked to sputtering death in the wet sand, but the moon had emerged again, just enough for Cai to see, and what the hell had he been thinking—of course the torch would go. He sent a prayer to the ancient hillfort goddess of the moon for her mercy. For not letting him dump his dearest friends and brethren into the battle in the pitch dark, to flail around as they might. So much for Cai as a strategist. Fen would have stopped him—would have known.

Desperately Cai plunged between Brother Cedric and the axe slicing down on him, deflecting it with the hilt of his sword. Cedric grunted, needing no second invitation. He jabbed as Cai had taught him, straight into the raider's undefended gut.

They were outnumbered. Without Fen, it mattered. The Vikings were regrouping, working out that they hadn't been leapt on by demons but by men—men in skirts, the puny castrated Christians who fell like wheat to their scythe. The first of them who took the time to draw in breath for laughter regretted it—Cai dived in past his unready shield and ran him through. He spun to face the next. This one was not laughing. His face was a blur in the moonlight, great thick plait unwinding as he whipped round for his opponent. He was lean and massive, copper gleaming dully in his hair. He focussed on Cai—God, amber eyes, cold as death—and snarled. "*Blóð ok sorg!*"

Cai lost peripheral vision. There was a tunnel, and he was rushing through it. The sounds of battle around him faded out. He raised his shield just in time for the whole weight of the Viking's sword to crash down on it. The raider followed up with an axe-blade swipe that nearly tore the shield from Cai's hand. Something punched him in the ribs. Hot pain consumed him, knocking him down to one knee in the sand. It was only for a moment. Then the pain burned out in rage and hate, and he surged up swinging.

He was back in the training yard with Fen. *Do you ever hold back on me? Don't you hold back on me!* Fen had sworn he didn't. Cai had believed him. But perhaps Fen couldn't help himself. Perhaps when it was flesh you had loved, you couldn't unleash your full Viking fury on it—not even to save it or teach it to save itself.

This Viking didn't love Cai at all. He was bulkier than Fen, a fraction taller—otherwise his exact equivalent, and Cai was learning the difference. His blade hit Cai's with the force of a rockfall. Muscles ripped in Cai's shoulders as he parried. He slipped away, got in one good stabbing thrust. The raider growled and retreated a step. Cai went after him. He would not allow himself to see how like Fen he was, so like that he had to be kin. That he had to be...

The step back had only been to gain a little space. Cai hadn't even slowed him down. The great blade flashed in the moonlight again and Cai flung his shield up—just in time to catch a blow so fierce that it deadened his arm. The shield flew from his grasp and landed in the sand. Cai spun away, the swift dancer's move that had saved him on the battlefield before. It worked—the Viking cleaved the air an inch behind him—but something was wrong. When he tried to recover, to whip back into the gap he'd left and fight on, shield or no shield, his legs wouldn't carry him. He staggered. The beach beneath him, good firm sand for a skirmish, gave a treacherous heave. It knocked him sideways. Down on one knee again, he watched as if from five miles out while the raider grinned, took a double-handed grip on his sword hilt and prepared his final blow.

Time stretched and doubled back on itself. Cai had been hearing—for some while now, if he thought about it—a shockingly familiar voice. Familiar as the smile lighting up the vulpine face of this warrior who was going to be his death. Cai raised his sword one more time. He scarcely knew why, except that he was his father's son, and Broc would have had an apoplexy to see him just kneeling here. The lively blade had turned to lead, and he could barely lift it. He thrust away the raider's plunging stroke and rolled out from under the next.

The voice rose again, breaking like waves through the blood-beat in his ears. Cai was down, finished. Bitter salt sand was in his mouth. He had no idea why he was hanging on, deflecting his opponent's frustrated strokes with his sword and then—last helpless gesture—with his arm. No idea...

Except that Fen was there. Fen, hacking a path towards him through the heaving sea of bodies. The voice had been his—roaring out threats and commands, orders to regroup. He was laying about him with *Blóðkraftr*, slaking the blade with Viking blood. Cai twisted like a cat and got out of the way of his assailant one more time. A cry of joy broke from him. Fen stopped dead—homed in on the sound, shoved the last barricade of raiders and monks aside—and came running.

Cai gave up the fight. It was such a relief, blissful as climax in its way. He thudded down onto the sand, air leaving his lungs in a whoosh. *Blóðkraftr* swept over his head, a scythe from heaven and hell. His assailant sprang back. Blade clashed on blade as Fen leapt after him, and then the unique, dreadful sound of flesh on flesh and bone. Hard-muscled impact and the snarls of men shedding their human skins in bloodlust and desire to rip one another apart.

Kindred flesh. On the edge of a faint, Cai clawed back. He struggled to his hands and knees. Kindred bone, kindred skin. Cai knew this—he knew Gunnar. Fen, his face a frenzied blank, had gone beyond such knowledge. Didn't recognise his brother. Cai lurched up. He threw himself at the entwined pair. "Fen, don't! Don't, in God's name! It's..."

One man fell. Blood staining his vision like ruby-red glass, mind going dark, Cai lost track of their differences, forgot that a cassock marked one and a salt-stained leather jerkin the other. On a beach a thousand years ago he had found Fen dressed in hides like this, his hair as wild as Gunnar's. He had found him dying. Which one was this on the sand?

Gunnar. Gunnar, because Fen was standing over him, sanity returning to his face. *Blóðkraftr*, scarlet from tip to hilt, was dripping in his hand. Gunnar, because now Fen was dropping to his knees beside the corpse, a cry like nothing Cai had ever heard before beginning to rip from his lungs.

Cai's training forced one last move out of him. Fen's back was unguarded. Scraping up his own sword from the sand, he staggered round to defend him. But there was no one there—no one who could make a difference anyway, not now. A handful of the raiders were retreating, splashing their way back to the boats. Others, who had reached the cliff path and found it undefended, were clambering up there to finish their night's work. And the beach was littered with the fallen—some in Viking leathers and hides, some in plain moonlit brown.

Fen was hunched over his brother. After that solitary wail he had fallen silent. Cai didn't know how to touch him. He tried to stumble to Fen's side, but his feet took him into the water, as if in some way he could get clean of this, clean and clear in the cold, redeeming sea.

The waves were marbled, veined with black. Cai recoiled from the drifting pattern. Who had poured ink into the lucid amber and polluted it so? He had a wild vision of the monstrous squid Theo said he had seen on his sea voyage here, and then a pure memory of Leof, poised in the scriptorium with a freshly cut quill in his hand. And then he remembered that bloodstains by moonlight showed black.

Cai leaned his hands on his thighs and struggled to stay upright. He surveyed the scene around him—the bodies, the scarlet-black tide. "Oh God," he said brokenly. "Oh Christ. No. Christ."

Chapter Fifteen

"I would do it again."

Fen was beside him in the water. Cai couldn't remember him getting there. But here he was. *Vengeance. You will have it one day, knee-deep in water and blood...* "What?" he asked stupidly, swaying.

"He was going to kill you. I would do it again."

"He was your brother. I...I tried to tell you."

"The madness of battle was on me. I could only see you. I would cut him down again, Cai."

"I didn't want that." Cai knew that was a lie as soon as it came off his tongue. What else had he been asking Fen to do up on the rocks before this battle? Why else had he run off, stinging with betrayal, when Fen had seen the Torleik sail and hidden his face? "Forgive me. I wanted you at my side. But not to..."

"I have killed my brother."

Cai followed him back to the shore. He waited while Fen crouched once more by the fallen man. Fen straightened out Gunnar's limbs, brushed back the thick hair from his face. In doing so he exposed the hole *Blóðkraftr* had torn in Gunnar's throat. He twisted away, retching as if he would tear up his heart by the roots.

Cai leaned over him, gripping his shoulder, stroking back hair from a noble Viking face in his turn. He wondered at the strangeness of it—one dead, one alive, one his mortal enemy and the other so dear to him he could hardly breathe. The entire world was becoming strange to Cai, seeming to lift gently off its moorings, as the magical Druids of ancient times had lifted the great stones for their monuments and sailed them away, riding serenely cross-legged on their backs. Had that been a story of Theo's? No, of Danan's, and she'd told it as truth, not a legend.

Fen choked and moaned, and Cai struggled back to himself. "Fen. My Fenrir."

"I am all right." Fen sat up. He used the sleeve of his cassock to wipe his eyes and his mouth. "Come on. We have to get back."

"Why? It... It's over, isn't it?"

"No." Fen raised an unsteady hand and pointed to the clifftop. Beyond it, a sullen light was spreading across the sky. "They're torching whatever's left standing up there. They'll do it for vengeance even if there's nothing to take. If anyone's still alive..."

"Oslaf."

"What?"

"Benedict's boy, the one I sent home. He came back to help us. And Hengist and the others..."

"Come on, then."

"And I have to let Aelfric go."

Fen pushed stiffly to his feet. "Are you insane?"

"Perhaps. But I don't want him trapped like a rat in there. I have to give him his chance, even if it's just to run away."

"Cai, are you all right?" Fen took gentle hold of him and surveyed him. "Did he hurt you?"

"Who?"

"Gods' sake... My brother. I saw him strike at you. Where are you injured?"

"Nowhere. Nothing. Just my arm, I think."

Fen rolled back his cassock sleeve. Only then did Cai realise that he was blood-daubed from elbow to wrist, an axe-cut so deep across his forearm that bone gleamed in the moonlight. The world drifted further still. "It isn't bothering me. We have to go."

"I can tourniquet and bind it."

Cai smiled despite the wasteland around them. "What the devil with?"

"I am girded with my subligaculum. A Viking is trained not to soil himself in battle. It is still clean."

The smile became raw, sobbing laughter. Cai closed his grip in the thick rope of hair at the back of Fen's neck. It was long enough for him to tie it back again, like Gunnar's, but finer, warm as lambskin. Cai turned him round, away from the sight of the brother he'd slain. Fen was calm again, back in his warrior's skin, but tears were still carving white tracks down the blood on his face.

"I love you," Cai said fiercely, still laughing. "I love that you would stand here and rip up your undergarments to bind my wounds. But we don't have time. We must go."

Their track back across the battlefield was strewn with the fallen. The first two were Vikings, one dead, the other locked in his body's last suffering, and Cai stood by dispassionately—serene on his floating Druid rock—while Fen drew his knife and finished him off. And the third was Wilfrid.

Cai drifted all the way out. He made his physician's checks, each in the right order. He felt for a pulse, pressed his ear to Wilf's chest and listened to the silence that had taken up eternal residence there, held his palm over the smiling lips and waited for the slightest warmth of breath. Fen paced angrily up and down the sand, swore hoarsely for the warrior goatherd, then stooped to draw his hood across his face.

"I wanted to train them," Cai said, his voice flat and grey. "I wanted them to be able to fight and defend themselves. I never wanted this, though. There's nothing in the whole bloody world I could ever want this much." He stopped. There was something wrong with his cassock. It was heavier on the left side than the right, its weight dragging at him. The fabric seemed odd—stiff and damp. It didn't matter. Fen grasped his arm and they ran on.

Halfway up the cliff path, Cai began to flag. He was drowsy, his legs going numb. Fen spun round to catch him as he stumbled, and he caught his hand gratefully, but then waved him back. "You go on. I need to catch my breath a minute."

"What's wrong? You look like death."

"Nothing. A bit sick and dizzy—damn arm's still bleeding."

"Let me bind it."

"Go on and help them. I'll be right behind you."

Not far behind, anyway. Cai was sure of that. Once the tide of weariness receded and he was in motion again, he was certain he hadn't let Fen get too far ahead of him. It was just that the cliff path had doubled in length, and even when he had toiled to the top of it, the monastery buildings were so far away that he could hardly see them at all. Sulphur-coloured clouds were blossoming over them, lit crimson from below. Before Cai could work out what this meant, howls from the darkness to his left drew his attention. He left the track and followed them. He'd retrieved his sword but wasn't sure he could lift it, so he unsheathed the knife from his girdle belt instead.

A raider was rolling with Eyulf in the remains of a barn, struggling to pin the lad down. Eyulf's cassock was already up over his thighs and he was shrieking like a pig at slaughter. His assailant, intent upon his business, didn't look up at Cai's approach. He made no sound as Cai's blade sank between his shoulders—dropped deadweight on top of his victim.

Cai dragged Eyulf out from under. He wasn't hurt, his linen cloth still in place, but he was hysterical, clinging to Cai when he tried to turn and leave. Cai paused for a moment, soothing him, then dealt him a judicious thump to the jaw.

Cai tried to pick him up and couldn't. That kind of strength had departed from him. He had no time to panic about it, though a kind of numb fear was spreading from his deepest entrails out, so he adapted—dragged the unconscious body by the shoulders instead, and buried him as deeply in the straw as he could, praying he would have sense to stay hidden there when he woke up. Then he continued on his way.

Yes, all his well-known tracks were longer. There was time for dynasties to rise and fall, all the little animals Leof had painted in Theo's manuscript margins to dance into the ark—not two by two, because Leof had never painted two of anything—but as best they might, and procreate and repopulate the world with exquisite hybrids and monsters, and Cai saw all these things as he slowly closed the gap between himself and the burning ruins. He had been away for a long time and was returning to a transformed world. Something had happened there during his absence. Addy had warned him that the Roman church would rise. Perhaps the time had come, because there was Abbot Aelfric. He was striding out undefended over open ground, and he was carrying a burning cross.

His faith was repelling the demons, just as he had claimed. Two of them were backing off before him, cringing and bowing. He was blasting Latin anathemas at them, his voice a buzzard's shriek that reached Cai in tatters on the hot wind.

No. Not demons—Vikings, and they were not in retreat. As Cai watched, one of them darted behind Aelfric and aimed a kick at his backside. Aelfric stumbled but marched on. The raiders began a mocking dance around him, now keeping pace with him, now trotting on ahead and resuming their mimicked gestures of fear. One of them crossed himself, starting at the groin, and both howled with laughter.

Cai couldn't save him. In this world where short roads extended forever, he couldn't get near him in time. He remembered Danan and the pyre, and for a moment was tempted to join the bestial dance. Then pity awoke in him, and he began to run.

He could pick out Aelfric's words now, rich with an inspired madness that might have made a saint of him in a different world. *Back, you heathen devils! Back to your burning pit, in the name of Christ!* He was flailing about him with the cross, oblivious to the burning shards of it showering down onto his head. The Vikings tired of the game. One of them shrugged at the other and casually plunged his sword through Aelfric's breast.

They would have taken Cai next, but strange guardian spirits were emerging from the smoke. One of them looked like a chimera of some kind, a four-footed beast with slender forequarters and a huge rump. The creature split into two and became Oslaf and Hengist, converging like furies upon the first raider. Next came Fen, transfigured by firelight, nothing but long strides and flashing blade as he bore down on the other Viking, grabbed him by the hair—kin or no kin—and impaled him.

Aelfric was still alive when Cai got to him. The lines of his life had been cut, but he was drifting. Cai had seen it before in the mortally injured, this short time of clear-minded waiting. He was lying on his back, starlight and smoke reflecting in his eyes. When Cai dropped to his knees beside him and eased him off the ground, he smiled. "You, abomination? Still alive?"

"Yes. Why did you do that?"

"My faith is strong. I set out to fight the demons with my holy fire."

Cai shifted him to ease his breathing. He took a thin strand of hair out of Aelfric's eyes. "You did it. They're gone."

"Don't humour me, abomination. But it was worth a try."

Cai looked down at him in surprise. Aelfric's spirit was in motion again now, beginning its departure.

"Yes," he said honestly. "I suppose it was."

"My faith is strong, but... Caius, is that God?"

"If you are seeing him—yes. Don't be scared."

"Seeing *him*?" Aelfric's eyes widened, and he broke into a wide and dazzled smile. "I have been wrong. Wrong about so many things. Ask the old witch to forgive me."

He was gone. Cai let the empty shell of him go. He stood up, wondering vaguely once more at the wet, heavy tug of his robes. Fen was there in front of him, propping up Hengist, who had trained well enough in the drill yard but turned primrose green in the wake of his first kill. "Fen, mind your back."

"It's all over. Those two were the last of them."

Cai looked around. From the burning heaps of rubble, men were emerging, running towards him. Seeing who was there and who was missing, frantically counting the gaps, Cai felt the chasm open under him, the gap between joy and unbearable grief. He jumped as someone took his hand. "Oslaf—what are you doing? Get up."

The boy was kneeling at Cai's feet. He kissed Cai's palm, filthy with blood as it was. "Can you be our abbot now? Really, now Aelfric is dead?"

Cai pulled his hand away. "No! It doesn't work like that. And..." He looked into the ring of faces gathering round him. They were marked with soot and bruises. Some still looked terrified, some triumphant. All they had in common was their focus on him, and a burning trust that melted his last grip on the world. "Why would you want me to? I've done nothing but lead you into danger. Wilf is dead on the beach down there because of me—God knows who else."

Hengist stepped forwards. "We know about our dead, Cai. It would have been all of us if not for you."

"Who else? Tell me."

"Demetrios, also on the beach. Aelfric's man Marcus, though he took three raider devils out with him. And—"

"Stop it."

Cai touched his numb lips. Had he said those words? No—he'd have heard the grim tally out to its end.

Fen had come to stand in front of him, gesturing the others back. His firelit gaze raked Cai over. "Stop it. There's something wrong. What is it, Cai?"

"Nothing. My arm, maybe."

No. More than that. If he traced his steps back to the beach, let his fading spirit slip between the corpses of his brethren to the place where he'd battled with Gunnar, he could remember. A blow to his ribs. Just a punch, he'd thought at the time, and wounded men had often reported that to him—a short-term ignorance of their damage, as if the flesh when given too much pain all at once simply thrust some of it aside, laid it away to understand later. Not a fist. A blade. Cai was pleased to have worked this out. He couldn't have Fen looking at him like that, not with such terror dawning in his eyes.

"It's here," he said, finding the rent in his cassock. "I don't think it's much, but..."

Fen caught him as he dropped. The turf and the burning sky exchanged places, and he was floating, the earth and Fen's arms pillowing him. He was stronger than he'd given himself credit for—even now he was aware, although it was like watching and hearing it all through thick fog. Fen laid him flat, easing his head down carefully. That was his last gentle gesture. He tried to haul Cai's cassock up by the hem, but it had tangled and caught on something. Swearing, he grabbed the cloth at Cai's waist and ripped. The homespun wool was tough and did not give easily, but Fen turned it to cobwebs, tearing it apart over the wound. Cai's body jerked as Fen leaned close, cleaning away enough blood to see. He tried to keep still. The pain was finding him now, though, bearing down on him like a *vikingr* horseman. He cried out, one hoarse yell.

"Help him! You, whatever you are called—Odleaf... And you, Cook—find me some wood, something to carry him on. Get him to the infirmary."

"The infirmary burned down, Brother Fen." That was poor Hengist. Cai wanted to tell Fen to stop snarling at his friends—that there was no need, no hurry. No point. He stared up into the circle of faces now drifting above him like scared clouds. He couldn't speak. Fen's hand came down hard on top of the gaping hole in his side. He went pale at the action, and Cai grabbed his wrist, making him press tighter.

"But all his things..." Oslaf leaned over him, shivering. "His cabinet and his medicines—I took them out. I carried them off and hid them in the cellar."

Fen's fist shot out. It closed in the neck of poor Oslaf's cassock. "Well, go and fetch them! Wait. You used to help him doctor people, didn't you? What does he need?"

"Sheep gut. Suture. And something to pack the wound. Oh, and it must be washed—he always made me boil the water first. And some of the poppy, to help with the pain."

Cai groaned. Between them they would kill him here, if he wasn't dead already. He wanted to let go, but it was just too damn annoying to hear them. He made a sign to Fen to raise him, and he dragged himself up far enough to speak, clinging to the strong arm. "There's no time to boil...bloody water! Sutures and a needle—now!"

He fell back. Fen's expression was almost comical, caught in transition between fear and hope. Cai began to hope himself. The wound was bad, but it was blood loss that had been bringing death in on him with soft-footed tread. If it could be stopped now... Oslaf had flown off like a well-aimed spear into the night. Cai stroked Fen's face, leaving a crimson trail. "Press harder with your hand. Push some cloth in and press harder."

Fen obeyed, his grimace making it easier for Cai to bear the new rush of pain. A time passed, measurable only in the thud of Fen's heart where Cai was leaning on his chest. Then the circle broke apart as Oslaf came shouldering back through. He was clutching Cai's leather medical bag. "Hold him, Brother Fen. I'll give him the poppy to calm him, then I'll stitch him up myself. I've watched him do it often enough. I can—"

"Give me the bag." Cai thrust out a hand for it. He had no doubt that Oslaf could learn to do it, but his first few tries would be cross-stitch, just as Cai's had been. Danan had made him practise on a dead sheep. "I said give it to me!"

"You can't do this yourself."

"Maybe not. Maybe I'll...die while you argue about it."

He snatched for the bag again. This time, to his relief, Fen caught it and dumped it on the ground beside him. "What do you need?"

"The sheep gut and that bone needle. Thread it for me. Prop me up."

Gunnar's blade had sliced him cleanly. He managed the first four stitches himself, his jaw clenched, head arching back onto Fen's shoulder. Blood flowed over his hands, and Oslaf, sobbing, kept wiping enough of it away for him to see.

"Don't cry, stupid boy. You'll have to be doctor here if this doesn't work, you hear me?" That hadn't helped—Oslaf wept harder. "You'll know more than I did when I started. Fen, lift me up a bit more. I can't—"

"Oslaf, give him the poppy."

"What? No. It'll make me incapable."

"I see how this is done now." Fen, still propping him, reached round and took the needle from his hand. It was slick with blood—Cai couldn't hold on to it. He opened his mouth to protest, and the neck of a glass vial slipped between his teeth. Oslaf, still weeping but surprisingly strong, held his mouth open and tipped the oily, bitter liquid down his throat.

Stupid boy. You've given me too much. But the truth was that Cai didn't know how it was meant to feel. He'd never used it on himself. He'd seen his patients drift off smiling in the drug's embrace, and he'd wondered, but the stuff was too precious for experimentation. Oslaf sat back, watching anxiously. Cai wanted to tell him there was nothing to worry about. He wanted to tell Fen, now drawing the edges of his wound together and neatly punching the needle through, how brave and beautiful he was. How quick to learn...

Cai turned his head and whispered it to him, ending it with a kiss, and Fen gave a kind of sobbing chuckle Cai could feel through his spine and kissed him back, roughly, not taking his eyes off his work. "Good stuff that old witch brews up for you, isn't it? Lie still."

Cai wanted nothing better. Fen had kissed him, here in front of everyone. Fen had come to rescue him from Gunnar—chosen him, and the horror attendant on that choice slipped away from Cai, just as every bad thing was slipping away. Even the pain was becoming a sweet fire. He hid his face against Fen's neck so no one could see that the next punch of the needle through his flesh was a pleasure to him, a shattering relief. He was in Fen's hands. Fen was stitching him together—drawing the dark down around him in warm, beating wings—making him whole.

Chapter Sixteen

At first there was only sky. It brightened and darkened, sometimes incredibly fast—the chariot of the sun driven westward by an insane charioteer, so maybe Fen had pushed aside old Lugh or Phoebus Apollo and seized the reins himself—and sometimes with an agonising slowness. There was one night that lasted for all eternity, and not all the kindly hands on him, not even the embrace that eventually closed round him, rocking him and stroking his hair, could make the stars give way to dawn. Then the passage of time began again, and Cai, throat sore from all the howling he had done but couldn't remember, surfaced enough to feel a little shame. To be aware of cold water trickling into his mouth, and his soiled clothing being peeled away from his body.

Only sky, and then a line appeared across it. One black bar and then another and another, and finally two more, cutting across the first ones lengthwise. Then there was a rich scent of dry straw and heather, and the sky began to vanish, one swathe at a time. The scents were pleasant, the sounds the workers made as they went about their business—muted, nevertheless hushed fiercely by someone from time to time—soothing to him, and he slept.

"You should have let Oslaf boil the water for you."

Cai considered this. There didn't seem to be any hurry. Fen, sitting cross-legged on the floor beside him, looked as if he had been there for hours. He was pale, Cai thought, and he hadn't bothered to keep himself as clean-shaven as he normally liked. He had lost weight.

Cai put out a hand. His arm was weak from the deep axe cut, but he knew that had been the least of his problems. Instead of turf or hard-packed earth, he felt smooth stone. He was no longer burning in the sun, or being flecked by autumn rain. He was warm, and the draughts that had made his bones ache had stopped. He lay watching Fen, who returned his gaze without expectation or hope.

"Have I had a fever?"

Fen leaned forwards. His expression changed indefinably—the

tiny shift of meltwater under ice. "Cai? You heard me?"

"Of course. What is it? You look dreadful."

"Those are the first sane words you've spoken in five days. You didn't know who I was."

"God. Five..." Cai tried to push himself up, and found that his limbs were made of overboiled mashed turnip. "Where am I?"

"Where the dormitory barn used to be."

"Is it...? Did it burn down?"

"Everything did. We've rigged up shelters from the ruins."

"Everything..."

Cai was about to ask more when the willow screen blocking the doorway was suddenly shifted aside. Oslaf entered cautiously, a bucket in one hand, Cai's medical bag over his shoulder. "I'll bathe him this time, Fen. You really ought to rest, if..."

The bucket clattered down. Water was too hard to haul up from the well to be lightly regarded, and Oslaf caught it on instinct before it could spill. Then he stumbled over to Cai, knelt and planted a fervent, noisy kiss to his brow. "My brother. We'd given you up."

"I seem to have caused trouble." Cai didn't have the strength to push Oslaf back, and submitted while the boy retrieved the bucket and began to wash him.

Fen had gone to stand in the far corner of the makeshift shelter. Oslaf glanced at him. "He's never left your side," he said quietly. "Apart from to help us build, and...other things. He hasn't slept."

Cai knew about the *other things*. He knew the hawthorns would be shadowing a new row of quiet heaps of earth. Wilf, Marcus, Demetrios... Who else? He drew breath to ask. Then he too looked at Fen. "Oslaf, I could really use some food."

"Well, I'm not sure you should start eating straight away. You always make us start with thin gruel and water, after—"

"Oslaf, dear." Cai patted the boy's face.

"What?"

"Just get out."

"Oh."

He disappeared, tugging the willow door back into place behind him. Cai lay still for a few moments. He touched the floor again, then the mattress beneath him. It was clean and dry and had been raised a little off the floor on some kind of frame to keep him clear of the cold stone. His probing fingers found the front of his cassock, also clean. Cai knew what an effort it took to wrestle a feverish man into one of those, or even a deadweight one. He had been scrupulously cared for.

"Fen."

The figure in the shadows stirred. He came to Cai's bedside slowly, a sculpture brought unexpectedly to life and still stiff in its limbs. Neither spoke. Then Cai summoned up all his strength and hitched his lead-weighted body to the far side of the bed.

Fen lay down beside him. He propped himself on one elbow and gazed into Cai's face, a scrutiny Cai returned with silent fervour. Fingertips brushed lips, new hollows under cheekbones and eyes, taking an inventory of damage. Together they tugged up Cai's robes far enough to examine the stitched-up hole in his side. They were matching scar for scar now—Cai stroked the place under Fen's ribs where his own blade had entered, and Fen bent to press four solemn kisses around the new wound, above, below, one to each side, as if in benediction, to set a seal on the life that had almost spilled itself from there. His hair was like warm silk on Cai's belly. If he'd touched him, brushed his lips an inch further south, Cai would have raised his flag for him, half-dead as he was. But Fen rested his brow for a moment, then shook with a convulsive yawn.

There was something better even than their coupling. Cai discovered it, drawing Fen's head down to his shoulder, tears stinging the roots of his lashes at the revelation. There was the place where all passion and strength had been spent. Fen was asleep the instant he lay down, warm as winter fire at Cai's side. There was the place where they would seek one another, beyond the furthest reach of desire. On battlefields, beaches, hollows in the dunes where they had loved one another till their coming was only dry spasms, scraping, painful... Beyond all of those places, here they would be. He pressed tighter into Fen's embrace. This place had forever in it. Time couldn't end it, nor even the limits of life. Not distance—not even the wastes of the wild North Sea.

When he was well enough, Fen took him outside to see the new world. He stood, leaning on Fen's arm, looking down across the sweep of green turf. The monastery Cai had helped rebuild had been only a shadow of Theo's, but there had been a church, a refectory, the remains of the hall where Theo and then Aelfric had kept their quarters. Cai had had his infirmary, and a dream of the restored scriptorium. A dormitory barn, and half a dozen outbuildings for their beasts and crops...

Now the place looked as it must have when the first pilgrim monks from Iona and the western coasts had come here. Every building had fallen. The brethren had made Cai his shelter in the corner of the dormitory, where two tumbled walls remained, but other than that they hadn't tried to restore what had been. They had started again. The stones from the ruins had been cleared, and all across the turf, small round huts were rising.

Beehive cells. Cai had admired the remains of them on the tidal islets, where the plain wooden cross marked the far edge of faith and devotion. They were easy to build, if you knew the art of corbelling. They needed no roof and contained no timbers for Vikings to burn down. They were pure in their way, returning to nature's simplest and most perfect shape, all the centuries of mathematical learning that had given birth to the right angle—how to make it, measure it, build with it—blown away on the sea wind. They were one step forwards from a cave, the most basic human habitation that could be endured.

"They had to have shelters," Fen said quietly. There was an edge of unease in his voice, as if he had read Cai's thoughts. "A man came from the village—that idiot who wanted to burn Danan. He still makes the huts for his beasts like this. He showed us how."

Cai squeezed his arm. "You did right. The village... Is it still standing?"

"More or less. And the men and women left when you told them to. They are grateful for their survival. That's why Godric came up here to help us. He seems a changed man."

Cai chuckled. "You should have checked his rump for the mark of Barda's sandal. This is good, Fen—all the things you've done. I am grateful too. And I have to get back to work."

"Worry about that when you can walk a straight line on your own."

"But...who is looking after the sick men? Where are they?"

"It was a sharp fight, beloved. Sometimes it happens this way. There were only survivors, who got away with scratches, and..."

"And the dead." Cai swallowed. Fen's arm went powerfully tight round his waist, and he braced himself not to huddle into his embrace, plead exhaustion and be taken back to the world behind the willow screen, where sickness had shielded him from all the things he didn't want to know. "Will you help me down to the churchyard?"

"Can you walk that far?"

"I don't know. But I have to see."

Five new mounds beneath the hawthorns. Cai, who had managed the walk but poured out the last of his strength, asked which one was Wilfrid's and knelt beside it. This was the season when the yarrow's long flowering made its blossoms significant and lovely on the open turf. Most of the summer's colour was fading back to green and tawny gold, but the yarrow shone bright on this overcast day, its tough, aromatic heads like a sprinkling of snow. It had feathery leaves. Crushing one between his fingers, Cai breathed in the scent of its oil, counting off its medicinal properties in his head to ward off newer knowledge. Fevers, bleeding, healing—one, two, three. It was no good. Marcus, Demetrios, Wilf. "Who else?" A cold pain struck him. "Not Eyulf."

"No. No, we've kept him away from you because he would have leapt on you like a dog and pulled out your stitches. One of these is Aelfric's. Your brethren wouldn't have him down in the crypt with Theo, and I thought him better out here."

"He'd have thought so too," Cai said dully, "at the very end. And the other?"

"Brother John died too."

"John? He shouldn't have been fighting. He was broken. He was..."

"I know. The noise scared him and he ran. It was a night when fighting was safer than trying to hide."

Cai choked faintly. "Much good that did Aelfric. Much good it did any of us."

Fen came to stand beside him. Cai rested his head against his thigh, and Fen roughly stroked his hair. "Much good it ever does. But what is the choice?"

"I thought you lived for the battle." Shame burned through Cai as soon as the words were out. "Forgive me. God, forgive me, Fen—your brother. Where does he lie?"

"I have to tell you about Gunnar." Again came that caress. Cai closed his eyes, surrendering, listening. "In the Dane Lands we are brought up to love whatever is strongest. So I loved my brother—without question, although he was savage, rapacious, so full of greed and bloodlust he wanted to swallow the whole world. A few months ago, he deposed old Sigurd. He took the Torleik for his own—violated all our laws of clan and rightful succession." Fen let go a painful breath and knelt stiffly at Cai's side. "Still I honoured him in death. Your brethren helped me. We placed him and the other *vikingr* fallen in the ship they left behind, and we torched it and cast it out to sea."

Beyond the grey clouds, the rain beginning to patter onto the fresh graves, Cai could see it. Viking burials were legend along the north shore. That beautiful boat, her final cargo laid out on her deck—the night, and the hungry flames reflecting off the water... "I grieve for you. Your love for him was more than the worship of brute power."

"That love has died in me. The decision to leave me here was his. He knew that I was still alive. He told the crew my injuries were hopeless and ordered them to leave. I was Sigurd's other heir, his only rival. He seized his opportunity. It's raining, Cai. Let me take you back."

"Wait. How do you know this? About Sigurd and what Gunnar did to him—what he did to you?"

"One of the Torleik fallen spoke to me before he died."

Fen stopped short. They were shoulder to shoulder, and Cai felt him swallow the rest as if it had been a stone. He sought Fen's hand blindly, wondering at its chill. "What more do you have to tell me?"

"Nothing of significance. Come back with me now. You're cold."

"No—*you* are. Fen—your brother abandoned you here, but the waves didn't get you. I did. I've lived at your side. I eat with you, breathe with you. I can feel whatever you're trying not to tell me now, bottled up inside you like water behind a dam."

"You feel too much." It was a low growl, and Fen turned to him, his grip closing hard. "What more would you have of me? Your brethren are dead here. If you want more bad tidings, we lost half our grain and all the beasts we'd hidden in the caves."

The news almost distracted Cai. His mind tried to seize the new problem—their reduced numbers, how far the food that remained could be spread amongst those left alive. "I can weather all that," he said grimly. "Did the *vikingr* take the animals?"

"No. Wilfrid was so eager for the fight that he didn't pen them in properly. They escaped."

"Then the goats will probably make their way home. And we might be able to round up the sheep. Yes, we can weather that—no thanks to you, shepherd." Cai laid a tender hand on Wilfrid's grave. "Now tell me the rest."

"When Gunnar took over from Sigurd, it threw the tribe into chaos. They fought among themselves until half their warrior chieftains were dead, and when the rival clans who live in the marshlands around knew their weakness, they moved in. They are besieged. They have no winter stores, and now—with Gunnar gone—they have no leader. Caius, beloved—"

"Quiet. I'm tired now. Please take me back."

Cai knew how to make a man love him. The mechanics of desire were simple. Theo had taught that plainly, to men thrown together night and day, most of them healthy and young. They could and did operate without permission from the mind or soul. A monk could be as devoted as he wished, and still be plagued by them, and it was not a source of shame. Control them as best you can—cold plunges, meditations, prayer—but all can still be lost. Even when the mind says no and means it, the flesh can have its way.

Fen's mind was certainly saying no. His mouth too, until Cai had clapped a hand across it. Fen had left him alone until darkness fell, and then he had come as always since the raid, to sleep beside him, warm him, make sure he came to no harm in the night. And Cai had seized him and begun to change his body's no to yes. Cai knew men's flesh and how it worked—knew this one best of all.

Fen fought his way out from under. He took hold of Cai's shoulders and dumped him down onto the bed. "What are you doing? Don't make me hurt you!"

"You are going back to them."

A terrible silence, Fen's eyes blazing down into his. "Caius. Stop."

"The next time we meet could be on a battlefield. Why the hell don't we start now?"

He smacked Fen hard across the face. Other demons could be called up too, and this one lived close to Fen's surface. He wasn't a tolerant man. The trick worked instantly—Fen cuffed him back. He had laughed until he wept when Cai had told him the doctrine of turning the other cheek. But he wasn't the same creature who had been marooned here in the spring. His eyes filled with tears. "Stop this."

Cai dragged him down into a kiss that tasted of blood. There was the surge of his erection. Even unwilling, Cai could command his body. Perhaps the soul would follow. "You are going home. Why? They betrayed you."

"My brother. Not my whole clan. They are starving, diseased. I can't abandon them."

"I can't let you go."

"Then come with me. Leave your brethren behind and sail with me. Can you?"

Cai stopped struggling. He lay still, his breath coming in great gulps. The prospect unrolled itself before him. At first it felt like an answer. He could taste the salt now, hear the rush of the wind as it had sung to him on their way back from Addy's island. It wouldn't be easy. He would be a Christian among hostile strangers, lucky to escape with his hide. But to be on shipboard with Fen, perhaps with one of those great dragon heads dipping and rising with the motion of the prow...

Leaving his brethren behind. Oslaf and Eyulf and the rest of them, the little community that had been smashed to pieces again and again, this time almost to oblivion. The men who looked to him to lead them, flawed though he was.

For many years now, Cai had thought of himself as a grown man. He had left his father's kingdom and come here, stiff with pride and independence. He had trained an army, fought and killed with them. He had taken a lover, in the teeth of hellfire doctrine and the religion he had vowed to serve.

But he had been a child. Adulthood didn't lie in action, or the assertion of his will. It was here in this moment. Fen couldn't have imposed it upon him more deeply. *Forget them so you can be with me...* Impossible. But Cai had asked that very thing of him.

Cai grew up fiercely, gasping at the pain of it. Fen was still holding him fast at the focus of that merciless gaze, making him see. No nobility, no fire. Just the slow, cold dawning of realisation. He had taken the men of Fara into his hands, and now he couldn't let them fall. "Go and look in the box in that far corner."

"What?"

"Just go and open it. I had Oslaf bring it up from the cellar, after you had talked to me by the graves and I knew what you were going to do."

Fen detached himself stiffly from their embrace. After a moment he returned, his expression wondering. In his left hand he clasped the magnificent helmet Cai had found on the beach and hidden away from them both. "You told me this had been lost."

"I picked it up from the beach that night. I put it away in a box in my infirmary."

"Well, I could have used it before now, you idiot."

"I know. I couldn't bear the sight of it." Despite his words, Cai took the beautifully worked thing from Fen, and when his lover knelt beside him, carefully drew it down over the shining red hair. "There. Now you look as you did when I first saw you. How you'll look when you become a stranger to me again."

"Cai, don't." Fen's voice cracked, giving the lie to the blank ferocity of the helmet's mask. "Take it off me, for God's sake."

"All right." Cai obeyed him. "But when you go, you will have that, and your shield and your sword." He buried his fists in Fen's hair. He drew his head down, barriers of resistance dropping inside him.

Fen kissed him with a tenderness that was new, even after all their exchanges. "Forgive me, Cai. I swear I will come back to you."

"Don't make any promises. You don't know what you'll find there."

"Nothing like you. Not ever."

"And..." Shifting, Cai took his weight more thoroughly, welcoming the blossom of pain in his side. "Understand me, love. You have to go now."

"What? No. I will wait till you're well. Till the rebuilding is done and you have some defences against—"

"Listen. I can behave myself like a good soldier—a good monk, a good leader, whatever kind of man I'm meant to be. I can do that, maybe for a day, maybe two. More, if I have to. But if you drag out your leaving any longer than that..."

"Don't." Another of those kisses, lingering, deep. "Oh, don't."

"If you drag it out, I'll fall. I'll weep at your feet in front of the very men I have to lead."

"You know," Fen said hoarsely, "making my decision wasn't

hard—not once I'd seen I had to. No, it was easy, because I pushed it away and made it little. I told myself I wouldn't leave for weeks—and it wouldn't really matter even then, because I would come back. I'd promised you that. Already in my mind I *was* back."

"And I won't let you promise."

"No."

"Won't let you push it away."

Fen's expression didn't alter. But two hot splashes hit Cai's face—just two, as if all the grief in the world had been distilled into them. The tears of a Viking warrior.

Cai wrapped his arms around him. That wasn't enough, and he lifted his thighs, groaning, and embraced him that way too. Fen's hard shaft pushed into the crease of his body, ploughing in tight behind his balls, the dear familiar trackway. Cai nodded, pressing consent to Fen's face and neck in mute kisses. Yes. Fen smelled of apples—he must have been helping to store the crop they had left up in the drying lofts. His skin was warm as if printed with the memory of sunlight, and Cai's ailing flesh yearned and opened to the sheer health and strength of it, starving for his heat. "Yes. Push in."

"Not like this. I'll get something."

"No. No wheat oil, no butter filched from Hengist's kitchen, no flax." They'd tried all of those and managed on less—on seawater, sweat, spit. "Not now. There isn't time."

Fen froze for an instant, confusion palpable. "No time? You want me to leave so soon as—"

"No, you idiot. I mean I can't wait for you."

"Oh..."

"What do you do to me? Don't let me come on my own, empty and alone like this."

"I'll hurt you."

"I want that, this once. Carve your shape into me. So I won't ever forget."

Chapter Seventeen

Eldra was magnificent and ready for her journey. There was no longer a barn or a stable to shelter her, so Cai had tied her to a post in the field to knock a week's worth of mud out of her sleek coat. His palm was raw from the many handfuls of straw the job had taken. Exhausted, he leaned back against the fence.

Yes, she was fine. Cai looked at her for something else to do, but she tipped her head at him and blew a derisive snort through clean pink nostrils. She knew she was good enough. That left Cai alone with the knowledge of his own failings, and the rest of the day on his hands.

No good. He pushed upright. If he'd still had Broc's chariot, he could have killed some time and truth in checking it over. Fittings to be polished, wheels squinted at from back and front to make sure they were properly aligned. Linseed oil to rub into leather till it was supple and resistant to salt sea winds. But the raiders had turned Broc's sacred heirloom to ash along with the monastery's ox-ploughs, carts and hay wagon. There was nothing to stand between Cai and the knowledge that Fenrir was leaving tomorrow at dawn.

All these preparations had been his way of staving off the truth. Irrational, because with every swipe of the straw across Eldra's coat he had made her more fit for her new owner, but this way he brought the racing minutes under some kind of control. If Cai was giving Fen a horse to aid his journey, it would be the best horse available. If he was providing supplies to send him on his way, they would be fresh and wholesome. And that reminded him—he had told Hengist to pack up some saddlebags with victuals, dried fish and oatcake that would serve Fen if his perishable food ran out on the long road south. Cai had better go and check there was enough. That Hengist was doing it right. Then another aspect of this departure would be his, a thing inside him, not a hook in his guts hauling them out.

He led Eldra up into the pasture at the top of the slope. It was drier here than anywhere else, so that even if she did choose to roll and besmirch herself, the damage wouldn't be too bad. What Cai wanted to do was let her go. He wanted to slap her on the rump and send her pelting off to some far distance where no one could ever retrieve her. He wanted to fasten up the gates of Fara, hide every loaf and apple in the place and tell Fen that if he wanted food, he damn well could stay here and grow it like anybody else.

Cai's throat contracted. He gave a low, wrenching moan he was grateful nobody could hear. No one but Eldra, anyway. She thumped him with her muzzle, right in his slow-healing stitches, then trotted away with her freshly groomed tail bannered high.

He took the clifftop path to avoid passing through the new huts. Since yesterday and his visit to the graves, he was formally up and about, the reprieve of sickness ended. He couldn't get from his bunk to the latrines without half a dozen interceptions, questions. *Brother Cai, Brother Cai.*

Abbot Cai.

He didn't mind. He knew most of the answers and remembered how it was. In troubled times, good to have a benign elder to direct your works, or simply bestow upon them a nod and a smile. Yes, the church would be rebuilt. No, there would be no canonical hours, only morning and evening prayers, as in Theo's time. Who was Cai to decide such things? He didn't know, but the answers came to him clearly and cleanly when they had to, based on common sense and his long acquaintance with these few surviving men. No one had ever asked Aelfric anything. Theo had usually travelled about at the heart of a small group, eager for his teachings and his word.

Cai had no teachings to offer, but he would do what he could. He just couldn't do it now, not until he had once more strangled into submission his infantile rage. A benign elder? Emerging onto the clifftop, taking deep breaths of the fresh breeze, Cai choked on bitter laughter. He felt like a child.

And, dear God, there was a ship on the horizon. He stumbled, grabbing at a fence post for balance. No. There wasn't a single thing, not a scrap of resistance left, inside him or in the remains of the monastery, to fight off another raid. "No..."

"No!"

Cai glanced down the track, startled at the echo. Fen was running towards him, as little like a monk as Cai had ever seen him—a proud, athletic figure, his cassock only incidental, a becoming second skin, even with a waxed-linen apron on top. "No, Cai," he called, coming into sight of him. "Not this time. Just take them and get them inland."

Make a run for it. Even now Cai's hillfort blood rebelled at the idea. Fen came to a breathless halt at his side, and Cai shielded his eyes, trying to make out the details of this new terror. It was one ship only. That was something, except that it was huge...

A vessel such as Cai had never seen. She was ungainly, more like a river barge than a seagoing carrier. She was magnificent, though. The sunlight was dancing off golden trimmings on her prow. Her sides were decked with purple cloths, and her sail... Cai took Fen's hand. He hadn't meant to—had meant to teach himself how not touching him would feel and start to live with it. But it was so natural, and natural as breathing the returning embrace of Fen's arm around his waist. So there they stood—lovers, brothers, comrades, watching the sea. "That sail. The sign on it—that's the bishop's crozier."

"His what?"

"His staff, you heathen. Do you see it—the spiral curving back on itself?"

"Yes. Who would bring such a ship out here?"

"I don't know. That's the emblem of the diocese at Hexham. Only the bishop himself would have the authority, or...well, a king, but that's even less likely than a bishop, this far north of civilisation."

"It looks as if it's heading to East Fara. The island."

Cai wasn't certain which of them had begun the walk down to the beach. Fen's hold on him distracted him from many things, quieted his mind even when he wished to stay alert, cogent, angry. He only came to surface again when the cliff track narrowed and Fen let him go, pushing him gently ahead to take the lead. Why were they coming here? Cai had a dozen things to do, and Fen from the look of him had been helping with the slaughter of their few remaining pigs. But as they made their way downslope, he saw that the vision of this strange, majestic ship had exerted its pull on others of his brethren too. One by one they appeared among the dunes, leaving their tasks behind them. Perhaps they were only relieved that the vessel hadn't heralded another raid, and wished to watch it out of sight. Or maybe, like Cai, they couldn't take their eyes off the misty place on the horizon where it was slowly fading, in flickering purples and flashes of sun.

The Fara brethren settled on the beach, on the dry sand and the scattered rocks where the seals liked to bask. Cai knew he should send them back to work. He was no Aelfric, but he shouldn't allow a reasonless midday idleness like this. They were working monks, and outside of mealtimes and prayer, their labours were mapped out for them—especially now, when barely a stone lay on a stone at Fara to show what the place was meant to be. There was no excuse for Cai himself to be here, hitching up the hem of his robes and scrambling onto a rock so he could see.

Fen took his elbow to give him a boost and steady him, and then he too clambered up and sat at Cai's side—to windward, Cai noted, shielding him, keeping him warm. "Is she still heading out?"

"I'm not sure. She seems to be just...hanging there. Drifting."

An attentive silence fell. The survivors of the last raid had been subdued men, but still when they came together there were murmurs about aching limbs, the occasional burst of laughter. They were quiet now, their attention fixed on the gilded ship.

She came about. The movement was imperceptible at first, and then the noonday sun caught her helm in a blaze. At first Cai was surprised by her new heading, but then everything faded away but her beauty. She was making for shore. All around him, the gathered men came to their feet, shielding their eyes to watch. Cai got up too, and he and Fen picked their way down past the rock pools and over constellations of pale cockleshells and barnacles until they were standing at the sea's edge.

The ship was too deep in the hull to draw very far into the shallows. A couple of hundred yards out, her crew trimmed the sail. They were vigorous men in neat uniforms, a match for any interested *vikingr* pirates. Cai could make them out clearly now, as well as the ancient gateway symbol on the canvas. Not just episcopal authority, then, but secular, and the highest in the land—the mark of the kingdom of Bernicia.

The vessel came to a standstill. First the crew ran to drop anchor, and then a burly quartet of them winched up a smaller craft, a tender-boat fit to make the run between ship and shore. In it was a solitary figure, balancing with fragile dignity while the tender swayed on its ropes and was lowered by slow, careful degrees into the water. Three of the crewmen scrambled down rope ladders and boarded it too. Two of them took up the oars, and the third stood behind the passenger, apparently as a kind of honour guard. All were heavily armed, showing rich purple cloth beneath their breastplates, their shields also marked with the crozier and gate.

Only when the tender was far enough inshore to rock on the breakers did Cai understand. "My God. Who have they got there?"

"They stopped off at Addy's island, didn't they? He told us they were after him to make him bishop."

"Didn't we agree he was mad?"

"Well, does he look sane to you?"

Addy—Aedar, the hermit of Fara—was sitting bolt upright in the boat. His hair and beard were streaming in the wind, untamed as ever, but over his cassock he was wearing a sumptuous gold and purple cloak. He had an air of having been bundled into it. In his hands he was clutching a staff, at once like his old shepherd's crook and entirely alien to it—the mark of the shepherd of souls, its old functional shape wrought out of use and into beauty, the bishop's spiralled crozier. He saw Cai and Fen, and used this mighty symbol of authority to wave at them, a broad grin breaking across his face. "My friends!" he yelled across the windswept distance between them. "I am pleased to see you. Wait there."

The oarsmen stopped their efforts and brought the boat to a smooth halt in the shallows. One of them promptly leapt out and held up his hands. The old man accepted his aid but waved off the attentions of the guardsman who was trying to hold his cloak and cassock out of the water. Once out of the boat, he hitched up his garments for himself, gave his escort a friendly nod and began to splash through the wavelets, digging his crozier into the sand for balance.

Cai wanted to run to him, but something held him still. Fen too was motionless beside him. They waited until Addy was right in front of them, and then the three stood and looked at one another, all of them stilled with wonder at the changes. Addy broke the seagull silence at last. "You see," he said sadly, "it's as I feared. They've come for me at last."

"Against your will?" Fen glanced at the soldiers, assessing his next fight. "Just make a signal. Caius and I will assist you."

"No, no." Addy chuckled and patted Fen's muscular arm. "What a wolf it is! No, I am here of my own will, if not of my own desire. They came in this great ugly boat of theirs. I tried to refuse, but the young man with them was insistent—quite insistent. He agreed to let me stop and say goodbye to my friends at Fara, but I fear he's anxious for my return. I mustn't keep him waiting long."

Cai followed Addy's swift glance back over his shoulder. Standing at the rail of the ship was a slender, fair-haired man. He was dressed quite differently to the soldiers, in a gorgeous cloak of scarlet, richly embroidered all over in gold. It was fastened at the shoulder with a brooch whose jewels flashed visibly even from this far away. He didn't look like a man much accustomed to having to wait.

Fen's distance vision was better than Cai's. "That lad in the prow," Cai said. "Is he wearing a crown?"

"Not by *vikingr* standards. Our chieftains have better than that. But..."

Cai racked his brains for a name. News came slowly to Fara, and borderlines and monarchs changed fast. "Addy—did King Ecgbert of Bernicia come to fetch you?"

"Aye, it seems so. A pleasant young man. He took my spade from me—I was digging my garden—and gave me this staff. Put this cloak on me with his own hands. Still I would have refused him. I love my solitude, my seals and my birds. But men like your new abbot are springing up everywhere, and I can't defeat them from here. So I shall go among them as a teacher and a leader, take up arms in my own way, and try what that will do." He adjusted his cloak, one-handed and awkward, as if it weighed more heavily on him than he could bear. "Oh, Caius. Tell your brethren to stand—the occasion doesn't warrant this."

Cai turned. Behind him on the sand, Hengist and Cedric and the others—even Eyulf, his mouth wide open in amazement—had drawn together into an orderly group and fallen to their knees.

"Some of them know of your legend, sir," Cai said hoarsely. "And all of them recognise the signs of your authority. It's what they wish."

"Well, it seems strange to me, but..." The old man fell silent. His attention focussed on the cliff and the green shoulder of Fara's great rock. "Caius. What happened here?"

"There was a raid. The worst we've ever known, and Aelfric was killed in it. So you don't need to worry about him anymore, but God help the rest of us—everything is gone."

"My son..." Addy tottered as if he would fall, but he gently rejected Cai's supporting hand. "There are so few of you. Who else has died?"

"Wilfrid, our goatherd. Marcus, one of Aelfric's men who fought bravely with us. Demetrios, our shepherd, and a brother called John, who was hurt in the first raid this spring and was meant to be protected. But I couldn't protect him." Suddenly his failure, and the tally of the dead, was too much for Cai. He covered his face.

"My son, I can't comfort you. I can't bring back your dead. All I have to give you is my blessing. Will you kneel for it—even though you are a soldier and the new leader of these men?"

Cai hesitated. It wasn't pride—he didn't have an ounce of pride left in him—but it seemed so strange, to be asked this under the clear northern sky, in the sunlight that shone on all men equally. Addy, who had entered his mind as a creature at one with wind, sun and rain, wouldn't have asked it. Perhaps it was part of his new work—and, after all, a king was watching. Cai wouldn't let him down. He dropped to his knees on the sand.

"And will even Fenrisulfr, the fierce warrior, kneel?"

Cai held his breath. Fen had changed, but could still flash out like a thunderbolt when occasion called. But Fen thumped down beside him, and the two knelt like their brethren, awaiting the old man's word.

Addy looked them over. Something about them seemed to please him. He smiled unsteadily and gave another awkward tug at his cloak. "Not boys anymore," he said. "Not the rolling pups who washed up on my island a few months ago. How did that come to be, Caius? From fighting your fellow man?"

"No. It came from fighting with myself."

"Aye. And so are all our lonely, worthy victories won. I don't have a faithless rebel monk and a murderous Viking here with me now. I have battle-forged men who..." he paused, long enough to push a strand of red hair back from Fen's brow, "...who have both understood the nature of sacrifice. Thank God."

Now Addy in turn fell to his knees. He went down hard, as if beneath the weight of something. "Thank God," he repeated. His back was turned to the guards and the king on the ship. "At last I can get this damned treasure of Fara out from under here and into worthy hands—quick, before anyone sees."

He reached into his cloak. Something tumbled out into his lap—a box so heavy that he barely caught it before it slid into the sand. Cai had no idea how he had carried it or even stood upright. The box—no, a casket, with hinges and elaborate fastenings—was made of solid gold. Not Hibernian or *vikingr*... Danan the magpie had taught Cai to recognise both, and this was richer than either, a deep buttery yellow that glowed in the sun. It was beautifully worked. All around its edges little creatures danced, beasts that might have found their way from Leof's imagination, when he was drawing things Theo had described to him but he had never seen. Horses with long noses and awkward-looking humps to their backs, another breed whose neck had stretched to monstrous length, and glimmering all around this fantastic bestiary, jewels in colours Cai could never have dreamed of, let alone believed could be captured in stone. He put out a hand to touch the marvellous thing. He found Fen's hand in his way, and instead of finishing the gesture, turned his palm up. Fen seized it, grasping tight.

Addy watched them, his expression hard to read. "Yes," he said after a moment. "Worth a *vikingr* raid or two in itself, though greater treasures are to be found nearer to home, as you've found out. Listen to me carefully. This is not the secret Theo told you of while he was dying. The treasure lies inside. Don't open it now—wait till I am gone and you're alone." He shifted, drawing the edge of his robe across the casket to conceal its rainbow fires. "It is a lovely thing. It holds a book. Theo had travelled to the east, right to the ends of the Mid-Earth Sea, and he found a place where rebel pagan priests were guarding a small library, barely more than a cellar. In it were relics—brands snatched from the burning of a temple called the Serapeum, which in its turn had held the ancient treasures of the greatest library of all. Did Theo ever speak to you of Alexandria?"

Cai cast his mind back. He grasped Fen's hand, his one anchor in this strangeness. "Yes. Not often, though—it seemed to give him pain."

"He was a man who minded such things. Alexandria burned too, and scattered the learning of centuries to the four winds. The Christian Roman emperors needed to wipe out such scholarship. Much of it came from the Jews, from Arabs, from pagan Greeks, and by Theo's time—our time—it had all been deemed heretical. And Theo himself was under suspicion of heresy. That's why he was banished to his post on the world's western edge, and why you monks of Fara got such a splendid abbot for a while."

Addy sighed, patting the box. "He was a saint, a holy fool with little thought of his own safety. He bought as many of these forbidden books as he could afford, and when he was exiled he chose just one to carry with him, as much as he could conceal about his person. The rest were destroyed. When I met him on my voyage back from Rome, he was still grieving, clutching this one relic to his breast as if it had been a child. We spent weeks aboard that ship, and by the time we parted, he trusted me. He had heard of the raids on the north-coast monasteries, heard to his sorrow that Christianity even in these far-flung lands was beginning to fear science, mathematics, astronomy, all the wisdom of the ancient world. So he left the book, and this glorious casket, with me. I buried it on my island, Fenrisulfr, and you slept within yards of it. You were quite right—there are hidden tunnels at the back of my cave. How could I trust either of you then, even if Theo had told you part of the truth? You were nothing but flotsam, thrown up on my shores by the wind and the sea."

Cai swallowed hard. "I still don't understand. This book—no matter how marvellous it is... Theo said it would bring peace and stop the raids. How can any book do that?"

"I've wondered the same thing. I had hoped—I still do hope—that Theo saw in you a wisdom that would grow to interpret his words. What else did he say to you?"

"That the secret wasn't even in the book. That it was in the binding." Cai drew a rough breath. "Oh, I have failed him. My wisdom *didn't* grow. I've tried all I can to be like him, but..."

"Hush. Who could be like him? Who could ever be like you? Each of us has his path. They run close together sometimes—for life, if we are fortunate—but they never cross. Do you understand?"

"No," Cai said miserably. He was faint and sick, the hole in his side aching fiercely. Fen disentangled his hand and put an arm round his shoulders instead, and Cai leaned gratefully into his warmth. "No."

"Poor boy. You're sick, and I have kept you talking out here in the cold. I must go now and be..." He paused, gathering up his staff and using it to push onto his feet. "Aedar, Bishop of Hexham, it seems. Understand this one thing only. I love my faith and my church, and shadows are falling upon it. Only men like you can keep a light of knowledge burning till the darkness has passed. Will you try?"

"I'll try. I don't know how, but..."

"It's enough. You won't be hindered by any more abbots from Canterbury, I believe. These north lands are considered beyond salvation now, and Rome won't throw good men after bad. Fara is yours." He straightened up, lifting his crozier high so its ivory curve caught the light. "I will bless you and your brethren now. They've waited long enough. Er, Caius, that boy..."

"Which one, sir? Eyulf?"

"The one who seems weak in his wits, unless he knows some

benefit to eating sand... You should bring him to me. Not now, but the next time we meet."

"Will there be a next time?"

"Of course. Creation being eternal, all things must happen in time." He raised his free hand, extending it towards the gathered men. "*Benedicat vos omnipotens Deus, Pater, et Filius, et Spiritus Sanctus...*"

Cai closed his eyes and tried to take the blessing in good part. Creation might be eternal, but he was only flesh. With a few exceptions, men did not live long in the harsh north. He had seen more than twenty summers. Broccus, barely sixteen years older, was considered an old man, and Cai knew the wound draining strength from him now would take its toll in years at the end of his life. Perhaps that was the nature of the blessing. Cai was certain he had seen his finest days, his hottest, sweetest hours.

He opened his eyes and found twenty golden ones staring back at him. A flock of the black-and-white ducks who haunted the Fara isles had gathered out of nowhere and waddled close to Addy until they formed a kind of honour guard, their faces at once comical and solemn. One was so close that its beak had gone under his robe.

Addy finished his blessing. He looked down and gave a groan of exasperation, as if this was a regular problem for him. "Ah, you fools—found me out here, have you?" He gathered up his hem and gently shooed out the intruder. He turned and began to walk away, and they followed him, sea-gilded rumps swinging. "You fools," he continued, addressing them as if no one else existed, his voice fading into the breeze. "Didn't I tell you? I am not really going away. Or, if I am, I will be back. If not, I never was here, or I always was and always will be—sometimes I can't remember which it is." He reached the water's edge. The king in the ship looked up eagerly, and the soldiers jumped down to assist him, but he hitched his robes up and waded out alone, the Addy ducks swimming in his wake.

Cai sent his brethren back to their work. At first he felt like an impostor, as he always did when ordering men older, better, longer-serving than himself, but then despite his pain and weariness, his voice firmed. *These north lands are considered beyond salvation now.* Perhaps he need not be so afraid, if Fara was already lost. Perhaps the lost souls who lived there could do worse than him as a leader. They went without a murmur, as if his commands were what they expected and desired.

They hadn't seemed to expect him to dismiss Fen too, any more than they'd intruded on their privacy in the makeshift shelter. Perhaps they thought an abbot could do as he wished, keep whoever he wanted close to him. Pushing back that bitter thought, Cai went back to Fen's side. He settled on the sand beside him and turned the precious casket in his hands. He and Fen were alone. It was time to open up the treasure of Fara. He turned the box so that its hasps were facing Fen. "Will you? I'm almost afraid."

Fen smiled, shook his head. "No. This is your abbot Theo's gift to you."

"The man I once knew was ready to kill for this."

"The man you once knew would have killed for just one of its jewels."

Cai looked up. Fen was gazing at him through strands of windblown hair, his eyes bright with sorrow and mischief. In some ways he was transfigured—in others just the same, unapologetically the man he had always been. With unsteady fingers, Cai unfastened the clasps. No fleck of rust could corrode the magnificent gold, and the box opened easily.

By contrast, the book inside was plain. Its cover, though made of good leather, was worn thin in patches that corresponded to fingermarks. How many hands must have lifted and opened it, over how many centuries, to wear away that thick hide? Lifting it out, Cai found how easily his own fingers fitted into the same gaps. Yes, the cover was almost worn away. A dirty leather strip was wrapped round the whole book to prevent it from falling apart. It was only loosely knotted—cradling the volume in one arm, he undid the strip and let it fall. A little sand went with it, skittering in the breeze for long enough to show its deep red tint, then flying off to vanish in the pale north-lands gold. Desert sand... Cai remembered now that Theo had talked of the hump-backed horses depicted on the casket's sides, not horses at all but beasts of burden called *cameli*. Maybe this book was a bestiary, an account of desert travels, or...

No. Nothing to do with palm trees or beasts. The first page was a diagram, beautifully laid out and labelled—first in a strange foreign scrawl, and then in crisp Latin—of the three heavenly bodies. Sol, Terra, Luna. Sun, Earth and Moon—with the sun at the centre, and the moon going stepdance around and around the round Earth. The next page showed a man in exotic robes kneeling at the foot of a building such as Cai had never seen before, nothing but four triangular faces that met at an apex. The man had a compass like Theo's, and he was busy taking measurements from this apex to a brilliant overhanging star.

Cai closed the book. He couldn't see for tears. Fen's arms went round him from behind, and he clutched him, hard enough to bruise, still keeping the volume held tenderly close to his chest. "Fen, it's Theo's book. The one he was copying bit by bit from memory."

"The *Gospel of Science*?"

"Yes. Oh, God—all his learning. All here."

"I'm glad. Is it what you imagined?"

"A thousand times more. But I still don't understand." Cai struggled round, leaned his brow against Fen's. It was a gesture of tenderness from the earliest days of their short time together, when words had almost failed, when two heads were better than one, when words and thoughts alike were both about to melt into a kiss. "I don't know how it can bring peace."

"Have you looked into the binding? Theo said the answer was there."

"Yes. Not in the book but in the binding… It scarcely has any left. The pages were all held together by…"

The dirty leather ribbon was still fluttering on the sand. The wind was about to take it. Fen shot out a hand and pinned it down, catching its tail at the last instant. "This?"

"Yes. It was tied round it, binding it all together." Realisation hit. "Oh, Fen. The binding."

It was nothing but a dirty ribbon, more tattered than the book itself. A cloud had passed before the sun, and not until it was gone did Cai make out the markings. He'd seen something like them on grave-marker stones in the older Saxon villages. A series of straight lines burned into the leather—mostly vertical, easy to carve into stones, broken by angles, horizontals. "This looks like lettering."

"It is. Runic. My people use a pure form, the Saxons a degraded one."

"Oh, of course."

"This is pure." Fen took the ribbon, passed it slowly through his fingers. "It's old, though—older almost than I can translate, and the first few letters are gone. Wait, though. I have it. *The cord...*" He turned the ribbon, held it to the light. "*The cord that binds the wolf where fetters fail.*"

His colour drained. Still clutching the ribbon, he sat down hard on the sand.

"Fen? What is it?"

"It is Gleipnir. In the legends of the Dane Lands, the people you call *vikingr*... No. It can't be."

"Tell me anyway."

"In *vikingr* legend, there is a great wolf. I have told you of him. I was named after him—Fenrisulfr. This wolf became troublesome, even to the gods—he was a god himself, you see—and so they tried to defeat him. They tied him with huge iron chains. But the wolf broke through those as if they had been spider webs."

Cai closed his hand on Fen's fist. It was chilly as marble. "A strong wolf."

"Yes, but a stupid one. The gods commanded the dwarves to create a new binding—thin as a ribbon of silk, but unbreakable. Now, this wolf being arrogant, he laughed when he saw it. And when the gods challenged him, he let himself be bound." Fen's voice softened and caught. "And he found out, as I have, that any strength may be conquered by the right chains. The ribbon was named Gleipnir. It passed into our legends as a symbol, a thing that could bind and defeat all *vikingr* power. It's what Sigurd was looking for, raiding so fiercely to find. I didn't realise. This is the treasure of Fara."

"This poor scrap of leather?"

"Yes. You don't understand what it means to us. More than gold, more than any plunder." Fen shivered, as if a ghost had touched him, a spectre from a future opening up to him for the first time. "If I have this... With this, I can command the Torleik. They will see it as their strength being returned to them. When the other tribes know that we have it, they will fear us. If I bear it home with me now, perhaps I can control them. Perhaps I can bring an end to the slaughter on these shores."

Cai didn't let go of his hand. "Eldra is ready for you. Hengist has prepared some travelling clothes and packed up supplies for your journey."

Fen glanced up. His gaze returned from wide inner vistas to the detail in front of him, and pain creased his brow. "I don't have to go now. We said tomorrow, didn't we?"

"Aye, but think what will happen. I am very tired—I've sat down here for too long. Halfway up the cliff, my strength will run out, and you will pick me up. Is it not so?"

"Yes, of course."

"I will protest and tell you I'm not a village maiden or a pig for you to run off with. And you will take no notice and carry me back to our shelter, and kick the willow door into place so no one can see. By that time your hold on me will have become more than I can bear."

"Yes." A terrible comprehension dawned in Fen's eyes. "And your weight in my arms, your warmth and your scent..."

"Yes. So you will lay me down, and even though I am half-dead from weariness, I will open my body to you, my heart, any thing of me you want, and we will struggle and fuck until sleep takes us. And wake in the knowledge that you must go, and I must stay here, and comfort each other for that until we are fucking again. Is it not so?"

Fen couldn't speak, but his silence gave Cai the answer he needed.

"And so it will go on. We will tear each other apart."

Fen lurched upright, a huge spring of a movement that almost knocked Cai over on the sand. "I will go. I will send someone down to help you home."

Gleipnir, that worn scrap of nothing, was fluttering from his hand. Cai caught the end of it. "This cord," he whispered, not looking up. "This thing that has the power to bind all Vikings... Won't it bind just one?"

"Yes. Yes, if you choose to use it that way."

Cai let go. He felt one last touch to his shoulder—a kiss, warm as life, to the top of his bowed head. Then he was alone.

Chapter Eighteen

"The tail of the *b* goes up, Godric, not down."

A bowing of the grizzled head. A frantic gnawing at the end of the quill, and another attempt. "There, priest. Better?"

"Much. But I should have reminded you, it's also on the other side. You've written me a *d*."

"D for damnation!" Godric jumped to his feet, sending quill, ink and pile of birch-barks flying. "Does this feed my cows? Does this get my slut of a wife to her hearthside to make me my broth? Does this...?" Running out of questions, he blew out his cheeks until he looked like one of the pufferfish that sometimes got caught in the cod nets, turned on his heel and stamped out.

"Never mind him, Abbot Cai."

Caius, who had buried his head in his hands, looked down from the pulpit. Barda, the slut of a wife, was smiling serenely at him. Godric was much changed these days, other than his tongue, and the two of them rubbed along peacefully. Ironically, Godric was one of Cai's brightest pupils. D for damnation? Cai was rather proud of him. "I don't mind him, Barda."

"Let him stump around his barnyard for a little while, scaring his hens. He'll be back."

"I know he will. How are you getting on?"

"Here." She lifted her birch-bark to show him. It was a clear autumn day, and the new church roof was still incomplete. Cool grey light shone in. "I have made you an *a*, a *b*, a *c*, and..." She paused, tracing the last letter to check the direction of its tail. "And a *d* for damnation."

Cai restrained himself. It didn't do to laugh, even when they were striving to amuse him. "Those are very fine. Perfect."

"But, you know, my husband is right."

A murmur ran around the dozen or so villagers assembled in the church. Astonished faces turned to Barda, who had certainly never accused Godric of such a thing before. She spread her broad hands, ink-stained from her labours. "I like to do this. I like the little marks, and the sounds you tell us they make, and I like it especially when you get bored and tell us a story instead. But it *doesn't* feed Godric's cows—and I do prefer stories to broth. Why do you teach us, Abbot Cai?"

Brother. Brother Cai, not abbot. But the villagers had caught the habit from the brethren of Fara, who now mingled freely among them, sharing their labours and lives. Cai felt like the rawest, rankest novice who ever fell in from the fields. He was weary, suddenly almost too tired to stand. This happened to him still, even two months after the raid. But Barda was gazing at him, her handsome face expectant. He'd told them to ask, hadn't he? *Ask, and if I know the answer, I'll tell you. Nothing is more dangerous than a darkened mind.* "I want you to be able to read," he said, leaning his arms on the pulpit. "If a day ever comes when a man stands among you and says, *do this, do thusly,* and tells you to obey because the Bible says it is so..." He paused, coughing. His lungs seemed too shallow these days. He felt as if one of them had knit into his scar.

"You want us to look at the Bible ourselves and see if it is true."

"Yes. Exactly, yes."

"Will we ever see a Bible, Abbot Cai?"

"You may come to the church and look at this one freely."

"Forgive me. You said that wasn't a Bible yet. That's what your brothers have written down, what they can remember of the old one."

"You're quite right. The old one was burned. When next summer comes, I hope we will have enough mead and barley to trade against a new one from the Tyne monasteries." He leaned forwards. "It is a good thing to remember, though. All the words in any Bible, no matter how sincere and holy, are words copied down from someone's memory of something very, very old. Copied and copied, put into other languages and copied once again."

"You want us to think for ourselves." Godric had come silently back into the church. He gave Barda a warning look and made his way back to his seat and makeshift writing desk. "Attend to him, woman. Don't I know better than anyone what comes of blind obedience?"

"Aye, well." Barda set down her quill and folded her arms. "You'll not be expecting it from me, then."

Snorts of laughter broke the holy silence. Cai had often wondered what Theo would make of the things that went on in his church now. Women brought colicky babies in at their breast. It was the only covered space of any size for miles around, and Cai allowed a small amount of trading there, exchanges and barters before the men set off to market. At night, he would spread out the *Gospel of Science* on the pulpit, light candles and torches in sinfully wasteful abundance, and teach his brethren how to calculate the distance to the moon.

"My friends," he said, "I think our lesson has gone as far as it can today. Friswide, can you bring more birch-bark strips from your timber supply tomorrow?"

"I can, Abbot Cai."

"Good. We'll go on from *d* for damnation then. In summer I'll buy you some parchment, and you'll be writing like monastic scholars."

After I've taught you Latin. Head spinning with exhaustion, Cai made his way down from the pulpit. He followed his students out of the church and sat on a rock outside its sheltered southern wall to wave them off. He recognised the futility of what he was trying to do. The illogic of it too—why not teach them to read and write in a language they already knew? But even if he succeeded with that, there'd be nothing for them to read. Latin, seeded here by a conquering army, brought to ripeness by the church, was now the language of learning—of domination—across the known world. It was a shame, because the Saxon language danced. It rolled out bright carpets of story by the village firesides at night, some in a slow-thumping poetic metre you could clap to. Cai should try to write some of it down. He should try to teach the children too, persist in getting their parents to spare them from farm work for just an hour a day. He had time. He had time for anything now.

The villagers were gone, and none of his brethren in sight. Curling up on the rock, Cai allowed the nagging cough that always lurked in his lungs to have its racking way with him. It sounded worse than it was, he hoped, and there was no blood. He just wasn't a husky great Viking who could spring back from such damage as if it had been a scratch.

That was a bad line of thought. When he could breathe again, he lifted his head and saw Danan down by the shoreline, plucking her herbs unmolested. The sight of her pleased him. It was for her sake, for the sake of every creature different, unknown, unable or unwilling to conform to the law of the church or any authority, that Cai would teach his villagers. He would teach his brethren, who could read their Bible but needed to look beyond it to the stars. There once had been a Christianity here—Addy's kind, the communion with eagles and seals—which had briefly blended with Danan's ways, with the ancient beliefs of these islands. Cai had no hope of restoring it. But Addy had told him to shed light, and so he would.

Yes, he had time, though he filled his empty hours diligently. He was strong enough now to help with the rebuilding, such as it was. No more halls, nothing at all that could be seen from the sea. The beehive huts crouched low—a primitive shelter, but sufficient. Cai had one of his own now, and the salvaged corner of the old rooms served as a kitchen and refectory. In his cell he was quite alone, and once his working day was done, he would turn over the pages of the *Gospel of Science* for himself, lost in the wonder of it, learning all he could. The book had a hiding place ready, a gap beneath Theo's tomb in the crypt. Cai wasn't sure who he feared more—Viking raiders, or the men of his own faith who might someday come to claim the wilderness. He would do as Theo had done. He would absorb enough to make a copy, so that if the day came, they would have to burn him too.

Another bad thought. Something in him stirred with yearning at the idea of the flames. Time—despite everything, he had too much time. The hours stretched. No matter how he worked, there were still great, barren patches in his days, sterile deserts when all he could do was escape to the beaches and walk. The sands were desolate now, winter blowing down in heaped grey clouds. Cai would walk for miles, looking eastward to the land of the Danes.

It was no good. He was hollowed out, sick, losing weight by the day no matter what he ate. He pushed Fen from his mind and saw his shape in every shadow. It had only been two months.

Harness jingled in the distance, and he sat up. His limbs were stiff, the cloudy sun much lower in the sky than when he'd settled here. Had he slept? His eyes were gritty and sore. Rubbing them, he tried to make out the source of the sound. He could hear men's voices now, and horses whinnying. Some kind of caravan was making its way across the mud flats. Two carts—no, three—and a couple of shaggy horses on a leading rein. Benighted traders, perhaps, hoping for a night's shelter at Fara. Or maybe a rare group of travelling players, come to tumble and juggle beanbags and frighten Eyulf into shrieking fits by pulling out coins from his ears. Aelfric had sent the last lot packing. Cai would welcome them, give them a supper. He barely had enough to feed his men as it was, but Theo—and Christ—had commended all kindness to strangers.

A show would do everyone, monks and villagers alike, a world of good. Cai got up and brushed off his robes. The leader of the group was driving a sturdy black pony at a sharp pace over the sands. He was well-matched to his beast, burly and dark haired. It took Cai a minute more to recognise his father.

Broccus slowed up in a flurry of mud-splash outside the monastery gate. Cai no longer kept it closed, his friends all being welcome and his enemies unstoppable now by means of any barricade. Nevertheless the old man halted. He raised a hand. Cai returned the gesture, wondering if he were still asleep. For once in his life, Broc had asked for permission.

He rattled up the track and came to a stop outside the church, the other drivers flanking him. Cai went to meet them. He had pulled up his hood against the sharp autumn wind, tucked his hands into the sleeves of his cassock. Broc looked down at him from the seat of his cart. He gave a derisory chuckle, much more familiar to Cai than the show of politeness at the gate. "Well, freeze my balls if it isn't my firstborn, looking every inch the monk."

The last time Broc had seen him, Cai had been wearing his travelling clothes. He'd never set eyes on him in his cassock. "What did you expect?"

"From the stories I've been hearing—chain mail perhaps, and a sword. I heard my godly son became a warrior. Took up arms and fought off Viking marauders—saved this place, for what it's worth. I heard they made you abbot."

Cai pushed back his hood. He didn't want to be angry. He didn't have the strength for it, and he hated the dull surge of rage the old man could make him feel. "Nobody made me anything. What do you want here?"

"I thought I'd come and look at my son's domain. See what made him give up a kingdom. So far I see a church with no roof and what I hope are your pigsties."

Cai began to walk away. A cold, thin rain was falling, and he could smell Fen in the folds of his damp robes. Laundry was less of a priority these days, though Hengist did his best. The scent was a reality. Broc had to be a bad dream. He'd vanish if Cai ignored him for long enough.

"Caius!"

Something different in that voice, as alien as the hesitation at the gate. Remonstrance, and a rasp of—what? Fear? Unable to imagine it, Cai turned back to see. But Broc was leaping down from the cart, his face hidden.

"Here!" he shouted, dragging down a sack and hefting it as if it weighed nothing. "Barley grain for your bread and your next planting. Half a dozen of those, and..." He gestured to his companions, who also began unloading their carts. "Where is your sheep pasture?"

Mutely Cai pointed uphill to the enclosure where three lonely beasts now grazed, the only remnants of Wilf's runaways. Broc's second wagon seemed to burst apart in a surge of bleating life, and Cai found himself knee-deep in the hardy little black-faced crossbreeds who thrived on the hillfort's bleak slopes. Before he could speak, Broc nodded to his companion, who whistled to a grizzled herding dog and turned the flock into a river, flowing away uphill. "Ten ewes and a tup, to restart your stock. Half a dozen sacks of corn. Half a dozen oats. Two decent-sized horses, fit for plough or cart."

"Why, Broccus?"

"Why what?"

"This. Now."

Broc balled his hands into fists. He braced them on his hips and looked about him. "I heard the last raid cleaned you out, that's all."

"I can't give you anything to pay for these."

"If I'd wanted barter, I'd have taken them to Traprain market, not this ruin. When I heard how boldly you'd fought, boy, and trained other men to do likewise..." Broc hesitated, then went on as if being forced to confession at sword point. "I was proud of you."

Cai came to stand in front of him. His heart was beating fast, the shrieks of dying friends and enemies resounding in his ears. "Proud of me?" He swallowed. "I came here a raw, ignorant brat. I have learned to read, write, speak Latin. I can doctor men and teach them. And now—now when you hear that I've broken my every vow, grabbed a sword and learned how to hack men to bits with it—*now* you're proud?"

Broc stared at him blankly. His face was Cai's, sculpted by a few more rounds of summer light and winter hail, a mirror of the future Cai had come here to avoid. "I should load these wagons back up and go, you brat."

"If you wish."

"Caius—what do you expect of *me*?"

Cai blinked. The old man sounded bitter, but the anger had vanished from his voice. "What do you mean?"

"When I said you looked like a monk, you asked me what I expected. You were right. It was a foolish thing to say." Broc ran a hand through his hair so that it stood up in a perplexed crest. "What do I look like to you? A saint? A priest? I am the man you have known all your life. I steal cattle, swive women, defend my hillfort. My boy ran away from me to become everything I am not. Forgive me, that my heart burned with joy to hear he had become a warrior."

He unhitched the two horses from their leading rein, tethered them with a wooden ground spike, and clambered back into the cart. He shouted at his herdsman, pointing off down the track to indicate that he should catch up with him there, and shook his pony's reins.

Cai watched his retreat. Dusk was falling, and it wouldn't take long for the mist to swallow him up. There would be no evidence for his existence, apart from some tracks in the turf.

Those, the two horses, the black-faced sheep now terrorising Wilf's three sorry survivors, and the lifesaving abundance piled up all around Cai's feet. Cai stood frozen for a few seconds more, and then he ran after him.

"Broccus! Broccus..." Cai couldn't run far anymore. It hadn't mattered until now. His lungs were too tight for him to throw his voice ahead of him, or at any rate Broc was affecting not to hear. Slipping on the muddy track, Cai forced his heavy limbs on. The wagons drew further ahead. Once they were on the flats, Cai would lose them. "Father!"

Broc reined in. He didn't turn or look down as Cai stumbled up to him, panting, grabbing at the cart shaft for support. "Father. These things you've brought..." A spasm of coughing seized him, and he tried again. "They're the difference between life and death. I tried my best, but...we haven't got enough. We'd have starved."

"Well? Am I taking them away from you?"

"You've got a long trip home. Will you stay?"

The old man's shoulder twitched. His grip on the reins relaxed. "What—in your pigsties? No. We'll bed down in one of the villagers' barns for the night."

"At least eat with us."

"Lentils and scurvy grass?"

"No." *Just as well you didn't turn up yesterday, though.* "A good fish supper tonight."

"Very well. Turn around, Gowan!" Broc held out a broad, calloused paw to his son. "You'd better climb up. What's the matter with you, boy? You look like a ghost that's been left out to bleach in the rain."

Only one cresset flickered in the church that night. The light was enough for the two men and the book they held between them. Cai had spared his brethren their lesson for that night, sending them off to their cells with an extra jug of ale in honour of Broc's visit. Then he had awkwardly asked the old man if he would come to the church—not to meet God, or anything so injurious to digestion. Just to see the book.

Broc was as uneasy as a bear, even in the stripped-back nave, which apart from its stark wooden cross now scarcely betrayed any signs of its function. He occupied old Martin's chair as if it had been his hillfort throne, thighs splayed, only a vague notion of courtesy preventing him from propping up his feet on the stool in front of him.

Cai sat on a bench at his side. "My abbot Theo brought this back from the East with him. He hid it with Addy—with Aedar, I mean, the new bishop—and Aedar gave it to me."

"From the East? Kent?"

"Further even than that. A land called Arabia, beyond the Mid-Earth Sea."

"Why did he leave it with you?"

"I'm still not sure. He told me I should learn and teach from it, spread light. And I will, as long as I'm able."

Broc's attention had been on the book. Now he looked up thoughtfully at his son. "As long as you're able? Why shouldn't that be for a long time yet?" Cai didn't reply, and the old man pursed his lips, brow furrowing. "You know, I'd thought there was no hurry, but...isn't it time you had a child?"

"A child?"

"Yes. A boy, an heir—someone to carry on what you are. I will raise him, if you are... If you couldn't keep him here."

Cai chuckled. "Well, I couldn't sit with him in my lap while I talked to my monks about chastity. Broc, you have dozens of sons. Go and tell them to get heirs."

"None of them are firstborn," Broccus returned grimly. Cai, who'd heard that sole argument for his value all his life, shook his head, and Broccus sighed. "I mean...none of them are my Caius. Could you not consider it, lad? If I sent you down the choicest of my women? I have one girl—good birth, willing, fertile as a springtime coney. Couldn't you bring yourself to have her just once?"

My Caius. Cai, who'd been about to snarl at the old man to mind his business, lost a breath as the words sank in. "Thank you," he said quietly. "I'm grateful. But...I couldn't lie with a woman. Not now."

Broccus blanched. "Are those rumours true, then? What have they done to you?"

"Nothing. No." Frowning, Cai gave his father an amused, disgusted grin. "No! Not for that reason."

"What, then? Oh, is her place taken?" Broc exhaled noisily. "I see. And around here, not by a woman, I assume."

"No. Not by a woman."

A silence followed, broken by the crackle of the torch in its cresset. "Which one is he, then?"

More silence. Cai clasped his hands round the back of his head and curled over until his fringe was brushing the *Gospel of Science*, the page where a small man was standing on the surface of the moon to demonstrate her phases, and Cai dearly wished he could join him there.

"I heard it said, not that I believed it, that you fought with a half-tame Viking at your side. I didn't see that kind of fox in your chicken coop tonight. Is he gone?"

"Yes."

"And is that why the bones of your back are sticking out like a starved hound's?"

How could the old man know that? Cai, returning from the moon, realised that for the first time in his grown-up life, his father's arm was around him. "No. I've been ill, that's all. I was wounded in the last raid."

"You took a blade?"

The old sod sounded more delighted than concerned. Still, his arm was warm, and as he had pointed out to Cai, he had never pretended to be other than he was. “Yes, a sword. Right through my side.”

“That’s a brave lad! Let me see the mark of it.”

“Not here. I’d have to hitch up my robes too high, and that’s unbecoming...”

“In the house of God.” Broc snorted. “I’m sure old Martius and Cernunnos wouldn’t faint to see your tackle. Never mind. Look at what that bastard Bren did to me in the last cattle raid!”

He pulled open the neck of his tunic, and Cai saw a livid scar snaking up his throat. He gave a low whistle. “You were lucky. That one missed your carotid by an inch.” Broc beamed as if he’d been given a gift, and Cai remembered he had marks of battle he *could* show without getting undressed. “A Viking I was fighting slashed my arm. Look.”

Broc whistled in his turn. “That must have gone to the bone.”

“Near enough. And here, where I fell from the scriptorium onto the rocks.”

“I can see grit in it still. This is where Edulf lobbed a javelin at me. That was a grand battle.” Broc rolled down his sleeve and sat nodding in satisfaction at the memories for a moment. “Next time you’re troubled with raiders, you should remember that I can raise an army. I have enemies all over these hills. They’d just as soon fight Vikings as fight me.”

An army... Cai hid a smile. That would be Broc himself in a chariot, and a handful of old-timers like himself on ponies. “Thank you. But I’m not sure if I’d stand up to another raid. We’ve lost so many men, and our best warrior is... He had to leave.”

“That damn Viking. Ah, you’d feel different once your blood was up.” Broc patted the open book, turned another couple of pages. “I bet you would fight for this, if nothing else.”

“Perhaps. It’s a fine thing, isn’t it?”

“Aye, fine enough. But your own Roman ancestors knew more than this. It’s these bloodless Christians who are trying to make such knowledge rare.” Stretching and yawning, Broc glanced at the night sky through the open rafters. “Still, it’s good that someone wrote it down. I must go while there’s still some light.”

Cai accompanied him as far as the door. Once there, the old man surveyed the darkening hillside, starred all over with faint light from the beehive cells. "Forgive me," he said—a low growl expressive of anything but remorse, but nevertheless a shock to Cai. "I have seen this place now. Your monks have told me how you built it up from less than nothing. You've done well. You should take care of that book, boy—and yourself."

The breeze snuffed Cai's lantern in the doorway to his cell. He thought about lighting it again, but then set it aside in its niche. He was tired. That was good. His one hope tonight was that he would drop into the profound sleep where all his memories of Fen seemed to be stored, fresh and vivid as if just laid down. Yes, tales with the ink still wet on them, of a monk and a Viking who met in combat and defied two worlds to live in love. Wild fantasy, of course, on a chill north-coast night with the wind moaning through every gap in the stonework. Awake, Cai was losing belief in the stories himself.

He stripped off his cassock and fumbled in the dark for his woollen nightshirt. Barda had made a batch of the garments for the monks when the autumn nights began to cool. A true ascetic would have refused her, but Cai had been too glad of the gift to refuse it for any of his brethren, who spent their nights warmer if itchier for her generosity. He shrugged into his and lay down. He would say his prayers later, he told himself. He would have the strength for them once he'd visited his dreams.

A shoulder touched his. Biting back a yelp of fright, Cai sprang out of his bunk. He retreated until the hut's curved wall stopped him, reaching for the sword that lived in here with him now that the armoury was gone. "Who is that?"

Silence. Had Broccus somehow made good on his offer to send him a girl? Perhaps he'd intended it all along, brought the poor lass with him, hidden under sheep or sacks of grain. With an effort Cai stopped the wild rush of speculation. "Speak, or you'll be sorry for it. Who is there?"

"Caius, it's...it's me. Oslaf."

Cai let go the sword along with a pent-up breath. The weapon thudded onto the earthen floor. "Oslaf? What in God's name are you doing here?" He grabbed at possibilities and found one that didn't make his hair stand on end. "Are you sick? Did you come here to find me?"

"I should say that, shouldn't I? That I felt ill, came here and...fell asleep on your bunk while I was waiting?"

Crouching, Cai sheathed the sword. He hung it up again, then retrieved the lantern from its niche and re-lit it by feel, his flint striking sparks before the wick caught. A soft glow filled the cell, revealing Oslaf sitting upright in the bunk, his hair dishevelled, his pallor lending credence to his story. And if it was true, he had kindly undressed in readiness for Cai's examination. He was an attractive lad, skinny but no longer starvation-thin. His skin was smooth and unmarred, a hazelnut brown in the lamplight, scattered with freckles.

"Oh God," Cai whispered. "You'd better tell me the truth."

"Not if you stand there like Judgement. I can't."

"Like Judgement?"

"As if you're about to point at me, call me an abomination and throw me out, like—"

"Oslaf!" Cai slung the lantern over a hook. He knelt on the bunk and took the boy into his arms, pulling up the blanket to warm him. "Of course I'm not. How can you?"

"I'm sorry. But you've been different lately. You know you have."

"Aye. And if you don't know why, no one does."

Oslaf laid his head on Cai's shoulder. Cai knew the nature of the convulsion that went through him—the heave of a grief too deep for tears, dry and terrible. He held him until it had passed. Oslaf said, "I do know." His voice was worn to rags. "I do know. I've been watching you, and I've seen you dying inside your skin, just like I did after Ben. When your father came tonight, I thought he was going to pick you up and take you home, like my grandmother did when you summoned her."

"Not Broc's style." Cai rocked the boy, pressed an absent kiss to his brow. "Still, he was kinder than I'd thought."

"Yes. He's like you. And you're *so* like him. I can see how you'll be when you're older—strong and tough, but compassionate too, and shining with your learning. I want to be with a man like that."

Cai frowned. This view of his resemblance to the old man was too startling to take in all at once. "You *will* be with me. As long as the Fara brethren are together—"

"No. With you as Benedict was with me. As you were with... Cai, I've grown afraid to say his name to you."

Cai knew why. He'd been walking around with his grief held before him like a frozen shield, deflecting all attempts at human kindness. "I'm sorry. Say it."

"With you like Fen was, then. What can be the harm? Yours is over the sea, and mine is..." He choked faintly. "Mine is under the earth. We can comfort each other. You don't need to show it in the daytime, Cai, not to the others. But I can come into your bed at night, and you can touch me—warm yourself on me, lose your pain for a while in my flesh. And...I can lose mine."

"No," Cai said softly. "You can't." Oslaf had lifted his head. He was nose-to-nose with Cai now. His lips were parted, his breath sweet with the mead that had given him the courage to come here. To kiss him would have been easy—the easiest thing in the world. But Cai knew he could lay him down here, wring pleasure from both their bodies from now until dawn, and make no real difference to either of them. "You can't lose it. You can only learn to live with it, and that's not the way."

Oslaf thumped a fist off his shoulder. "Why not? What *is* the bloody way?"

"I don't know. I'm beginning to think...time. Only time."

"That's no use to me. I want you now."

"Lie down."

Oslaf sucked a breath. Despite his declarations, he was rigid in Cai's arms. Fear as well as arousal rolled off him in waves. Cai turned him so that he was lying with his back pressed to Cai's belly. Once more he adjusted the blanket to cover the poor naked limbs.

"When I lie here at night," he said, "I have so many stories about Fen that go through my head. I can't seem to get at them during the day." Oslaf had lapsed into listening stillness, and Cai stroked his hair. "I certainly can't tell them to anyone else. That's why I've been...such a block of ice, I suppose. Is it like that with Benedict too?"

"Yes. But I don't want to think about it. I just want—"

"You do."

"No! Why can't you be like the others? They're afraid to say his name to me, and I don't want to make them weep and pat my head and not know what to do with themselves by saying it to them."

"It's always so when someone dies or...goes away. Death is too big for us. We jump to get out of its way."

"Not you, though."

Cai held him tight. "No, not me. Tell me a story about Benedict. Just one."

"If you will tell me one about Fen."

Shrugging, Cai nodded. Oslaf's hair was soft. His body was lithe, coming to a fine, strong maturity. Everything about him was sweet and good and right, and utterly wrong. "Very well. You first."

"I don't know where to start."

"From the beginning, if you like."

"The beginning..." Suddenly Oslaf twisted over onto his back, pushed his fringe out of his eyes and looked into the long-vanished world beyond the stone hut's roof. His head was pillowed comfortably on Cai's arm. "I remember. My brother Bertwald brought me here. He hated you lot, you know—he thought you were going to whip me or crucify me for the good of my soul. And as I was half-dragging him up the track, this fine tall man—not even in a cassock—it was a hot day, I remember, and Theo must have let him work in a shirt... This fine tall man pulled his ox to a halt in the field and asked us if we were all right. Well, Bertie's a farmer too, and I had to stand there in the blazing heat for an hour while the two of them talked about how Ben got his plough rows so straight."

Oslaf chuckled. "Bertie was almost a convert, though I'm not sure he knew what to. And my first night here, when I had bad dreams and woke up shouting for my grandmother... Ben had the cell next to mine. I hadn't really looked at him at supper or during prayers. He knocked on my door, and I was so surprised to see my ploughman there. He sat on the edge of my bunk and talked to me until I fell asleep—all about Theo, everything I'd learn to be and do..."

In the first faint silvering of dawn, Cai left the hut. He paused for a moment in the doorway. Oslaf was curled up tight in the blanket, sleeping with the thoroughness of exhausted grief.

Cai hadn't told a single story about Fen. He smiled, pulling the willow screen over the door. Oslaf had talked all night. After a while he had forgotten Cai was there and begun to address something or someone beyond the hut's confines, and he had confided to that vast and merciful unknown the whole history of his time with Ben, from their first awkward kiss to the alien misery of Ben's estrangement from him, a deeper hell than any Aelfric could have devised. Cai had let him run on. He had taken the boy's drooping head on his shoulder when finally he had lapsed into sleep, and lain wide-eyed himself.

Maybe it was just lack of sleep that was gilding the sunrise, but Cai had never seen a more beautiful one at Fara. The silver was turning to a fresh rose gold. The eastern horizon was clear, a thin arc of sun already poised over the water. Once the whole orb had risen, Cai's duties would begin—leading his brethren in prayers, seeing they all got a sufficient breakfast, assigning them their labours for the day. Such a sunrise should be seen from the dunes. He had just enough time.

The tide had swept the beach clean. The only marks on it were those of the water's pure dance, ripples and sandbanks whose crests were beginning to dry out already and catch diamond light from the sun. This was Cai's earliest memory of it. Benedict had been instrumental in his own first days here—had brought him down to the sands to show him that his new life was not all self-discipline and Latin verbs. Cai, itching for exercise, had run like a lunatic along the shoreline, splashing his new cassock to the waist. The sand had been like a blank canvas and so had he, for all his turbulent upbringing with Broc. Now when he settled among the long grasses and looked down, every inch of the strand was marked for him in event. Here the sea had brought Fen to him. Here they had fought, and once boldly fucked in the open, a thick sea mist keeping their secret. Here Fen had taken Gleipnir, the cord that could bind when fetters failed, and kissed Cai on the head and walked away.

Cai had done everything he could. He had filled his days, and endless insomniac nights, with every good action Theo could ever have prescribed for him. He had worked until his body failed, and then strapped his mind to the plough and read and learned until his vision had turned to dazzle. He had subdued his sorrows in the griefs of others—sat with new widows and widowers, with mothers of stillborn children. He had taught his brethren and the villagers, guided their minds and physicked their bodies.

He might as well have sat here on the dunes and moped from dawn till dusk, for all the good he'd done himself. The weary pain inside him had never ceased, and he was so lonely he wanted to fill up his pockets with rocks and walk out into the sea. Fen had imagined a moon-bridge that brought souls together before they met in the flesh. Perhaps Cai could follow the track of this rising sun on the water, leave his aching skin and bones behind him with his cassock and...

He jerked upright, scattering sand, sliding halfway down the dune before he could stop himself. What was he thinking? He had spent the night immersed in Oslaf's griefs—had begun to mix them with his own. Fen wasn't lying cold and still beneath the soil. He was vividly alive somewhere, perhaps riding Eldra hard across the Dane Land marshes, pursuing his duty as sincerely as Cai had tried to follow his own.

Tried and failed. He couldn't do it anymore. What was the point of it all, if one day Fen came home and *he* was lying under the damn hawthorns? Cai had seen the look in his father's eyes, unsentimental and accurate, sizing him up. His lung was sticking to the inside of his ribs, or so it felt, and each day it hurt him more to breathe. He'd known it to happen with deep wounds like this one—scar tissue forming too fast, too abundantly, binding and strangling where it should heal.

He scrambled back up the dunes. If he was going to follow the track of the dawn sun, it had better be soon. *Now,* his racing heart told him. *Go now. Go now.* He could take one of the ponies Broc had brought. No. If he was going to leave Fara, desert his brethren, he'd take nothing with him but the clothes on his back. A huge, sick exultation rose up in him. He would go. Each step he took—down the long track to the Tyne, and then further south still, down maybe as far as Eboracum where trading ships set out across the North Sea—would carry him closer to Fen. God, it was strange—now that he'd made his decision, he could almost catch his lover's scent in the air. A sense of his own failure clawed at him, but he was past caring.

"Fen," he gasped, stumbling out onto the slope where the beehive cells lay curled and dreaming in the day's first light. "Fen, I'm on my way."

Chapter Nineteen

Leaving was easy after all. Cai did it in a handful of sun-shadowed minutes, in still waters at the turn of the monastery's tide. He shooed Oslaf gently out of his bed, before it could be said that the abbot of Fara had a new friend and a short memory, and he washed and dressed himself as if for any day.

He breakfasted with his men, noting with detached approval that Oslaf had colour in his face and that he went back for a second slice of Hengist's fresh bread. He met the boy's grateful gaze steadily. Afterwards he sat with Hengist among the grain sacks Broccus had brought, which were piled up in the covered part of the church for want of other space, and the two of them went through the tough, basic arithmetic of supply and demand. There would be enough to last the winter—just. If there were no more raids.

When Cai left the church, a blazing autumn day was unfurling its wings. The sunlight held a crystal chill of summer's end. The shadows were blue-black, deep. The men of Fara had gone to the fields, or to help in the villagers' dairy and barns. The place was as still as a starling's nest with all its noisy fledglings flown. Cai changed into his travelling clothes and unhitched his sword from the wall of his hut. After a short tussle with his conscience, he took one of Broc's horses after all. The others had survived the raid, and maybe this one could be spared. Leading it to a drystone wall so he could clamber on—a leap he had used to make without thinking—Cai reflected that he had no choice. Even this much exertion had left him coughing and fighting for air. He was going to the Dane Lands, and if he tried it on foot he would get as far as Godric's southern pastures and probably die there amongst his cows. Everything was silent. He turned the horse's head towards the track that led out across the mud flats.

He rode until the sun was high. When it began to beat upon his skull in silent hammer strokes, it finally occurred to him to wonder why he'd brought no water. Well, there were streams everywhere. He would stop and find one, if he could overcome the need in him, insistent as his pulse, to travel south, and south, and south. Water was easy.

Not so food. Cai touched the place where his satchel would normally hang on journeys like this. He hadn't brought it. He'd set out with nothing at all. He hadn't thought as far ahead as paying for his passage on board ship. He could work it, he supposed, as a physician on one of the big merchant vessels, or simply as a deckhand.

"First you have to get there."

Cai reined in, gasping. There on the track ahead of him a woman was standing. There were no trees or cover for miles around. This was the first lonely moorland stretch of Cai's journey, and to be there she must have dropped from the sky. She was familiar. Cai rubbed his eyes. "Danan?"

"Who else? Stop that horse before you trample me."

Cai dismounted, hanging on to the beast's mane until he was sure his legs would bear him. The old woman was planted squarely in his path, and the trouble Cai was having—another sign of failing health, perhaps, distortions of his vision—was that she no longer seemed old. She was boldly upright. Her hair, though still white as banners of falling snow, drifted in sunny abundance. Her expression was ageless, stern as the angel's at Eden's gate.

"I had thought better of you," she said. "And old Addy certainly did."

"What are you doing out here? What has Addy got to do with...?" Cai remembered his manners. No matter how she appeared to him, she was frail and alone, and no better equipped for a journey than he was. "I'm sorry. Where were you going? Can I take you?"

"And interrupt your flight?"

"Danan, I don't understand."

"You're leaving, aren't you? Your men, and the holy lands of Fara, and the book."

Cai left one arm hooked round the horse's neck. That way it would look as though he were standing here easily, not about to drop to his knees on the track. "How do you know about the book?"

"I know everything that happens in this land. Don't you realise that by now? I am always everywhere, just like the wind and the sea."

"That's..." Cai shook his head. "That's what Addy told the ducks."

"And what did they think?"

"I don't know. They just waddled after him, but..."

"They seemed to understand it better than you. Caius, you can't leave Fara. You know that yourself, or why have you come out here in your shirtsleeves, without enough food to get you to the next town?"

"I just wasn't thinking. I have to go on."

"You won't make it."

Yes. Cai knew. No need for a dying man to pack his bread and cheese. He couldn't even raise a flicker of denial. "Please let me use up what's left of myself as I wish."

"In search of your Viking." Danan came and took Cai's arm. She led him off the track, and Cai went with her helplessly, wondering at the wiry strength buoying him up. "Sit down here with me." He subsided onto the flank of a beautiful green mound he hadn't noticed before, and she settled beside him, producing from somewhere in her robes a leather flask. "Drink. And listen. It was good of you to come and rescue me from Aelfric's pyre, even if I didn't need your aid."

"Well, it was Fen who really... What do you mean, you didn't need me? You were about to be roasted alive."

"It was Addy who said I should wait and let you try your powers—or at any rate, see what would happen if you didn't. He's an old fool. I damn near suffocated, and I singed my robes. Still, you came at last, didn't you?"

"If I had the least idea what you were talking about..." Cai didn't mind too much. The sun was warm, the mossy slope beneath him comfortable. He took a deep draught from the flask she offered him, and made a face. "Good Christ, woman. What was that?"

"Just something to sustain you for a while. You'll need it. Yes, it was good of you, and I am grateful. So I will give you one last prophecy."

Cai chuckled. "I swear—if you tell me the Vikings are coming..."

"Ah. Did you see it for yourself, boy? Are you getting that kind of power, as your life ebbs? It does happen sometimes, with people of your—"

"Danan, I was joking. *Please* tell me you are too."

"Forget Vikings, then, and hear me about just one. Turn back, Caius of Fara. Get on your horse and ride home before something much worse than your own little sorrows comes to pass."

"One Viking?" Cai jumped to his feet. His blood heated and

coursed in his veins. He remembered fighting up through fever clouds while he was ill, fighting Fen's grip with a bestial strength that seemed to return to him now. "Which one? Tell me!"

"The one whose loss you've grieved over." Danan took his hand. The shimmering cobwebs of restored youth had blown away from her. She was ancient again, and her eyes held sorrow enough for both of them. "You don't need to mourn him anymore. He's come home."

All the way back to Fara, Cai was looking out to sea. Time after time he rode his snorting mount—Swift, he named her halfway home, to bring down the right kind of spirit on her—up the side of a dune, reined her in and scanned the blazing waters. It was too bright for him to see. A Viking fleet of any size could have been concealed in the light, in the troughs between the dancing waves. An hour passed and then another, Cai leaning low over Swift's neck, scarcely aware of the ground she covered or the thunder of her hooves. The jolting hurt him, but his pain had become a bright, cold fire, a kind of unearthly singing.

The light had changed. The track snaked inland here. Cai halted Swift on the brow of a hill. Scents of gorse rose up at him in clouds, all the sweeter for a touch of frost that morning. Now he could look out as far as the horizon, out to Addy's island and beyond. He could see every detail, down to the rainbow beaks of the fat little short-winged birds sitting placidly on their rocks. Black-and-white ducks plied their serene course along the shoreline, and a vast sea eagle—Addy's, perhaps, relieved of its fishing duties—sailed in wide circles overhead. A Christian monk was not supposed to take counsel from bird omens, but Cai would swear to it that no harm could come by water today. The North Sea was peaceful, not a ship in sight...

But an army bearing down on him by land.

Cai reined Swift in at the start of her downhill plunge and sat motionless. What poison had Danan slipped him, to bring on a vision like this? He wiped his eyes, but there they still were—a moving cloud of men and horses, chariots and mounted soldiers, crossing the coastal plain that stretched from Berewic in the north to Fara.

But Fara was not their target. Now Cai could see brightly coloured tunics, metal helmets, manes of long, thick hair. Vikings, dozens upon dozens of them, their ships exchanged for war carts, their motives transformed. Cai had heard for years of places further north than Berewic still, up in the wilds of Scotia, where the pirates came to raid and never left, settled and began new conquests from the land. No, not Fara this time—Fara had nothing. The coast had been scavenged, its bones picked clean, and this army was turning inland—for the Saxon farms and villages, for the strongholds of chieftains like Broccus. Not a raid. An invasion.

And a force was riding out to meet them. Cai froze, his hands clamping tight on the reins. Was he looking through veils of time to a battle played out here five hundred years before? Not since then had a Roman standard been raised in defence of the north coast. With dreamlike slowness, Cai recognised the ancient sign his father had treasured up in the barn along with his chariots—a time-blackened eagle, the letters SPQR worn away almost to nothing beneath it. The Senate and the People of Rome, about as far away from home as they could get... The lead chariot was Broc's. From somewhere amongst the hills and scattered villages, the forts and the elderly warlords who ruled them, Cai's father had raised an army.

Cai broke into laughter, startling a lark from the gorse. The old man had threatened to, hadn't he? Cai had taken it as an empty boast, part of his dream of a noble past. Broc had underestimated him, and he'd returned the favour, years of mutual disdain piling up between them.

His laughter died. Yes, Broc had done more than gather a dozen or so of his hoary friends and their carts. He was leading at least fifty men over the plain from the foothills, and at a cracking pace. They looked good. Cai would have backed them against anything short of the enemy they were facing. They were outnumbered—by how many, Cai couldn't tell from this distance. Maybe not many. Not enough at any rate for Broc to see sense and back off. The fight would take place—farmers and cowherds against Vikings.

Cai couldn't let it. All he'd learned from clash after clash with the wolves from the sea was that he couldn't win, and nor could any landsman. Broc could fight them to a standstill as Cai himself had done, spill out the best blood of the ancient forts to do it, and the next tide would bring in another pack.

He was closer to Fara than he had thought. He must have ridden for miles under the influence of Danan's potion. The effects were draining from him now, but one more hard gallop would do it.

He didn't stop to consider just what it would do until he was back on the mud flats again. Swift was slackening her pace, the magic of her name wearing off, foam rising on her neck and flanks. That was no good, no use to Cai, and he signalled frantically to Gareth, who had appeared on the track at the sound of his approach.

"Is Fen here?" Cai yelled, as soon as Swift carried him into earshot. "Did he come back?"

"Caius, where did you go? We've been searching for you all day. There's a horde of *vikingr* horsemen on their way down from the north, and—"

"Yes, I know. Did Fen come to warn you about them?"

Gareth's gaze clouded in something Cai fought not to see as pity. "No. No sign of him."

"Well, look out for him. The other mare Broc gave us—is she in the paddock?"

"Yes, I think so. But—"

"Gareth. Fetch me the horse."

Cai slithered off Swift's back and stood with his hands propped on his knees. By the time Gareth came running down from the paddock, he had caught his breath. "Thanks," he said, grinning, reaching out to grab the fresh beast's halter. "Help me get the bridle off this one and onto..." He was running short of inspiration, but Broc's other gift still had a long green strand hanging from her startled mouth. "Onto Clover."

"Clover? All right. But why, Caius? They're plough horses, not... What are you going to do?"

"I'm not sure. But if it goes wrong, and you see the *vikingr* troops making for this place, you take your brethren and leave."

"Can't we give them a fight for it?"

"Not this many of them." Cai shook his head, grinning. "How you've changed, my friend! No. This time you run and hide—together, separately, whatever is safest. Take nothing but the book. Here—give me a leg up."

"You're not well. You shouldn't be galloping about the countryside on your own."

"I know. I just have to try this one thing."

Once settled on his new mount's broad back, Cai paused. This mare was bigger than Swift, but raw-boned and awkward. And Cai hadn't chosen the best name for her either. "Clover the warhorse," he said doubtfully. Well, he had ridden Broc's ponies into skirmishes for cattle and land since he was big enough to lift a sword. He shook her reins and set her to a lumbering canter. Gareth held out a hand, and Cai squeezed it in passing. "Don't worry!" he called back over his shoulder. "Fen is on his way. Watch the fields, and if the battle turns against us, run!"

He drove the mare hard through the open gates of Fara and down past the village. The villagers—his friends now, Barda and Friswide and even Godric, Wynn the smith and a small mob of children—came tumbling out of their barns and huts to call to him, "*Vikingr, vikingr!*"

Cai didn't slow down. He waved at them, slewing the horse around them. Soon the fields gave way to the vast coastal plain he had seen from the cliffs above Fara, where the raiding army and Broc's were closing upon one another fast. Taking one deep breath and then another, Cai aimed for the centre—the narrowing patch of land between them—and rode on.

Chapter Twenty

A strange, wild faith was kindling inside Cai at last. It was nothing like Leof's, nothing even Theo could have taught him. Its fires had first touched him during the storm, when he had been shipwrecked and Fen had pulled him from the waves. He had been nothing but a heartbeat in a skeleton, nothing but breathing flesh, and so it was now. His purpose was only to meet the next rush of sunlit wind against his face, and the next, as the horse bore him onwards.

Fen was near. Cai knew it, as certainly as if he were back in the sea with that strong arm reaching down for him. Perhaps he was already at Fara, dishing out orders and chivvying the brethren into action. The very air was sweeter in Cai's lungs for his closeness. The perfection of the moment wrapped him round.

He could hear voices now. He could make out separate figures through the glimmering light. At the head of the Viking force, a vast charioteer was tearing across the plain. His hair flew out behind him, thick as a sheepskin. When he raised his arm and roared, a noisy chorus roared back at him.

Sigurd! Sigurd! Sigurd!

Sigurd, Fen's warlord. The leader of the Torleik clan, deposed by Fen's brother and cast out. How had Gunnar ever managed to defeat such a bear of a man? Well, he had risen from his ashes. His warriors were yelling his name like a battle cry, like the song of a war god. His two-horse chariot was flying full pelt towards Broc's front line, so fast that he was opening a gap between himself and his own men.

Only one horseman was able to keep up with him. The beautiful horse he was riding kept perfect pace with the chariot. The contrast between him and Sigurd could not have been greater—the one a solid wall of muscle, flesh and fur, the other a lean, graceful shape whose flag of copper hair seemed to take light from the sun.

Cai saw and understood. The burgeoning faith in his heart snapped out, a candle snuffed in brutal fingers. Clover sensed the change in him and lost momentum, and he let her falter to a halt right in the middle of the plain.

"Caius! Damn you, boy—get the hell out of my way."

Cai didn't move. He couldn't turn his head—not even for his father. He had let Fen go. The sorrow of that had eaten him alive. But nothing in his loneliness had taught him what it would be to see him return as his enemy. Despair seized him, colder than death.

And Fen had seen him too. He peeled away from Sigurd's side, his magnificent russet-red cloak floating out behind him. Briefly the sight of him wiped Cai's mind clean of anything but his beauty. Cai had fallen in love with a Viking, a warrior. The warrior had taken on a cassock and gone about his duties at Fara as a monk, but he was a Viking still, and now for the first time Cai saw him restored. His throat went dry as dust. Fen was heading straight for him. So be it. Cai wouldn't so much as draw his sword. Even now, a voice of unbreakable trust told him Fen would strike neatly, end his life fast and cleanly.

"Gleipnir! Bring back Gleipnir!"

That wasn't Broc's voice or Fen's. It wasn't in Cai's own tongue, but the words of the Dane Lands were part of his heart's language now. Sigurd's troops were slowing up, all of them gazing after Fen. And Fen was holding at arm's length a thin banner, a streamer flying behind him on the wind.

"Fenrisulfr!" Sigurd was hauling his chariot to a stop. His mouth was open, his face a blank of outrage and dismay. "Fenrir, you devil—bring Gleipnir back."

"No!" Fen rode Eldra full tilt to Cai's side. He didn't stop there, but reined her in hard so that she made a circle round him, one then another, as if seeking to shield him not only from Sigurd but from someone behind him. At last Cai broke his paralysis and saw Broccus pounding down on him, howling with rage at the sight of his son in league with an enemy soldier. "No!" Fen yelled again, brandishing the ribbon. "*Hætta!* All of you stop!" And then, in full view of his warlord and his Viking comrades, he held out the ribbon to Cai.

"Take it," he said quietly. "Take it now, beloved. Can you translate to the Celts for me?"

If I can speak at all. Cai took the fluttering strip of leather in a numbed-out grasp. "I will try."

"Hold that up. Let them see I've given Gleipnir to you. Sigurd!"

A roar like an avalanche came back. Cai could barely pick out words from it, but Sigurd's livid face gave him the gist. Still, not one of the Viking men moved. Cai didn't understand. He and Fen were an easy target out here. If Sigurd wanted Gleipnir, he could come and get it, unless... He lifted the ribbon as Fen had told him. He gestured with it, letting the wind make it fly.

The Viking men fell back.

"Fen. What's going on?"

"Tell the others what I say. Sigurd, stop this fight! There won't be a battle here today."

Strong, simple words. Lost in disbelief, Cai turned to his father and the mismatched group of chieftains and farmers hauling up to a disorganised halt all around him. He could translate easily. "Stop," he cried, the beginnings of a grin tugging at his mouth. "Stop the battle. Nobody fights today."

"Sigurd, I couldn't stop you from coming here. But no Torleik warrior will lay hands on the man who saved my life. Who became to me more than a brother. Nor will they harm his tribe, or his..." Fen looked quickly from Broc to Cai, making the connection, "...or his family."

These words were harder to convey, but Cai did his best, blushing with pleasure at the sound of them. "Fenrir forbids the Torleik to harm me. I am his... More than his brother. So they won't harm my tribe either. Not even you, old man."

"Caius, you whelp. Is that Viking on my bloody horse?"

"No. On mine, since you gave her to me. She's called Eldra now." Cai stopped, distracted by a rumble of hooves and wheels. Sigurd had finally broken rank. "Fen, is he frightened of Gleipnir? Take it back."

"No. I have to make him frightened of me—it's long past time." Fen waited. He manoeuvred Eldra so that she stood fearlessly between Sigurd's oncoming chariot and Cai, and as Sigurd tried to rush past him, seized his rein. A sound of disbelief rose from the *vikingr* troops, and Cai understood that this was Fen's challenge—a head-on contest for leadership, one warlord to another. "Sigurd, I have given Gleipnir to this man, to do with as he wishes. He is worthy."

"Worthy? You have given our power to him, you traitor."

"This poor strip of leather? You believe that?"

Sigurd's face suffused with rage. He tried to jerk the rein free, but Fen held fast. "Of course not. But *they* all do, and so I can command them."

"Not anymore. I give my allegiance to the Britons, and they aren't easy prey, not now. There will be resistance..." Fen paused, glancing in amusement at Broc's army. Some looked like fierce Roman soldiers. Others were brandishing pitchforks. "As you'll find out, if you start a fight. Go back and tell them that. Now."

Cai braced. Sigurd's brow lowered until he looked ready to spit thunderbolts. Fen was going to lose this standoff, surely. Cai would live with the results. He wrapped Gleipnir round his wrist and reached for his sword. It wouldn't be a bad end, to vanish fighting underneath a wave of *vikingr* wrath. To drown there with Fen by his side.

"Traitor," Sigurd repeated, but his voice rasped on it. He shook his rein again, and this time Fen let him go. Cai watched in disbelief as he pulled his horses round and began to retreat.

Fen brought Eldra snorting and prancing to Clover's side. "Holy gods almighty," he declared, swallowing audibly. "I never thought that would work."

"*You* never did..."

"Oh, Cai. Listen to me, please." He laid a hand on Cai's arm, and Cai put his own hand on top, heat rushing through him at the touch. "When I left you... I promise you, beloved, I thought I could help my people. I thought I *had* to. For nothing less would I have..."

He faltered. Cai squeezed his fingers. "I know."

"But when I got there, Sigurd wasn't in exile. He'd come back, and he was rousing an invasion force to come here and ravage this country for everything we need at home. I tried to stop him. I told him the only way to mend things was to mend our land. But winter is coming. The Torleik are starving."

"And he wouldn't listen to you."

"No. When he knew I had Gleipnir, he put all his faith in it and set out here. So all I could do was ride with him, then take my chance once I got here. I've backed him down in front of his men now, and given you Gleipnir."

"What happens now?"

"He'll obey me. And you, if you're strong enough."

"What do you want me to do?"

"Speak to them—my men and yours."

Cai nodded. Fen was so close that he could catch his longed-for scent in the air. He would have done anything. "I will. What else?"

"What else?"

"Something more you want to ask me, love. I can see it in your eyes."

Fen shivered. "Breath wasn't worth drawing for me once I'd left you behind. I want your forgiveness. To stand once again at your side."

"Yes. Always. Go back to Sigurd now, though."

"Oh, gods. Why?"

Cai raised the hand he held. He pressed its knuckles to his lips, in full view of Broc's warrior's and Sigurd's. "Because if I'm going to speak to him, you'll have to translate for *me*."

Caius held the sacred relic high. It was like a powerful wave, he thought, rushing up a wide, lonely shore. The *vikingr* warriors shifted like kelp in the currents, leaning towards it yearningly, shrinking back when the wind made it swing round towards them. Only Fen sat proud and still. He had taken up a place by Sigurd's chariot. The warlord was waiting. He looked tired, as if some vital essence had passed out of him. Off to Cai's left, Broc was waiting too. It was time.

Cai rode Clover slowly into the middle of the sun-blown turf. When he moved, he felt invisible shapes move with him in the wind, keeping close to him, casting no shadows. *Leof,* he thought, for the first time with no pain. *Theo—now I know how the treasure of Fara can bring peace.*

"Hear me!" he called. For a moment he wanted to laugh. Who was he, to stand between armies and demand that they listen to him? Then the breeze caught Gleipnir, and it tugged in his fist like a living thing, a sea serpent coiling. He let it fly out like a banner. The runic words burned into it seemed to swirl and dance around him. The cord that binds the wolf...

"Hear me. I wield Gleipnir. No man will fight here today." He waited for the roar of derision, but none came. Sigurd was frowning, listening to Fen for translation, and as for Broccus... Once more Cai swallowed down laughter. He'd never seen such a face before. One of Broc's hounds could have spoken and astonished him less. "I wield Gleipnir, and...I command you to look around you. Look at the men gathered here—*vikingr* and old Roman, Saxon farmers, and..." he patted himself on the chest, then gestured at the looming rock of Fara, "...and my kind too, the soldiers of Christ. Each convinced the land belongs to them. At least these *vikingr* pirates know they're invaders. The rest of us have forgotten—we are too."

A rumble from the hillfort warriors. Cai turned to them—to Broc, meeting the dark eyes that were so like his own. "Yes. The waves of change break on this shore, over and over again. There never was such thing as a pureblood Briton, and..." He paused. Maybe Danan's draught was working on him still. He seemed to stand on a brink. There would be a time when conflicts like this one would devour a whole nation. A world. "And there never will be, Broc. Not even you."

The flickering visions faded. All that was left was the light, the sea air, the vast sky above him owned only by the wind. "Look at this land," he said. "It's huge. It's empty—I can walk for days and not meet another living soul." Clover shifted, and he let her turn so that he too could see the great wide spaces of his home. "There's room for every one of you here—for settlers, not raiders. Men who will come to build houses and farms, sustain themselves by work, not theft and plunder. No, Broc—listen. We too came here as conquerors. Our Roman fathers tried to seize the land and...and they found they could only become a part of it. At least—the only ones left are men like you, who did, who stayed and had children and..."

Cai jerked his head up. He had started to speak to Broccus only, and the Vikings were waiting. "And now I tell you, men like me—Christians, who say they serve the word of Christ but have gone deaf to its meaning—are starting to put out the lights of learning and freedom. I won't let anyone—*vikingr* or Saxon, Roman or Celt—bring down that darkness. Not while I have a breath in my lungs."

Gleipnir stopped its dance. It fluttered down and lay tamely over Clover's neck. If there had been any magic in it, the power was spent. And Cai was finished too. He sat quietly, letting Clover shake her head and snort. Whatever would come next would come.

"Caius!"

Cai turned. Fen was looking up from low-voiced conference with Sigurd, and he was smiling. Cai knew that smile. *Good luck with this one, monk...*

"Sigurd has something to say to you. He says..." The grin widened. "He couldn't care less about learning and freedom. But he'll take the land, if you're giving it away."

Cai shook his head. His answering smile rose up. "Not mine to give. If it's anyone's, it's my father's. I'm sure he'll be willing to step forwards now and deal with Sigurd for it—by negotiation." He shot a glance at Broc, who was puce, his mouth hanging open. "Or they could fight. They're pretty well matched up, aren't they—his farmers and your pirates. They'd do a grand job of wiping each other out."

Caius left the battleground. He touched his heels to Clover's sides and turned her head towards the sea. Was it a battleground that lay behind him, or a chamber of council, roofless and open to the light? For himself, he couldn't care anymore. He was done. He had all his work cut out to stay aboard his rocking mount as she surged to a choppy gallop and took him away.

Other hoofbeats, faster and lighter. Cai cared about those. Still he didn't look back. No plough horse could make such a sound. He risked closing his eyes for a moment. Instantly vertigo grabbed him and he opened them again, and it had been enough—Fen was right there at his side. Eldra fell into effortless pace, a swan beside a hard-swimming Addy duck.

Fen put out a hand. "Where are we going?"

"I don't know. The dunes. Just...away."

"Yes. Good."

"Not too fast. Clover can't keep up." *And nor can I. Why is it so hard to breathe?*

"You called your warhorse Clover?"

"It was short notice. Just ride."

Off the coastal plain and into the hills, where earth turned to sand beneath the turf, where marram whipped freshly in the wind. Where salt and the manes of white horses made the air crackle with life, sustaining Cai a little longer—long enough to gallop after Fen deep into the maze of crests and sandy troughs.

"Here," he called, when his hold on Clover's reins began to slip. "Fen, stop here."

Eldra came snorting to a halt. Fen turned her neatly and brought her to stand beside Clover. "Is it far enough?"

"Yes. It'll have to be."

"Cai..." Fen took hold of his shoulder once more. He looked into Cai's face. Cai didn't dare look back. "What's wrong?"

"Nothing. Can you see them from here—Sigurd and my father?"

"If I ride back up this crest. Wait a moment. Yes."

"Are they fighting?"

"No. They're still where we left them. They're...talking, I think, if you'll believe it."

Cai chuckled. "Just barely. If you're here, though—who's translating?"

"Does Broccus speak Latin?"

"A little."

"Well, Sigurd speaks a little less, but maybe it's enough. Your father seems to be drawing something on the ground."

"Partitioning his lands, perhaps."

"Does he really own them?"

"Not an acre. But if that's what it takes..."

"Yes. Sigurd won't ask to see his deeds. Cai...?" Fen leapt off Eldra. He came running down the dune and took hold of Clover's bridle. "Why are you so pale? You were mending when I left, weren't you?" He reached up. Cai began to dismount. Fen would help him down, and then he would be fine. But something went wrong between Clover's broad back and the sand. The noise of the sea had got inside his head. When he tried to tell Fen about this—to lean down and find his embrace—his eyes filled with salt water too, blinding him. And then the sun went black.

My only grief is that I can't deceive you. Cai lay listening to the thud of a heart that was now so much stronger than his own. He was curled up with Fen in the sheltering arm of the dunes. The wind was growing chilly as the dusk came down, but he could scarcely feel it. He had awoken wrapped in a beautiful cloak, its soft red wool drawn closely all round him. Fen had been holding it there, holding him. Briefly he had tried to lie. But the damn cough had started, racking him, for the first time bringing blood.

"Why is it happening?"

"The wound's healing badly, I think." Cai was calm now. His words no longer came in crimson rags. His head was on Fen's shoulder. "Binding up one of my lungs."

"What can I do? I will bring you a physician."

Cai smiled at the imperious tone. "Knock one over the head and bring him to me hogtied?"

"If necessary."

"It isn't. I've had the opinion of the best doctor for miles around. The only one, as it happens. It's all right, love. It doesn't even bother me now."

"It doesn't hurt?"

"It did until today."

Fen took his face between his hands. He brushed back Cai's fringe, wiped a trace of blood from his lips with the pad of his thumb. He was so lovely to Cai in the fading light—his haughty features softened, the breeze blowing his hair to kestrel's-wing feathers across his brow. "But it will get better?"

Cai couldn't deceive him. He could hold his peace, though. He buried his hands in the heavy, warm hair, kissed the sculpted profile where the setting sun was limning it in gold.

Fen shuddered deeply and moved to lie over him, bearing his weight on his arms. "Tell me the truth," he growled. "I'll take your silence for your answer otherwise."

"Don't. Just touch me. I have been hungry for you."

"And I for you. I have starved. Why did we do it?"

"We thought we had our duty."

"Yes. But I missed weeks of you, months of..."

Months of whatever I have left. Cai captured Fen's mouth before the words could come. "Never again," he whispered, between one fervid kiss and the next. "My only duty is to you."

"And mine to you."

Solstice to solstice, hand to hand... Their rough interchange called into Cai's head the words of the vow, the chant Danan had begun for them and then stopped when she caught sight of their futures. She had been right—Fen hadn't had a year and a day to give, and now neither did Cai. And yet here they were. He wrapped his arms round Fen's shoulders, and something tugged at his wrist, restricting him. "Fen, I've still got... Look. Gleipnir."

"Bury it. Chuck it in the sea. It took me away from you."

"And brought you back. Give me your hand, love."

"I've told you, I don't want..."

"No. To finish what Danan started."

Fen caught his breath. Carefully he unwound the relic from

around Cai's arm. "The handfasting?"

"Yes. I know the words."

"Then say them." Fen wrapped the ribbon tight round their joined wrists—awkward, and not in the intricate pattern Danan had begun, but it was tight and hot and it would do.

"It feels like using up the last of the magic in it."

"If it's so, then you can only use it once. Not like Danan's ribbon—not just for a year and a day."

"I would never take your freedom, Fen."

"You *are* my freedom. Bind us. Bind the wolf."

Cai swallowed. "Solstice to solstice, hand to hand, from blood-mother earth to the heart of man..." He couldn't go on. Instead he hung on to his end of the strand, and Fen grasped the other, tighter and tighter until their veins ached and pounded with the force of pent-up pulse.

Then Fen released them both, gasping. "Can I love you? Can I have you without hurting you?"

"I don't care if it bloody kills me. Find a way."

Fen undid Cai's shirt. He knelt over him, unthreading its leather fastening one loop at a time. With the same deliberation he pulled out its hem from Cai's belt, and lifted, exposing his belly. Cai hadn't looked at his own flesh in daylight in months. He didn't look down now—kept his gaze fixed on Fen's, reading there all the changes in himself, the message of the wound that hadn't healed. Fen caressed the scar. Cai arched his back in response, his skin sending wild mixed signals of pleasure and pain to swirl around in his head, raising waves of goose bumps, suddenly lifting his cock. "God. I wasn't sure I could anymore."

"That'll be the last thing to go, if I know my Caius." Fen's grin was too bright, and he swiped the heel of one hand across his eyes before returning his attention to his task. "Sit up a little way. I want this shirt off you."

Cai shivered in the wind, until Fen drew the cloak round him tighter and leaned over him, shielding him, kissing his shoulders. He brushed the flat of his palm over Cai's groin, teasing and promising before he tore his belt buckle open and pushed his hand down inside.

His grip was perfect. He had learned Cai's body in the waves of Addy's island, in the summer hayfields, in these dunes. He knew the tender dip between his balls where a light touch was unbearable but an outright grasp, a squeeze of one finger into the sensitive gap, would wring out cries of pleasure, call up climax even from exhausted flesh.

Cai writhed and clutched at him. "Yes. Like that. No."

Fen gave a muffled grunt of laughter. "Yes? No?"

"It wasn't just your hand I missed on all those nights. It was all of you."

"I want you comfortable on a bunk somewhere before you get...all of me."

"Not like that. I mean I want you in my arms."

"I don't want to put weight on you."

"Beside me, then. I'm still good for that. Oh, God, Fen, please."

Fen stretched out at his side. Cai drew him in so that they were sharing the warmth of the beautiful cloak. He undid the wolf's-head belt, and Fen's fingers tangled with his in the urgent undoing of his leggings. He gasped with impatience—his Viking was girded for battle, another of those cunningly worked bronze cock-pieces shielding his manhood, stitched into his subligaculum. "That can't help you now."

"Help me? It's strangling me. Help me get it off."

Between them they unwound him. Cai sobbed in relief as at last the garment was out of the way and Fen shoved his hips forwards, his hand on Cai's backside holding him still to receive the long, shuddering stroke. Held and braced like this, Cai could push back. He groaned beneath the next thrust and the next, an anvil where the white-hot fetters of the wolf were being forged, and then he hurled himself into the fire, all pain and injury and shadowing death forgotten.

Fen clutched him close. Their mouths met roughly, muffling howls of climax. Sand shifted under them, receiving their struggle, cushioning its aftermath as Cai rolled up and onto his lover's body, hammering out the last of his strength. He fell and Fen caught him, easing him into the endless embrace of the dunes.

"Cai, when did Addy come home?"

Cai stopped brushing sand out of his clothes. There was little point to it anyway—he'd be washing it out of his crevices for weeks. He thought of the weeks, and the washes, perhaps down in the sapphire pools, Fen splashing and complaining of the cold beside him. How many days might be left to him? It didn't matter, he decided. His lung was tight and aching now. The next fit of coughing might tear him apart and finish it, and he'd never think himself short-changed, not after...

He looked up at Fen, who was standing on the crest that overlooked the plain, holding the two horses. He had just retrieved them. They had wandered off placidly together, united in their good opinion of the turf at the foot of the dunes. The plain was now deserted. Had Broc and Sigurd too found peace for the sake of good land?

His passion-fogged brain cleared a little. "Addy? He didn't—not that I know."

"Look."

Cai stumbled up to join him. Fen's arm closed tight round his waist. He pointed off into the dusk. "There. Down by the islets, the place where you said the first monks from Hibernia settled. Near the green mounds."

Cai leaned on him to look. The night was falling fast, the light shifting before his eyes could adjust. He'd never really noticed that the ancient beehive cells were surrounded by mounds, but they were. In the spring they were covered with every scented and dancing shoreline flower you could imagine—celandine, harebells and yarrow, sea pinks and thyme, snowy drifts of scurvy grass. It must always have been such a beautiful place, its sanctity held, deep and potent, in its very rocks. And yes—down by the worn wooden cross, a frail but vigorous figure in a plain brown cassock. "I can see him. I didn't hear anything about him coming home—he's still the bishop of Hexham."

Fen broke into laughter. "Perhaps they threw him out. He's got a girl with him."

The girl was leading Addy by the hand. The old man was following her serenely. The sun dipped down between two bands of cloud and threw one final bright lance across Fara and the sea. Cai's distance vision was no match for Fen's, but suddenly the whole scene crystallised. She was wearing a green robe. Her hair blazed around her like an aura, and in this light Cai couldn't tell if it was fair or...

Fair or white. "Fen, that's Danan."

"What—your old salamander from the fire?"

Salamander, witch, hare. Traveller by unknown tunnels beneath the sea and currents of air in the night. "She's wearing all her jewellery. She made me trade for it over the years, but she never put it on, just hid it like a dragon in a cave. Do you see her earrings?"

"Yes, but..."

"Those are coral flowers in Roman gold."

"It's her daughter, then. Her granddaughter."

She doesn't have one, as far as I know. But the lives of our fellow souls are strange to us, most of them hidden like a dragon's gold, and perhaps Fen is right. Cai leaned his brow on Fen's shoulder, and shuddered in pleasure as the grip around him tightened. "What is she doing with Addy?"

"I don't know, but he seems pleased about it. Look, they've seen us."

The girl raised her free hand. It was gleaming from wrist to elbow with Danan's horde of bracelets, and her smile was just as bright. Addy's too, when he turned and waved to them. They were standing at the foot of the largest green mound. Slowly, as if in a dream, Cai lifted his hand and waved back.

"Cai, look at all the seals."

"Seals? Where?"

"All over the rocks there. I thought they *were* the rocks. Is it a haul-out time?"

"No. The tide's wrong. God—listen to them."

The seals began to sing. Hundreds of them—grey, mottled, inky-wet black, from smallest pups to mountainous grand-dams—were congregated on the rocks of Fara. They tipped up their sleek heads. The noise that rose up should have been a raucous clatter, huffing and barking, echoing off the cliffs. Instead it took flight on the wind and whirled up to fill the dusk from sea to zenith like a mermaid's song of worship to the sky. And when Cai looked back to find Danan and Addy, they were gone.

Chapter Twenty-One

In the dead of winter, a king came to Fara. The first Cai knew of it, he was standing in Cai's study, a puzzled frown quirking his fair brows. Cai rubbed his eyes. He glanced down at the *Gospel of Science* spread out upon his desk. The candles had burned low. A sudden dark had come down.

Mortification touched Cai. He hadn't seen the change from afternoon to twilight. Fen was standing by his chair, a reassuring hand upon his shoulder. Cai had been preparing his brethren's lesson for that night. He'd fallen fast asleep over a treatise on how rainbows came out of white light. "Fen...I'm sorry."

"You need your rest. This is King Ecgbert of Bernicia, who's come a great distance to see you. Your Majesty, this is Abbot Caius of Fara."

Perhaps Cai was dreaming. He could see prisms and bands of coloured light in water still. Fen's quiet courtesy was perfect, all the more so for the uncompromising fire that lay beneath it, but Cai couldn't get used to his own title. And other than a dream, there was no explanation for the golden-haired vision in front of him. He took the best breath he could and stood up. Fen knew better than to aid him unless he asked, but his warmth was at Cai's shoulder, a kind of exterior strength held in trust. He rested his hands on the desk. "I'm honoured by your visit, sire. And at a great loss to account for it. But please, sit by the fire. Have you been offered food and drink?"

"Your assistant has asked for hot mead to be brought. Will you come and sit also? I wish to speak to you."

Cai could make the walk from his desk to the circle of chairs round the fire. The room wasn't large, nothing like Fara's old scriptorium, and different in its function. Cai called it his study, but all were welcome here. It was a kind of roundhouse, built in half-Celtic, half-Dane Lands style. A fire burned in the centre, and Cai taught his brethren and the villagers in the nimbus of its comfortable warmth. It had risen in the space of a week, to the sound of conflicting Saxon and *vikingr* work songs.

The king had taken a seat, his coronet glimmering, blue and scarlet garments exotic in the firelight. Cai settled near to him, careful not to wince, smiling at Fen to come and sit at his side.

"I had thought to have audience with you alone, Abbot Caius."

Cai shrugged. The assumptions of men—even kings—were so much dust to him now, cobwebs in the wind. "This is Fenrisulfr. You may speak as freely before him as to myself."

Ecgbert raised one eyebrow. "He is Alexander too?"

Yes, except that this Hephaistion could never have been spared to rule in Asia on his own. Cai remembered Theo's stories, and how the younger monks would weep at the tales of their separation.

Fen came and sat, his face composed, eyes glimmering with amusement. Ecgbert looked them over, plainly trying to work them out. Fen was in his cassock—every inch a monk, and yet somehow every inch a splendid Viking too.

"He is my friend and companion—my most valued helpmeet. Now, tell me what has brought a king to this lonely place."

"I have been here once before, you know."

"Yes. I remember."

"I was on board ship, and I saw you—you and your companion—on the shore."

"You came to fetch Addy. Forgive me—Aedar of Fara."

"Yes. And it's news of Aedar that brings me back now." The young king spread his palms and looked into them as if searching for words. "This is difficult. He spoke very often of you, especially when he was... I know he was your friend."

Fen leaned forwards. "I will tell, if it is better."

"Yes, then. If you would."

Fen reached for Cai's hand. Cai returned his grasp on instinct, as if they had been alone. Many fireside hours had passed for Cai thus, hours when the feel of drowning inside his own lungs had put him past thought or speech, and that grip had been a lifeline. "What's happened, Fen?"

"Addy's dead," Fen said simply. He laced his fingers through Cai's. "He was a good bishop, but his heart was here. And when he knew his days were drawing to a close, he asked King Ecgbert to bring his remains back to Fara."

"Fara? To his island, or...?"

"No. To Fara monastery. He asked that his body be placed in your keeping."

Cai gazed into the fire. "When did he die?"

But here even Fen faltered. "It was four weeks ago," Ecgbert supplied. "He was well cared for and peaceful to the end."

"But that can't be. I saw..." Cai trailed off. Reluctantly he let go of Fen's hand, and the two sat in silence, gaze locked on gaze. What *had* they seen? Cai had fallen sick that night, worn out by his long ride, and Addy and Danan had flickered through his fever dreams until memory had merged with delirium. "Did you do it? Did you bring his body here?"

"Yes, just as he asked. His casket is on his funeral bier, under supervision by my personal guard. I have come to ask permission to place him in the crypt of your church."

"Granted. Granted, of course. I will come and see it's done at once." Cai ran his hands over his hair. He had met old Addy only twice, but still a bitter grief knifed through him. *You said we would meet one more time. The world is darker for your death.* "This land is unsettled and dangerous, Your Majesty. I have never known a king come so far on such a mission, even for one of his bishops. Why?"

Ecgbert sighed. He looked as if he would have liked to pull off his gold coronet and scratch in bewilderment. "This too is hard for me. I'm a man of Christian faith, but I have also striven to educate myself. And yet now I have seen things that..." He shook his head. "Yes, I am rational. But Aedar's body hasn't decomposed. He lay in state for three days in Hexham crypt, and we have taken two weeks on our journey here. I travelled with his casket because I had to see for myself. But it is true."

The scientist in Cai awoke. He too had seen things that had challenged his bright, plain view of the world, part of his inheritance from Broc. But dead men soon faded, reaching out to meet the earth halfway. "I'm a physician," he said. "Tell me—was the crypt in Hexham cold? You've had a cold journey of it up here, I know."

"Aye, we have. But this is different, Abbot. He looks as if he's sleeping."

"Was there rigor mortis?"

"His attending doctors argued over that. If so, it was quick, and now..."

Cai gestured him impatiently to silence. King or no king, if some idiotic, beautiful mistake had been made... "These attending doctors did make quite sure he was dead?"

"There's no breath, no pulse."

"I will come and see. There may be a catalepsy or some hypothermic state. All men rot, Your Majesty."

He set off well enough. Pain and hope were sparking in his blood, a stimulating mix. He knew he should have paused at the door, let Ecgbert precede him, but to hell with that—he marched out into the dark and made it halfway down the hill to the torchlit church before the breath scraped in his lungs. Fen was there instantly. Oh, not a second too soon—catching him, restraining the stumble that would have dropped him to his knees. Speaking to him gently, too low for Ecgbert to hear. "Cai, slow down."

"I have to get there."

"Will you let me help you, then?"

"Yes, love. Thank you. Just...please don't let him see."

It was too late—Ecgbert had caught up with them. He looked them over with the pity Cai had struggled so hard to avoid. With Fen's aid, he had managed—kept his faintness and battles for air out of sight of his brethren, a feat that grew harder every day, his determination hardening with it.

"I fear you don't have your health, Abbot Cai."

"It's nothing. A pleurisy." He moved on, Fen's arm around him. Fen had learned an unobtrusive hold that kept him on his feet. He had promised to use it until Cai told him to stop, until his failing body took the choice from him. He kept it in place until they were on the frosty path to the church, and then let him go so he could make the final stretch on his own.

Cai was glad of it. News of the arrival had spread, and brought not only as many of the brethren as could be spared from their tasks down to see, but half the population of the villages as well. Quite a crowd was shifting about, the flames of the cressets lighting up faces of wonder, cynicism, blank incomprehension. As Cai approached, all turned to him, the cluster of bodies parting. Did they think he had answers for them? Well, perhaps he did. Ecgbert was a man of faith, but it was not the same faith as Cai's. Perhaps only the pure faith of a Saxon king could keep dead flesh incorruptible. What would happen when a man who had read Theo's *Gospel of Science* looked inside?

The bier had been lifted from its cart and carried inside the church. Around it, the king's honour guard stood at attention. They were clad in royal livery and well-enough armed to deter any attention their rich attire brought down, but they too had had a long trek through the dark. They were looking disdainfully at the farmers, women and children milling about in what once had been—as it should be still, Cai knew, by ecclesiastical law—an enclave of holy men.

Hunger and cold did nothing to ease relations. Cai smiled and nodded at Hengist, who had been doing his best to bring some order to the crowd. He stopped in the doorway and clapped his hands. "Gentlemen," he said into the ensuing silence, looking at the guards. "These people are my friends and my brethren, and much excited by the news you bring. Show patience to them. You must be in need of food and drink. Has anyone—"

"I have." Hengist stepped forwards, flushed with eagerness. He had a real kitchen again—another work of Celtic and *vikingr* hands—and could barely contain his desire to refresh the royal visitors. "Mead and hot flatbreads. Gareth and Eyulf are fetching them now, and our evening broth is ready at your command."

"My command..." Cai shook his head. Ecgbert would think he ran this place like a Roman fort. "Thank you, Hengist. Now, the rest of you...take orderly places around the church, just as when you come to prayers. This is a solemn occasion."

Hard for him to say, when Godric's rosy wife was standing before him, beaming from ear to ear, one laughing infant peering at him from her skirts, the baby in her arms flailing and crowing at the fun of it all. "Abbot Cai, they say he died in the odour of sanctity. Can it be so?"

"I don't know." Cai said that to them often—always disappointing them but increasing their respect for his answers when they came. Not knowing didn't scare him as it once had. He didn't know if he would last out these torchlit minutes, even with Fen's warm presence at his back. His chest was tight, a coppery taste in his throat. "It's a very wide world, Barda, isn't it? I have come to see. Now, my friends, be mindful—we are in the presence of a king."

Poor Ecgbert, for all his gold and brocade, had almost been forgotten. Now he stepped forwards, and Cai's brethren and friends did him honour after their own fashion, ceasing to shuffle and murmur, touching fringes, bowing heads. Nobody knelt. Distractedly Cai wondered if their education was taking effect, and whether it would bring them in the end to liberty or destruction.

He had to open the coffin. That was what he had come here to do. Why was he suddenly reluctant? It was best, wasn't it, to dispel any illusions beginning to gather around the old man's death? He went and laid his hand upon the casket. It was a very plain one. Cai caressed the grain of the wood—Addy's choice, he was sure, not the gorgeous Northumbrian king's.

"My friend," he said quietly. "I'm sorry you died so far from your seals and your birds. Forgive me for disturbing your rest."

Footsteps pounded on the turf outside. Cai didn't have to look to recognise Eyulf's uneven, shambling gait. He turned in time to see the boy gallop into the church. Hengist had clearly sent him off like an arrow for supplies, and he was coming back the same way. His arms were piled high with wineskins and loaves wrapped in linen. He couldn't possibly see.

The night had spread a fine, barely visible carpet of frost into the church. Eyulf tried to slow, and his feet shot out from under him. Before anybody could move or try to catch him, he had crashed to his backside on the flags. His loaves and flagons went flying. The next thing Cai heard was the deep hollow thud of his skull cracking off Addy's bier.

Cai put a hand to his mouth. Fen crossed his arms—turned aside and hid his eyes. All around the church, jaws were dropping, the first snorts of laughter—echoes of the one Cai was still fighting to restrain—breaking out.

Cai bit his lip. "Hush," he commanded, his voice unsteady. He strode over and knelt by the poor boy. So much for the solemn occasion. "For the love of God, Eyulf. Don't you know that's King Ecgbert over there?" Eyulf was flat on his back, staring up at the newly thatched roof. "Well, never mind. Are you hurt? Sit up and let me see."

"Brother Cai?"

Eyulf hadn't moved. His gaze was still fixed on the rafters, or some fascinating point beyond them. Cai hadn't heard himself called *Brother* for such a long time. He smiled at the sound of it. And then he realised who had said the words. "Eyulf?"

Eyulf looked at him. Not through him, or past him, or with dim comprehension that someone was there. Not as a sheep or an ox. "Brother Cai," he repeated, his voice rough but clear. "Caius." He sat up, Cai putting a hand to his elbow in wonder and easing him upright. "It's Caius, isn't it? My friend."

Cai had never heard him form a single complete word. "Yes," he said faintly. "Yes, I'm your friend."

"You hid me in the barn, Cai. You saved me from the raider. And Fenrir..." He twisted to look at Fen, who had crouched wide-eyed beside him, and broke into laughter. "Do you remember?" Growling, he twisted his face into the old mask that meant *Viking.* "And yet Brother Fen caught me when I fell down from the tower."

He started to struggle to his feet. Cai helped him, oblivious to the surge of pain in his lungs. "Eyulf, is it...? Is it you?"

"Yes!" Eyulf beamed at him. He stared around him. "I have been lost in the dark for so long. But here are all my brethren... I knew you were there. My God—all those years, and not a cross word from any one of you. Not one single act of unkindness. My God, my God..."

He began to sob. Cai took hold of him, and he collapsed into his arms. Cai placed a hand on his skull. He looked across his shoulder to the gaping villagers, to the monks who did not know whether to laugh or burst into tears with the boy—to the poor bewildered king, and finally to Fen, who would see that his words were brought into action. Fara was not a Roman fort, but Fen was now Cai's general. Cai loved him more than sunlight, more than breath.

"I do not wish this coffin opened," he said. "Do you understand me? The man inside it was my friend. And His Majesty Ecgbert, king of this realm, has declared and witnessed that Aedar has died and remained incorruptible. Who are we to doubt his word? Go back to your work and your homes now, all of you, and be at peace."

"Fen, what are we doing here? Oh, God—did I fall asleep again?"

"No. You did well."

"I fell asleep. Please not at the table."

"No. You were a perfect host—good enough for a king. You just became tired at the end, and I brought you away."

"Carried me."

"You weigh less than a goat wet through. Does it shame you?"

"No. No, never. I just don't want the others to see."

"No one saw."

"Why... Why did you bring me here?"

"You know why."

Cai lifted his head. Fen had made him comfortable on the stone flags. Only one torch was burning in the church now, its light low and fitful. Fen had found a blanket from somewhere and sat him at the foot of Addy's coffin—settled down beside him and held him in his arms.

"Is this my free-thinking heathen? You look good in that cassock, but..." Cai paused and waited till the need to cough had passed by. He didn't have the strength for another seizure. He remembered now—he hadn't gone to sleep. His throat and lungs had closed, and Fen had helped him out into the air, and he had gasped and choked until scarlet had splashed onto Fen's sleeve, and then he had known nothing. The stains were still there. "You told me the other day you're not sure you believe in any god."

"Well, I've never met one. I did meet Addy, though."

Cai caressed the broad chest. "Fen—Eyulf banged his head."

"Yes. He was little better than a beast, and we left him telling Ecgbert of Bernicia about his political views. But you're right—he banged his head."

"Is that what you think I should do—crack my skull off this poor old man's coffin?"

"Of course not. I have just brought you here to pass the night. Addy deserves our vigil."

"He does. But I can't keep my eyes open."

"Then sleep, beloved."

Cai burrowed back into the deep, sacred warmth of his embrace. He knew what was happening to him. He tried to fight it—the sudden lapses into sleep, the dark that awaited him after each struggle for breath—but it was merciful, the long, slow process of his body shutting down. *Not tonight,* he prayed—to God or to Addy or Fen, sinking his fingers into Fen's robes and hanging on. It was always his last cry on the brink of the dark. *Not tonight. One more morning with him, one more waking in his arms.*

A long grey time passed. Immeasurable, deep, a limitless sea fret shot through with scents like sunlight, a tang of sex-heated skin... Cai woke up in the dawn, his prayer granted.

Oh Christ, for the last time. Sunrise gold was pouring through the little unglazed arch at the east end. Fen was sleeping peacefully, and something inside Cai had reached its end. The sense of his lung being stitched into his ribs, the unremitting pain that had stopped him from standing upright for months... All that was gone, and in its place was a void. A floating, dreadful freedom. He couldn't draw breath.

He lurched upright. He tore out of Fen's embrace and staggered a few steps—crashed to his knees on the flagstones, then hauled up again and ran for the doors. He had to get outside. He wanted the sun on his face—one last sight of winter dawn. Tearing the doors open, he fell out into the day.

His lungs inflated, frosty air blazing deep into his chest. An ecstatic heat filled the void. He let the breath go in a wail and sucked the next one in. Strength flooded him. He wasn't torn or broken. He was free.

When Fen reached him, his face a blank of terror, he was standing with his arms stretched to the sun. "Caius! Cai, what is it?"

Cai couldn't tell him. He whirled to face him—seized his face between his hands and kissed him. He had breath for it. He had breath for everything. Kiss after kiss, until Fen was laughing and cursing him, demanding he explain. Cai had no explanation. He flung his arms round his lover—his tall, proud, solid Viking—and swept him off his feet.

Epilogue

In the Year of Our Lord 692, the flood of pilgrims to Addy's shrine overwhelmed the monks' ability to feed and house them all. And although Fara monastery, uniquely among the north-shore holy lands, had its own formidable guard—warrior monks and proud Dane settlers who now called themselves Britons—the Viking raids still swept the coast. Fara had two treasures, now too precious to be risked at any cost. There was the body of Aedar, which whether or not it was still whole in its coffin every few months was reported to have restored someone's sight, set some lame man walking on his withered limbs or revived a dying child. Miracle, or only the faith of the thousands who came there, burning with hope and belief? It scarcely mattered. The healing was the same, and Aedar of Fara was called a saint.

And then there was the book. Many deputations had come from the south, men sent by the new bishop of Hexham, and even from the Canterbury heartlands of the new Roman church. The *Gospel of Science*, blasphemous or not, was too precious a thing to be left in the hands of half-heathen monks in the north. It should be taken to the proper authorities, submitted for examination. The deputations came and put their case, and then they went away.

But still the raids went on, and so one morning at the perfect pitch of spring, a strange procession set out from the lonely rock of Fara. At its heart, flanked by outriders in cassocks and animal hides, was Addy's funeral bier, the coffin worn silkily smooth by all the hands that had touched it. Behind it, fat and old but still as burly as a bear, the Viking warlord Sigurd proudly rode. And at his side, not ceasing to remind him with haughty gesture and look that he had still more reason for his pride, the mighty chieftain Broccus kept his place. The two old men were deadly rivals, and intimate, mead-swilling friends.

The hawthorns were flowering, great, pungent heaps of white blossom with pink hearts all round the monastery graves. Cai and Fen, at the head of the exodus, drew their horses to a halt for a moment. Fen snapped off one thorny branch and passed it to his abbot, who took it from him tenderly, their hands lingering over the touch.

Behind them they left the great monastic school established by Caius of Fara. Cai didn't fear for its future. All around it on the plain were new, thriving villages, their roundhouse huts enlivened by the shouts of first-generation children, in some of whose faces Saxon blood had merged into the Dane. Viking and Saxon still guarded the land, and martial arts were taught along with Latin, Greek and studies of the stars. Fara's new abbot Oslaf was young, but seasoned in fires few older men would have borne and survived.

"This place that we're going to—this new citadel up on its cliff..."

Cai rode on a few paces. The sunlight was brilliant, the whole coastal plain laid out and glimmering beyond the salt flats and dunes. The air was sweet in his lungs. He breathed in the hawthorn and waited for Fen, who had loved his reborn body with such skill and devotion all night, to finish his thought.

"You do realise they just followed a cow."

"Who did?"

"The founding monks. They prayed for a sign about where they should put their new church, and a bloody cow turned up, and they just followed it."

"Well, what of it? Perhaps the cow knew best."

Fen gave a snort. "Well, I see why we're taking our priceless holy relics out of danger there, then. Speaking of which..."

"Don't worry. Eyulf has the book. He asked if he could read it as we went, if he travelled with the linen in the cart. By the way, there was no need for you to call the latest ambassador from Canterbury *quite* what you did." Cai smiled. "Cow or no cow, beloved, you can be sure the monks chose their place well. A great rock by a river, out of reach of raiders—defensible water supply, three sides protected by the cliffs..."

"Oh, Abbot Cai—how like a soldier you sound."

"Well, it isn't Abbot Cai anymore. I am just a monk again, and Addy's guardian. And I am not the only one transformed."

Cai didn't need to explain. Fen brought Eldra into perfect step beside him, and they rode on, so close their knees would brush from time to time, always within reach of an outstretched hand. Fen the warrior, now Fen the teacher, a companion and equal beyond any yearning heart's dream. A warrior still, his sword belt slung over his cassock, his great wolf's-head sword ready to meet trouble as it came. He was Cai's general—his right-hand man and faithful lover, their passion as fresh as their first wild collision in the island waves.

Cai glanced back at the procession. It gave him a reason to steady himself on Fen's arm—just the briefest touch, a promise. "Lover, is there nothing you regret? Not your homeland? Not the freedom of the sea?"

Fen caught his hand—a promise kept—and held on. "I have often wondered," he said, "about the true meaning of Gleipnir. It was nothing but a scrap of leather—lost again now."

"Yes. I think we left it in the dunes."

"But you see, I still have it. To me you *are* home—my tribe, my honour. To me you are Gleipnir—the cord that binds the wolf where fetters fail. Forever, my beloved Cai."

About the Author

Bestselling British author Harper Fox has established herself as a firm favourite with readers of M/M romance. Over the past three years, she's delivered thirteen critically acclaimed novels, novellas and short stories, including *Scrap Metal* (Rainbow Awards Honourable Mention), *The Salisbury Key* (CAPA nominated) and *Life After Joe* (Band of Thebes Best LGBT Book, 2011). Harper takes her inspiration from a wide range of British settings—wild countryside, edgy urban and most things in between—and loves to use these backdrops for stories about sexy gay men sharing passion, adventure and happy endings.

Harper's recent move to rural Cornwall is inspiring her with ideas for many stories to come. When not writing, she's helping longtime partner Jane with the demolition/reconstruction of their tumbledown Cornish farmhouse, and answering the demands of her three imperious cats.

To find out more about Harper and see updates on her current projects, please visit www.harperfox.net.

Enjoy the following excerpt for Scrap Metal:

It was almost dark by the time we set off, the only light left in the sky a serpent of rose gold across the sea. Our famed Arran sunsets had been wiped out by rain for so long that I was reluctant to spoil it, but I flicked the quad bike's beams to full as we left the track and struck out over the fields.

I took it easy in deference to my passenger. It was a long time since Archie had deigned to hell around on a bike with me, but I knew it was a rough ride. The quads were single-seaters technically, one and a half at a stretch—or a crush, more like it. The pillion either hung on to the back of the saddle, or...

I hit a tussock and bounced the bike hard. Cameron gave a startled yelp then burst into wild laughter. I pulled up, grinning too. God, what a sound—unfettered, like a kid's. "Sorry. You okay?"

"Aye. Nearly went crack over nips into yon bloody bush, but I'm fine."

"Crack over nips, eh? What a nice Larkhall lad." I let the engine idle. "I know we've barely met and all, but if you hang on to me, you'll be safer."

"You don't mind?"

"Course not."

He put his arms around me tentatively. I gave his hand an encouraging pat—it was only a business arrangement after all, never sparking the slightest frisson in me when Kenzie was hitching a ride—and he closed his grip.

That was better. We had a lot of ground to cover, and now I could give it some welly. After the first good bump or two, he got the idea and hung on properly. I picked up speed and felt him duck his head against my shoulder to shelter from the wind. "All right back there?"

"Yes. Go faster if you like."

I chuckled. "Fun, is it?"

"Hell, yeah."

I closed my fist on the throttle and took off. His grip was powerful. Whatever the reasons for his loss of weight, they hadn't yet impinged on the essential inner force of him. I could take a lot of his skinny warmth at my back, I decided, gunning the quad up to the last crest before the long slope towards the cliff's edge and the sea. From there I'd get an idea of the task ahead, how far the flock had scattered, if any looked like they had new lambs at foot. Fill up the bale feeders, see to any casualties, begin the endless round of fence checks...

"God almighty. Stop."

I braked so hard he nearly went over my shoulder. "What? Did I hit something?"

"No. I just want to see... It's so beautiful."

"Jesus." I snapped off the engine. "You scared me."

"Sorry. But look at it."

I was looking. I looked at this landscape every day, through sea frets, rain, or just the mists of my exhaustion. I didn't need him to tell me it was lovely, on those rare days when it cracked open its casket of jewels.

Or did I? That serpent band of light had found its reflection, its shimmering twin, in the sea. The air between them was on fire, casting the cliffs in bronze, throwing a weird burnished radiance right into the zenith. Ailsa Craig island burned on the horizon, its sugarloaf turned into a pyramid, as if Giza had set sail from its sands and paused here on some unimaginable journey, to Atlantis maybe. Yes, I'd been looking. But I hadn't seen it in months.

Cam dismounted from the bike and came to stand beside me. "Incredible place," he said softly. "What's it called?"

"Just Seacliff, as far as I know—like the family. Seacliff Farm."

"Seriously? That's wild. Crazy romantic."

I stole a glance at him. The transfiguring light had caught him too. If anything deserved to be on the cover of a book...

"Not really," I said, gruff in proportion with my desire to tell him so. To undo my grip on the quad's handlebars and reach for him. I did let go with one hand, but only to point at the glittering water then the towering faces of rock that lined the shore. "It's pretty basic really. Sea. Cliff." I turned in the saddle and gestured back the way we'd come, where Harry's windows had taken the sunset, almost as if he'd put on all the lights and kindled a comfortable fire. "Farm."

"Nichol, did you ever see...?" Cam paused, and I frowned at the unsteady hitch in his voice. I couldn't have upset him, could I? "Did you ever see a film called *Young Frankenstein*?"

"Yeah, of course. It's one of my favourites."

"Do you remember when Igor's driving Professor Frankenstein home to the castle, and they hear something howling, and the girl says, 'Werewolf!'? And Frankenstein says, 'Werewolf?', and..."

"And Igor starts pointing and says, 'There, wolf. There, castle.' Okay, okay, I get it." I shook my head, helplessly mirroring his smile. "Fair enough. I don't know how I got so blind to it all. Or so grumpy about it, for that matter."

"Are you kidding me? You must have been through hell."

His voice had changed completely. Now its huskiness was

something else—a sympathy that passed like a blade through my hard-won defences. God, and I wasn't going to have to reach for him—he had put out a hand to me, careful but unafraid. I held very still while he brushed his fingertips across my fringe.

"Were you very lonely?"

Desolate. I hadn't known till now. I didn't bloody want to know. If I let that come to surface, he would see it. He was a stranger, a runaway. A criminal, to take the view that Archie Drummond would, an unknown who had broken into my life and would like as not be gone in the morning.

"Sometimes," I managed. I couldn't say more. If I opened my mouth again, he would see how badly I wanted him to kiss it.

Oh, God. He saw anyway. A sweet concentration gathered in his eyes. He leaned a little towards me. I heard the wind in the gorse, the whisper of the sea far below us then nothing but the pulse of my own blood.

CPSIA information can be obtained at www.ICGtesting.com
Printed in the USA
LVOW13s2028280514

387624LV00008BA/1247/P